RUNNING WITH CROWS

The Life and Death of a Black and Tan

A Novel By

DJ Kelly

The photographs of the Dixon Residence (cover and interior) and Dunlavin Garda barracks were kindly provided by Dr Chris Lawlor. The portraits of William Mitchell were generously provided by his family. The cover design is by Esther Kezia Harding.

First Published in the United Kingdom 2013 by UK Arts Council funded FeedARead Publishing

This book is lovingly and gratefully dedicated to my husband, Terry Beddows, for his patient encouragement, story editing and sage advice on all things military.

CONTENTS

FOREWORD

Between the initial declaration, in January 1919, of an independent Irish Republic, and the creation, in December 1921, of the Irish Free State, there occurred a state of conflict known variously as *Cogadh na Saoirse; The Irish War of Independence; The Anglo-Irish War* or *The Black and Tan War*. This war was characterised by outrages and bloody reprisals on both sides. The creation of the Irish Republic was, like all births, painful. Those fighting for the nationalist cause tended to select, as their principal targets, officers of the Royal Irish Constabulary.

Of necessity, the RIC was quickly augmented by temporary constables – men recruited in Britain from the ranks of ex-servicemen of The Great War who could find no employment back in the 'land fit for heroes'. Demobilised officers were subsequently recruited also, initially to provide an officer cadre for the temporary constables. Whilst the temporary constables were assigned to police barracks around Ireland to assist the regular Irish constables in upholding the law, their officers (known as the ADRIC, the auxiliaries, or temporary cadets) became a law unto themselves. They operated like hit squads, terrorising innocent citizens and snatching, torturing and even killing those whom they suspected of involvement with the self-designated *Irish Republican Army*.

To the Irish populace however, all these temporary policemen, whether constable or auxiliary, were known as the 'Black and Tans', from the mismatched appearance of their hastily assembled uniforms. There is no evidence to support the popular myth that *The Tans* included a greater number of criminals than did any other police force before or since. They were however battle-hardened ex-combatants, many of whom had turned to hard drink to dull the memory of their recent experiences in the trenches of the Western Front.

This novel does not seek to present yet another view of the *War of Independence*, but rather to tell the forgotten story of one man – William Mitchell, the *only* member of the British Crown forces to be executed for murder during that war. Those few accounts of the wider aspects of the conflict which actually refer to Mitchell, generally do so inaccurately, describing him as 'an Englishman' or 'an auxiliary'. Neither statement is true.

The truth is that Temporary Constable Mitchell was Irish. History relates that, in the main, it was the auxiliaries who carried out the worst of the atrocities during the conflict. One company of auxiliaries in particular, operating out of Dublin Castle, was known as 'the murder squad'. Although three members of that squad were tried for murder – one of them twice – all were acquitted. Another auxiliary was found guilty of murder but insane. Not a single auxiliary was ever executed. In the case of Temporary Constable Mitchell however, it seems that the outcome of his trial was never in any doubt.

Records relating to Mitchell, his trial and his execution were not easy to find, and indeed confirming his identity and tracing his antecedents proved difficult in the extreme, but two years of painstaking research has uncovered a unique and hitherto untold story. Accounts of the crime, the court martial proceedings and Mitchell's military service are taken from contemporaneous official records. Other details of Mitchell's life have been provided by living family members.

The principal characters named in this story were real people, most of whom appear in their true identities. Some incidental characters have had their names changed or withheld to avoid causing needless offence or distress to their living descendants. Other minor characters are wholly fictional and were created by me to add both colour and credence to what I hope is an intriguing yet faithful account of the life and death of a Black and Tan.

DJ Kelly
2013

'Police and military will patrol the country at least five nights a week. They are not to confine themselves to the main roads, but make across the country, lie in ambush when civilians are seen approaching and shout: 'hands up!' Should the order not be immediately obeyed, shoot, and shoot with effect. If the persons approaching carry their hands in their pockets, or are in any way suspicious-looking, shoot them down. You may make mistakes occasionally, and innocent persons may be shot, but that cannot be helped, and you are bound to get the right parties sometime. The more you shoot, the better I will like you, and I assure you no policeman will get into trouble for shooting any man and I will guarantee that your names will not be given at the inquest.'

– Words attributed to Lieutenant-Colonel Gerald Bryce Ferguson Smyth, RIC Divisional Commander for Munster, by Constable Jeremiah Mee, the Banbridge-born spokesman for the RIC men who mutinied at Listowel Barracks in County Kerry on 19th June 1920, and are as reported in Freeman's Journal on 10 July 1920.

ACKNOWLEDGEMENTS

I should like to express my gratitude firstly to three formidable women: my cousin, Jane Potter of Belfast, who provided the inspiration for the story and doggedly pursued enquiries in Dublin; my cousin Mary Downes of Ocean Shores, Australia, who is a dab hand at internet research, and to my daughter, psychologist and writer Amy Beddows, for her patience and diligence in proof reading my work. My thanks are due also to 'D' – you know who you are – for the invaluable inside information; to Dr Chris Lawlor, Dunlavin-based historian, educator and author, and to the kind folks posting on the Royal Irish Constabulary Forum and The Great War Forum.

Lancer 7539 W. Mitchell
In uniform with 'kettle' in breast pocket
1914

Chapter 1 – **The Joy**

The sorry ruins of Dublin's elegant Custom House smouldered still on the quayside, yet the black waters of the Liffey lapped by unconcernedly. The sun was rising and wary citizens began to appear and go about their business as best they could on an otherwise pleasant June morning.

As the military vehicle sped along the quay on its way out to Phibsborough, the handcuffed prisoner in the back strained to take a last glimpse at his native city. He noted they were taking a roundabout route along the north bank of the Liffey, presumably to avoid the Republican areas with their many roadblocks. All too soon the vehicle reached the North Circular Road and the entrance to Mountjoy Gaol. Shortly the reception process was under way.

'One on – from Arbour Hill,' the escort reported, handing over the paperwork to the warder seated behind the large desk.

Then the same laborious registration process, undergone two months before at Arbour Hill, was now repeated. The warder confirmed the prisoner's details as he completed his log:

'William Mitchell, thirty-three years old, temporary constable in the RIC ...'

'*Former* constable,' the prisoner interrupted, 'I was dismissed.'

'Religion?'

'Church of Ireland.'

'Place of birth?'

'Dublin.'

The army escort departed and Prisoner Mitchell was left standing in the reception area to await the weighing in, the medical, and the compulsory bath. That was typical of the army, he reflected, hurry up and wait. They had roused him from his cell at Arbour Hill Military Prison at the crack of dawn and had hurried him across the city to Mountjoy with all haste and now he had to wait.

The first thing he noticed about Mountjoy was the smell. It was the unmistakable stench of urine, not dissimilar to the stink of the foul tanneries of his adolescence. Arbour Hill, by comparison, had not smelled bad. Of course Arbour Hill was a military prison and therefore had been organised like any army camp, with well-scrubbed floors and well-scrubbed prisoners. Military prisons in the field were a different matter again, of course, as well he knew. Even the army abandoned its normal standards of cleanliness and hygiene during war. Perhaps the same was true here in Mountjoy, or *The Joy*, as the ever ironic Dubliners called it. Dublin was at war these days, after all. Perhaps *The Joy* wasn't always this pungent – perhaps.

All around him, the early morning routine of the prison bustled along. Staff came to the reception area and went away again. Prisoner-orderlies shuffled to and fro. Their whistling, the clink of keys and the slamming of iron doors were magnified in this echo chamber which was the heart of *The Joy*. All were oblivious to the plight of the lone standing man – a tall man, ex-soldier, ex-policeman, a condemned man whose trepidation grew as he waited. He knew *The Joy* had seen so many executions of late that such an event must now be almost commonplace. That Prisoner Mitchell was to die here was a prospect remarkable only to himself.

The warder manning the reception desk arose from his seat only once and that was at the arrival of the Roman Catholic chaplain. The appearance of the priest prompted the warder's gesture of respect. However, the black biretta on the priest's head was somewhat unsettling to Mitchell. What the priest wore for consoling and absolving Catholic prisoners gave him the solemn look of a Judge passing the death sentence.

Glancing quickly away down each of the wings, Mitchell thought the layout of the prison impressively well-conceived. From where he stood he could see in every direction. He saw three landings on each of four wings, comprising hundreds of cell doors, all of them visible to the warders from their vantage point here in the central hall.

This gaol was also far bigger than Arbour Hill. He recalled his mother once telling him how Mountjoy had been built to hold the many men, women and children who were to be transported to Australia. These cells, he thought, would have held the ancestors of those fearless *dinkums* he had met during the war – the heroes of

2

Gallipoli. The thought saddened him. Dublin was a harsh mother who did not treat her children kindly.

A police escort arrived with another prisoner. The middle-aged man also smelled of urine and had the look of a well-practised drunk, the sort of drunk which Prisoner Mitchell had seen every day of his Dublin childhood. Through the happy glaze of permanent intoxication, the drunk sang snatches of 'I'll Take You Home Again Kathleen' as he was booked in.

'One on – from the courthouse,' the escort announced.

'Name?' the warder demanded.

'John McCormack,' the drunk answered.

'Patrick O'Donnell,' the escort corrected, 'sixty-two years'

'Trade?' the warder asked.

'Balladeer,' answered the prisoner, grinning amiably.

'No trade,' the escort said.

'Address?'

'Broadway, New York,' the drunk giggled.

'No fixed abode,' the escort intoned wearily.

The drunk who thought himself John McCormack continued to serenade the warders as the log was completed and the papers signed. After a few moments however, he fell silent, began to turn green and then vomited over both escort and reception desk. For only the second time that morning the reception warder leaped from his seat. To a sound cursing and an equally sound kicking, the drunk was dragged off to the washrooms and a prison orderly was sent off for a bucket of hot water and a mop.

When eventually taken to the washrooms himself, Mitchell had his dark green police uniform taken away from him and exchanged for prison garb of blue shirt and heavy woollen trousers. The trousers were not long enough for his height, for he was a good few inches taller than the average Dubliner, but the warder could find none which were a better fit.

He was surprised they had let him remain in uniform this long, since he had been dismissed from the Royal Irish Constabulary back in February, immediately after the preliminary enquiry. At Arbour Hill, remand prisoners had been permitted to wear their civilian clothes, but he had none, for his own suit was still held in evidence, as was his hat. The pathologist had cut so many holes in them when testing for bloodstains they would not have been wearable in any case. He was glad to have been able to wear uniform at his trial though, if only to create an impression of belonging to the constabulary.

Belonging? He had never actually felt a sense of belonging anywhere. He had lived in many places. He had even been to the other side of the world and back, without finding anywhere he could truly say he belonged. Here he was again however, right back where he had started out, in North Dublin, his birthplace. Yet he had certainly never felt he belonged here.

'Never go back, Mitch, keep going forward in life,' a friend had once said. He would have done better to have heeded his friend's advice. Well, he had no friends now, not a single one. He never seemed able to keep friends, and he certainly wasn't going to make any friends here in *The Joy*, not in the one week he had left on this earth.

At Abancourt Military prison, the prisoners had all been herded together into tents to sleep. He had shared a tent with the Australians and had experienced a sort of fellowship there. He now learned that, as a condemned prisoner at *The Joy*, he would not be sharing a cell with any other felon. He would not be allowed to fraternise with the other inmates at all, although this was more for his own safety than for punishment, they told him. He was not of *their* fraternity in any case. Unlike many of the inmates, he was not here for espousing Republicanism in the face of the occupying foe. Indeed, as a former *Black and Tan*, he *was* the foe. And yet like them he was also an Irishman, albeit not a Catholic.

He suspected that fact was why they had assigned him a Protestant warder to watch over him night and day and be his final companion. Prison Officer Boyd was an ex-combatant too, he said, as they got acquainted. Boyd knew how it had been. Thus the two men had something of a bond from the outset. Prisoner Mitchell reckoned Boyd must have been amongst the oldest men to have fought at the Somme, for he looked to be in his fifties. The other warder who was to guard him was much younger.

'They usually call me Mitch,' their new charge informed them.

'Well, they call us all sorts, but sure, Boyd and Dwyer will do,' Boyd said.

Dwyer would be a Catholic, Mitch thought, if his name was anything to go by. He looked very young to be a prison warder, early

4

twenties maybe. Dwyer seemed to regard Mitch with curiosity rather than animosity. Doubtless though, he'd be telling his Ma and Da he was guarding a *Tan*. That would give the Dwyers something to talk about over supper, after grace was said.

'Am I going to have the pleasure of your company for the next week, then, gentlemen?' Mitch asked.

'Yes, I'm afraid so, Mitch, night and day. We'll get to know each other fairly well, so we will,' Boyd replied affably.

'Will I never get a moment to meself, then?'

Dwyer now piped up:

'You're not supposed to. It's in case, you ... you know ...'

'Now lad!' Boyd warned.

'I know,' Mitch smiled wryly, 'in case I try to cheat the hangman out of his fee. Well, I promise you, I won't do that. Mr Ellis will get his supper and his pint of porter, yes, and his thirty pieces of silver too.'

Mitch looked around him at the cell. It must have been three cells at one time. He could see where two doors had been bricked up and the walls separating the cells had been knocked through. There were two bunks in a tier arrangement at one end and a separate single one at the other. In the centre there was a small, square wooden table and three wooden chairs, but not very much else. Tin mugs with cutlery stored in them adorned a corner shelf. The cell was not very clean and the walls were covered in messages scratched into the chipped green paint by former occupants. Some had left political statements. One had been simply marking off the days. Mitch wondered if that had been a countdown to release or to execution.

'So this is what a condemned cell looks like?' he said, 'I've always wondered.'

'No, this isn't actually the condemned cell,' Boyd told him, 'that's occupied by Maher, one of the other condemned prisoners here at the moment. You and Foley, the other condemned man, each get one of the treble cells. We use these for prisoners who need to be kept on twenty-four hour watch. This is bigger than the condemned cell though. It's 'cause we've had so many condemned prisoners through here of late.'

'We had six hanged last mo...' Dwyer began, but a look from Boyd cut him short.

'Time was,' Boyd added, 'you'd have had four warders to keep you company; two for the day and two for the night, but we don't

5

go home at the end of our shifts any more. These days we're all sleeping up at the prison, for reasons of personal safety. And we're terrible short staffed too. Not all of us made it back from the war, and those of us who did come back didn't come back the same.'

Boyd's shortness of breath, the wheezy, staccato delivery of his speech and the deep rise and fall of his chest left Mitch in little doubt that Boyd had been gassed in the trenches.

'It's good that you had a job waiting for you, at least' Mitch said, 'though I don't suppose you enjoy being in a death cell any more than I do.'

'Well now Mitch, it may surprise you to know I actually volunteered for this duty,' Boyd said.

Mitch was surprised. Boyd continued:

'Let's just say that there's things go on elsewhere in this prison that I wouldn't want to be party to – things I wouldn't want to be held to account for when the British leave.'

At eleven o'clock that morning, Mitch was accompanied on the obligatory morning exercise by his two warders. There was no-one else in the exercise yard. The prison authorities had decided it would be safer if *The Tan* did not associate with the Republican prisoners. To do them credit, Boyd and Dwyer marched around in the same senseless circles on the same uneven concrete along with him. He supposed this would be the only exercise the three of them would get.

He noticed that, when leaving or re-entering the wing, the prisoners had to be signed in and signed out. The escort must call out either 'one off' or 'one on', as appropriate. Mitch though this must be a custom peculiar to civilian prisons.

The lunch when it came was disgusting. It was a thin, grey gruel, made with water. Mitch thought it might once have passed within sight of some meat or vegetables, though it clearly contained none. It was accompanied by a thick hunk of equally grey bread but no butter. Mitch could not eat it. Boyd assured him the supper would be better however, as condemned prisoners did not usually get the standard prison fare. Those men under death sentence usually ate better than the rest of the convict population, Boyd explained. However, though the prison had been expecting Mitch's arrival, he hadn't been expected so early in the day. In these troubled days, most transfer prisoners arrived at night to attract less attention from sympathetic city crowds. No provision had therefore been made for Mitch to have a special lunch.

6

Mitch was touched when Dwyer offered to share with him his own ham sandwich, or 'hang sangwich' as he pronounced it, and Boyd offered one of his apples. Boyd didn't eat much these days, he said, because of his ulcer. Mitch declined their offers. He wasn't really hungry anyway.

There was a further period of outdoor exercise after lunch. Again it was just Mitch and his two gaolers, circling the yard. He could hear 'John McCormack' singing in his cell somewhere, clearly recovered now from the *hurling* and the beating. The man actually had a fine tenor voice. His vocal chords seemed unaffected, either by his drinking or by his incarceration, and his song rang out pure and clear around the prison. 'Kathleen Mavourneen' was not an easy song to sing either.

Mitch guessed the two other condemned men must take their exercise at a different time, to avoid meeting *The Tan*. That made sense, he supposed. He understood that generally prisoners were not allowed to speak to each other at all. British civilian prisons imposed what they called the *silent and separate* system. Denial of human discourse was considered both a punishment and a precaution against conspiracy. Furthermore, introspection encouraged reflection and remorse – or so it was believed. Mitch knew though that prolonged lack of company would have driven him insane. Fortunately, the condemned men were exempt from this inhumane regulation. Foley and Maher would be allowed to engage in conversation with each other but Mitch's only companions would be Boyd and Dwyer.

Mitch learned he would not be allowed access to newspapers, a privilege he had enjoyed whilst on remand at Arbour Hill, but that he could borrow books from the prison library if he wished. He had never been a great one for books however and now didn't seem the time to start any novels. Boyd and Dwyer had brought card games and a set of dominoes to help while away the evenings with their charge. He guessed it mustn't be easy trying to cheer or console a man who knew the hour of his own death. There were others who would be in charge of his spirituality it seemed.

'There are two Church of Ireland chaplains here, you know,' Boyd advised him, 'Reverend Greer and Reverend Verschoyle. And I know you're not Catholic but the Little Sisters of Mercy come around every day and will visit anyone, if you'd like a little chat or a prayer with them.'

'Jesus no, keep the nuns away from me!' Mitch spluttered, recalling an unhappy childhood encounter with the women in black.

'An' me an' all,' Dwyer muttered under his breath, 'for ye'll get no mercy there.'

The supper was a great improvement on the lunch. Boyd told Mitch he could request any preferred foods, within reason, and, with the Medical Officer's agreement, they would be supplied. He was even allowed a bottle of stout with his supper – just one though. Also, the warders would make him tea whenever he fancied a cup. He had only to ask. All of this was on account of his condemned status. Mitch thought that, in many respects bar the obvious one, being condemned was a little better than being on remand.

As night fell, the lights in the cell were lowered, though not extinguished entirely, and Mitch stripped to his underwear and turned in on the single bunk. The pillow and blanket smelled of stale sweat and this brought back a long suppressed memory of an unsavoury *estaminet* in France.

Regulations required one of his two warders to remain awake and seated at the table through the night whilst the other slept in one of the bunks. Boyd and Dwyer took half the night vigil each. Thoughtfully, they endeavoured not to wake Mitch when they made the changeover. Having learned only that morning of the court's verdict and sentence, Mitch had not expected sleep to come to him at all. However, perhaps because the strain of waiting and the uncertainty were now at an end, and in spite of Boyd's laboured nocturnal breathing, Mitch actually slept very soundly indeed.

The following morning, he managed to eat three slices of buttered toast with the tea Boyd made him.

'What day is it today?' he asked Boyd, 'I've lost track now and I didn't see a newspaper for a couple of days.'

'It's Tuesday the thirty-first of May,' Boyd said.

'Nineteen twenty-one,' Dwyer added helpfully.

'He knows that, lad,' Boyd said dismissively, 'Oh, and the governor will be around to see you this morning, Mitch. He visits all the condemned men daily.'

'Who is governor here?' Mitch asked.

'Mr. Munro. He's a good man, a kind man, though he has a terrible lot on his plate these days.'

'So, it's Tuesday already. Just six more days to go,' Mitch said, thoughtfully, 'you know, I wuz born on a Tuesday, and, unless my solicitor can pull a very big rabbit out of his hat, I'm going to die on a Tuesday too. That's a coincidence, isn't it?'

'Like Solomon Grundy,' Dwyer chimed in.

'How is that like Solomon Grundy, ya eejit?' Boyd scoffed, 'sure, didn't *he* arrive on a Monday and was dead by the following Sunday?'

'What was *he* in for? Mitch asked.

'No,' said Dwyer, earnestly, 'he wasn't a prisoner; he was a fellah in a nursery rhyme'.

'I know who he was,' Mitch grinned, surprised to find himself still able to joke about anything.

Charles Munro was shorter and more slightly built than Mitch had expected and Boyd was right, he seemed to have the cares of the world upon his shoulders. Mitch had expected him to be Irish, but of course, like most men in positions of authority in Dublin, Munro was an Englishman. To Mitch's surprise, Munro shook hands with him on entering the cell and chatted freely, clearly trying to establish a degree of rapport and to put a condemned man at his ease.

Munro had lost his brother Hector at the first battle of the Somme, he told him. Hector had been a gifted writer, he added. Had Mitch heard of 'Saki' perhaps? No, Mitch was sorry to say he hadn't. Munro himself had been desperate to enlist, he said, but the authorities had refused to release him from his post at Mountjoy.

Mitch told the governor he was awaiting word from his solicitor, who was working on an appeal. Munro seemed genuine in wishing him the best of luck, before he headed off to see Maher and Foley. Mitch had liked Munro's voice. It was an educated voice, which hinted at an upper middle-class upbringing, rather like the voices of some of the officers Mitch had served under in the war, yet softer, kinder and full of compassion. Munro's accent moreover was cultured and region-less.

Something which had been nagging at Mitch since his trial suddenly became clear in his mind. Accents – that was what had been bothering him. The question of accents had not been raised at his hearing, either by the prosecution counsel or by the defence. At no stage in the trial had the witnesses been asked what accents the two armed men had used. How could they have overlooked such an important point? He resolved to mention this to his solicitor the moment he saw him. He wondered how soon Mr Byrne would come to see him.

Byrne did not call that day however, nor indeed the following day, to Mitch's disappointment. Governor Munro called in each day on his round though. Mitch was greatly surprised when Munro turned up with a gramophone and some records.

'Mrs Munro and my three daughters love music,' he explained, 'and it suddenly occurred to me that it might equally cheer you chaps here on D wing to have a bit of music.'

Dwyer's face was a picture of delight. Boyd and Mitch both expressed their thanks and Munro departed with a look of satisfaction on his face. This act of thoughtfulness seemed to please him as much if not more than it did the recipients of his kindness. The three men immediately began to browse the selection of records he had left for them.

'Ah great,' Boyd exclaimed, 'I thought it might all be that classical stuff, but there's some rare auld Irish ballads amongst this lot. Mitch, you have a look and see if there's anything you fancy. Now Dwyer, do you know how this thing works, lad?'

Dwyer certainly did know how it worked, for hadn't he spent hours gazing into the window of the music shop in Grafton Street, watching a certain elegant young lady demonstrating them for the well-heeled customers? He couldn't wait to get his hands on the gramophone, though Boyd urged him to go easy with it.

Mitch was pleased to find one of his favourite songs, 'Whispering' by *Whispering Jack Smith*. Dwyer gave the gramophone handle a half dozen or so turns, placed the record on the turntable and lowered the needle carefully onto the record. As the machine crackled into life, Dwyer opened the little wooden doors at the front to allow the sound to escape into the cell. Soon the three men were crooning along with *Whispering Jack*:

'Whispering while you cuddle near me,
Whispering so no-one can hear me ...'

The rather ludicrous situation of a prisoner and his two gaolers, incongruously singing a love song together, soon occurred to them and reduced them all to laughter. Boyd found both a recording of the *real* John McCormack taking *his* Kathleen home again, and also another favourite ballad of Mitch's, 'The World is Waiting for the Sunrise'. Mitch had Dwyer play that one several times.

'Dear one, the world is waiting for the sunrise,
Ev'ry rose is covered with dew,
And as the world is waiting for the sunrise
So my heart is calling for you.'

The following day, Mitch's solicitor appeared at last. Dwyer escorted Mitch to the interview room where Edward Byrne was waiting for him. Byrne looked grave.

'Hello Mr Mitchell. How are you? Well, I hope?'

Mitch nodded.

'Mr Reardon and I met on Monday to discuss your case and we felt we had good grounds for appeal. Mr Reardon was keen to be involved at the appeal stage, so I went yesterday to lodge the application with the Judge Advocate's office, but er ...'

'But ...?' Mitch's heart began to sink.

'Well, you must understand that neither Mr Reardon nor I have been involved in court martial proceedings before and, well, I don't know how to tell you this, but ... I am very sorry to have to advise you that there *is* no right of appeal, not under martial law.'

'So that's it, the end of the line, is it?' Mitch was deflated.

'Yes, I'm afraid so. I do apologise if we have given you false hope, and I am so very sorry that we have clearly let you down. Perhaps though, if you were to write a memorial to the Chief Secretary, that might at least delay matters?'

'Do you think it'd change their minds – about hanging me, I mean?'

'Well, you never know,' Byrne looked neither hopeful nor convincing, 'after all, things are moving ahead quite quickly now, with the peace process and everything. There will be a new Irish state soon. If you were still here ... attitudes might change ... people will want to move on and the past will be forgotten. Your case might then be of less importance... perhaps.'

Mitch looked into Byrne's eyes. The man looked genuinely distraught for him.

'So much for them telling us no constable would get in trouble for shooting any man,' Mitch smiled sardonically, 'well, never mind. Thank you, Mr Byrne, but maybe it would be best if I wuz forgotten.'

'Well, it's up to you. I truly am sorry, Mr Mitchell.'

'Don't distress yourself now, Mr Byrne. You and Mr Reardon did your best for me,' Mitch said as he shook the solicitor's hand, 'better luck next time, eh?'

Dwyer walked Mitch back to his cell in silence. Boyd looked up expectantly as they entered. Following behind Mitch, Dwyer quickly shook his head.

'Will I make us a nice cuppa tea?' Dwyer asked.

'Not for me,' Mitch said, throwing himself down on his bunk, 'and I won't manage no lunch neither.'

The two warders tiptoed around him for most of the day, and a bright sunny day it was too – on the outside. As the morning wore on into afternoon and the sun moved around Mountjoy's outstretched wings, shafts of light stole defiantly into the cell and onto the bunk where Mitch lay, immobile in his gloom. He had declined to go to the exercise yards. The warders would not compel him.

'Will I put on a bit of music to cheer us up, Mitch?' Boyd asked.

'Please, don't,' Mitch said, 'I don't think I could bear it right now.'

They let him be for the rest of the day.

The following morning, Mitch seemed to have shaken off his torpor. He ate his breakfast and accepted a second cup of Boyd's good strong tea. Then he and his two warders went out for their obligatory exercise.

On the landing they passed two prisoners coming back to D wing from the exercise yard. Mitch guessed they must be Maher and Foley, the other two condemned men. Maher looked to be about Mitch's age, but Foley looked a good ten years younger. The three prisoners exchanged glances. Nothing more than this would be permitted. Maher and Foley seemed to be aware who Mitch was too. They each nodded to him. Mitch nodded back. It was a brief gesture of acknowledgement between men who were on opposing sides in the conflict but who shared a common prospect – the premature termination of their lives.

He then noticed that their escorts were not in regular prison uniform. Their guards were in fact members of the Auxiliary Division of the Royal Irish Constabulary, and so were probably Englishmen. That struck him as odd at first. He then reasoned however that feelings were running high in this Anglo-Irish War and the authorities would

12

not rely on the Irish prison guards to participate in the execution of their own compatriots. Equally, the authorities would not trust the auxiliaries to guard a fellow RIC man, even were he a *former* constable. Governor Munro really did have his work cut out for him, Mitch thought. If the auxiliaries knew who Mitch was, they gave no sign of acknowledgement to a fellow RIC man. Well, why would they? They were officers, after all.

There had been a uniformed auxiliary at Arbour Hill too, not as a guard however but as one of the prisoners. A very tall, square-jawed man, he was referred to as 'The Major' and had seemed vaguely familiar to Mitch, though they had not spoken of course. Mitch had never discovered who he was nor why he was there. The auxiliaries were the officer class of the temporary RIC and, although also referred to as *Black and Tans*, they operated separately from the constables and didn't associate with them, not even when shared circumstances threw them together. Presumably preoccupied with his own predicament, the auxiliary had given Mitch little more than a disdainful glance and, in any case, Mitch had no regard for officers. That he was here at all was, he felt, due in part to the whim and the spite of officers.

Once outside, Mitch walked around in the regulation fashion for a little while, but then asked if he might be allowed to just lean against the wall. Of course he might. He was a condemned man. They would deny him little. He tilted his head back and felt the sun and the breeze on his face. The unpleasant odours of the prison did not extend out of doors. Here he could smell the familiar air of Dublin. It was the smell of industry, oil and traffic, with a background scent of the river and perhaps also a hint of the sea. He fancied he could smell Monto and Summerhill, his old districts. It was the smell of abattoirs, of blood and death, poverty and decay. He had but days left to live and his senses seemed the keener for that.

'Boyd,' he asked, 'what did Maher and Foley do?'

'Well now,' Boyd answered, 'they were charged with killing two RIC men – trying to rescue another IRA fellah they were. They were tried twice for it and each time the jury could not agree a verdict. Then it was decided to try them a third time, under court martial and without a jury this time, and then they were found guilty, of course.'

Guilty, and with no right of appeal, Mitch thought.

'They've been in here a year now,' Dwyer added.

'That Maher must be a rare auld crack shot though,' Boyd added, 'for a lotta witnesses said he was three miles away when the policemen were killed.'

Mitch was aware, from the newspapers he had read at Arbour Hill, that public opinion lately had called for condemned men to endure hard labour rather than be unoccupied in prison. Even the do-gooders thought it cruel to allow them so much idle time for fearful contemplation of the horror which was to befall them. What did they know? Only a condemned man knew the truth of it. Mitch felt that the time he might spend just thinking, in these his final days, was in fact very precious to him. He had a great deal to consider. He needed to think over his life, to come to terms with what had happened and to try to make sense of things, while indeed he still had the ability to think – while he still had a head on his shoulders.

He thought Maher and Foley had walked upright with the righteous air of men of conscience. They walked like heroes. He himself was neither a man of conscience, nor was he a hero, but if they could face death bravely, then so could he.

As Boyd and Dwyer walked him back to his cell, he was surprised to find himself whistling 'The World is Waiting for the Sunrise.'

Chapter Two – **Monto**

It was the drunkard, being ejected from *The Green Kilt* public house, who declared that if Dublin had an arse it would be here in Monto.

'In that case,' said the cynical publican 'you'll just be passing through, I suppose?

It was a story that five-year-old William Mitchell loved to hear his father Joe repeat. Joe told it often, for he never failed to be tickled by it himself. He wasn't offended by jokes or insults about the Dublin district where he lived for, unlike his wife and children, Joe wasn't Dublin-born. Joe Mitchell was a Londoner – a Bermondsey boy – who had exchanged the slums of south London for those of north Dublin when, in 1886, he had been posted there with the 16th, the Queen's Royal Lancers.

Like all of Her Majesty's soldiers based in Dublin, Joe spent his off duty hours carousing in one of the city's many public houses. *The Green Kilt* was just one of his usual haunts. It was in Dublin's Monto district that Joe had met and married twenty-three year old Georgina More, the sixth of seven children born to confectioner John More and his wife Jane Warren. Joe and Georgina's courtship had been a short one and their marriage rather a rushed one. Their nuptials had taken place at St George's parish church on the eighteenth of September 1887 – just ten weeks before William's birth. Georgina's brother Ben, a sugar boiler at Lemon's Sweet Factory, had acted as Joe's best man, and her elder married sister, Jessie Shields, had been Georgina's witness.

It was evident that the More girls had a bit of an eye for a soldier, for Jessie had also married a man in British uniform the previous year. Her husband, Danny Shields, was a Londonderry man, a private in the Highland Light Infantry, which regiment was also stationed in Dublin. Starting off what seemed to be a family tradition, the birth of the Shields' first child had also occurred rather soon after

15

their wedding. In Jessie's case however, her son had put in an appearance just *two days* after his parents' marriage. As Joe Mitchell would jest, little William Arthur Shields was almost in time to be a page boy at his parents' nuptials.

In Monto, as Dubliners called the area around Montgomery Street, such family events did not always conform to the proper order of things and so few eyebrows were raised. Danny Shields had returned to his barracks after their marriage whilst Jessie and her new baby had continued to live with her parents in their tiny, single-story terraced house at eighty-four Innisfallen Parade. Following the birth of Joe and Georgina's son the following year however, it was clear the little More house could not accommodate any more family members, so Joe had secured a room in a nearby tenement block in Lower Gardiner Street for his own wife and son, whilst he, like Danny Shields, stayed in Barracks.

The fact that Jessie and Georgina's sons were born less than a year apart meant they grew up to be friends as well as cousins. That both were named William, after their respective grandfathers, did not cause the least confusion. By the time the two lads had enough speech to acknowledge each other, William Arthur Shields had become known to all as 'Artie' and had soon nick-named his younger cousin 'Mitch'. Georgina had soon gone on to provide Mitch with three siblings, Joseph junior, Margaret and John, and Jessie too had produced Annie, a sister for Artie.

Mitch always roared at his father's jokes, but especially at his story about the drunk and Monto, not because he fully understood it, but because it had the word 'arse' in it, and that was a dangerous word. At least it was dangerous for Mitch, since the repetition of it usually earned him a slap from his mother. Mitch was attracted by danger however, and indeed there was plenty of it to be found in Monto.

Once a magnificent and wealthy district of the Georgian city, Monto was now just a wizened spectre of its former self. The five-storey terraced houses, which now kept the sun off the ragged street urchins at their play, had once been the fashionable residences of the Dublin gentry. Although it was hard for Joe Mitchell to imagine, the aristocrats, professional men and administrators of British colonial rule in Ireland had once gazed out of these tall sash windows. They had probably surveyed their neighbourhood through pristine lace curtains, rather than through dirty, cracked panes, as Joe now did. Indeed, there was a time when the Mitchells, the Mores and their like might have

16

looked and felt out of place walking *these* streets. However, all beauty fades in time and, for Monto, the disintegration had been triggered more by political events than by natural degradation.

Dublin's downfall had been the dissolution of the Irish parliament many years before. The entire upper strata of Dublin society had vanished, many withdrawing to their principal residences in England, leaving one of Britain's finest cities to decay. Ordinary Dubliners, who had earned a living from service to the Dublin élite had suddenly found themselves unemployed. The city's working class, their ranks swelled by the thousands who migrated in from the countryside in the famine years, had no comfortable country estates to which *they* might retreat of course.

The elegant, towering terraced homes had soon been snapped up by unscrupulous landlords who subdivided the storeys, and in many cases even divided the rooms themselves, renting them out to the city's poor and labouring classes. The Irish press labelled Monto as 'Europe's largest slum'. Such reports angered Joe and Georgina, who detected in them the clear implication that it was the local inhabitants themselves who were to blame for the district's squalor, rather than the criminally neglectful landlords. The tone of the reporting was that Dublin's ailing poor lived as they did out of choice. The newspapers further reported, probably truthfully, that of the district's twenty five thousand families, some twenty thousand households each occupied a single room. In that respect, the Mitchell family would concede they lived as the majority did.

It was in one such shabby, crumbling tenement, at number nine Lower Gardiner Street, that Joe Mitchell maintained his growing family. In better times, Lower Gardiner Street had been favoured by the city's legal profession and other eminent citizens. No less a personage than the French consul had occupied the entire house at number thirty-seven. Joe knew this because the house still bore a barely legible, blackened brass plate announcing the fact. He pointed this out to Mitch with a strange, vicarious pride. Joe said it was just as well the plaque no longer gleamed, for if it did it would have been stolen long since.

In this wide cobbled street, Joe would tell his son, where shoeless boys now chalked out football pitches, a queue of hackney carriages had once patiently awaited their turn to convey the barristers to the law courts. Joe fancied the carriage springs would have creaked something terrible, what with the combined weight of the lawyers' massive legal brains and their bulging judicial files.

Joe had a colourful way of explaining things which enabled his son to picture the scene. Mitch could imagine stiff-wigged gentlemen, standing on their steps, waving up a cab, whilst their elegantly dressed lady wives waved them off with snow-white lace kerchiefs. The flights of stone steps, which had once been scrubbed daily for the shiny-shoed solicitors, nowadays served as squatting places for gossiping women and their bawling infants, and, worse still, were urinated on nightly by drunks and dossers.

It must be said that there were far worse buildings and much greater squalor in the Monto than that experienced by the Mitchells and the Shields. As might be expected for a Protestant family with regular incomes, they lived very slightly better than many of the neighbourhood's other residents. As Mitch often heard his mother and Aunt Jessie remark, there were many, mainly Catholic families in the neighbourhood with ten and even twenty children and goodness knows how they managed. Georgina and Jessie did not attribute the more modest growth rate of their own families to any divine grace bestowed on Protestants however, but rather to the frequent absence of their husbands on military duties.

Being on good terms with William Trench, the property agent who collected his rent, Joe had learned from him something of the history of number nine. The whole of the house in which the Mitchells now shared a single room had formerly been occupied by one Henry Concannon, a barrister-at-law. According to Trench, who was a bit of a history buff, Concannon had married Maria, daughter of one Count de Lusi. Mrs Concannon had been heiress to vast estates across seven counties of Ireland. Joe had eagerly lapped up all this rent-collector related history. If number nine had been good enough for a countess back then, he felt it was certainly good enough for the Mitchells now.

Joe wondered what those wealthy aristocrats would have thought had they seen the circumstances under which nine families, comprising thirty-nine individuals, now occupied the Concannons' former residence. Some of those families shared their rooms, and sometimes their beds also, with unrelated lodgers, in order to meet the rent. When Joe came home one day to find someone had removed every alternate stair baluster in the building for firewood, he pictured Mr Concannon spinning in his grave. With every subsequent indignity which befell

18

number nine, Joe would wonder what 'spinning top' Concannon would have made of it.

Tenement dwellers were not as settled as had been their illustrious predecessors, but would come and go as their own fortunes waxed and waned. Indeed, Joe Mitchell's family had not lived in Dublin continuously. He had once quit the army and taken his wife and baby son Mitch to his native Bermondsey, but he had found there only sporadic labouring work, inadequate to maintain them. The attraction of regular army pay had persuaded Joe to re-enlist and, since most of her Majesty's troops continued to be based in England's most troublesome dominion, the army had brought the Mitchells back once again to Monto. It seemed a difficult place from which to break free.

The military was a safe option for Joe Mitchell, since work for unskilled men was sparse in all of Britain's industrialised cities. In both London and Dublin, unemployment, poverty, drunkenness and ill-health stalked the streets. It was a given that men in regular employment would spend as much as a quarter of their income on drink. Ironically though, it was those without employment who probably had greatest need of drink. Joe Mitchell's army pay was meagre but steady, so they were at least safe from eviction or starvation which threatened a great many in Monto.

It had come as a shock to Mitch the first time he had witnessed an eviction. He had seen bailiffs remove all the furniture from the room of Mrs O'Loughlin, who lived across the street, and pile it up on the pavement. The distraught woman had emptied the contents of her chamber pot from her fourth floor window down onto the heads of the bailiffs, in a defiant but futile gesture. The neighbours had taken in the youngest of her ten children. Mitch never discovered where Mrs O'Loughlin had gone, but she never returned to Lower Gardiner Street and her children were gradually dispersed. The realisation that a family might be dispossessed and thrown out, destitute, onto the street, had disturbed Mitch greatly and for some time after he had suffered nightmares about this happening to him.

The tenement room occupied by the Mitchells was situated at the front of the five storey house, one floor up from street level, and had a tall sash window which overlooked the bustle of the street below. The window had originally boasted nine panes of hand-blown glass, though two of these were now missing and had been replaced with rags and cardboard. Although the elegant picture rails and dado rails had long since been torn off and burned in the grate by former tenants, some

19

ornate plasterwork still remained on three sides of the ceiling, testifying to the fact that this had once been an elegant first-floor drawing room, occupying the entire width of the house. On a chimney wall which, if William Trench were to be believed, had once famously accommodated the Concannon's priceless *Caravaggio*, there now hung only cobwebs. Joe hadn't liked to show his ignorance by asking what a *Caravaggio* was.

The Mitchell's single room was sparsely furnished, and was dominated by the one large iron bed which now accommodated Georgina, Joe when home from barracks, five year old Mitch, three year old Joey, two year old Margaret and baby John. A small deal table and two spindle-back chairs enabled the couple to sit down to their meals, Georgina with Margaret on her lap. The elder children meanwhile would stand elbow to elbow at the table to eat. A rickety wooden wall shelf held their mis-matched china and cutlery, whilst most of their clothes were accommodated inside a single, old chest of drawers. Coats, shawls and aprons hung from hooks on the inside of the door.

Toilet and water facilities for the residents of all the tenements were located on the ground floor, out in the back garden of the house, and were shared by all. Most families however avoided nocturnal trips up and down the stairs by judicious use of chamber pots, which had to be emptied out downstairs in the mornings. In the Mitchells' case, a single, large, enamel bucket in the corner of their room served all the family as a toilet. Although heavy when full, only one trip downstairs was necessary to empty it. Georgina was slim, but she was also strong.

Water for drinking and personal washing had to be carried *up* the stairs several times a day however, as did the turf which Georgina purchased from the turf dealer's shed located on what had once been a neat green, to the rear of the Gardiner Street houses. The turf kept the little fireplace in their room glowing, providing a little comfort and also serving as the family's only cooking facility.

The fact that most families cooked over an open fire dictated the nature of their meals. Even had the Mitchells been able to afford a joint of meat, they would have been hard placed to roast it. The small fireplaces facilitated only the stewing of cheaper cuts. Perhaps because of this, Mitch developed a lifelong, nostalgic fondness for a particularly modest type of stew, known in Dublin as a coddle. No matter how mean were its ingredients, the smell, sight and sound of a

20

stew bubbling in the pot would always bring him cheer. A bowl of coddle and a cut of bread, and his mother's reassurance that they would never be evicted, was all the young Mitch required to be happy.

Mitch's best friend during his early childhood was his cousin Artie Shields. The Shields eventually moved out of the More house at Inisfallen Parade and rented a room in a tenement just around the corner in Summerhill. In their early years, Artie and Mitch were inseparable. As they played, invariably out of doors, they learned the unwritten rules of the street gangs. The gangs however were changeable entities. One day, they would run with the Gardiner Street boys and would engage in stone throwing against the children of Mecklenburg Street; the next day the Gardiner Street toughs would form an alliance with the Summerhill boys against the Mecklenburg gang.

Sometimes however their alliances would be along religious lines, the *proddy-dogs* waging a holy war on the *cat-licks*. However, it was not just the children who fought in the streets. Pitched battles would sometimes erupt amongst adults also, to the annoyance of local shopkeepers, whose windows were put at risk. In Monto, there seemed to be no hard and fast rules for conflict.

Although sporadic violence could erupt over any minor issue, all Monto residents were united in their avoidance of a common foe – the local constabulary. The officers of the Dublin Metropolitan Police, or *peelers* as they were known, were the scourge of the battling adults and children alike and, in Monto at least, were not exactly acknowledged as the saviours of the people. Unfortunately, the *peelers* had a disconcerting facility for appearing suddenly out of nowhere.

As the younger of the two cousins, Mitch was happy to follow Artie's lead into daring pursuits, whether it be tying strings of tin cans to cats' tails and releasing them down the alleys or relieving the local shopkeepers of the odd comestible item. Mitch was in awe of his naughty cousin, who was both funny and clever. For his part, Artie enjoyed having a compliant sidekick.

Artie had worked out a plan, whereby he would enter a shop, followed shortly afterwards by the innocent looking Mitch, who would promptly trip up and fall to the floor with a clatter. Whilst Mitch roared in feigned shock and pain, his appealing tousled hair and freckled cheeks never failed to attract the concern of the shopkeeper and lady customers. In the confusion Artie might pocket a couple of apples, a handful of dried fruit or even a chocolate bar for them to share later.

Whilst Artie was the brains of the duo and usually managed to look out for Mitch, Mitch was never quite as quick or as successful in his own right. Artie was the planner and Mitch his adoring disciple. Inevitably, the day came when Artie had to start school however, and so Mitch found himself latching onto some of the other boys around the streets, boys who did not share Artie's concern for keeping Mitch out of trouble.

Mitch's first brush with the law occurred when he was given a leg up by some of the bigger boys in order to clamber over the high convent wall. Once inside the convent garden, he was to gather up wind-fallen apples and throw them back over to the big boys. No thought had been given by Mitch as to how he would then climb back over the wall unaided, and so, when the nuns spotted him and ran out, the other boys disappeared with their fruity booty, leaving Mitch to his fate.

It was the burly Sergeant Lynch who retrieved a tearful Mitch and conveyed him, by means of a firm grip on the lad's ear, back to his tenement in disgrace. Glancing out of her open window, Georgina had seen them coming down the street, and so had worked up an appropriate degree of rage by the time she met them down at the street door. Sergeant Lynch explained what had happened.

'Now don't be too hard on the boy, Mrs Mitchell, for 'twas just the windfalls he was after. It was trespassing, rather than stealing, and sure the little fellah didn't get so much as a sniff of an apple for himself. What's more, Mrs Mitchell,' he added ironically, 'he's already had an almighty thrashing at the hands of the Little Sisters of Mercy.'

As the front door closed, shutting out the sunlight from the dark hallway, the departing constable heard Mitch yell out, as his mother delivered his second walloping of the day.

Like a sad little stray dog, Mitch would spend most afternoons waiting outside the school entrance for his cousin Artie to emerge. Another regular character who also waited at the school gates was *Aul' Snuffer*, a little old man who sold the children sweets from a basket strapped to the handlebars of his bicycle. *Snuffer* was so named by the children for the unfortunate cleft palate which impeded his speech and caused him to pronounce each word with an involuntary whistle of air down his nose.

Snuffer had a reasonable set of dentures, but his upper set was broken into two halves, each half thus being capable of independent movement, and they clacked loudly when he spoke. *Snuffer* made a modest living by purchasing a selection of the more popular of Lemon's sweets, which he would divide up and wrap into smaller paper twists and sell to the school children at a small mark up. Artie and Mitch would gain great amusement by interrogating *Snuffer* about the variety of sweets.

'What sweets d'ye have today?' Artie would ask, and all the queuing children would get set to giggle, as *Snuffer* snuffed and clacked his way through:

'Thisss ss-pineapple rock-k-klak; themss ss-bon ss-bons, and thisss ...,' he indicated the Turkish delight, 'iss-nutty shite.'

Mitch had to seek out his own amusement whilst Artie was in school however and it was not difficult for him to slip his mother's apron strings, whilst she was out in the back garden beating her washing in the laundry tub. She would leave Mitch in charge of his younger siblings in the garden, whilst she climbed the tenement stairs with the big basket of laundry. Of course, he would have absented himself by the time she returned. Georgina's whole day was punctuated by trips up and down the stairs, carrying either one or several infants plus baskets of laundry, shopping or turf, and of course the enamel bucket. She counted herself lucky to be living just one flight up. She had to be constantly on the move however, for, if the children were left alone for too long in the room, they might be in danger from the unguarded fire and, if they were left too long unattended in the yard, they might wander off.

Some of the older women in the tenement would keep an eye on the infants if asked, but there were so many children constantly running and out of the building that the women's vigilance could not always be relied upon. It was a small relief for Georgina therefore when Mitch did go off to play, albeit with a warning from her not to leave the street, so she might keep an eye on him from time to time from her window. Seemingly impervious to his mother's warnings to stay away from the big, bad boys, and apparently lacking any sense of self preservation, Mitch was soon in trouble again.

This time, when Georgina Mitchell was summoned to the front door of the tenement, to be confronted again by the imposing figure of Sergeant Lynch, his truncheon was firmly entwined in the coat loop of a fairly unrecognisable Mitch. The boy was coated from head to toe in unspeakably pungent, black muck. The sergeant explained that Mitch had been dared to steal the coalman's horse and to ride it off down the road. The big boys had unharnessed the horse whilst the coalman was tipping his sacks down a cellar coal hole, and they had hoisted Mitch onto the beast's back. With a cry of 'Yee hah!' from Mitch, and several sharp slaps to the horse's flanks from the big boys, the nag had taken off down Summerhill.

The sergeant said that Mitch might have the makings of a jockey one day, though he had come a bit of a cropper at *Beechers Brook*, as the children called the slaughterhouse gore-pit at the bottom of the hill. Summerhill was renowned for its stock pens, abattoirs and meat processing establishments. Indeed piles of offal usually lay in the streets, causing the rainwater to run red in the gutters. The unholy stench of gore and carcasses was highly prevalent in Summerhill, especially in high summer, but Georgina did not want it in the house as well.

Again she found herself apologising for her son's latest misdemeanour and again, as the door closed on the sergeant, the darkened communal hallway rang with the echoes of a well-slapped backside and the hapless lad's yells of indignation.

The day that Sergeant Lynch returned Mitch from a warehouse property, where the bigger boys had broken in to wreak some minor damage, Georgina realised that thrashing was an ineffective deterrent. She decided to try reasoning with the boy. She knelt down wearily in front of Mitch to impart the only piece of advice he was ever to remember, though not perhaps to heed:

'Come here to me, ye little fecker, ye'll be the ruination of me, bringin' the peelers to me door all the time! Now listen here to me and mind my words, William Mitchell. If ye carry on like this ye'll meet a bad end. Them as runs with the crows will be shot with the crows. Just you remember *that* now!'

Through such regular acquaintance, Sergeant Lynch had by now developed a bit of a soft spot for little Mitch and more than a little tender feeling for his mother, who, despite the harshness of her daily household labours and the demands of her four children, was nonetheless still a young and attractive woman. The sergeant suggested he might take Mitch to the police station one day and have him help out the constables with grooming the horses, since the boy seemed to be fascinated by even the biggest of four-legged beasts. Georgina was grateful and relieved to be rid of the boy for a whole day. The Sergeant said he understood how a boy might fall into bad ways when his soldier father was so often absent from the family home and not there to mete out discipline or set a solid example to the boy.

'Sure an' don't worry your lovely head, Mrs Mitchell,' he reassured her, 'for I'll take great care of the little chisler, that I will.'

Mitch did spend a day, and indeed quite a few days, helping out with the police horses. He never tired of shovelling up the horse droppings from their stalls, so long as he was allowed to groom the horses with the curry brush. A constable had to hold him aloft whilst he carried out the grooming of the main body of the horses, but it was a task which was enjoyed as much by the kindly constables as by the enthusiastic boy, and certainly by the horse. Sergeant Lynch meanwhile looked on with a gratified grin.

When the horses had been groomed, fed and watered, and the stable yard sluiced down with a hose, a constable would lift Mitch onto one of the calmer horses and parade him around the yard. The constable would sing galloping or hunting songs, whilst ensuring Mitch did not fall off. Mitch would rear up and down on the beast's back and whoop with delight. In his head he would be a soldier riding into battle or a cowboy rounding up cattle. Mitch provided as welcome a diversion for the constables as the horses did for Mitch.

At the end of the day, it was an exhausted but happy little boy who would either be collected by his mother or walked home by Sergeant Lynch. Mitch's erstwhile nemesis gradually came to be viewed by him as someone he might trust. Georgina was happy that Mitch might develop a respect for the law and learn to differentiate between right and wrong.

On the last of Mitch's visits to the police yard however, the day did not end well. After the horses had been groomed and the constable had given Mitch his ride, Sergeant Lynch took Mitch into the station offices to wash his hands. He then sat the lad at a table in one of the cells with a mug of warm, milky tea and a biscuit. The sergeant left, closing the cell door firmly behind him, which seemed curious, but did not worry Mitch unduly, for he had his tea and biscuit to enjoy. Shortly afterwards, he heard the sergeant returning and he heard also his mother's voice.

'The little fellah's down here, having a nice cup o' tay,' he heard the sergeant say, but it was another cell door which opened and closed again, and not the one in which Mitch sat.

Mitch heard some scuffles and his mother protesting,

'Ah, no! Sergeant!'

Next, he heard the sergeants' voice cajoling, 'Ah come on now, missus, sure there's no harm in it!'

The scuffling continued for some time, and was followed by his mother's suppressed squealing and rhythmic grunting noises from the sergeant. Mitch was greatly alarmed. He tried to open the heavy iron cell door, but could not. He began to call out for his mammy. His tears began to flow and his cries became louder and louder until at last he heard the grating of iron doors once more and the Sergeant's boots coming. He stepped back as the cell door was opened and his mother entered. She appeared distressed and dishevelled as she scooped Mitch up into her arms and carried him out of the cell. Without a word to the Sergeant, she hurried Mitch out of the station and straight home.

Mitch's Auntie Jessie came over that evening with Artie and his younger siblings, and there was much serious discussion between the sisters, to which Mitch and Artie were not privy as they were sent out to play. Mitch never fully discovered what had happened, but he was never taken to the police station again and, somehow, he knew he should not ask why.

Later that week, Mitch's father arrived at the tenement in civilian dress, as was usual for his off duty days, and there seemed to be more earnest discussion going on. Mitch's uncle Danny later joined them and the two men put on their coats and went out. Mitch supposed they were going drinking together, as they often did, but he was in bed and asleep long before they returned. Things seemed to return to normal thereafter, and the strange events surrounding his last visit to the police station were never spoken of. He could not be sure, but he feared that whatever had upset his mother had been his fault.

Mitch did not see Sergeant Lynch patrolling down Lower Gardiner Street again. In fact, it was to be some three or four years before he next saw the sergeant. Mitch knew him at once, although of course the former constable did not recognise the boy, who was now grown quite a bit taller. Lynch was no longer in uniform but was one of a squad of bailiffs, engaged in evicting a family from their Gloucester Street tenement, not on this occasion it seemed, for nonpayment of rent, but because the landlord had decided to convert the ground floor front rooms into more profitable shop premises.

When Mitch was ten, he found himself increasingly put in charge of his younger siblings. Johnnie was no longer the baby, for Georgina had now added little George to her brood, and Jessie had two more boys. Georgina was pregnant yet again however and now relied on her children to do the fetching and carrying for her. Her latest pregnancy was taking its toll on her health and Aunt Jessie came over to ensure Georgina had sufficient rest. Jessie sent the children out to play each day, ordering Mitch to look after the younger ones. Little Joey was now nine, Margaret seven, Johnny five and George was two. Aunt Jessie told Mitch to be especially careful looking after Johnny, who suffered from asthma and who sometimes had episodes where he could not breathe. Johnny was not to be allowed to get overexcited, she instructed.

Margaret was quite a sensible girl and did her best to help her mother with shopping and preparing food. Margaret also had a strong sense of responsibility and did not question what had to be done. Therefore Mitch delegated his childminding responsibilities to Margaret whenever he could, so that he could enjoy running with the other boys in the street. He found it irritating however that, wherever he went and whatever rough and tumble games he was playing, his sister would be keeping up, standing on the sidelines with George in her arms and brother Joey would have little Johnnie's hand in his.

Joey would try to join in with his bigger brother's games which irritated Mitch even more. Unlike his cousin Artie, Mitch had no need of a junior sidekick. Mitch wanted to run with the big boys. He didn't want infants tagging along, for that was demeaning. He ran where the gang ran and had no compunction about trying to outrun his siblings. Invariably however, they would catch him up eventually.

One grey, drizzly September day, a day which Mitch was never to forget, he was running with his gang up Summerhill, and as usual Margaret and his younger brothers were running up the hill behind him in an effort to keep up, when he heard Margaret cry out. He looked back and saw that his sister was on her knees on the pavement, her arms around Johnny. Mitch could see Johnny's arms flailing and immediately realised that something was wrong. He ran back down to them and saw that the exertion of running up the hill had brought on an asthma attack in the five-year old. Johnny was highly distressed and seemed to be turning blue in his efforts to breathe. Neither Mitch nor Margaret knew what to do and could only utter soothing words to the infant. To cap it all, the steady, soft rain had now become a torrent and soon the children were soaked through.

'We have to get home *now*, Mitch,' Margaret warned, 'or mammy will kill us!'

Mitch suspected his mother would likely kill *him*, for he was the one nominally in charge of the brood. He picked up Johnny and, with George clutched to Margaret's hip and Joey holding her hand, they began to run through the rainy streets, back to Lower Gardiner Street. As Mitch led the way up the wet and greasy stone steps however, he slipped and his legs went from under him. Clutching Johnny with one hand and putting out his other to break his fall, he landed heavily and painfully on one knee on the threshold. The force of the fall caused him to lose his grip on little Johnny, who fell forward out of Mitch's arms, hitting his head sharply against the door frame.

This greatly increased Johnny's distress and he began to howl loudly between his frantic gasps for air. By the time the children had reached their first-floor room they were all soaked to the skin and the younger ones were all crying. A weary Georgina raised herself from the bed, to be confronted by a sorry sight. Summoning sufficient of her dwindling energy to rise and give Mitch and Margaret each a hard slap, she ordered Margaret to get George and Joey out of their wet clothes whilst she set about trying to calm Johnny.

Once warmed by the fire, the children were soon calm and comfortable again, save Johnny however, who continued to cry at intervals. His cry sounded strange to Georgina, as it was more high pitched than usual, more like the braying of an animal. The listless infant now felt hot and dry to the touch. One minute he was floppy, the next he would throw out his limbs and arch his neck backwards in an alarming fashion, making it difficult for Georgina even to hold him, let alone comfort him.

As the evening wore on, Johnny was fretful and kept shading his eyes from the lamp light. Georgina kept inspecting him to see if he had any rash or other signs. She feared it might be measles or even chicken pox, which she declared was a bad thing to have with a pregnant woman in the house. She could find no clues upon his skin as to what ailed him, though the poor little mite continued to wail throughout the night.

28

The following day, Georgina left Mitch in charge again, this time ordering him to remain indoors with the children, on pain of a sound thrashing, while she took Johnny down to the hospital. Mitch was happy enough to comply, since it was again raining heavily, and as he too had been greatly alarmed at Johnny's condition. He feared he might have been the cause of it. He had not mentioned to his mother about Johnny's accidental bump on the head, since it had only been a bit of a bump and as the little redness which had ensued had not been noticed, given all Johnny's other symptoms.

Johnny never returned from the hospital however. He died several days later. It was a deeply shocked Mitch who fearfully asked his father why Johnny had died. Joe told him that it was from something called *meningitis*. Through his own tears, Joe assured him it was just one of those illnesses that children sometimes caught, especially here in Monto. Joe assured him that it could not have been avoided, but this did little to assuage Mitch's guilt.

A funeral was hastily arranged, though the children did not attend. Mitch could not believe he would never see his five year old brother again. He now wished with all his heart that he had spent more time playing with little Johnny, in the way that Artie had always included Mitch in his games and japes. Mitch now recalled the hurt he had felt when Artie had gradually drifted away from him, choosing instead to run with his own class mates after school. He wondered if Johnny had felt the same sort of hurt at his older brother's constant rejection of him. The thought that he ought to have been kinder to his little brother during his short life was to weigh heavily upon Mitch's mind for a long time.

If Mitch was saddened at Johnny's death, Georgina was devastated beyond all consoling and took to her bed, crying, for several days. The children crept around, trying not to upset her further, and were probably the best behaved they had ever been. Although infant death was a common occurrence for Monto families, it was not something Georgina had experienced personally, and nor was it something she had expected. Fate still had more heartache in store for the Mitchells however for, just days after little Johnny's burial, Georgina lost the baby she had been carrying. Between endless cups of tea, Aunt Jessie had ascribed this to the shock of Johnny's death. Shock, she declared, could do the strangest things. It could turn a person's hair white overnight and could cause an unborn baby to return to its maker before it had even set one tiny foot in this world.

29

With his mother confined to bed once more, Mitch's sense of guilt was overwhelming.

A few days later, Georgina herself was admitted to the North Dublin Union hospital, suffering from a fever arising out of the miscarriage. Mitch could not sleep for the thought that, like Johnnie, she might not return. With Aunt Jessie and her children spending several days in their tenement room however, Mitch and his siblings had some distraction and soon Georgina was home again. Things gradually returned to normal. However, the double tragedy had left Mitch with a morbid fear and deep distrust of hospitals and doctors.

Mitch had never really given a thought to how his father occupied himself when he was not at home. He knew his father was a soldier and that he was in the 16th, the Queen's Own Royal Lancers. He understood that, when not at home with them in the tenement, Joe lived at the Island Bridge Barracks, but Mitch did not really understand what that entailed. He imagined his cavalryman father grooming, feeding and exercising horses all day long, as the constables seemingly did in the police barracks. Mitch thought this must be a grand job to have. When he was twelve however, he would unexpectedly see his father in a new light.

One Saturday morning, Aunt Jessie arrived, with Artie and the rest of her brood. The two mothers and their collective band of youngsters set off walking up to Mountjoy Square. There was an archway stretched across the street, with '1900' marked out upon it in flowers. Mitch's schoolmaster had already explained to the class that this was a special year, as it was the start of a new decade and, more excitingly, the start of a new century. He had also told them that the Queen was coming to visit Ireland. Mitch had heard about Queen Victoria of course, and suspected she must live in constant danger, since he and a hundred other schoolboys sang lustily each morning to God, asking him to save her.

Joe Mitchell also used to sing to his children a stirring song about being 'the soldiers of the Queen, my lads'. Mitch asked his father if the Queen would be dripping with precious jewels and travelling in a gold coach when she visited Dublin, but Joe Mitchell's irreverent response was to sing several verses of 'She'll Be Coming Round the Mountain'. Unlikely though it seemed, this suggested to Mitch that she might in fact be wearing pink pyjamas and riding six white horses when she came. He was to be disappointed.

30

Upon their arrival at Mountjoy Square, the children and their mothers found the pavements crowded with people, most of them clutching flags. Mitch and Artie wanted flags to wave too, but Georgina dismissed their pleas, given the outrageous cost. After a very long wait, during which Joey had to relieve himself surreptitiously, incurring the wrath of a smartly dressed man with sodden shoes, they eventually heard a military band coming along the road from the direction of the docks.

The high pitched sound of flutes and the clash of cymbals was enthralling to Artie and Mitch but there was also something rather terrifying about the rat-a-tat of the drums and in particular the booming of the big regimental bass drum which seemed to be beating within Mitch's chest. Mitch loved the sight of the huge horses with their identically uniformed riders, as regiment after regiment passed in due order. When a division of scarlet-coated men appeared, the sun glinting off their highly polished brass buttons, and their tall hats blacker than black, Georgina pushed her children forward against the barriers and whooped:

'Look boys, there's yer da!'

Mitch did indeed glimpse his own father trotting past, resplendent in the scarlet dress uniform of the 16th, the Queen's Own Royal Lancers. Georgina informed her children that the 16th were also known as *The Scarlet Lancers*. Joe Mitchell could not acknowledge his family but his eyes darted in their direction and he sat even higher in the saddle as he spotted the look of astonishment and delight on Mitch's face. Mitch was enthralled. His father had his *own* horse, and clearly his work entailed him riding around on it, dressed in that magnificent red coat with all the fancy buttons and gold work. The headgear, which his mother later explained was called a *czapska*, made his lanky father look even taller and more imposing.

Furthermore, Trooper Joseph Mitchell had a band marching in front of him. Mitch decided therefore that his father must be very important indeed. Utterly spellbound by the spectacle, he barely noticed the black carriage containing the dumpy little old lady, clad in drab mourning clothes, which followed shortly behind Joe Mitchell.

Mitch could not wait for his father to come home so he could question him about his life at the barracks. When Mitch eventually had the opportunity to do so, Joe laughed at his son's wonderment, and told him it was not as exciting as it looked and, in fact, it was 'all bull

31

and spit and polish'. Mitch was seduced however, and was now convinced where his own future lay.

Soon, Joe Mitchell and the 16th Lancers were preparing to set sail for South Africa, where, he informed his spellbound sons, he would be fighting 'the boars'. Georgina said she hoped he would bring back a good joint or two of pork in that case, for her children could do with fattening up.

Chapter three – **Wild Irish Rose**

Monto was not only Europe's largest slum, it was also Europe's biggest red light district. The proximity of so many British Army barracks and also the docks provided a massive customer base for the local brothels. The *kip houses,* where the prostitutes slept during the day, were not located apart from the general community but were interspersed within it and were generally run by hard-faced madams, or *kip keepers.*

Mitch had only the sketchiest notion of what went on in these establishments, though he understood, from his mother's and Aunt Jessie's discussions, that most of the women who lived there had arrived from the country as innocent and fresh-faced girls, hoping to earn a respectable living as domestic servants or shop girls, but had fallen into a baser trade.

The residents of Monto did not universally condemn the working girls, but referred to them as 'the unfortunates'. From Mitch's limited acquaintance with them, the girls seemed to be useful contributors to the community. Most of them had hearts of gold and they were very kind to the local children, giving them the odd coin and even, on occasions, taking the barefoot ones to the market to buy them shoes. Some of the girls had their own children, though no fathers seemed to be around, and the *Monto Babes,* as they were known, did not always remain with their mothers but often had to be 'given up'. Aunt Jessie said the girls probably showered on other folks' children the love they could not give to their own babies.

Georgina Mitchell was perhaps more judgemental than her neighbours however and was continually warning her children not to be speaking to '*them hooers*'. She considered the girls not so much unfortunate but rather feckless. Joe Mitchell took a kinder view however and would not agree with his wife on the issue. After all, many of the girls had sunk to their present low because they had become pregnant by British soldiers – soldiers who, unlike himself, had not done the honourable thing and married them. Mitch paid no

33

heed to his mother's disapproval, as he found associating with the girls to be quite profitable.

Whenever a boat arrived at the city's docks, Mitch and the other local kids would run to notify the working girls of its arrival and would be paid for the information. The first the local residents would learn of the ship's arrival would be the sight of a giggling band of young women racing each other down Lower Gardiner Street to be first at the dockside. This would be the signal for pub landlords to tap new barrels and their wives would start to prepare food, for the Monto pubs would fulfil the sailors' *other* demands.

Fourteen year old Mitch was now lean and athletic and was taller than most of his contemporaries, so he would usually be amongst the first to sprint back from the docks and seek out some of his preferred girls to alert them to the arrival of new business. Most of the working girls were scarcely older than Mitch himself. There were few who were beyond their early twenties. In fact, they seemed to disappear as soon as, in his mother's words, 'the bloom was gone from the rose'. There were older prostitutes in Dublin, but these 'gutties' lived rough, camping out in the bushes alongside some of army barracks. Mitch naïvely supposed that most of the girls left the profession as soon as they found a regular sweetheart or perhaps when they had enough money to return to their home counties and settle down.

Mitch's absolute favourite amongst the *unfortunates* was Rose Cassidy. Sixteen year old Rose had arrived in Dublin from the north only a matter of weeks before Mitch had begun running errands for her. Rose adored clothes, especially hats, but had failed to find her dream job in a grand Dublin gown shop or milliner's. She had soon been seduced by the fine clothes given to her on temporary loan by Nellie Brannigan, who kept the *kip* where Rose now stayed. Of course the clothes, board and lodging all had to be paid for, so much of the money Rose earned, from the trade Nellie Brannigan taught her, had to be paid over to Nellie.

Being tall for his age, and taking after his father in looks and bearing, Mitch found favour with Rose, who tipped him most generously for his early alerts when a boat docked. Rose was, in Mitch's opinion, a stunner. She was fairly petite with a pale and beautiful face, framed by dark auburn curls. What attracted him to Rose Cassidy most of all however was her lively and playful nature and her instant and infectious laughter. She would bestow her warm smile upon him as readily as she would her coins. In fact, Rose was Mitch's ideal, a true Irish beauty.

Of course, he had only the vaguest idea of what it was that Rose and her clients got up to back at Nellie Brannigan's, or what went on when they were on board ships or in the alleyways behind the pubs. Monto being what it was, he had seen couples moving rhythmically and urgently in darkened corners of the tenement hallways, and indeed had been aware of his own parents' mechanical movements sometimes in the shared family bed in the dark of night. However, he did not know the *exact* mechanics of it all. What he knew of love making however was little more than a combination of exaggerated adolescent rumour and his own imagination. He could not imagine that those rough sailors and soldiers, whom he knew to be Rose's clients, would expect her to adopt the demeaning and ridiculous postures he had observed of those anonymous couples in dark alleyways. He persuaded himself that men would be content to pay Rose generously simply to allow them to look at her unclothed. That much he could understand, as he himself often imagined Rose unclothed, and the thought distracted him and made him feel hot.

Some afternoons, after school, he would linger around the steps outside Rose's *kip* at the lower end of Lower Gardiner Street. When she awoke and threw open her window, she would catch sight of him, though he would jump to his feet and try to look as though he had simply been passing by. Rose would call to him and ask him to run an errand for her. She would lower money in an old tin can on a string and ask him to fetch cigarettes or sometimes a half bottle of gin for her and the other girls with whom she shared a room. He would complete his errand in double quick time and she would always tell him to keep the change.

Sometimes, if he were lucky, she would come downstairs to sit alongside him on the steps and share her cigarettes with him. The spring days now were warm and she would wear only the thinnest of cotton blouses. He could feel her skin, still warm from sleep, as she leaned her arm against his. She would show an interest in him, asking him what he would do when he left school in the summer. He was flattered to be asked. Nobody else ever asked him. He told her he wanted to be a soldier. She had laughed, but in a nice way, telling him he would make a fine, handsome soldier and that, when she saw him in his smart uniform she would surely give him a free one. 'A free what?'

35

he had asked innocently, then immediately he had blushed as he grasped her meaning, more or less, and they had both laughed at his innocence.

One day, Rose asked him if he would like to escape the Monto for a while and come out to the country with her on the following Sunday. Naturally he agreed. He could think of nothing he would like better.

Sunday could not come around quick enough for Mitch and he was up bright and early. Pulling across the old blanket which was draped over a string and served as a modesty curtain in the Mitchell's room, he poured freshly boiled water from the kettle into the enamel basin and washed himself, before pulling on the cleanest shirt he could find. He decided his everyday trousers would do, with a bit of a sponge down, for indeed he had no others. He polished his boots with a rag. He thanked God he had long trousers, for some of his classmates were still in humiliatingly short ones. He did not own any ties, but he knew where his father kept his, and he silently removed one from the drawer, folding it up and putting it in his pocket.

He left the tenement before anyone else was awake and headed down the street to Nellie Brannigan's. He had to kill an hour or so, as Rose was still lying in after her busiest night of the week. He hoped none of his neighbours would spot him, as they passed on their way to church. Soon however, Rose appeared at the door, in her Sunday best white blouse and immaculate skirt. She kept an outfit for Sunday best, even though she no longer went to mass on Sundays. She carried a knitted woollen shawl, and a smart straw boater sat neatly upon her head. Straightening Mitch's tie and taking him by the arm, she steered him off towards the tram stop.

Mitch and Rose sat on the top deck of the tram, giggling like two children, as they watched the grey, slate roofs of the city gradually give way to the green fields and whitewashed cottages of the countryside. Mitch had little idea of where they were when Rose said it was time to alight, but clearly she was familiar with the area. They walked hand in hand along verdant pathways through the woods, and Rose pointed out trees and birds which Mitch had never seen before. She teased him for his city boy naivety and laughed at his surprised reaction when she tried to slip a young hawthorn leaf into his mouth.

'Sure it won't harm ye!' she laughed, 'and it has a nice taste, so it does. Where I come from, we call the young spring leaves 'bread and cheese' and the farmers eat them to stave off hunger when they're out in the fields.'

Mitch asked her where 'home' was. She told him how she had forsaken the rural simplicity of County Fermanagh for the sophistication of Dublin. She told him how she had walked along Sackville Street, gazing into the windows of the high class dress shops, and how she had thought she had arrived at the place where her dreams would come true. However, they had not needed a Fermanagh girl, no matter how pretty, to sell their fine gowns to the ladies of the city. She had been re-directed to the sweat shops of the garment district instead, but even there, she had found women queuing around the block, a hundred hopefuls for each vacancy.

She had sought directions to a cheap lodging house and had then ended up at Nellie Brannigan's. Her beautiful face clouded over with the telling of it all, but then, a second later, she smiled her radiant smile at him once more, as they had now reached a little stream. Stooping, she unlaced her boots, removed her hat and stockings and hitched up her long skirt, then stepped, shrieking with delight, into the cool, running water. Her unrestrained and melodic laughter competed with the delicious sound of the trickling stream.

Mitch removed his own boots and socks, rolled up his trouser legs and followed her into the water. He glanced in admiration at her shapely legs, the exposure of which seemed to cause her not the slightest embarrassment. The clean air and clear, cold water were so refreshing, and the city seemed a very long way away.

Soon Rosie had tired of the stream, both paddling in it and drinking from it, and she patted her legs dry gently with her woollen shawl then spread it under a tree and lay down upon it to rest. She beckoned him to lie beside her. She asked him if this were not the most idyllic place in the world. He said it was, particularly since she was in it. He blushed as soon as he had uttered the words, for he was unused to expressing himself in this way. However, lying here next to Rose and saying endearing things to her somehow seemed the most natural thing in the world.

Nor did he feel the slightest bit uncomfortable when Rose leaned over him and kissed him. He responded eagerly, trying to act in a gentle fashion, and to behave as little as possible like the rough sailors and soldiers he imagined she normally had to kiss. However, it was Rose who pressed her soft lips urgently against his. She also pressed the full length of her body against his and her rapid breathing excited

37

him. He was aware of her slowly unbuttoning first his shirt and then his trousers, and sliding her hand with gentle if alarming intimacy inside his clothing. She then pulled away from him and started to remove her blouse.

Soon, Rose was completely naked and was sitting astride him. Her beautiful auburn hair, now loosened, cascaded down over her shoulders and caressed her bare breasts, every bit as boldly as Mitch now longed to do. He could hear his own heart pounding, like the bass drum of an army parade. He prayed he would not die from the excitement – not yet at least. Rose took his hands and ran them slowly over her body, from the small, hard breasts, down over the soft whiteness of her belly and into the warmth between her slender thighs. Her bosom rose and fell with the quickness of her breathing and his own breathing echoed her passion, as his young body discovered its natural response. Gently, she leaned over him, guided his lips to her breasts and coaxed him to please her in ways familiar to her, but new to him.

Next, Rose reached down and began to caress him intimately and rhythmically. Judging the moment to be right, she now sat astride him again and enfolded him in the inner warmth of her body. Rose moved her body on top of him with greater and greater urgency, until his loud sighs told her that he had reached the point of ecstasy. They lay, still, warm and naked, in each other's arms, uncaring lest anyone venture by, and indeed no-one did, as the afternoon turned to evening. Eventually, the sun began to set and a chill fell upon their young skin, telling them it was time to return to the city.

'Well,' Rose teased him as they dressed, 'yer a skinny lad for one who'd be a soldier. Tell yer ma she should put some more meat in yer coddle, so she should.'

Fired with the confidence of his newly discovered sexuality, Mitch drew her to him, asked her who she thought she was calling a lad, and suggested he was in fact a man now, for he believed he had put some meat into *her* coddle. She pretended to be outraged at his impudence, and they both burst out laughing.

Serious now, Mitch asked her if he were different from her clients. She reassured him at once, explaining that he was the only one she had ever kissed. He was her boyfriend. She did not kiss clients. Mitch was happy with the distinction. He sat with a protective arm about her all the way back on the tram. As their destination came into view, he asked her:

'Rose, will you be my *mot*?'

'What the devil is that when it's at home?' she asked.

'My *mot*, my girlfriend. That's what we say in Dublin. A fellah calls his girl his *mot*. You know, like them butterfly things you get at night, hanging around a lamp.'

'Is that what they say? Well then, I'll be the *mot* to your flame, Mitch. I'll be your girl, so I will.'

Mitch was deeply in love with Rose. He now saw her most Sundays. Sometimes she would sneak him into her room at the *kip*, though they had to be vigilant, for Nellie Brannigan did not encourage visits from boyfriends. Sometimes they would take the tram out to their own special place in the countryside and make love. Other times they would just walk around Dublin's better streets together, sharing a dream of a better life. Their trysts had to be daylight occurrences of course, for the nights belonged to Rose's business clients, the thought of whom Mitch tried to banish from his mind. Now, when he saw the rough sailors and their women in doorways, he understood exactly what it was they did, how it felt and why couples were so urgent in pursuit of this particular intimacy.

He diverted himself with the dream that, when he became a soldier and had money in his pocket, he would marry Rose and support her, so that she would not have to consort with the sailors ever again. They would have children – not too many mind – and would live happily ever after. For now however, they simply enjoyed their stolen moments of love making.

He sometimes found himself gazing at his mother, and wondering if there had been a time when she too had been a young and mischievous girl, who had made love with breathless abandon to his father. He looked at her now, a still attractive woman, but with hands red from cleaning their miserable, decaying room. Her unkempt dark hair was fading to silver at her temples and infants clung habitually to her skirts. No, he could not imagine she had ever been as carefree, impetuous and passionate as his Rose.

Rose had a truly wild side to her nature. Sometimes however, she alarmed him with her dare-devil tricks. One Saturday afternoon, Mitch saw her standing outside the Royal Barracks with Teresa, one of her friends from the *kip*. Rose beckoned Mitch over and, when he reached them, she made him bend down so that she and Teresa might climb up on his back and from there scale the wall of the barracks, since the guard at the front would not let the working girls enter the premises looking for custom. Both Mitch and the plan collapsed however, as they all took a fit of the giggles. The guard spotted them and chased them away. Mitch was reminded of his own early bad experience scaling the convent wall for apples. Rose soon got her own back on the surly guard at the barracks however, when she knocked off his hat from behind with a carefully aimed stone, and she and Mitch made rude gestures at him before easily outrunning him, since he could not stray far from his post.

Sometimes it would be Mitch who was the butt of her japes, like the time when they had been making love in the woods and had heard a Sunday school party heading their way on a nature ramble. Rose had been first to her feet, joking that the children might see more of nature than their teacher had intended, and she had run off into bushes to hide, taking not only her own clothes but Mitch's too. Mitch had been forced to hide behind a large oak tree. As the group passed on both sides of the tree, he had clung to it, praying that the children would not glance back and spot his nakedness. They did not, fortunately.

When they were alone together, Mitch would sing to Rose. Rose told him he had a good voice. No-one had told him that before. He would sing her favourite song, one of the latest ballads, which they heard being sung around the local pubs and which seemed entirely appropriate:

'My wild Irish Rose,
The sweetest flower that grows.
You may search everywhere,
But none can compare
With my wild Irish rose.'

Owing to his height, Mitch sometimes succeeded in persuading publicans he was old enough to be served beer. He would bring the drinks outside to share with Rose. Rose would pay of course. It was ironic that she looked, and indeed she was too young to be admitted to the local bars, yet was old enough for the bars' patrons to take their custom to her after closing time.

If Rose hated what she had to do to make a living, she never disclosed her unhappiness to Mitch. As he grew fonder of Rose however, he began to resent what she did and he was also uncomfortable with the fact that she was, by necessity, so generous

40

towards him. It was she who paid for their outings, since he had not a penny to his name. In Rose's country philosophy however, money was like manure – no good, she said, unless it be spread around. Rose was almost reckless in her bounty, however.

She would impulsively buy them both a chocolate bar if they were passing a confectioner's shop. When particularly flush, she would take him to a café and treat him to a good meal. She even took him to a gentleman's outfitters on one occasion and bought him a quality shirt to wear. He felt uncomfortable accepting her generosity, yet he felt more than comfortable in the soft, creamy cotton shirt. He had never seen nor felt, let alone worn, the like of it. Rose would spot gaily coloured hair ribbons for Teresa or for their neighbour's little girls and would rush into the shop to buy them without a moment's hesitation. If she had the money, Rose would spend it.

Mitch's *mot* seemed to live her life at a frenetic pace, as if it might end tomorrow. She put him in mind of the dizzy mayflies they saw on their country rambles, trying to cram a lot of living into a single day. She seemed to derive great pleasure from lavishing her money on others. Mitch wondered if her benevolence made her feel she had a status above that of a common 'brasser'. Certainly her profuse spending seemed to compensate for the distasteful and demeaning side of her life. She would tell Mitch that life was too short for regrets and that he should savour every moment of it. It seemed nothing could dampen her spirits, nothing, that was, save the prospect of what awful fate might one day befall her. On one occasion, after a frantic and intense afternoon's love making in their own little sylvan glade, as she lay in Mitch's arms, her cheerful face clouded over suddenly and she made a strange request of him.

'Promise me,' she entreated, 'you won't ever let them *Magdaleens* get their hands on me. Will you do that for me, Mitch? Don't let them nuns get their hands on me and put me in the laundry. And don't let them cut my hair, for I couldn't bear it, so I couldn't. And don't let them send me to *The Lock*, neither, for nobody ever comes back from there. Will you promise me that, Mitch?'

Mitch was taken aback by her sudden fearfulness. He had cause to dislike nuns himself. He knew the Magdalene sisters ran an institution in Gloucester Street, for he had seen of some of the 'fallen' women who had been incarcerated there. Their shaven heads and pale, haunted faces might just be glimpsed through basement windows as they laboured away in the confines of the steaming laundry. It was generally supposed that they had sunk to such a degree of wickedness that they had to be confined in cellars so as not to contaminate some supposedly innocent and respectable world on the outside. The Monto – innocent and respectable? That was a laugh.

He was unfamiliar with the term *The Lock* however, and was not sure what she meant. He guessed she must mean the local police lock-up. He could see the thought disturbed Rose however so he did not explore her fears further and risk spoiling the magic of their afternoon together. He promised her solemnly that he would always love her and would always protect her to the best of his ability.

Mitch's school days were now drawing to a close but he could not wait for the end of his final term, so he decided to absent himself. At five foot nine inches now, he appeared a couple of years older than he actually was, so he did not attract the attention of either the *peelers* or the school truancy officers as he hung around the streets with some of his equally disenchanted classmates. Ironically, the offence the boys were committing in missing school was known locally as *mitching*, therefore Mitch felt almost obliged to do it.

He had been disappointed to learn that it would not be possible for him to join the army before his fifteenth birthday, which was not until the first of December. He supposed that, had he stuck at school and obtained his school leaving certificate, he might have been taken on with the army as a scholar, but he didn't want to exchange once classroom for another. He felt he had outgrown schooling and he wanted to get on with the business of being a man. The impatient optimism of his youth persuaded him that adult life was simply out there, awaiting his participation.

He persuaded a local greengrocer to take him on as a messenger boy, which was just a boy's job but was perhaps a first step towards adult employment. It gave him some pocket money and a modest feeling of independence. It did mean however, that he was not free in the afternoons to see Rose. Afternoons and early evenings were his busiest times for making deliveries to the housewives who had placed their orders earlier in the day. He was not now free until the evenings, which was when Rose started work. However, he still had his Sundays with Rose to look forward to.

Several days went by when Mitch did not see Rose around the Monto as he cycled the streets making his deliveries, and nor did he see her around the area in the evenings, which was unusual. He was familiar with her usual nocturnal haunts around the barracks and outside the pubs but did not see here there either. One Sunday came and went without Rose appearing either at her window or doorway, then another, and then the summer was at an end. Rose no longer came and sat out on her step and he began to worry that she might have tired of her schoolboy lover and be avoiding him.

He wondered whether she had decided to return to Fermanagh, but he could not believe she would have done so without saying goodbye. Taking his courage in his hands, he ventured to knock on Nellie Brannigan's door, to enquire if Rose were alright. To his relief, it was Rose's friend, Teresa, and not the sour-faced auld *kip keeper* herself, who answered. Teresa looked grave when she saw Mitch. She told him Rose had fallen ill and that Nellie had called in the doctor. He had diagnosed syphilis and had sent Rose to the Westmoreland Hospital. Teresa said she had been over there several times, but they would not let her visit Rose as she was not a relative. She advised Mitch that, if he went, he should claim to be Rose's brother.

Alarmed, and annoyed with himself for not having made the enquiry earlier, Mitch followed Teresa's directions and headed over to Townsend Street, where he eventually located the hospital at its corner with Luke Street. The discreet brass plaque announced the rôle of the *Westmoreland Lock Hospital* as being for the treatment of venereal diseases. He soon found himself being interrogated by a stern woman at the reception desk, just as Teresa had warned, but he told her he was Rose's brother, and eventually he was sent up to the appropriate ward. As he made his way past long rows of beds, he was taken aback at the condition of some of the women patients but could not at first see his Rose. Then he spotted her in one of the beds at the far end of the ward.

On reaching her bedside, he was immediately shocked at her appearance. Rose lay, motionless and almost as white as the bed sheets which enveloped her now thin frame. Her skin appeared almost translucent. There were dark rings around her eyes and flat, livid red sores around her mouth. She seemed to be only semi-conscious and was hot and feverish to his touch. A nurse was by his side immediately, issuing a stern warning that the patient was infectious and that he should not touch her. As the nurse walked away down the ward however, Mitch placed a hand gently on Rose's brow and smoothed back her damp, matted hair. To his horror, strands of it came away in his hand.

Rose half opened her eyes. They no longer sparkled in recognition of him, though it appeared as if she were trying to force a smile. Was this the inevitable decline to which his mother and aunt had alluded? Had 'the bloom' gone from *his* Rose? He wondered if this loss of looks was the price she would pay for her profession. As he reflected on all of this, Rose's eyes remained very slightly open, yet she seemed to be sleeping. He guessed she must be heavily medicated. He sat beside her bed for a couple of hours, stroking her hand whenever the nurses were not looking. He thought how much the loss of her beautiful hair would hurt her when she recovered. He placed his lips close to her ear and softly sang to her.

'My Wild Irish Rose
The dearest flower that grows.
Some day for my sake
She may let me take
The bloom from my wild Irish Rose...'

The lyrics now took on a particular poignancy for him. His sorrow at her lamentable condition choked his voice into respectful silence. It did not seem that she would awake whilst he remained however, and so, with a heavy heart, he tiptoed away.

The following evening, Mitch counted out his earnings and purchased some chocolate for Rose, to add to the fruit he had stolen from one of his deliveries. He did not have enough to buy some flowers, as they were quite expensive at that season, so, as he passed the flower seller's kiosk in Merrion Square, he surreptitiously relieved the florist of a bunch of red roses and headed back to the hospital. He felt a sharp pang of guilt as he realised that these were the first gifts he had ever given Rose, and some of them were stolen. The knowledge that he had never been able to repay her generosity stung his masculine pride.

Once again, he was interrogated by the receptionist before she would allow him in. He made his way up the stairs and down the ward but was dismayed to find Rose's bed empty and freshly made up. He sought out the stern ward nurse and asked her where he might find Rose Cassidy. The nurse's expression, seemingly starched to match her collar and cap, now darkened and she led him back down the ward to her nurse's station.

'I'm afraid your sister passed away in the early hours of this morning, Master Cassidy. Will you advise your parents and have them get in touch regarding the funeral arrangements?' she said, completely without emotion.

Mitch could only nod. He was dumbstruck. How could Rose be dead? How could she have gone so quickly? He wondered if the nurse might be lying to him, but then he could not imagine why she would do so. He felt a wave of nausea pass over him. The nurse saw him begin to sway and eased him into her chair. She took the gifts from him, placed them on her desk and gently guided his head down between his knees, rubbing his hands, partly to comfort him and also to increase his circulation and prevent him fainting away completely.

After a few moments, he felt able to sit upright again, and the nurse said she would just have to leave him for a moment to get the ward book from her cabinet. First however, she asked him for details of Rose's next of kin. Without hesitation, Mitch told her the hospital should contact Mrs Brannigan, at 37 Lower Gardiner Street, then, when the nurse went for the ward book, he quickly slipped away.

Rose's death affected Mitch, even more than had the death of his little brother, Johnny. It was not as though death were an uncommon occurrence in Monto – far from it. Mitch had even seen dead bodies lying in the street from time to time. Many families lost infants and babies. Infant mortality was particularly high in the overcrowded tenements. Mitch and Artie had once inveigled their way into a house where a wake was being held for an old woman they did not know. They had gazed respectfully at the deceased in her coffin before stuffing themselves with as much food and drink as they could.

Rose's death was different however. She had not been some sickly infant or feeble old woman. She had been the liveliest creature he had ever known. Rose had been an irrepressible spirit, full of life and fun and only sixteen years old. How could she possibly be dead? It hit him hard. For the next few days, he was quiet and withdrawn. Even his mother remarked upon his depressed state, but his Aunt Jessie attributed it to moody adolescence, since she could hardly get two words out of Artie these days either.

Gradually however, Mitch's melancholy began to turn to anger. The joy of life had gone out of him, leaving a void within him which slowly gestated pain and resentment. He could tell no-one of the tragic end to his secret relationship with Rose but must grieve in silence. His

45

sorrow, like a canker, slowly grew. The pain of his loss would not ease.

Around him, the neighbourhood with its bustle and drama served only to heighten his feeling of isolation. He had never felt he belonged in Monto. He lived *in* Monto but yet was not *of* it. He did not belong to the majority Catholic community and, although he shared their poverty, he did not accept it as they did. He would never be able to integrate into that community, for he was different. He was the son of a Protestant Englishman. What should have been an advantage was in some ways a distinct disadvantage. He had attended a Protestant Church school, with smaller classes than the Catholic schools, and therefore he ought to have had better prospects. The Mitchells lived in the same miserable, grimy tenements as the Catholic families and yet they might have had cause to expect better.

His father however was just a soldier. Joe Mitchell was not really a part of that English élite which ruled Ireland. He was just the means by which they ruled, and so no-one expected Mitch to rise above his father's station. In fact, to do so might be a betrayal of one's kin. Mitch could write far better than his parents could. He had beautiful handwriting. His mother said so, and so he would write any note or letter his parents needed to be written. He hoped his handwriting might help him to get on in life one day. However, he could not see that happening here in Monto.

He hadn't enjoyed any close friendships since Artie had started school ahead of him. School had ensured Artie always remained a year above him and beyond his association. Artie now had friends his own age. After Mitch's own disastrous escapades with the other neighbourhood boys and his subsequent dealings with the *peelers*, Mitch had not trusted anyone else. He had no friends in his own class at school.

Of course, Rose had been his friend and confidante, as well as his lover. They had shared each other's hopes and fears, but Monto had taken her from him. This accursed place, with its relentless poverty and sickness, crushed both the hope and the life out of its desperate people and offered them only short-lived pleasures for which they might pay most dearly.

It caused Mitch great frustration that he looked like an adult and felt like an adult, yet he had no adult's job, no adult's voice. He had little money, no independence and no prospect of escape. Monto now revolted him. It was holding him back. He hated living in these shabby

46

streets. He hated living in one room, without personal comfort or privacy. He would gladly fly the nest, had he the means to fly and somewhere to go.

During one of Aunt Jessie's visits, Mitch lay on the bed, trying desperately to read a copy of *Boys' Own*, whilst the younger Mitchell and Shields children continually ran around, bumping into the bed frame. He tried to ignore their childish laughter and to blank out the women's idle fireside chatter, none of which gossip interested him in the slightest. It was a cold day outside and, since he had no warm coat to wear and no money to take him anywhere warm, he had no choice but to remain indoors.

Cabin fever was making him feel listless, but suddenly he was aware that his aunt was speaking of a woman from Summerhill who had, she said in a grave and knowing way, 'gone to *The Lock*'. He immediately recalled Rose's expressed fear of *The Lock* and he now began to take note of their talk. The women's conversation had moved on however, and so he felt moved to ask his aunt what she had meant by 'gone to *The Lock*'. Glancing across at the younger children, to ensure they were not listening, Jessie replied in conspiratorial tones.

'The Lock Hospital, you know, the Westmoreland Lock, up in Townsend Street. It's where all the *brassers* end up, though they don't stay there long,' she said.

Mitch must have looked uncomprehending, for his aunt willingly expanded on her explanation.

'You know, they're sent there with the *veneerul* diseases and, of course they never get better, so the doctors and nurses see them off by smutherin' them wid a pillow. They're allowed to do it though. What's this they call it, Georgie?' she looked at her sister for a prompt, '*euphemised* or something, isn't it?'

Georgina confirmed that this was indeed what was rumoured and she expressed the view that it was probably a kindness for the women, not that anyone cared for their sort anyway. She added that, as in all hospitals, you knew you were done for when they moved you to one of the beds furthest down the ward. Apparently, it was convenient to have those souls who were closest to death located nearest to the back exit. That way, they wouldn't distress the other sick ones by carrying the dead all the way down the ward.

Mitch felt as if he had been struck by a lightning bolt. He got up from the bed and slammed the door on his way out. The women nodded to each other, as if to confirm their diagnosis of chronic adolescence.

Oblivious now to the bitter wind which stung his ears and to the cold rain which diluted his tears, Mitch walked down to the Liffey. He could hardly contain his anger. He stood for a long time watching the dark, oily waters ebb and flow and observing the activity surrounding the boats. He thought about Rose and the way she had died. She had not been ill for long before she died. Had she been killed by the medical staff? Was such a thing possible, or was it just a scurrilous rumour? Could the hospital authorities really get away with that? Then again, if they had killed Rose, would there be any proof of their crime? Would he ever know the truth?

His thoughts turned blacker as the sun set. He fantasised about finding the medic who had killed his Rose and about slowly killing *him*. He now realised what Rose had meant when she had asked him never to let them put her in 'The Lock'. Had those nurses in any way been kind to his Rose, or had she in fact suffered death at their hands? Maybe they had thought it a kindness. Maybe he should have been there earlier to speak up for Rose. Perhaps Rose's death was not the fault of the medical staff. Maybe it was the *Kip-keepers* like Nellie Brannigan, and the awful clients Rose had been forced to service, who had been responsible for her death. As he watched the seamen coming and going between pubs and ships, his heartache and his anger grew.

He wandered around the dockside for hours. He had not eaten since early that morning but he was not aware of his hunger. What should have been an empty stomach was instead a tight knot of tension and resentment. Drunks were now wandering out of the pubs. Some were with women, laughing raucously at some obscene joke or other. Others, more inebriated and less capable, walked alone, trying to make their way back to their ships. He saw one shadowy figure in front of him, a short, stocky man, clad in the unmistakable woollen cap and jacket of the seaman. The man made his way unsteadily down the alley at the side of the pub he had just left, maintaining his balance by keeping one hand on the wall as he went along. Finding a quiet spot, the mariner began to urinate, swaying somewhat as, of necessity, he relinquished his grip on the wall.

Mitch felt a gross contempt welling up inside him for this brutish man, this frequenter of prostitutes, this despoiler of beautiful young girls like Rose. He waited until the man had apparently finished and then, on impulse, he stepped forward, put a hand on the man's

48

shoulder and whirled him around. He threw his fist into the surprised face of the stranger, who fell to the ground like a sack of turf. It felt satisfying to see the man go down. Mitch pulled him to his feet and continued to pummel him viciously. The man looked stunned, but was too dulled by drink to fight back. Again he fell to the ground. Mitch kicked him into unconsciousness then, looking up and down the alley to ensure no-one had witnessed the attack, he went through the man's jacket, found his bulging wallet and pocketed it.

Several blocks away, in the light from a gas lamp, Mitch was surprised at how much money there was in the wallet. He threw the empty wallet into the gutter then, pocketing the notes, he noticed the welcoming lights of a nearby bar so he crossed the road and went in. The landlady did not seem to be fooled by Mitch's height and looked questioningly at his flushed, youthful face. However, the sight of the wad of notes in his bruised hand dispelled her caution and she immediately drew him a pint of beer. His anger temporarily assuaged, he now felt ravenously hungry and so ordered a plate of stew and sat at a table by the glowing hearth to eat it.

The stew was extremely good and the beer relaxed him. The pain he had felt for some days now was dissipating slightly. He reflected on what had happened. It had been easy – too easy, but he now felt strangely elated. He felt he had somehow taken control. He had been involved in fights before, and had usually given a good account of himself, but only with other boys, not with an adult. He had rarely been the aggressor before but had usually been on the defensive. Of course he realised that taking advantage of a drunken man was not an honourable thing to do, but then he persuaded himself his victim had not been an honourable man.

For the first time in his life, Mitch had money in his possession, and a sizeable amount too. It probably represented a whole month's pay for the seaman. He justified his actions with the conviction that the man would have probably spent the money foolishly anyway, on drink and women. Mitch had saved him from a series of hangovers and perhaps also from contracting some incurable condition or other. The idea did not salve his conscience entirely, but he decided that guilt would not get him out of Monto, whereas money might – and he had to get out.

A beacon of hope presented itself soon however, when Joe Mitchell returned, gaunt and weary, from the glory and the gore of the war in South Africa and declared, not for the first time, that he had had enough of the army. What did come as a surprise to Mitch however, but a most welcome one, was when his father announced they were all going to relocate to London and he would find work there. Of course this was not the first time the family had tried their luck in Joe Mitchell's birth place, but Mitch had been very young the last time and had no recollection at all of the brief period they had spent in Bermondsey.

That particular venture had not been a success apparently. Ironically enough, that had been because many Irishmen had settled in Joe's old district back then, and he had been disappointed to find that labourers had been plentiful but labouring jobs few. The available accommodation had been more affordable to groups of young labourers who pooled their wages and shared rented rooms, than to a married man with a single wage and a wife and two young sons to support. Things had not worked out for them on that occasion, and so Joe had rejoined his old regiment and had taken his family back to Dublin.

Now however, a cousin of Joe's had assured him the employment situation in South London was much improved. There was plenty of work in the existing industries and a number of food processing manufacturers were now setting up factories in the district too. The plan was for Joe to go on ahead and, as soon as he had a job and accommodation, Georgina and the children would follow. That day could not come soon enough for Mitch.

He delivered his very last greengrocery order, which would be a little light this week, since he had helped himself to some of the apples, knowing he would be on his way out of there even before the theft would be reported. He cycled down Summerhill on the greengrocer's bicycle and took a last look at the grey, slate rooftops of the grubby tenements. He took in the vista of grey washing, threaded onto poles, angled as if in mock salute out of many of the grimy windows; the crucified shirts hanging limply above the noisy streets. Beneath them, the ill-clad, barefoot children played in mud and horse droppings. Smoking chimneys disgorged their black smuts onto damp sheets, while elderly women with racking coughs sat upon the steps, their hungry and inconsolable grandchildren swaddled to them in dirty shawls. How he hated Monto. There was nothing about the place that he would miss; not a damned thing. He felt no connection to the place and vowed never to return.

Mitch's Uncle Danny had also left the army after his exploits in South Africa and had found a low paid labouring job locally. His wife Jessie complained that the pay was so poor it would not keep them, but Artie was working too now. They might just scrape by until their next child Annie left school.

Jessie was devastated at the prospect of her sister leaving. She had wanted Danny to go with Joe, so that both families might remain close, but Danny had no connections with London and did not want to leave Ireland. Jessie had wept at the news of their imminent departure, for she would greatly miss her favourite sister and her nephews and niece. Georgina had tried to comfort her but Jessie was convinced she would never see any of them again. Artie, who, like Mitch, had started out as an errand boy for a local tradesman, was now doing a man's job, labouring alongside his father, a fact which had widened the gap between the youths still further. This convinced Mitch that, if he had any future at all, it would be in London.

Chapter four – **Bermondsey Days**

Mitch was not sure exactly what he had expected of Bermondsey, but if he had hoped it would smell any sweeter than Monto, then he was certainly disappointed. The first thing which had struck him about the place, as indeed it did all newcomers to the area, was *the stink*. For Mitch, the pungency of the Summerhill slaughterhouses was now eclipsed in his memory by the all pervading reek of Bermondsey's tan pits. If Monto's odour of freshly slaughtered flesh had offended his senses, the new stench of hides, scraped of their putrefaction and soaked in the collected urine of London's horse population and dog faeces lifted from the capital's streets, was an outright assault on them.

The stinking refuse from the many tanneries was collected daily and transported for further processing to the nearby glue works, which in turn contributed its own particular brand of vile odour. Incredibly, it seemed that some bright spark once had the idea of setting up a vinegar works in Bermondsey, partly out of a flawed belief that fumes from its brew house would somehow neutralise the insanitary smells of the industries around it. If anything, the harsh waft of acetic acid on the breeze merely added to the choking, noxious cocktail.

Nor were the sights of Bermondsey any less unpleasant than the smells. The tangible effluvium of the various industries spewed out of the factories via the many creeks and glugged into the nearby Thames. Barefoot children were just as much in evidence here as they had been in Dublin and, contrary to popular myth, the streets were not paved with gold, but were adorned with the same filth as in Ireland's capital.

Depending upon the strength and direction of the wind however, more pleasant aromas might be detected in the air from time to time. Bermondsey boasted a vast spice mill for grinding a variety of fragrant substances, freshly transported from other continents to the London docks. The Mitchell children had never seen sacks of cloves or cardamoms before. The brightly coloured hillocks of powdered ginger, cinnamon, turmeric and cayenne pepper could be glimpsed within the mill sheds and their aromatic, oriental scents detected on the river breezes. Such exotic cargoes would arrive at the local wharves and, after initial processing in the spice mill, would be conveyed the short distance to the pickling sheds.

As Mitch and his siblings gradually explored their new territory, they saw that the huge paper sacks of sugar delivered to the pickle works and jam factories were liable to burst if dropped and that quick-witted and light-fingered youngsters might profit from this. Georgina was pleased with the hatfuls and pocketfuls of sugar they sometimes brought home, for although sugar was an expensive commodity it was unthinkable to drink tea without it.

The youngsters were surprised to see also that the local river, the Neckinger, which flowed through the tanneries and dye works, ran alternately indigo blue or khaki yellow, depending upon the nature of the goods being dyed on any particular day. The Neckinger was no clearer or fresher than the black waters of the Liffey. It was merely harder to spell.

Mitch was pleased to find that Bermondsey had as many horses as Dublin. Despite the expansion of the railways, horse-drawn wagons were still the primary form of transportation for collecting the raw materials arriving at the docks and also for delivery of the finished products. Of course this meant that generous deposits of horse dung lay around the streets, adding yet another layer of effluent to the district and providing a source of infection to the barefoot children.

Bermondsey was a far noisier place than Monto had been. Metals were processed locally, at both the brass foundry and the tin box company. This added another deafening dimension to the local environment but enabled foodstuffs produced in the area to be preserved and packaged on the spot. Insalubrious Bermondsey did not seem to Mitch to be the ideal location for food industries, yet their recent proliferation along the nearby stretch of waterfront had led to the area becoming known as 'London's larder'. This was according to Mitch's brother Joey who now found himself work in one of the food canneries. Joe had secured jobs for himself and for Mitch in a tannery in nearby Grange Road. Three wages coming in meant the Mitchells could now afford not one but two rented rooms in a tenement. Crosby Row, off Long Lane, where the Mitchells now lived, was set in a network of grubby alleys and grimy courts which were little better than those of Dublin's Monto district.

Predictably perhaps, since her husband was released from the army and living at home full time now, Georgina soon increased her brood by another child, a daughter, whom she named Jessie, after the sister she was missing so much. Not long after little Jessie's birth, Georgina received a letter from Dublin advising that her sister Jessie's husband Danny had passed away unexpectedly. Only thirty-seven years of age, he had contracted meningitis – the same illness which had done for Georgina's son Johnny. Like little Johnny Mitchell, Danny Shields had spent his last few days on earth in the insanitary, overcrowded hospital at the North Dublin Union Workhouse.

Joe and Georgina were not in a position to send very much money to assist Jessie, but knew she would be grateful for whatever they could spare. The letter from Jessie went on to say that Artie was now labouring and was putting in all the hours he could manage, so they would not starve at least. Mitch was quite disturbed to learn of his Uncle Danny's death. It further confirmed his conviction that people in Dublin's Monto had but a tenuous grasp on life. He decided his father had done the right thing in moving them to London.

Mitch and his father both now worked as general labourers for CW Martin & Co at the *Alaska Seal Fur Factory*. Despite its name, the factory processed not only seal furs, but also beaver pelts, goatskins and cow hides. Mitch's was not a boy's job, as his previous one had been, but a real man's job. He hauled heavy bags of lime from the dry storage area and tipped them into the lime pits, where the caustic nature of the lime ensured the hairs were gradually burned from the animal skins. Of course the lime had a similar effect upon his own skin.

He also poured stinking alum and other foul substances into the tanning pits, where barefoot workers trod the hides to in order to soften them. As unpleasant as his own task was, he thought the job of the youths who stamped the hides was far worse. The fifteen year old hoped his job would be a step along the way towards his independence, even though the money he earned was less than he had hoped for. The hours were disappointingly long and the nature of the work most distasteful. He thought he would never become accustomed to the fishy stench of the seal skins, a stench which pervaded even his clothes and hair. His fellow workers assured him that he would not notice this eventually – perhaps after twenty or so years at the work.

Nor had Mitch realised how much derision his Irish accent would attract. Nobody actually had difficulty understanding his speech; they just felt it necessary to mock his flat, Dublin vowels. His pronunciation of 'worse' as 'wairse', 'mean' as 'meeyan' and 'south' as 'saywtt', singled him out for continual mimicry and ridicule. His fellow workers never seemed to tire of imitating his speech. He consciously avoided using certain words which he knew they would pick up on. He was by no means the only Irish-born worker in the factory of course, but he was the youngest and most recently arrived. This made him a natural target for cruel tricks which went beyond the ragging that was part of any normal workplace induction.

His first day initiation involved a dunking in one of the stinking pits, where he struggled to hold his breath as he re-surfaced amongst the foul, gelatinous sealskins and the clinging shreds of viscous flesh. This caused the other leatherworkers and supervisors enormous amusement. It also ruined his only good shirt. The shirt was the beautiful cotton one Rose had bought him. He had unwisely chosen to wear it on his first day, in the hope that he would make an impression and perhaps be selected for a particularly good position. The shirt was his only tangible memento of his beloved Rose.

As he climbed out of the pit and the stinking chemicals drained out of his ears, he distinctly heard someone refer to him as an 'Irish turd'. This comment greatly increased the mirth of his fellow workers. It also increased his own anger. His skin burned and his eyes stung as he cursed them all silently. He cursed the shavers, the blubberers and the finishers, the foremen and the supervisors. He even cursed the wealthy manufacturing Martin family themselves. That the men in charge should let this sort of cruel and barbaric behaviour happen was unforgivable. He promised himself revenge, no matter how long it took.

He had to work on for the rest of his first day in his sodden, sticky clothes and, though he washed them out thoroughly that night, leaving them to air before the fire, his trousers were still slightly damp and malodorous when he put them on again the next morning. His lesson learned, he wore one of his father's old shirts on his second day. The only protective clothing supplied to the workers was a large, heavy and stiff leather apron. He hated this. He hated also the sacking which he and the other leather workers had to wrap around their legs to absorb the dust rising from the white lime as they poured it into the stinking pits. The lime dust rose to coat their faces, their hair, their arms, and made them look like living corpses. The heavy wooden clogs, which were also compulsory wear, gradually blistered the tops of his feet. He absorbed the stinging chemicals through those blisters as well as through the blisters on his hands. The lime and urea caused his eyes to stream and his supervisor's continual racist jibes also stung him. He soon decided that factory work was not for him. For the moment however he could see no way out of it.

Joe Mitchell felt Mitch's disappointment and tried to reconcile his son to what he considered fairly typical of the 'high spirits' a youth might invariably encounter in a new job. After all, everyone had to start at the bottom and work their way up the ladder. That way, he assured him, when Mitch eventually found a better job he would appreciate it all the more.

Joe explained also that the people of south London were, in some ways, a race apart. He told Mitch that, very long ago, long before there were houses and factories thereabouts, the whole area had been bleak marshland. The now thriving towns and villages, such as Southwark and Bermondsey, had once been just small settlements dotted around the flood plain of the Thames. It was hard to imagine now, Joe said, but these busy places had just been tiny hamlets back then, perched on small islets or even just on banks of mud, sedge and reeds.

As Joe's late father, William Mitchell, a Bermondsey dyer, had told the history of the place to him, so Joe now repeated to his own son the story of how criminals on the run from the law in the City had found a refuge in these marshy places. Here, south of the river, where the city authorities had held no legal jurisdiction, many criminal enterprises had grown up, including numerous unlicensed *shebeens*, houses of ill repute and bear-baiting dens. Sordid though they were, these establishments had attracted a great many clients – mostly *toffs* – who crossed the river in search of licentious entertainment.

Whilst the capital had expanded outwards from the original city limits *north* of the river, the wealthy and the respectable working classes had not chosen to settle in the districts *south* of the river. These were the badlands, where the poorly-drained bog and the tidal-stink were considered fit only for the establishment of prisons and lunatic asylums. Back in those times, it was only criminals and society's detritus which had ended up down here. Later on however, the area had become the obvious location for the more malodorous industries, chief amongst them being the skin trade, and had attracted the lower

56

echelons of working folk to set up home south of the river. South London had not managed to shake off its insalubrious and villainous reputation.

'So lad,' Joe summed up, 'as often 'appens, the nature of the land comes out in the nature of the people, and the folks 'ere in *sarf lannen* is 'ard as nails. They have only contempt for outsiders. It's not a soft life around 'ere, son, but you 'ave to remember that where there's muck there's money. Just give it a chance, mate.'

Mitch didn't want to disappoint his father, but he decided he would not be giving it much of a chance. He didn't think he would be able to endure the unpleasant work, or the bullying, for very much longer.

However, Mitch did determine to try to sound more like his Londoner father, imitating Joe's speech patterns and trying to eradicate his own Dublin accent. Soon things did begin to improve. Whether due to chance, or to his father having had a *sarf lannen* word in someone's ear, Mitch soon found himself moved away from the pits and over to the loading yards where Joe worked. Here, he was to assist the packers and loaders. This was much cleaner work. Mitch passed his sixteenth birthday working alongside his father, where there was no blatant bullying, just harmless banter.

When Joe's foreman got to know Mitch and learned that he was literate, he sent him out with the car men who delivered the finished pelts to the local furriers. Not only was the wiry Mitch strong enough and tall enough to lift the bales of pelts on and off the carts, but he was smart enough to interpret the delivery notices for the mostly elderly drivers. He had good handwriting and a sharp eye to spot any deficiencies between the invoices and the goods.

The car men knew the area and local businesses well enough of course, but their lack of education meant they sometimes had difficulty deciphering the dispatchers' handwriting and checking over the written goods receipts. This task was much more acceptable to Mitch, who liked getting out in the fresh air, away from the gruesome tanning yards. He also enjoyed helping the car men with their horses. The men would let him harness up the horses and would also let him take the reins from time to time. He quickly got the hang of steering the large carts around corners and applying a half brake on a downward incline.

Mitch was also quick to learn his way around the area, acquainting himself with all the main routes and with the many back lanes which might be used to save time or avoid traffic congestion.

Bermondsey was very heavily congested, especially at peak times of the day. It only took the collapse of one half starved nag to hold up the traffic and bring Bermondsey to a halt for an hour or more. Knowing the back streets and short cuts saved time on the round and enabled the car men to slip into a pub for a crafty pint. Mitch would mind the horses whilst they did so. The car men would then doze quietly on the carts whilst Mitch assisted the warehousemen to load and unload at each port of call.

Gradually, Mitch established a rapport with the skin merchants' store men whom he met on his round. He also assimilated useful information from them. They were happy to show off their expertise in differentiating between the various types of skins. Mitch learned to tell the difference between the ermine and the red Brazilian otter pelts which were stacked up in the warehouses awaiting despatch to the furriers where they would be made up into coats and jackets. The store men enjoyed demonstrating their skill in determining the best pelts from those of lesser quality. Mitch also saw, hanging in the furriers' warehouses, the racks of finished fur garments awaiting collection.

The furriers' machinists and finishers, mostly young women, who spent their breaks outside in the delivery areas gossiping and smoking, were also keen to chat to the good looking new youth. They tried to impress him with accounts of how much they had seen *their* coats selling for in West End stores. Although they did not enjoy a fair share in the profits of this highly profitable industry, nevertheless they felt the value of the end product reflected their own worth as skilled machinists. Mitch noted the wholesale prices of the pelts on his receipts and compared them with the retail sale prices on the labels of the finished garments. He was surprised to note the furriers' impressive profit margins. Most of the furriers to whom the pelts were addressed had German names, such as *Russ & Winkler; Poland* and *Fentenstein* and their labels claimed connections with Leipzig, Hamburg, Berlin and Paris – places he had learned about at school and which sounded exotic to him.

He also delivered smaller skins and off cuts to some of the Bermondsey hatters, such as the well-known *Christy's*. In time, Mitch became acquainted with some of the delivery lads from the wool merchants who supplied the wool felt for *Christy's* famous hats. One of those wool delivery lads, Harry Bailey, invited Mitch to join him for a drink at a pub up Bermondsey Street. As he got ready for his first night out in London, it was with some relief that Mitch felt he was perhaps beginning to fit in at long last.

Five miles away – as the crow flies – in a mews in the more fashionable district of Kensington, another youth, over six feet tall, broadly built and square-jawed, is leaning against the half door of a stable, whittling idly at a piece of beech wood. He watches his sixty-one year old father who, with some difficulty, is trying to coax the last of the horses into their loose boxes for the night. The youth does not offer to assist him. They are discussing the youth's plans for his future and the older man remarks that his son does not seem to have inherited his father's interest in horses. He urges him therefore to stick with his carpentry apprenticeship, since he will need some sort of skilled trade if he is to make a success of his life. The youth replies, dismissively, that he believes life has more excitement in store for him than stabling horses or woodworking. He declares that he does not belong here. He is better than this. The older man nods wearily. His work finished for the day, he goes indoors, as the light is now fading.

The youth remains, glancing around at the stables and the small apartments above them where the coachmen and the grooms live very modestly. When the youth is certain that no-one is watching, he enters one of the stables. He approaches a horse, which whinnies softly, but is not fearful at his approach. The youth pauses for a moment, and then throws down the stick. Suddenly, and with great violence, he kicks out, catching the horse savagely on one of its back legs. The horse screams in pain as its leg collapses lame beneath it. The youth quickly crosses the mews and disappears into the night.

When Mitch arrived at *The Tanners'* public house, Harry Bailey was already there in the tap room with another youth and was just getting the beers in. As soon as Mitch joined them, they made their way to a quiet corner table. Harry introduced Benny Hyman, who, he explained, worked as a costermonger down the Old Kent Road. Mitch was unsure what a costermonger was but, from the conversation, it soon became clear that Benny and his father hawked fruit and vegetables from barrows which they pushed around the streets.

Harry, whom Mitch estimated to be perhaps a couple of years older than himself, was a short, stocky youth with blond hair, blue eyes and a toothy grin. He grinned a great deal and had a lively and amusing way about him. He also seemed to be dressed very smartly for a night out at a fairly rough pub. Mitch had taken to Harry immediately, though he noticed he was not the only one to do so. He observed that Harry's smart appearance and his laughter were attracting the attention of the barmaids and of a couple of young women over in the snug. Mitch was just wondering how Harry could afford his smart woollen coat and suit on a delivery man's pay, when Harry spoke.

'So, Mitch,' he said, 'are you ... wossname?'

'Am I ... what?' Mitch asked, puzzled.

'You know, Irish, or what?'

Mitch replied that he was, and wondered what sort of jibe might be coming next.

'Only, our Benny here is a Jew boy,' Harry continued, 'see, 'is family arrived in London's east end originally, from Russia, when Benny wuz just a small boy, dincha Benny? But then they came sarf of the river. Nah they lives in Paradise Street over by Rovver'ive. As for me, I'm a bit of a mongrel, I s'pose – 'didn't never know *my* family. Grew up in a horffnidge, didn't I?'

Harry's cheery grin did not diminish as he spoke of his humble origins, which suggested he was not unduly upset about them. Mitch explained he had arrived the previous year from Dublin, though his father was a Bermondsey boy. Gradually, the empty glasses on their table increased, as did Mitch's ease with his new friends. Benny had a noticeable accent that was foreign to Mitch's ears. Benny explained that his first language had been Yiddish. He had not had much schooling, he said, but had picked up his English on the street. Perhaps because of this, Benny was quite fluent in the east end rhyming slang.

Once the argot adopted by criminals to avoid having their conversation overheard by police informants, rhyming slang was now becoming popular amongst the youth of all London's working class districts. It was an ever changing patois, which, as it developed, incorporated the names of famous people and of common domestic items. Mitch was familiar with some of the phrases, since his father used the odd one from time to time, but he found it challenging trying to work out the ones he did not know, sprinkled liberally as they were throughout Harry and Benny's chatter. He thought he should make the effort to pick up the lingo however, if only to blend in.

The two girls who had been watching them from across in the snug apparently knew Harry from the wool factory and Harry now waved them over into the tap room. Giggling, they approached to give Harry's new friend the once over. Harry effected the introductions.

'Ladies, you know me old china, Benny, and this 'ere's Mitch. Mitch, allow me to introduce Lily and h'Edie. They're very good girls, they are – so good they'll touch yer knob fer a tanner!'

The girls feigned shock at Harry's lewd recommendation and squawked with laughter. Although genuinely embarrassed at Harry's coarseness in front of the girls, Mitch couldn't help but admire his ease with them. Keen to be thought one of the lads, he quickly dismissed his embarrassment and replied;

'Not mine, they won't, Harry – mine'll cost 'em a shillin'!'

The girls shrieked even more, looked Mitch up and down approvingly and tripped away again in a haze of cheap scent, leaving the three friends to resume their conversation.

Harry said he lived down Neckinger Road. Mitch guessed this must be near the river of the same name, which was familiar to him as it provided a tidal stream into the tan pits and nearby dye works. Mitch asked if Neckinger were a German name, since it didn't sound very English to his Irish ears. Harry explained that, according to local lore, the name of the place had originally been 'neck-incher' as it referred to the gallows which had once stood by the river. Benny demonstrated this with a grim gesture indicating a rope stretching his neck, causing his eyes to bulge and his tongue to protrude. Mitch immediately shivered. This confirmed his father's assertions that Bermondsey had a dark and criminal past.

To establish common ground, Mitch informed them that his father had been born in *Ship & Mermaid Row*, a grim little alley situated not far from an old burial ground. He told them of the rumour that prisoners who had starved to death in Marshalsea prison and the destitute dead of St Olave's Workhouse lay side by side in unmarked graves down in that burial ground.

Harry said he had heard that too, and added that beneath the stinking alleys of Bermondsey there also lay long forgotten plague pits. Locals would not dig the earth down there, he said, for fear of releasing the plague once more. The three youths laughed at the horror of it all and agreed they wouldn't want to go walking around Bermondsey's ancient streets alone on a dark night.

Harry asked Mitch what he thought of 'Bamsie', as he called his 'manor'. Mitch said he liked it well enough, which was completely untrue of course, but added, more convincingly, that things had improved greatly at the *Alaska* since he had graduated from the putrid pits to the pony carts. Of course, he added, the pay could have been better. Harry nodded sympathetically and said that he too was poorly paid. Benny caught Mitch's sideways glance at his friend's silk tie.

'You're wondering how he can manage this sort of *schmatter* on a delivery boy's wage, I suppose?' Benny asked with a lop-sided smile.

'This what?' Mitch asked.

'*Schmatter* – that's east end speak for clothes,' Harry translated, 'Benny means me *whistle* an' me *weasel* – the suit and the coat. Dahn 'ere, we says *whistle an' flute* for a suit. Yer *weasel and stoat* is yer coat. Just *whistle* and *weasel* for short though. It's so's the pleece can't foller what yer sayin' and won't be askin' yer for no receipt.'

Mitch admitted he had indeed been admiring Harry's clothes. He recognised the smart felt hat as one of *Christy's* finest, since he had seen them in *Christy's* warehouse and also in the West End shop windows and he knew what they cost. Harry now confided that he and Benny had a little 'sideline' going – something which earned them some easy money. He asked if Mitch would like to be a part of it, and earn a little extra himself, so that he too might wear 'dapper duds' like Harry's. Mitch said he would be interested, so long as it didn't involve him squelching about all day in bare feet in a tub full of sealskins. Harry leaned forward and with a conspiratorial gesture, he confided the secret of their success;

'Benny and me 'as a mate, a ... wossname?' he clicked his fingers at Benny for a prompt, 'a *lumper*, who reggly puts us in the way of some import surplus goods, which we 'as to collect and which Benny's dad minds for us in 'is yard until I can arrange collection by a geezer I know wot pays us top prices.'

Mitch had no idea what a *lumper* was, but did not want to show his continuing ignorance. He asked what his own part in the transaction would be.

'Well, our reggla driver 'as gorn away for a bit, on a lickle 'oliday, yer might say,' Harry expanded, 'so we could use a bloke wot can 'andle a 'orse an' cart, and so, if yer up fer it, we can cut yer in on the deal, cash in 'and, sweet as a nut, and no questions arsed.'

62

It sounded pretty straight forward, or at least it did until Harry mentioned that Mitch would have to *provide* the horse and cart. Mitch wondered why Harry did not do the driving himself, since he must have the same access to transport as Mitch did. However, he did not want to turn down the chance of some extra money.

'Of course, if that's beyond yer,' Harry said, seeing Mitch's thoughtful expression, 'we can allus find someone else.'

Mitch assured them he should be able to 'borrow' a horse and cart from somewhere, probably from the *Alaska* yard, since the factory premises were guarded at night, but the stable yard was not. In premises stacked high with valuable animal skins, it was unlikely any thief would steal a horse.

'That's the ticket!' said Harry, grinning broadly as he handed Benny some coins, 'fetch us three more pints o' pigs, Benny'.

'Pigs', Mitch worked out, would be 'pig's ear' – beer. Yes, he felt he was indeed fitting in now.

The following Friday night, Mitch turned up at the appointed rendezvous, a small terraced house down near the Phoenix wharf. He had purloined one of the *Alaska*'s more biddable nags, one that knew him and gave no trouble when unexpectedly roused from slumber and removed from its stable. Mitch had experienced no difficulty manoeuvring the horse between the shafts of a small cart and persuading it to head for the docks.

The *lumper* turned out to be a longshoreman, a dock labourer, and the mysterious goods turned out to be bundles of animal pelts, loosely wrapped in grubby, knotted sheets.

'Jayzus, these aren't stolen from the *Alaska*, are they?' Mitch asked, alarmed.

'Nah,' Harry explained, 'these is imported ones. They've been treated overseas already and brought in by ship, then left sittin' in crates in a ware'ouse, waitin' fer auction, so the *lumpers* just knocks an 'ole in the bottom of each crate and lifts out an 'andful. Then they turns the crates upright again. When the crates is collected and delivered, right way up, to the furriers, no-one notices the 'ole in the bottom. They don't clock the fact that each crate is a few skins short, neither. In fact, Martins would thank you for this, Mitch, 'cause these imported skins is in competition with the ones bein' processed dahn the *Alaska*. They shouldn't allow these imports really. It's wossname – damagin' British businesses, innit?'

Assisted by the *lumper*, the three youths carried half a dozen or so bales from the house, loaded them onto the cart, and then headed off, with Mitch driving, for Benny's father's yard. It was a moonless night and, although Mitch was now familiar with the area, the alleys looked very different in the dark.

He fully expected to see a *peeler* around each corner and indeed there were figures lurking in the shadows around some of the alleyways, but he guessed they too were on some illicit business of their own. The three youths had consumed a few beers before the pubs closed, which had given them some Dutch courage, but nevertheless felt spooked when they passed the churchyard.

'Wotchu bringin' us dahn 'ere for, Mitch?' Harry joked, 'it's a dead end!'

'Keep an eye out for the Bamsie banshee!' Mitch warned.

'Nah,' said Harry, 'it's the 'eadless h'executed ghosts of the Marshalsea prison you 'as to watch out for, 'cause they digs their way out at midnight and hides behind 'eadstones, waitin' for folks to pass by, then they jumps aht, grabs yer and pulls yer dahn inter the graves wiv 'em!'

'Leave orf 'arry,' Benny implored, looking fearfully around him.

Soon, they arrived at Benny's dad's yard, where they offloaded the bundles of skins amongst the stacks of empty fruit and vegetable boxes. Mitch then set off alone to return the horse and cart before the dawn broke.

The following week, Mitch and his friends met up at the pub again by arrangement. Harry produced a handful of money from his pocket and divided it equally between Mitch and Benny. He then gave Benny some additional coins and sent him to the bar to buy them each a beer. Mitch thought his share represented a lot of money for a night's work. Then again, since he knew the value of the pelts it occurred to him that someone further along the supply chain must be making an enormous profit. Harry never divulged what his own cut had been and neither Mitch nor Benny asked him. Harry was the man with the contacts, after all. All things considered, Mitch decided he had done well out of the venture and was not averse to repeating the experience.

When an opportunity presented itself and he found himself alone back in the tenement, he unscrewed the knob from the frame of the iron bed he now shared with his brothers George and Joey, slipped his money down into the hollow frame and quickly screwed the knob firmly back on again. Several more such operations were carried out over the next few months, and all went smoothly enough.

The nature of the goods varied with each trip. Sometimes the load was bales of lightweight silks, which took no time or effort at all to load. Sometimes it would be cartons of drugs, medicines or chemicals. Whatever commodity was passed on, the remuneration was usually generous. No type of goods seemed to be beyond the handling capabilities of Harry's *geezer*. The consignment which netted them their biggest return however was one which Harry described as 'kettles' but which turned out to be silver fob watches.

'*Kettle on the 'ob* – fob,' Benny explained to a bewildered Mitch, winking conspiratorially and stuffing one of the watches into Mitch's pocket when he was sure Harry was not looking.

'Right,' said Harry, as Mitch dropped them off before returning the horse and cart, 'see you next week, but at a different pub this time, just to be on the safe side.'

'Which one?' Mitch asked.

'The *Lord Nelson* over Union Street. They turns a blind eye to everythin' in there!' Harry joked.

Unable to spend his money on too many conspicuous items which his parents might question, Mitch nonetheless manage to acquire a couple of new shirts and a warm coat, and of course he now had plenty of money to spend on drink and cigarettes.

Having money had other benefits too. As Harry had promised, Lily and Edie could be quite obliging around the back of the pub after closing, especially after they had been stood an evening's drinks and a bite of supper. Mitch now felt life was being good to him at last. He had cash in his pockets, and plenty more put by in his bedstead, and he also had a good social life now.

He handed over all of his factory earnings to his parents for his keep and he told them he had secured a second weekend job as a night porter in a hotel up West, which seemed to satisfy them as to where he went at weekends and how he funded his drinking. Harry had been most affable and generous towards him when first they had met, so now Mitch was glad he was able to buy his share of the drinks in the pub and feel on an equal footing with his friends. Harry declared that the three were now 'entreeprenooers' and moreover, they were contributing to the local economy.

The supply of varied and valuable goods available from the docks did not seem likely ever to run out. The same could not be said for Mitch's luck however.

In the very early hours of one Saturday morning, Mitch had made it back unseen to the cart yard after dropping off firstly their latest load and then his two cohorts, and he had just tied up the sleepy horse in the stall when he turned around to see a figure standing behind him, silhouetted against the light. The sight of the policeman, and, hovering behind him, CW Martin's night watchman, almost stopped Mitch's heart. He thought about running, but found himself trapped in the stall alongside the horse.

Later that morning, Mitch found himself sitting in a cell at Tooley Street Police Station, charged with taking away the horse and cart, even though he protested that he had actually been bringing them back. Naturally, the police did not believe his feeble story of wanting to teach himself to handle a horse and cart in order to expand his range of useful skills.

The cell reminded him of a similar one he had experienced Dublin many years earlier. The vague memories of that episode from his childhood, or perhaps it was just the damp chill of the lockup, caused him to shudder. The following Monday morning saw him climbing the steep, narrow stairs up from the darkness of the cells into the brightly lit dock of Tower Bridge Magistrates' court.

The proceedings did not take long. The constable gave evidence of how CW Martin's night watchman had alerted him to the inexplicably missing horse and cart and how, whilst they were discussing its absence, they had seen the accused returning the aforesaid horse and cart. However, in the absence also of any conceivable nefarious motive for Mitch having taken and returned the horse and cart without the consent of his employers, and possibly also because luncheon now beckoned, the magistrate felt inclined to accept Mitch's plea of not guilty to theft.

The magistrate had also been swayed by Joe Mitchell's evidence that his eldest son, who had missed out on his soldier father's discipline in the recent past owing to Joe's participation in the South Africa Campaign, wished also to join the army. Joe pleaded that a criminal record would harm his son's ambition to serve his Queen and country. Joe Mitchell had worn his campaign medal. Mitch had worn a remorseful expression. Mitch was duly discharged. He was fortunate also in that he did not lose his job at the *Alaska*.

Mitch's profuse apology proffered outside the courthouse was cut short by an unexpectedly sudden and hard slap across the face, delivered by his angry father.

'Don't ever cause me and yer mother this much worry and shame again!' Joe Mitchell yelled at his shocked son, who wondered what sort of discipline his father would have meted out, had he known the true reason for Mitch being in possession of the horse and cart.

Joe's anger was soon forgotten however and Mitch and his partners in crime were soon moving on to greater things. Having decided that an unlawfully borrowed horse and cart represented too great a risk, made too much noise and attracted too much attention, it now occurred to them that, rather than bringing stolen goods all the way back from the docks, it might be both more profitable and less risky to cut the *lumpers* and the docks out of the picture. The three friends decided to burgle local factories themselves and transport the goods to Hyman's Rotherhithe yard, using Hyman's two handcarts for the purpose.

This was where Mitch's knowledge of the layout at the *Alaska* works came in handy. Although the factory workers operated around the clock in shifts, the warehouse staff did not. Mitch was able to climb over the rear gates at midnight and open them to let his cohorts into the storage areas with their barrows. He identified the best skins to steal and, once their handcarts were fully laden and out in the alley, he bolted the gates behind Harry and Benny, then climbed back out. Barrow boys were often to be seen out and about in the early morning, collecting produce from the markets, so the friends' presence on the streets with fully laden handcarts did not arouse any suspicion whatsoever. Mitch felt quite smug the following Monday when, upon arriving for work at the factory, he heard of the weekend robbery. He almost felt avenged for his earlier ill treatment at the factory – almost.

Harry's inside knowledge of the wool warehouses facilitated their thefts from those premises also, and Mitch's familiarity with the layout of the various furriers' storage premises led them on to even more valuable booty. There were numerous furriers and other sales outlets which Mitch and Harry visited during their delivery rounds and they now ensured they acquainted themselves with the access points and security arrangements at each location.

Furs were pleasingly light to transport too. Thus the friends' criminal activities went from strength to strength and Mitch's hoard of cash increased beyond the diminishing capacity of the brass bedstead.

To retrieve some of his money, he merely had to unscrew the brass foot from the bed and ease the money out from below. He still could not seem to spend his money as fast as he came by it however. By the age of seventeen, Mitch had amassed what seemed to him to be a small fortune.

Indeed it was Mitch's wealth that was preoccupying his thoughts on his return home in the early hours one Saturday morning and which prevented him noticing that the lights were still on in his parents' rooms in the Crosby Row tenements. It came as a complete shock to him when he entered to find a uniformed policeman sitting in the Mitchells' only armchair. Mitch tried his best to control his rising panic and assume an air of surprised innocence, but his parents' grave expressions told him that they, at least, saw through that feigned innocence, much as they had done when he was an infant, getting into minor scrapes with his cousin Artie.

'This officer's come to 'ave a word wi' you Mitch,' his father said, 'to see if you've noticed any strange goins on, bein' as you reggly walks past them west end furriers on your way 'ome from yer night job, and bein' as 'ow them furriers keeps gettin' robbed.'

Mitch registered his father's warning look. The policeman asked Mitch where he had been, and Mitch gave him the name of the first hotel he could think of – *The Hotel Cecil*.

'Ain't that the big posh place in The Strand?' the policemen asked.

Mitch confirmed that it was. The officer stood up to leave and said he would be contacting *The Cecil* to confirm Mitch's employment there and might well be back to see him again. When the door closed behind the policeman, Joe advised his son that he did not appreciate having his home searched by the police. Mitch felt his cheeks colour.

'He didn't find anything though?' Mitch asked fearfully.

'No, he didn't, but I did,' Joe looked darkly disappointed as he produced from his pocket the silver fob watch Benny had given Mitch.

Mitch tried to explain that the watch had been a gift from his friend, but since he had not mentioned it before, Joe Mitchell did not believe his son's explanation for one minute. Joe said they would discuss it later, after he had caught a few more hours' sleep. Mitch climbed into his shared bed, trying not to disturb his sleeping brothers. He could not sleep himself however for worrying how he was going to get out of his new predicament. No more was said about the policeman's visit but, later that day, Joe announced he would be taking Mitch over to have a look at the Abbey Street army parade ground. Joe had heard the local Surrey regiment was recruiting. A spell in the army would do him no harm, Joe said. Mitch did not demur. A combination of shame, worry and fatigue made him compliant. From Abbey Street, they were directed down to New Cross to the Army recruitment office.

Having undergone a brief medical, which found him underweight for his height but otherwise fit, and having completed Army form B217, falsely declaring himself to be eighteen, Mitch was duly enlisted as a Private in *The Queen's Royal Regiment*, also known as *The Royal West Surrey Regiment* and was directed to report for posting two days hence. It had all happened so quickly. Mitch was officially in the army now. Any trepidation he felt about what the military life would be like and whether it would suit him was calmed by the knowledge that, wherever the army posted him, it would be away from here. Wherever he would next find himself might be better than Bermondsey, or it might be worse, but it would at least be somewhere different.

Chapter Five – **The Mutton Lancers**

'Allah hu Akbar,
Allah hu Akbar.'

The voice of the *muezzin* voice rang out clear and pure from the minaret of the nearby mosque. Mitch knew the words and the tune of the Mahommedans' call to prayer by heart now, and he found it quite haunting. Of course, starting off at dawn as it did, it was not always appreciated by the soldiers in the barracks. Whilst he supposed it sounded as sweet and familiar to the Mahommedans as the Sunday church bells did to a Christian, unlike the weekly church bells, the call of the *muezzin* at the Sialkot mosque rang out five times a day, every day.

Mitch stretched out on his *charpai*, his face turned towards the high ceiling of the barrack room, where, he now noticed, the *punkah* had ceased to sway. The lazy *punkah wallah* had doubtless succumbed to sleep himself. The morning was comfortably cool however, so neither Mitch nor any of his comrades felt moved to rise and give the native a good kicking. Instead, Mitch lay dozing as he awaited the arrival of the regimental barber.

Soon, the *nai* and his assistants would come creeping like silent shadows around the block room, as they did each day before reveille, to shave the men whilst they slept. The *dhobee* would appear next and tiptoe around, silently collecting all their discarded clothing from the floor and leaving freshly washed and ironed replacements by each bed. Thus each man would have a clean uniform to climb into after his ablutions.

Mitch's throat was dry. It would be an hour or so yet until the *char wallah* came to make them the early cup of tea which would see them through early parade until breakfast time. The tea was always hot, sweet and milky. The *char wallah*'s method was to boil up the tea leaves, water, milk and sugar all together and dispense the well-brewed *char* from several big brass *samovars* into tin mugs. Mitch had learned to drink it Indian-style, sucking it through clenched teeth to sieve out the leaves. The tea was most refreshing, especially to men who had put away a pint or three of the canteen beer the night before, as naturally Mitch had.

He now hauled himself upright on the rickety *charpai*, pulled back the gauzy mosquito netting and reached out for his *lota*. Another couple of things Mitch had learned, by experience, were firstly to keep a *lota* of water by his bed, in case dehydration awoke him in the night, and secondly to keep his *lota* covered. Mosquitoes would lay their eggs in the smallest amount of still water.

His furry throat now lubricated, he lay back again and thought how content he was with his present situation. His father had been right about the bull, spit and polish of army life, of course. The endless drills, cleaning of weapons and kit inspections were monotonous, it was true, but there was something comforting about the daily routine and the regular meals.

Beyond the requirement to maintain his weapon and his items of kit, Mitch had neither to take responsibility for himself nor to make decisions. The army took care of everything. He thought that was probably why so many of the older hands had re-enlisted once their time was served. Discipline in *The Queen's* was most strictly upheld but Mitch didn't mind that. Within the firm guidelines and regulations of army life, he found a kind of security he had not enjoyed in either Dublin or London. The poverty and uncertainty that had characterised life in *Civvy Street* did not trouble him here.

Glancing along the row of sleeping soldiers, he now saw Kempie's long legs and huge feet protruding over the edge of his *charpai*, beyond the protection of his fine gauze mosquito net. The sight made Mitch smile. The Indian wooden bed was a flimsy affair, perfectly suitable for the short and slightly-built plains Indian of course, but woefully inadequate for a solidly built, Anglo-Saxon labouring man.

'Kempie!' Mitch warned in a loud whisper, 'yer plates are stickin' out, mate!'

With a loud snort, the big man eased his great frame over onto his back and bent his knees to withdraw his feet inside the netting. Kempie had enough problems with his feet without having them nibbled by mosquitoes during the night, Mitch thought.

Mitch liked his *charpai* in spite of its rickety wooden framework and the string base which had to be re-strung when it went too slack to support the sleeper. It was the first bed he had ever had to himself. Until he had left home he had always shared a bed with his brothers. He had shared clothes with them too. Back home, it had been a case of the first one up laying claim to the least worn underwear and least holey socks. Now however, he had his own bed and bedding, set within his own regulation space in the barrack room. He had his own trunk and his own army-issue clothing, from white cotton undergarments to smart new uniform and stout boots, and every item marked with his own regimental number: 8475.

Somehow, along with all the uniform and kit, came a sense of self. When Mitch put on his uniform he felt he was his own man at last. Best of all he loved the helmet. Made of lightweight cork, it was the same 'home service' helmet the regiment wore back in England, except out here it was covered in khaki cotton, and there was a detachable white cotton cover for when it was to be worn with dress uniform.

He now wondered if it had been more than economic necessity which had kept his father returning to the army life. He guessed his father would have preferred the orderliness and camaraderie of the barrack room to the cramped chaos of his family's tenement room in Dublin. Joe's pay would have been apportioned, so that Georgina received her fair share, and with this, she would maintain their home and the shrieking, restless children. For Joe however, up at the Island Bridge barracks, all meals and requirements would have been decided and provided for him. With no significant decisions to make, no family finances to balance and his own portion of his pay to spend on beer, it was no wonder Joe had been content to be a soldier.

When Mitch thought about the arrangements for army pay apportionment, this seemed a much better arrangement than that by which most Dublin men handed over the bulk of their pay to the local publicans, often leaving their families without bread on the table. It was the violence to which this gave rise, the drunken men dismissing their wives' complaints with a clenched fist, which had characterised life back in Monto.

Mitch had arrived in India in March of 1907, along with one hundred and thirty seven other privates, eight corporals, six sergeants, two lieutenants and a chaplain. Theirs was not the only regiment on

72

board ship when they had sailed from Southampton to Bombay. Spending twenty-one days at sea had been an adventure in itself for Mitch, whose only previous experience at sea had been his leaving Ireland on the packed overnight ferry out of Kingstown. The Atlantic and Indian Oceans had however been very different from the Irish Sea. Once his seasickness had subsided, he had marvelled at the vast expanses of water to be seen in all directions.

Their Colour Sergeant had shown some of the men a globe in the purser's office and this had given them an idea of just how far around the world they would be travelling. Mitch's excitement at the prospect of what might lie ahead had been somewhat dulled by boredom though, as the days spent confined on board turned into weeks. The troops had passed the time at sea mainly playing card games, and, since he was no novice at gambling, Mitch had earned himself a decent amount of cash. He envisaged this would come in handy when they reached their destination.

Their quarters on board had been cramped and uncomfortable, with most of the other ranks sleeping on thin straw palliasses on the hard wooden decks. Despite this, the drill sergeants had found sufficient space on the open decks to exercise the men several times a day. By the time of their approach to Port Said, the sea breezes were becoming noticeably milder and they had been ordered to change into their lightweight Indian khaki for day wear, with their regimental dress reserved for the evenings. The latter included a scarlet cotton, five-buttoned, loose-fitting frock jacket, with side vents and smart piping on the cuffs.

Mitch wore his regimental dress with pride, and recalled how he had felt when he had seen his father, also clad in scarlet uniform, riding on horseback through Dublin and stealing the attention away from Queen Victoria. Joe's eldest boy had never imagined he would one day be wearing the Queen's scarlet too, and would be heading to another continent as his father had done. The warm air currents over the emerald Indian Ocean; the widening blue skies and the smart red uniform had coloured his heart with optimism.

The troops had docked at the port of Bombay in what was described as the cold season, yet it had been hotter than a Dublin summer. During their brief stopover in the trooping sheds by the docks, they had a chance to change their winnings into Indian money with the local *Parsee* money changers. Mitch learned that a *rupee* was worth one shilling and four pence, whilst an *anna* equated to a penny and a *pice* was worth roughly a farthing.

His first sight of India had astonished him. Although barefoot children were a common sight in Dublin and London, here in Bombay people wore fewer clothes than would be considered decent back home. The women wore brightly coloured fabrics wrapped around themselves from head to toe, yet they still managed to reveal naked brown waists as they moved about, whilst many of the men wore nothing but a couple of lengths of cotton wrapped about their loins and heads.

When wandering around the bazaar stalls, Mitch and his comrades had even come face to face with a holy man who was totally naked, save for a tin cup which he wore on a string around his neck. What surprised Mitch most however was that his nakedness had attracted so little attention from bystanders.

From Bombay, the troops had proceeded in stages, via the clearing station at Deolali, to Sialkot in the north eastern reaches of the Punjab. The journey across the interior, albeit mostly by rail, had taken days and had been exhausting but thrilling. Mitch had never seen, heard or smelled any place like it. Hanging out of the train window, he had been aware of towns and cities long before they appeared, since each had a very particular odour which was carried on the hot breezes across the scorched plains. The sweet-sour smell of rotting fruit, combined with that of human and animal ordure, would be the first clue to the approaching settlement. As the train entered each town, the odour would gradually be replaced by the more appealing scent of wood fires and the aromas of onions and spices frying.

At each station stop, small boys plied a variety of snacks from the platforms and the troops eagerly purchased slices of fresh pineapple, sticks of sugar cane or glasses of lime water and sherbet. Mitch had been advised by an outgoing old India hand he had met at Deolali, that there was nothing better for slaking one's thirst in India's searingly arid climate than a mug of sweet, milky tea. A man's urge might be for an ice cold beer, but the effects of this on a dehydrated man would be violent stomach cramps. Only a cup of *char*, served at blood heat, would safely refresh a body, the old hand had warned.

Mitch and his comrades bought *samosas* from the station vendors. These were deep fried, highly spiced pasties containing meat or vegetables and were very tasty. They left Mitch's gums tingling pleasantly. Even hotter were the newspaper twists of *chaat* which

74

comprised mostly fried spiced nuts, chickpeas and morsels of batter. These were very cheap indeed, though they did not always remain long in the system.

To their consternation, Mitch and the others found that the *water closets* on Indian trains consisted simply of holes in the cubicle floors, over which a man must squat to do his business. If one were unwise enough to look down, the sight of railway sleepers speeding away beneath the carriage could be unsettling and did nothing to alleviate either travel sickness or a common malady known variously as the *Bombay Trots* or the *Delhi Belly*.

During the journey, Mitch had become better acquainted with some of the other men of his company. Most of the men of *The Queen's* were London-based, but given the cosmopolitan nature of south London, a significant proportion had originated from the provinces. Mitch had been assigned to B Company of the 1st Battalion and during the long rail journey north he made sure he shared the rail carriage with the two friends he had made at Longmoor training camp. Thomas Lewis, an intelligent and well-read Welshman, had early on been nick-named 'The Prof'. Charlie Kemp, a Hertfordshire lad, was not as quick-witted as Prof, but was equally likeable. More significantly however, Kempie was quite the tallest man Mitch had ever seen.

The old soldier at Deolalie had also warned him that fighting and bullying were rife at Sialkot Cantonment, and he had advised Mitch to attach himself to the biggest man he could find and make an ally of him. Mitch had certainly done that. After the unpleasantness his Irish accent had caused him at The Alaska, Mitch could appreciate the wisdom of this advice, even though he was by now managing to sound much more *sarf lannen*. At six feet eight inches tall, and with hands like coal shovels, Kempie was far and away the biggest man in the regiment. Prof, being slightly built and studious and therefore ripe for baiting, was also pleased to enjoy Kempie's protection. The three had formed a strong friendship from the outset.

Lying on his *charpai* in the blockhouse in Sialkot, Mitch decided he had no regrets whatsoever about having joined the regiment. How else would he have seen India? He lay back and submitted to the careful ministrations of the regimental barber. The army encouraged the men to maintain good personal hygiene habits. Luckily, hot water was plentiful in the barracks and it was refreshing to be able to take a shower, rather than trying to wash in a kettleful of water poured into a basin behind a blanket, as Mitch had done in the Dublin and Bermondsey tenements. A year and a half of training at Longmoor, the army camp situated on the Hampshire heath lands, had prepared the men well for the routine of army life, though not by any means for the rigours of the Indian climate.

The constant drilling, parading and route marching were exhausting enough for the British troops in the heat of India without them having to undertake routine domestic tasks as well. It was fortunate therefore that the regiment had a support team of locals to see to their needs. When Mitch and his comrades would return later in the morning from the parade ground, their barrack room would have been swept and tidied by the sweepers, leaving the soldiers free to enjoy a relaxed breakfast after their exertions.

All the services provided by the natives were well worth the few *annas* stopped from their monthly pay. Labour was very cheap in India and the local economy depended upon servicing the needs of the vast army base. This inter-dependent relationship had so far kept a lid on any simmering desire the locals might have to rise up against their masters.

Drilling and parading apart, the social life of the private soldier at Sialkot cantonment revolved mainly around the canteen, a long cool building with high ceilings and shaded verandas. All day, every day, a *durzee* sat, cross-legged out on the veranda, pausing only occasionally from his darning and tailoring, to hawk up and deliver a thumping volley of spittle into the dust. His personal habits might not be genteel, but he was a fine tailor, and had made a couple of first class civilian suits for Mitch. Mitch thought he would enjoy upstaging Harry Bailey when, if ever, he got to visit Bermondsey again. It was a clean-shaven and smartly uniformed Mitch who polished off his *char* and headed out with his comrades to the vast parade ground for the early morning parade.

Sialkot cantonment was a large, self-contained and well-run military base, situated adjacent to, but separate from, the ancient city of Sialkot. The camp enjoyed breathtaking views of the snow-covered peaks of Kashmir above them and a surrounding panorama of the many foothills, through which the fast-flowing Chenab River carved out a green channel. The almost constant sunshine made the clear Chenab sparkle. This was a real, life-giving river, not an industrial cess pit like the Liffey or the Neckinger. To Mitch, the expansive views

76

represented a world far removed from the towering tenements of Monto or Bermondsey. Until he had embarked from Southampton, he had never in fact seen so much sky. In both Dublin and London, the sky had existed only in narrow grey strips, seemingly supported by the tall, crumbling old buildings. Even the woodlands on Dublin's outskirts had had very little sky visible through the canopy of deciduous tree foliage. India however had big skies.

Mitch did not mind the early start to the day. In fact he loved the scent of wood smoke which snaked its way into camp on the early morning breeze. From every village and settlement in every green valley hereabouts, cocks were now crowing and the natives were burning charcoal fires to heat their breakfast.

The Indian's breakfast generally consisted of torn up morsels of charcoal-flavoured wheaten *chuppatis*, saved from the previous night's supper and revived by being soaked in hot milk. Mitch envied the camp natives their breakfast which smelled so good. As he and his comrades drilled up and down the massive parade ground, they had a sustaining but bland dish of oatmeal to look forward to. He promised himself he would sample a traditional Indian breakfast for himself sometime soon.

The day's parade was invariably followed by musketry practice. Mitch enjoyed this greatly and moreover had become quite a good shot with both pistol and rifle. There was a great emphasis placed on drilling and musketry at present, for in the coming autumn the regiment was due to compete against others in field trials. Their performance would be judged by Major General Mahon, the Commander of the Sialkot Brigade. *The Queen's*, and Mitch's battalion in particular, had an enviable reputation to maintain, since the battalion had won the prestigious *Kitchener's Cup* two years earlier and had high hopes of again acquitting themselves with honour in the forthcoming competition. As the Indian day wore on, the weather warmed and the humidity rose, so the troops retreated under orders to the canteen for lunch and to rest up before fatigues resumed in the relative cool of late afternoon.

Prof drew his friends' attention to the latest notices displayed around the canteen warning the men to be alert for any signs of disaffection amongst the locals. The British forces in India were being expanded significantly this year, since 1907 marked the fiftieth anniversary of the Indian mutiny. The mutiny had been a black period in the history of the British in India, during which native *sepoys* had risen up against their colonial masters. Mitch recalled learning about it at school back in Dublin. His classroom had boasted a huge map, with the extent of the British Empire highlighted in red. Britain, Ireland included, had sat proudly at its heart. Because the empire straddled the various time and datelines, the British could boast, with jingoistic pride, that the sun never set on their vast empire. By far the largest area of red on the map had been India. A land of ruby red, set in an emerald sea, India was so often described as being the jewel in Queen Victoria's crown. Mitch was proud now to be a guardian of that crown.

Mitch's Protestant school teacher back in Dublin, proud of his status as a British subject, had told his pupils stirring stories of the brave resistance of the British soldiers, civil servants, and *memsahibs* during the mutiny. He had spoken of the tragic fate of men, women and infants hacked to death in their homes and churches, and of the administration's brutal revenge, when mutinous *sepoys* were strapped to the barrels of cannon and blown, in pieces, into the hereafter.

Having now gained more understanding of the continent from first-hand contact with the Indian natives, Mitch realised that this form of retribution had been more than merely a momentary cruelty. The Mahommedans believed they could not enter paradise with a mutilated corpse. Prof Lewis had explained that the followers of Islam had to meet their maker in one piece or be damned for eternity. For this reason, they always buried their dead. Of those poor wretches blown apart by cannon however, there had been little left to bury. It seemed unsurprising therefore that resentment should still exist amongst the Mahommedans hereabouts. Mitch could understand why the Indians had long memories for such matters. Back at the canteen it was the day's topic of conversation between the three friends.

'You see, it's a very different culture from ours, boys,' Prof explained, 'no better, no worse, mind, just different. And different again are the Hindus. They don't bury their dead, but burn them on bonfires and in public too. In fact, they used to encourage a dead man's widow to throw herself onto the husband's funeral pyre and burn herself to death.'

'Never!' exclaimed the incredulous Kempie, 'what'd she want to do that for?'

'Well, the thinkin' behind it was that it must be her fault he died, as she hadn't looked after him well enough in life, and in any case her life would be worthless without him, so of course she had to die too,' Prof expanded, 'though I reckon it was really because the husband's family wouldn't want to support her. Anyway, the British administration stamped out the custom. *Suttee* is what they called it.'

'Sooty? You're havin' us on, aren't you, Prof?' Mitch declared.

'No, straight up,' the Welshman insisted, 'it still happens from time to time, even though it's illegal now.'

'Well burnin' the dead has become popular back in Blighty too,' Kempie chipped in, 'an' it makes sense, for they'll run outa land for buryin' people eventually.'

'It's not the only option for disposin' of the dead, though,' Prof continued, 'and you've heard tell of the Parsees, haven't you, like the money-lenders we met in Bombay?'

His two friends confirmed they had.

'Well, they're fire-worshippers, they are, and they have these big towers, see, 'towers of silence' they call them, and they lay the dead out on top of them for the vultures to consume. That way, all life is returned to the earth. It works well enough, until a vulture tries to make off with a heavy bit, like an arm or a leg or somethin', loses his grip and drops it into a garden where a family's having their lunch. Then it's not very nice,' Prof explained.

'Now I *know* yer havin' us on, boy!' Kempie spluttered, 'sooty widows and giant bird tables! I'm not as soft as I look, y'know!'

Mitch realised that he and his comrades did not have an entirely unfettered view of Indian life from the cantonment however. Apart from when travelling on leave, the troops were barred from the cities and large towns. They were not allowed to frequent local bazaars, other than the *Saddar bazaar*, which had been built and designated specifically for their use. It was not just Indian society from which they were excluded either, for they were discouraged also from fraternising with the European civilian community. Whilst the British administrators and their *memsahibs* felt secure knowing that there were many British troops present in India to safeguard their empire, they had no desire whatsoever to associate with or even to gaze upon them.

Moreover, Lady Curzon, wife of the previous Viceroy of India, had not endeared herself to the troops when she was reported to have declared at some dinner party that the two ugliest things in India were the water buffalo and the British private soldier. The resounding response of those old hands, who had actually seen the Vicereine at the Delhi Durbar of 1903, was that, given a choice between consorting with the lanky, po-faced daughter of an American shopkeeper or forming a liaison with a water buffalo, they would choose to bestow their favours upon the four legged option.

The segregation of the military from civilian life was no great hardship, however, since the soldiers could find just about anything they required in the *Saddar Bazaar*, with its shops, bars and official brothel. The troops had been given repeated warnings lately to be careful when out and about in the bazaar though. It seemed the approaching anniversary had stirred up new hopes of Indian nationalism. It had started early in the year, in the cool season, as revolutions often did in this part of the world. Nobody in their right mind went around demonstrating or shouting in the fierce head of summer of course, for if they did, they would soon be *out* of their minds. Earlier that month, the houses of some Europeans in India had come under attack and sporadic riots and strikes had broken out. The British administration had moved swiftly to impose a harsh crackdown, and Mitch had seen reports in the Indian press of police and troops firing upon unarmed civilians.

As Prof had observed however, one could appreciate the anxiety of the British administration, not only in India, but around the dominions. Other citizens of the empire with dreams of independence would be watching the British response with interest. Mitch guessed developments would certainly be followed by the Irish nationalists. Britain could not, would not, let her empire break up. Violence would be met with violence. Any stirrings of insurrection would be quenched immediately and decisively. Mitch thought he would be more comfortable quelling any outbreaks of rebellion here in India than doing so back in Dublin amongst his fellow Irishmen.

Mitch admired Prof for his learning. Indeed, Prof was sufficiently educated, though not sufficiently wealthy, to have applied for a commission. He loved to read the newspapers and spent much time in the soldiers' reading room, where books and periodicals were freely available to the men. He had a talent for absorbing and interpreting news and for explaining current events and developments in terms his comrades could understand. It was Prof who had encouraged Mitch to attend the regimental schoolmaster's classes where they might learn, amongst other subjects, Hindustani. He had sold the idea to Mitch by persuading him they should look to their future, and consider what they would do when eventually they left the army.

There were many opportunities for a time-served soldier in India, according to Prof. Good men were needed to run the railways and to manage tea and tobacco plantations. A man might do well for himself if he kept his nose clean and set about improving himself. A knowledge of local languages was essential however, if they were to assert their control over the locals in their employ. Also, if they passed their general certificate in Hindustani, they would earn a fifty rupee award, which was the equivalent of almost four months' pay and was, as Prof had put it, better than a poke in the eye with a burnt stick. Kempie had declined to enrol for lessons however, for his education thus far had been sparse, or, as Kempie preferred to say, he had in fact forgotten more than ever he had learned.

The obligatory exercises in camp included horse drill. With his love of horses, Mitch had quickly perfected all the skills and techniques necessary to become a fully competent horseman. He loved both the equestrian drills and learning to care for the horses.

His own mount, *Raja*, was young and spirited but responsive to training. Like all the Lancers, Mitch learned how to ride his own steed whilst simultaneously leading two riderless horses alongside. Although it was never mentioned, this was a technique each man might need in battle, should some of their colleagues be killed, since the dead lancers' horses would be too valuable, and too useful a resource to the enemy, to be left behind on the battlefield. Having fared well in the equestrian training at Longmoor, Mitch had assumed, wrongly as it turned out, that he would be spending all of his time overseas in the saddle. Most of the journeys he had made thus far however had been by train, and the numerous manoeuvres in which he had participated had been mostly route marches.

The Queen's were also referred to by other regiments as the 'Mutton Lancers', this nickname having arisen from the lamb and flag on their badges. It also reflected their long history as a mounted regiment. Whilst the *Queen's* still kept many horses and maintained their equestrian skills, they were not really a regiment of lancers these days, but were infantrymen. In fact, they were now a part of the British Infantry's Northern (India) Command. Whenever Mitch did get an opportunity to get back into the saddle however he leaped at the chance, quite literally.

Although Prof was grateful to the regiment for his living and for the opportunity to further his studies, he did not see his future with the army. He saw himself riding his own horse around acres of lush plantations where he would manage teams of natives. He would find himself a nice little *half-chat* girl, he would say, and would settle down in a large, cool bungalow, with servants to prepare him Indian food and wait on his every whim. He declared he would never go back to Wales, where all that awaited him was the miserable work of a coal hewer – the sort of backbreaking labour which had ended his father's life prematurely. Prof had dreamed of going to university but circumstances had forced him to progress from school to the mines to support his mother and younger siblings. Soon he had realised he too would die young, either of injury or depression, if he remained underground. He had decided to travel to London in the hope of finding employment more fitting for a clever, if unqualified youth. When his money had run out however, he had little option but to enlist and *The Queen's* had been recruiting.

'Never go backwards in life, Mitch' Prof urged, 'big mistake, that. Always move forward and follow your dreams. Life is like the great Indian plain, stretching ahead of us, with a rainbow at its end. Travel along that plain as far as you can get, Mitch. You might not reach the rainbow, but you'll have got somewhere different at least. If you go back to where you started out, you'll just die an unfulfilled and bitter man.'

This advice sounded good enough, and Mitch promised himself he would never settle back in either Dublin or Bermondsey, not now he had seen India. He had gone far beyond the horizons of his boyhood experience, beyond his own expectation, and he liked what he saw.

Mitch had learned some unusual riding techniques since he had come to India. There were *tent-pegging* exercises, where each man galloped along at speed and, leaning over the side of his mount, speared a block of wood with the end of a sharp lance and charged off with it. From using a lance for this exercise, Mitch had progressed to using a sword, which, since it was considerably shorter, necessitated more daring acrobatics and more careful balancing. The original purpose of this procedure had been to uproot tent pegs or slash guy ropes in enemy camps during an attack, but it had evolved into an exercise designed to improve the men's agility and manoeuvrability on horseback.

Other exercises involved riding beneath the branches of fruit trees and spearing apples. In the regiment, this was known as *lemon-sticking*, though, since lemons did not grow in this location, apples were the chosen fruit. *Pig-sticking* was another traditional activity which Mitch believed might have more practical applications, since in the not too distant forests one might encounter wild boar, which were reputed to taste far superior even to the pork supplied by the local *bacon-wallah*.

Mitch loved it when the Pathan tribesmen occasionally came down from the north-western frontier to entertain the troops with breathtaking equestrian displays. These men spent most of their lives in the saddle and could hang sideways off their mounts, using the horse's body as a shield against enemy rifle fire, whilst simultaneously firing their own weapons effectively, from an almost impossible angle, between the horse's legs. The tribesman presented a wild, brave and romantic figure, dressed in thin white cotton *kurta* and *shalwar,* his head protected only by a starched cotton *pugree* and his scarlet silk sash billowing out behind, as he raced at breakneck speed along the parade ground. These native horsemen did not have stout army boots like the men of *The Queen's* but wore instead open-toed sandals made of thick leather.

Now in his twentieth year, Mitch was no longer the skinny, gangly youth who had left Dublin three years earlier. He had developed muscle on his lean frame from all the exercises and marches and from the regular army food. The mess grub was not fancy, but it was nourishing, plentiful and in regular supply. At Longmoor camp the most usual offering of the army's mass catering had been hot stews – Mitch's favourite kind of food. Similar army fare was served up in India also, though Mitch preferred the local food on offer in the *Saddar Bazaar.* He had grown to love the spicy and fragrant Indian stews and the soft breads, which drew their charcoal flavour from the clay ovens. Until he had tasted Indian food, Mitch had supposed the colourful mounds of spices piled high in the Bermondsey spice mills were only of use to the pickling industry. He had no idea they might add so much flavour and colour to cooked meals too.

As the spring weather became hotter, Mitch began to experience hitherto unknown sensations. Sweat trickled down into the small of his back and between his toes, bringing an awareness of those areas of the body which did not normally warrant a second thought in the cold climes of northern Europe. He was aware of his body developing from the pallor of youth into bronzed manhood. The sun warmed his bones through the thin Indian cotton of his uniform and the scented breezes of evening caressed his skin, bringing a heightened sense of self-awareness. There was something undeniably sensuous and stirring about India.

Despite the revulsion he had long held for the arrangements made for sating the soldier's baser desires, Mitch found himself remembering the pleasure of his trysts with Rose. Sometimes he would wonder if such pleasure might be found in the brothel down at the *Saddar Bazaar*. He decided however that the memory of Rose was still too raw, and that associating with the local prostitutes would not be for him. In any case, the men had to undergo another sort of 'parade' from time to time. Known as the 'short arms parade', this involved the troops standing in line whilst the medical officer inspected each man's genitals, to ensure none of them had caught a disease from the women in the brothels. Their NCO assured the men that they should remain disease free so long as they used the official establishment. In the regimental brothel, the girls too were inspected regularly and treated if necessary, and carbolic soap, fresh water and towels were provided for both men and girls. Mitch thought it a shame such precautions did not exist in civilian brothels back in *Blighty*.

The NCO also warned that infection was a dead certainty if they consorted with the 'sand rats', or rough prostitutes who hung around outside the cantonment. Any signs of infection which were spotted during the 'short arms inspection' would be recorded by the MO's assistant and the infected men would be hauled out of the line for immediate treatment. Mitch didn't know exactly what the treatment involved, but some of his comrades delighted in providing lurid accounts of the unfortunate man being held down, his member being fixed in what was commonly called a 'clap-trap' and mercury being administered via a very large syringe. After so graphic a description, whether true or not, Mitch, Kempie and Prof needed no further cautioning on the issue.

That evening, their day's fatigues completed, the three friends repaired to the canteen for their meal. As was the case most evenings, they washed the day's dust from their throats with some of the local beer. Brewed at the large brewery up in the Murree Hills north of Rawalpindi, the local ale was fairly palatable, but its most appealing feature was that it was cheap. The troops referred to beer as 'neck oil' and indeed many a military neck was well-oiled most evenings in camp. The canteen opening hours were not as generous as civilian licensing hours and so the men's drinking time was limited to the extent that it would be difficult to drink oneself into insensibility before 'stop-tap' was called. This was a wise precaution, given the early start the men had most days.

Thursday was the only full day in the week which was completely free for leisure pursuits. Sunday afternoons, after church parade, were given over to rest time but Thursday was their only full day off as such. There were no parades on Thursdays, no fatigues or other military duties and the men were free to swim in the swimming tanks, to play sports or to seek out the diversions of the *Saddar Bazaar*. For this Thursday however, Prof had a plan. Unlikely as it seemed, the three friends were going to a tea dance.

Chapter 6 – **The Dog and the Rabbit**

On Thursday afternoon, following an enjoyable morning playing football, Mitch, Kempie and Prof, showered and spruced themselves up and headed for the local Temperance Hall. The dance kicked off at five o'clock, as the sun was sinking low in the sky and the cool breezes began to set in. As was usual, Kempie had had a devil of a time trying to slick down his dark hair with pomade. One wayward lock at the crown insisted on popping skywards every now and again. Mitch assured him that, since he was the tallest person in Sialkot, no-one would see, let alone notice, the top of his head.

The three friends looked very smart in their mess dress as they filed in and took their seats at one of the tables down the left-hand side of the hall. It looked for a time as though this would be a men-only gathering, as that side of the hall was ablaze with scarlet tunics. Gradually however, the seats to the right of the dais began to fill up with young women, each accompanied by her mother or an aunt to act as chaperone.

A rather formidable and blowsy middle-aged lady now took the stage and advised the assembly of the rules of engagement. There would be dancing to the delightful tunes of Ronnie Maitland and his band, followed later on by tea, sandwiches and home-made cakes. The men might approach the young ladies to request a dance. Whether or not their invitations were accepted however would be decided by the ladies' chaperones. No alcohol was to be consumed and no couple was to leave the hall but must remain in the company of the chaperones at all times during the course of the evening. The men were exhorted to behave with decorum at all times and to respect the ladies.

Prof whispered that it was just like Treorchy on a Saturday night. Seeing the girls all on parade in their best afternoon frocks, Mitch recalled something Rose used to say when she would put on her hat and feather boa and head down to the docks looking for clients:

'C'mon then, let the dog see the rabbit!'

Soon the band struck up their first song of the afternoon. To the amusement of all, it was 'Teddy Bears' Picnic', and the friends started to inspect the girls, albeit from across the hall. They tried not to stare, but inevitably their gaze made the girls feel uncomfortable. Mitch thought this was more to do with the arrangement of the room than the bad manners of the men.

There were no officers present of course, only other ranks. The officers also attended tea dances, but the ladies who were rustled up for *their* inspection were of the 'top drawer' variety. It was clear that this afternoon's females would be considered 'second rankers'. Nevertheless, there were some fine looking young women present, Mitch noticed. All the women were from the Anglo-Indian community, whose earnest desire was that their daughters should secure an English husband, preferably an officer, but failing that a private would do.

Mitch felt a degree of sadness for the Anglo-Indians. They were descended from the offspring of European, mostly British, soldiers or East India Company men, some high-ranking, some low, who had married or had liaisons with Indian women. Being of mixed-race, they stood apart from the two dominant communities: the British civil and military administration and the fully indigenous Indian community, and it seemed to Mitch they were not fully accepted by either. As he became acquainted with this small but proud Anglo-Indian community, he began to resent the dismissive way the *pukkah* Englishmen referred to them as 'half-chats'.

These largely respectable folks embraced the British culture and the Christian faith. Many had British surnames, and many held good positions in the railways and other institutions, yet they were not welcomed into all areas of British social life in India. Mitch thought this most unfair, since no-one could be held responsible for the circumstances of their birth. In some way, it reminded him of the status of Irish Protestants, who did not fit in with the Irish Catholic community, but were neither highly regarded nor fully trusted by the British establishment either. The situation for the Anglo-Indians was rather worse however, in a culture where a man's status was assessed additionally according to the pallor of his skin.

After a few more ironic tunes were played, such as 'Follow The Colours' and 'Anchors Aweigh', some more obvious dance tunes ensued and one or two men dared to cross the divide and invite girls onto the floor. Soon, Mitch spotted a particularly striking girl on the dance floor. Unfortunately, she was already dancing with someone else. Mitch bided his time however and, when he spotted the soldier steering the girl back to her womenfolk, whilst he set off to get her a cup of tea, Mitch swooped.

The band had just struck up 'The Ragtime Dance' and the girl was pleased to continue dancing, especially as Mitch was much better looking than her first dance partner. She was slightly built and very nimble on her feet, Mitch observed. As they stepped around the dance floor, he took in her rich auburn hair and very pale green eyes. Her full lips, which owed nothing to rouge and her even white teeth were complimented by the most stunning pale cinnamon-coloured skin. Her simple white lace tea dress was of the latest, less structured style and she filled it nicely. As they passed her unlucky former dance partner, who was juggling two cups and saucers and two slices of Dundee cake, Mitch threw him a conciliatory smile.

After several giddy canters around to 'The Monkeys Have no Tails in the Zamboanga' and 'Wait Till the Sun Shines, Nellie', Mitch's dance partner indicated she needed tea. Cannier than his predecessor, Mitch took his girl with him to the tea table. They made their introductions by the tea urn. She was Irene Grover, she told him, and her father worked, somewhat predictably, as a supervisor on the railways. She filled two plates with daintily trimmed cucumber sandwiches and slices of Victoria sponge cake and Mitch carried their teas as they headed back to her table.

Irene's mother, Olive, smiled approvingly at Mitch and he did his best to impress her by taking her teacup back to the urn for a re-fill. Irene was the middle one of three sisters, Olive told him. Sadly they had no sons in the family, she explained, but she was hopeful one day to have grandsons. Mitch cast an eye over the Grover girls, the youngest of whom was every bit as attractive as Irene, though the eldest had somewhat darker skin than her mother and sisters and was both taller and a bit on the hefty side.

Mitch now remembered his mates. Glancing across to where he had left them, he saw them, looking across at him with studied envy. Excusing himself for a second, he crossed the divide once again and ushered Prof and Kempie out of their chairs and across to the Grover's table, where he introduced them to the ladies. Mrs Grover was happy for the friends to be seated at her table and Mitch surreptitiously slicked down Kempie's recalcitrant cowlick as the big man lowered himself onto a rather small chair.

Soon Prof was impressing Irene's younger sister, Millicent, with his knowledge of Indian politics, whilst Kempie was focusing his own brand of embarrassed and inarticulate conversation on Constance, the eldest girl, who seemed nevertheless to be hanging on his every word. After more dancing and endless cups of tea, Olive Grover declared it would be in order for the three friends to come calling upon her daughters. She suggested they might like to come to the Grover household for tea on Sunday. Arrangements having been made for this, Olive rose and escorted her lambs home, leaving the three friends standing respectfully to attention.

The next three days passed slowly, with the usual routine, including the daily parades so loathed by the men. Sunday brought the most detested of all, the obligatory church parade. The men assembled on the parade ground – Church of England in the front rank, and 'odds and sods' to the rear – and marched along to the Mall. Mitch felt this obvious display of arms and men was probably designed to remind the locals they were under British sovereignty, and to show that the soldiers were prepared to respond immediately if called to arms, even on the Lord's day. At the end of the Mall, the soldiers who were Catholics branched off to their place of worship whilst the C of E and Methodists filed into the cavernous Holy Trinity Church. There they sat through the standard service and sang a few hymns.

Church attendance in India differed from that back at Longmoor camp in one major respect. Out here, the men would each be fully armed with rifle, side arm and forty rounds of ball ammunition. Each man worshipped with his rifle propped against the hymn book rest in front of him. Irreverent though this seemed it had been deemed a necessary precaution ever since the mutiny. Mitch presumed that, during the unexpected uprising of half century ago, soldiers had been caught out in church without weaponry. Clearly, that would not be allowed to happen again. The cool, white interior of the church was a pleasant enough refuge from the heat of an Indian spring.

This particular Sunday saw a slight change from the usual routine. At four o'clock that afternoon, their weapons safely locked away at the barracks, Mitch, Kempie and Prof took a horse-drawn *gharee* over to *Railway Colony*. The Grover house was not at all as Mitch had expected. Located down an alleyway beside the railway tracks, *Railway Colony* consisted of several blocks of single storey, cube shaped, concrete block houses, nestling in the shadow of the station's tall water tower. The three friends had to sidestep around dozing bullocks and avoid stepping in mounds of animal droppings, in order to reach the front door. Although the three friends shared poor working class roots themselves, they had expected a railway supervisor, especially one with English ancestry, to live in rather more salubrious surroundings than this.

Once inside the small and immaculate parlour however, there were familiar little touches of Englishness which doubtless singled out the homes of the Anglo-Indians from those of the majority of Indians. A framed portrait of the late Queen Victoria glowered disapprovingly over them from one wall. On the opposite wall was a hand-tinted portrait of an equally stern, long-dead Grover man in uniform. On the tea table, which took up most of the little parlour, was a pure white cotton table cloth, hand embroidered with scenes of regency ladies in crinolines and bonnets, wandering amidst cottage garden flowers. The many sharp creases in the tablecloth betrayed the fact that it was normally kept folded and hence reserved for special occasions only. In pride of place in the centre of the table was a rather battered biscuit tin, the lid of which boasted a view of the Houses of Parliament, beneath blue summer skies.

The girls' father, Basil Grover, was introduced to the guests and seemed very happy indeed to welcome them into his mostly female household. Mitch noticed his clipped English syllables and rather old-fashioned vocabulary. He seemed like a man from a different age – an affable, lower middle class Englishman, but with distinguished white hair and moustache gracing a face which was the colour of a well-worn, tan leather glove.

Mr Grover bombarded the young soldiers with questions about 'the old country' although it was soon obvious that neither he nor any family member within living memory had ever set foot in England. He seemed to have the idea that all English families were affluent and had large houses, big gardens and servants. Overlooking the fact that his daughters' suitors were simple soldiers, he enquired as to the positions held by their fathers.

Prof responded, as only Prof could, imaginatively though with a small degree of truth, that his own father had been a 'mover and shaker' in the coal industry, whilst Mitch's had been a military man who had fought in South Africa, and Kempie's had been farming in Hertfordshire. This seemed to please their host, who insisted on the formality of addressing them respectively as Thomas, William and Charles. His accent did not seem far removed from Prof's Welsh lilt,

90

though he pronounced the 'h' in Thomas, which Prof did not seem to mind.

Soon, Prof had Basil Grover deep in conversation about the threat from nationalist politics and the likely plight of the Anglo-Indian community in an independent India. Mitch had to smile to himself as he noticed Kempie tentatively seeking to grasp the tiny gilt handles of the dainty, violet patterned, bone china teacup between his large, banana-like fingers. Several times, Kempie had tried, unsuccessfully, to cross his long legs, but they posed a significant hazard to traffic in and out of the little parlour, so he had given up and tucked them uncomfortably beneath his chair instead.

Soon Olive Grover appeared with a selection of sandwiches. These were, she announced grandly, ham and tongue. She placed on the table also an open jar of Crosse & Blackwell's Piccalilli and a long silver spoon and invited the guests to help themselves to the pickle. Mitch chose a tongue sandwich and took the jar of piccalilli. He examined the label and realised it had been manufactured in Bermondsey, doubtless with spices taken there from India, before finding its way, in its final incarnation, back to India again. This was indeed a well travelled pickle. He guessed the bright yellow preserve would have been distributed to the outreaches of empire for the enjoyment of the homesick expatriate British community.

It occurred to him that the piccalilli must therefore have been expensive and had perhaps been purchased by Olive especially for her British guests. He somehow felt guilty, and also a little sad, that it probably cost his hosts dearly, in many respects, to retain their tenuous connections with the British culture that meant so much to them. That they should feel such loyalty to a place they had never been, and to a British community which in most ways excluded them, made him also feel inexplicably angry, both for them and at them.

After tea and genial conversation, the family and their guests took a walk along the side of the railway tracks and watched a very big sun setting over a very wide horizon. It gave the three soldiers the opportunity of getting to know the sisters, albeit under the watchful eye of their parents. Mitch saw the golden rays of the diminishing sunlight reflected in Irene's hair. Her eyes were the colour of jade and shone as she gazed excitedly at him. She was certainly a beautiful girl, and he liked it that she laughed a lot. There was a definite sparkle about her and he could tell she was very keen on him. What he was not yet sure of was whether he felt the same about her.

The outing had given the three soldiers much to talk about that evening back in their barracks and this was just the first of several pleasant Sunday visits the friends would make to the Grover household.

If the courting process moved along slowly in India, the army however did not. There was much hustle and bustle in camp over the next couple of weeks, as the bulk of the regiment prepared for their annual move up to the hills. Not all the men would be going up together. Two companies would head north for the first six weeks of the hot season. The remaining companies would be released half way through the summer when the first two companies returned to Sialkot to relieve them.

It wasn't just the military which decamped to the hills for the summer. The civilian administration did so too. All over the continent in fact, British institutions were packing up everything they needed to maintain their operations through the summer months, loading their essentials onto wagons, mules or camels, and heading to their own personally allocated northern hill stations to avoid the blistering heat that was to come. Much of the colonial furniture was designed with brass handles on the sides to facilitate its transport on the backs of camels. Campaign chests, campaign chairs and folding desks were transported northwards, as were filing cabinets complete with their contents.

In advance of the main column however, British *memsahibs* and their children, accompanied by their retinue of servants, would set off for the hills and establish themselves in bungalows, to await the arrival of their men folk a couple of weeks later. The process was a vast but well-planned undertaking, intended to minimise disruption to the smooth administration of the largest nation in the British Empire. Favourite plants, such as roses and geraniums, were potted up and carried to the hills, where the terracotta pots would be arranged in neat order, two pots to each of the many steps leading up to the bungalows. This gave the hill resorts a decidedly English air. To see these transported English gardens, one might just think oneself in Guildford rather than Gulmarg.

On the twenty-third of April, the military exodus for the hills commenced. The logistics of such a move was as complicated and well organised as any wartime military campaign. The Army Service Corps despatched the baggage train of *The Queen's* to Barian, the regiment's

92

summer home, and this was followed two days later by six companies of soldiers, including Mitch and his comrades of B company.

The army's transport and catering services had left twelve hours ahead of the main body of men, in order that refreshments might be made available during the men's march, and overnight camps established along the route. The regimental bandsmen went with the catering corps. Mitch was not sure why this was but speculated that there might be a rule compelling bandsmen to travel with their instruments, just as fighting men always carried their own rifles. As he was soon to find out however, the reason for the bandsmen's early departure was not one of military importance.

B Company proceeded by rail to Rawalpindi, from where they commenced the long march which was to get them to Barian by the second of May. Breakfasting on *char* and *samosas* at the station before they set off on foot, they had covered around fourteen miles of the muscle-gripping uphill march before their stomachs began again to grumble loudly.

Mitch thought he could hear a brass band playing somewhere up ahead of them. Prof confirmed he could hear it too. Soon, the strains of the children's nursery rhyme 'Polly Put the Kettle On' could be heard loud and clear. The message was not lost on the bemused men, who began to march at the double, as they realised their band, and more importantly their lunch, were just around the next *khudside*. Whilst the men rested through the heat of the afternoon, the caterers and musicians packed up their mules and set off once again, ahead of the main body, to be ready in position for the evening rest halt.

The long service men said Sialkot was one of the best billets in India, owing to its congenial climate and stunning views and, moreover, to its particularly good hill stations. The friends learned that many more troops were stationed over on the north-western side of India, where they were constantly in danger of attack from hostile tribesmen. By comparison however, there seemed to be very little trouble here at the frontier with Kashmir. The main threat to the stability of the British Empire here in the north-east seemed to be from petty, and sometimes not so petty, pilfering.

In Sialkot, Mitch and his comrades usually kept their personal effects in heavy wooden padlocked boxes at the foot of their beds and yet still items went missing from time to time. The most valuable items which thieves might seek out in the camp though were the rifles. British army issue Lee-Enfields would fetch a high price on the local black market, and it was said that any tribesman would exchange his daughter for one of the new Sniders. Each soldier knew that any rifle lost or stolen would quickly make its way across to the north-west frontier, to be used by the Pukhtoons against British troops. Any man who lost his rifle or allowed it to be stolen would therefore be in serious trouble.

Back at the Sialkot cantonment, the rifles would be stored overnight in the guard rooms, chained up to iron racks which were in turn concreted into the ground. Each man would first remove his bolt and bayonet and these would be kept separately but equally securely in the barrack room lockers, as a further precaution against theft. When the company was out on manoeuvres or route marches however, different overnight arrangements prevailed. Since the soldiers had to sleep under canvas, each man had first to dig a trench, wrap his rifle in sacking and bury it in the trench, loosely backfilling with soil and placing on top the ground mat and palliasse, upon which he would sleep. Mitch now realised why his father had often referred to his bed as his 'pit'.

This rifle burial was an unpopular practice for two reasons. Firstly, the weapon would have to be thoroughly cleaned and oiled early each morning before parade, and secondly, the white ants which would emerge from the disturbed earth during the night could eat clean through the ground mats and straw mattresses before gnawing at the soldiers' soft, white hides. It was all too common, especially in hot weather, for ant bites to turn septic. Many men contracted a most unpleasant and potentially lethal fever in this way, and it was not unknown for an entire company of strong fighting men to be decimated by a regiment of tiny ants.

Despite such rigours, the men eventually arrived, exhausted but cheerful, at their summer camp. Barian camp was less substantial than the cantonment camp, consisting of row upon row of large, white, pagoda-shaped tents, arranged in neat looking rows. Mitch and his comrades were disappointed, as they had expected something more permanent, given that the regiment came up here every summer.

The views from the camp were sufficiently breathtaking however to make up for their disappointment. The snow-capped peaks of Kashmir were even nearer to them now and the men were surprised that the snow clung picturesquely to the mountain tops even in summertime. As they sat around camp fires after dinner, chatting and smoking, Mitch learned that the hills around them were home not only to the usual foxes and pheasants, but also to rhesus monkeys and leopards. The men were warned to keep their eyes peeled if wandering around the countryside, as the monkey and the leopard were each in their own way potentially troublesome.

The following day's routine followed a similar pattern to that back at Sialkot, with early morning parade – a level parade ground had been established even here amongst the hills – followed by breakfast, then more musketry practice and then lunch. That afternoon, the men were surprised to see another group of wagons, drawn by camels and mules, arrive at the camp. They were even more surprised to see familiar native faces amongst the wagon train. Many of the service industries provided to the army down in Sialkot: the butcher, the baker and the shoe and saddle maker; the *durzee* and the *dhobee*; the barber and the *char wallahs*, and even the girls from the regimental brothel, had all followed the colours too, in order to pursue their support rôle in the hills. They had their own tents and were soon plying their respective trades from under canvas.

The summer passed most pleasantly for the men up at Barian and almost without a hitch. One Sunday, a party of Afridis came riding into the camp. They held official looking government warrants permitting them to trade salt from the salt mines of Kohat, far to the west. Despite the loud protests of the camp-following merchants, the Afridis were allowed to mingle with the soldiers and to trade not only salt but a variety of wares.

Some of them sold eggs, which, as they demonstrated by breaking them into a greased degh over a charcoal fire, were without exception double yolkers. These came, they claimed, from the two-headed chickens which might be found only in their village. Few of the men believed this but many bought the eggs anyway, to the consternation of the *undee wallah* whose prices they were undercutting and whose eggs contained only one yolk.

The Afridis had a number of fine horses with them and also some attractive womenfolk and were welcomed into the camp, as they promised the troops a most entertaining evening. They quickly set up their equipment and saddled up their steeds. They proved to be highly skilled horsemen and some were also nimble acrobats and tightrope walkers. They had also brought their own homebrewed country liquor which, despite the misgivings of the quartermaster, they were allowed to dispense generously to the men. Later on, the entertainment was turned over to the Afridi women, who danced, scantily-clad and in a most sultry and provocative fashion around the camp fires – to the disgust of the ladies from the regimental brothel. All in all, it was indeed a most diverting evening.

The following morning, however, there were a great many sore heads in camp. When a somewhat feeble reveille was sounded, it was with some difficulty that many of the men dragged themselves from their tents. Mitch thought he must have slept with his mouth open all night, for his throat felt like sandpaper. Prof complained he had never before had such a sore head, and even Kempie, whose capacity for alcohol consumption seemed to be in proportion to his body size, said he felt as though he had been clubbed about the head with a malt shovel.

Mitch did not think he would survive the early morning parade with just one cup of tea inside him, but the morning's routine was soon abandoned when it was discovered that almost every rifle in the camp was missing. Also missing were the Afridis. At first, it did not seem possible that the tribesmen could have removed so much weaponry during the night, without anyone hearing or seeing them, nor that they could have smuggled them past the camp guards. It was soon suspected however that the alcohol the Afridis had been sharing out so liberally had been drugged.

The camp natives now suggested the thieves had been Adam Khel Afridis, notorious gun runners who ran half a dozen gun factories back in their village, Dara Adam Khel, over in the tribal territories. It would be their intention, the camp followers declared with scathing indignation, not just to sell the weapons to their Pukhtoon rebel cousins, but also to take some of the rifles apart in order to study and copy them.

A party of soldiers was sent off immediately to try and track down the thieves, even though the Afridis had the clearest of head starts, and of course clear heads. Next, the company signallers were despatched to the highest hills to signal warnings ahead to the various military stations. It seemed the wily Afridis had decided to split up and head off in different directions. Eventually, some of the thieves were apprehended near the Khyber Pass and were summarily hanged, and so some, though not all of the weapons were retrieved. However, the honour of the regiment had been slighted and the men knew they would have to work very hard to restore their reputation. The smug attitude of the native camp followers took some time to dissipate also.

In late October, the men of C and F companies packed up and left Barian in order to proceed, via Rawalpindi, further south to Delhi. The remaining companies, B Company included, set out on the ninth of November to return to Sialkot. The three friends were sorry to leave the stunning beauty of the hills, but as Kempie pointed out, they would get to see their girls again.

There were indeed more invitations to the Grover household for tea and more Sunday walks for the three couples, with Olive and Basil in tow as ever, of course. Kempie and his Connie had reached an understanding that, when his time was served, they would marry. Army rules did not permit other ranks to marry without the CO's permission, and this was very rarely given during the period of a man's overseas service. It was a different matter where officers were concerned of course. Olive and Basil seemed blissfully happy at the prospect of marrying off the eldest, and darkest, of their three daughters and did not hesitate to give their permission. A thrilled Connie was already planning her distant nuptials.

Prof said little about his relationship with the seventeen year old Millie, but Mitch knew that the Welshman's feelings ran deep and silent, as so often did his thoughts. As for Mitch, he liked being seen out with Irene, as she was the most beautiful of the three sisters, if not indeed the most beautiful girl in *Railway Colony*. He could not say why it was though that he did not see his future with her. Perhaps it was simply that, as lovely as she was, she was not Rose.

Irene was however besotted with Mitch, of that there was no doubt. He could see it in her eyes. She was always eager to please him, to flatter him. He could hear it in her voice and see it in her gait. As the Sunday group walked along by the railway tracks, she would link arms with him, daringly pressing herself close him and laughing coquettishly in an effort to hold his attention. He did not feel as comfortable as she clearly did to be indulging in such flirtatious behaviour whilst her parents followed so close behind. However he knew he would have thrown caution to the wind, had he been as smitten with Irene as she obviously was with him.

Mitch had wondered if her ardour might have cooled off whilst he was away in Barian, but, if anything, his absence had made that particular heart grow much fonder. It was difficult to discuss exactly how they felt about each other though, when they went everywhere in a six-some, with her parents trailing along behind to maintain propriety. Only handholding was allowed, never a kiss or anything more intimate. One Sunday however, Irene whispered to Mitch that she would like to see him later that night – alone if possible. Mitch had been surprised that she would risk her reputation in this way, and he was not persuaded that it was a good idea, but he felt he at least he owed her an explanation of his feelings, and to do so he needed privacy.

It was easy enough for Mitch to slip out of camp after dark, and, with the connivance of her sisters, Irene managed to arrange her pillows in the bed she shared with them, to deceive her mother into thinking she was soundly asleep in between her siblings.

The couple met by a small lake in the moonlight. Irene threw herself into Mitch's arms immediately. All the things he had planned to say to her, in order to let her down gently, went right out of his head as he felt her warmth against him. Immediately, she was declaring her love for him and kissing him warmly, preventing him from offering any argument. As they slid down onto the cooling grass, Irene unbuttoned and removed his shirt and immediately he felt the pleasant evening breeze caressing his shoulders. As she pressed herself against him and allowed him to slip the silk blouse from her shoulders, some of the passion Mitch had felt with Rose now returned. Perhaps Irene was the one after all. Perhaps she was to be part of his future. She did not have that restless and mischievous spirit which had so attracted him to Rose, but she was fervent and eager to please him. Perhaps that would be enough.

They made love in the moonlight, with only a solitary owl to hoot disapproval at their coupling. Mitch felt her wince suddenly and he was immediately concerned he had unintentionally hurt her. It had not occurred to him that this might be her first time, but then he realised that of course it would. Unlike the impulsive and experienced Rose, Irene was a virgin. She was a nice girl, from a poor but decent family, and she loved him. Irene sensed he was not at besotted as she, but she was so desperate for his love she was willing to give herself to him anyway. Before he had realised the nature of her sacrifice, the taking of Irene's virginity was achieved.

They lay back on the damp grass gazing up at the breathtaking Indian night sky with its ancient planets and shooting stars. Mitch glanced across at Irene and read her expression. She looked happy and satisfied. He feared that she saw their intimacy as a bond, as the start of a loving relationship and perhaps as a way out of *Railway Colony*. He felt uneasy. He now held her protectively and told her how guilty he felt. Her parents had been good to him, and he felt he had betrayed their trust. Irene said it didn't matter, so long as he loved her. Naturally, he told her he did, even though he was not entirely convinced of the fact. It was too late however. In taking her innocence, he had committed himself to her, or so she believed. She had clearly interpreted his lust as a betrothal.

As they walked back towards her house, Irene's mood was one of elation and optimism, and yet somehow she looked so pale and so vulnerable. Mitch simply felt emotionally confused.

Five thousand miles away, as the crow flies, in one of Bloemfontein's white, colonial residential districts, it is late afternoon and the sun is on the decline in a heat-hazy sky. The arrival of his employer attracts the attention of a small black stable boy. The tall, square-jawed young man dismounts from his large horse, wordlessly hands the reins to the boy and pauses to smack the trail dust from his new South African Constabulary uniform, before climbing the short flight of steps up to the veranda of his home.

Once inside, in the relative cool of the bungalow's dark interior, he removes his revolver and holster, and locks them away in the secure cabinet. Pouring himself a whisky and soda, he takes a long draught. Slowly opening the buttons on his uniform shirt, he lowers himself wearily into a cane chair. Reclining languorously, he calls out and a houseboy appears, barefoot but otherwise clad in starched, white cotton uniform. The constable regards the handsome black youth for a moment, then raises a leg and indicates he wants the boy to remove his riding boots. The youth approaches, turns his back on the constable and, bending down, he raises the constable's leg between his knees and begins to tug the boot free.

The constable raises his other leg and begins to caress the youth's buttocks with his still booted foot. Having removed both of the constable's boots, the youth stands to one side and looks at him, sheepishly. The Constable stands up, retrieves his drink and, picking up the whisky bottle, gestures towards the bedroom across the hallway. The youth, still looking uncomfortable, turns and heads into the bedroom obediently however, to be followed by the constable.

The 1st Battalion of *The Queen's* was busy that month as the day of the Northern Command field trials drew near. They were due to compete against others of the fifty British and one hundred and fifty

Indian battalions. In the recent past, the regiments had competed for the *Kitchener Cup*, the army in India's infantry efficiency competition. This had involved hugely exhausting exercises in marching, running and target shooting. As their NCO never tired of telling his men, *The Queen's* had covered themselves in glory a couple of years back when they had won the army's most coveted trophy. However, they now learned the competition had been abandoned as it was nowadays deemed to be too tough a contest.

Mitch thought it typical of his luck that, just as he was at the peak of his fitness and had all the necessary skills to compete for the honour of his regiment, this, the most prestigious of competitions should be set aside. There would still be field trials, but they would be far less gruelling than the *Kitchener Cup* contest. In fact all the men, save those who were in the hospital wing, were obliged to take part in the trials. The men could understand why the army had decided to make the competition less stringent, but couldn't see why they didn't continue to award the cup.

The trials now involved an eight mile march – in the *Kitchener Cup* competition, it would have been fifteen miles – and then the troops would advance for one mile in skirmishing order. Next they would fire at will at targets positioned around the woodland. This involved not only the skills that had been drilled into the men but also a good degree of personal judgement, as they had to firstly spot the targets, then estimate for themselves the distances involved and accurately set the field guns. The skirmishes were short and sharp and Mitch felt he was truly in his element. Prof and Kempie kept close to Mitch during this phase, since he was the best shot and also the most adept of them at guessing firing distances. The final phase was a free-for-all charge however, which all the men entered into with wild and vocal enthusiasm.

The NCOs' shrill whistles now heralded the end of the trials and the serving of lunch. The scattered men herded enthusiastically around the catering corps' enormous *degchis*, or *dixies* as the army cooks called the big Indian cooking pots, and were served hot soup. Although it was still the hottest part of the day, soup was the best thing to sustain the men on their exhausting eight mile march back to the Cantonment. The friends realised how much more rigorous the fifteen mile return march would have been. They were suitably awed by their predecessors' achievements.

Major General Mahon's report on the performance of *The Queen's* was posted in the mess during the next few days and was read eagerly by all the men:

'This is the third time I have had the honour of inspecting this splendid regiment and it is, if possible, better than last time. Their training and instruction, both at drill and manoeuvres, are all that can be expected. Their discipline is strict but the men are all happy in, and proud of their regiment. There is a very marked *esprit de corps* throughout the regiment. They are fit for active service anywhere.'

'What's *esprit de corps* mean?' Kempie asked Prof as they washed the dust from their throats in the canteen that evening.

'Well, it's French and it means that no man in the regiment would hesitate to buy his friends a beer,' Prof explained, 'so, your round it is then, Kempie.'

Although Lord Kitchener's trophy was no longer up for grabs, it was announced a fortnight later that Brigadier General Pink had decided this year to award silver medals, stamped at his own expense, to those men who had scored highest in the trials. To his astonishment and delight, Mitch was one of the recipients. Having worn his valued award in the canteen and been obliged to buy copious amounts of beer for his friends, he now wrapped the medal carefully in a pair of socks and placed it in the bottom of his locked box, in the hope that any pilfering native who might succeed in gaining access to his belongings would not notice it.

In early December, it was announced that six of the companies, B Company included, would be quitting Sialkot on the ninth of the month and heading south, via Delhi, to Agra. They would be following in the footsteps of C and F companies, who had left a few weeks beforehand. Prof informed Mitch and Kempie that Agra was situated down on the plains, south of Delhi and a great many miles from Sialkot, so he could not imagine they would be kept down there beyond the spring as it would be far too hot by then.

As the men were packing up to leave however, a new draft of recruits, including one hundred and fifty privates, arrived from England to take their place. Mitch and his friends were surprised at this, as they had assumed they would be returning to Sialkot, but it now seemed unlikely that would be the case. Prof and Kempie were saddened at leaving their girls behind. Only Mitch was excited at the prospect of seeing somewhere new.

The Grovers gave the three soldiers a small send off with tea and home-made cakes and Olive Grover hugged the boys goodbye with as much emotion as if they were her own sons. Olive's display of unrestrained affection made Mitch feel slightly uncomfortable however.

The three friends bid their girls farewell. Propriety still did not allow a public display of kissing at the Grovers' gate and, as Mitch closed the gate behind them and grasped Irene's hands in a somewhat formal gesture of farewell, he noted the look of resigned desperation in her eyes. He had been unable to utter the sort of words which would have reassured her. Torn between not wanting to hurt her feelings and not wishing her to assume too much commitment on his part, he assured her they would be back at the start of the hot season. Unconvinced, Irene smiled and nodded weakly. Mitch did not look back as he, Kempie and Prof walked away from *Railway Colony*, back along the railway tracks to the cantonment.

Chapter 7 – **Mutton Curry**

The six companies began their journey with several days' route march down to Rawalpindi, where they entrained for Delhi. After an overnight stay in the Delhi barracks, they set off by rail again south towards Agra. Like the cantonment at Sialkot, the permanent military installation in Agra consisted of long low barrack blocks, laid out with precise symmetry, and all the usual offices, such as latrines, shower blocks, canteen and mess facilities, school room and library, plus the separate officer's quarters and mess.

In fact, the layout was so similar to that of Sialkot, that the men had no difficulty finding their way around. Mitch guessed that all the military cantonments in India must be laid out to the same basic plan. With such precision of planning, he could understand how the British had come to rule an empire. The routine was certainly the same as it had been at Sialkot, with parades, drills, kit inspections, route marches and so on.

The cantonment even had its own *Saddar bazaar*, and that too seemed to be laid out to a similar plan to that of its Sialkot counterpart. The men had no idea how long they would be in Agra, but hoped that they would be moved to one of the hill stations once the hot weather came. This proved not to be the case however, as they were soon advised it would be companies C, F and H who would leave in April by train for Dehra Dun to commence their route march to the hill station at Kailana.

To their dismay, the men of B Company learned they were indeed destined to spend the summer in the heat of Agra. On a positive note however, Mitch and Prof learned also that they had passed their examinations. Mitch had been awarded a 3rd class certificate of education and was granted his financial award for his proficiency in Hindustani. The third class certificate meant he now met the basic requirements for promotion to non-commissioned rank. Prof of course had achieved the higher 2nd class certificate in addition to his awards for Hindustani and Farsi. They had good cause to celebrate with Kempie, who enjoyed having such smart friends.

The men of B Company now found themselves with three weeks' accumulated leave and those amongst the men who had been careful with their money now made plans to do some leisure travelling. They had the option of staying at one of the *soldiers' homes* if they wished. These were guesthouses, mainly established by retired long service men who had stayed on in India. The rates offered to soldiers in these establishments were reasonable, the food well suited to army tastes and a plentiful supply of best beer was always available. Mitch, Kempie and Prof decided to spend their first week of freedom in camp, taking the opportunity to see the sights around Agra, but thereafter they planned to take themselves back to the relative cool of the hills.

Hiring a horse drawn *tonga*, they naturally headed for the area's principal attraction, the white marble palace which had entranced many generations of travellers to India. They had heard a great deal spoken about the magnificence of the *Taj Mahal* and they were not disappointed. Their first sight of the majestic mausoleum, set against a periwinkle blue sky, took them rather by surprise as it came into view, for it exceeded all their expectations. The massive, white onion-shaped dome, guarded by four tall sentry-like minarets, sat in pride of place, visible for miles around, on the banks of the wide, grey-green Yamuna River.

As the three friends descended from the *tonga,* they were immediately besieged by hawkers, beggars and would-be guides. Selecting the smartest looking youth with the best English to be their guide, and having negotiated a price for his services, they set off to approach the monument on foot. The three friends sat on a low marble seat, from which the *Taj* might be viewed along the length of the ditches in front of it, whilst the youth intoned his speech about the history of the place.

He took them from its inception in 1653 as the tomb of *Mumtaz Mahal*, favourite wife of the Mogul emperor *Shah Jehan*, through the number of marble blocks used and the number of precious jewels set into its walls, to the number of men involved in, and indeed killed during its construction. The soldiers had no idea if the boy's figures were accurate, but they could appreciate the place was quite magical and impressive nonetheless.

Kempie's attention however was taken by something much closer to hand. On one of the long strips of lawn leading up to the palace, a large white bullock, goaded by a thin-legged native with a stick, was engaged in pulling a small grass cutting machine. The vast expanse of grass having been neatly trimmed, the native now unharnessed the bullock from the machine and turned him around, allowing him to eat the grass cuttings directly from the open collection area of the machine.

'Would you look at that,' Kempie exclaimed, 'isn't that the most brilliant thing you've ever seen?'

'It is indeed,' Prof agreed, 'and so beautiful, how the smooth whiteness catches the sunlight.'

'No, not the palace, boy,' Kempie corrected him, 'that grass-cutting cow. That's entirely self fuelling that is. No motor needed and no fuel, apart from the grass. The cow cuts the grass, and then the cow eats the grass and gets the energy to cut more grass. No expense is involved. They must have been doing this for generations. So simple, that is.'

Mitch and Prof laughed at the object of their friend's wonderment.

'You can take the boy out of the farm ...' Prof joked.

As they wandered around the base of the monument, the youth indicated all the many empty niches, from which precious stones had been prised by thieves over the centuries. Close up, they could see that the porous white marble was grubby and devoid of its valuable encrusting up to a height where one man might reach when perched on another's shoulders.

'*Chauray*!' the youth spat in disgust at the thieves who had despoilt his national treasure.

The friends decided to take the knowledgeable youth with them in the *tonga* along the twenty two miles to the next tourist site which he had assured them they must see.

Fatehpur Sikri was a palace-city complex, made entirely from local red sandstone, and it covered a vast area. It turned out to be, not one palace, but several, with fortified walls and no fewer than nine entrance gates. The youth explained that the city had not been occupied for very long after its construction but had in fact been abandoned in 1585 when the water supply had run out. Prof suggested this lack of forward planning was the reason why no Mogul empire existed today. His observation did not sit well with the youth however.

Next, the youth indicated a great victory arch with inscriptions in Arabic style characters. Unlike the Koranic verses which adorned the *Taj Mahal*, this, he told them, was a Christian text. He translated:

'Isa – that is Jesus, you know – said the world is a bridge: pass over it, but build no houses upon it. He who hopes for an hour may hope for eternity. The world endures but an hour. Spend it in prayer, for the rest is unseen.'

'That's good advice,' Prof agreed, 'the world is a bridge. Don't stop to build houses but keep going. Isn't that what I've been telling you boys all along?'

The youth now showed them the halls of public audience. The *diwan-i-am* was where the emperor Akbar would receive petitions from the common people; the *diwan-i-khas* was where he would receive notables and holy men. Mitch and Prof recognised the words, *am* – common, and *khas* – special, from their Hindustani lessons. It seemed this Akbar was a pretty egalitarian ruler who liked to welcome men of all religions to his palace and would discuss their respective faiths with them.

Next, they came to a raised, balustraded courtyard which had four separate palaces arranged beneath it. They learned that Akbar had a Mahommedan wife and a Hindu wife then a third who was of the Christian faith, and that this fact both pleased and appeased all the peoples of his empire. Akbar occupied one of the palaces and his wives each occupied another. Prof reminded Mitch they had learned the word *akbar* – meaning 'mighty' – in their lessons also. This was certainly an educational trip, they decided.

A set of sandstone steps led up from the raised courtyard to an even higher area. The youth took them up the steps and they found themselves at a small balcony which was shaded from the sun by a *chatri,* a domed stone canopy. It had splendid views of the countryside around and also enjoyed balmy breezes from all directions.

'What's this – the crow's nest?' Kempie asked, gazing at the flat plains all around them.

'No,' said the youth, 'this is the *love* nest. Here, one cannot be seen from below. Emperor Akbar would bring one of his wives up here and would make love to her on a sumptuous silken *diwan* and, since the other wives could not see them, so they would not be jealous.'

The friends found themselves liking the sound of this Akbar fellow and his hauntingly romantic but deserted red city. The youth led Kempie and Prof back down the steps, but Mitch remained for a moment or two alone. A strange and overwhelming feeling of timelessness had suddenly come over him. He felt as if he were a speck on the cheek of time itself, unimportant and humble against the vastness of India and the might of the ancient civilisation which had been here before him. It occurred to him that this place, this deserted palace, with its empty halls, vanished splendour and ghostly shadows, represented what he loved about India. He felt the magic and awe of the place and was gripped by it. He suddenly understood also why he could not marry Irene.

Unlike Prof, he saw no future for himself here in India. He would never be a wise and powerful Mogul emperor, living in a splendid palace, with all its luxury, intrigue and romance. He would never enjoy great wealth or great respect. Equally however, he could not see himself being married to Irene and raising a mixed-race child back in that dismal concrete *Railway Colony*, with no prospects of anything better.

He could not bear the thought of any child of his being treated shabbily by both the British and Indian communities, as the Grovers clearly were. He did not wish to feel, for any son of his own, the sadness, frustration and anger he had felt for the Anglo-Indian community. Nor could he see himself or, worse, his future descendants talking longingly and fondly of a revered but ungrateful 'old country'. He had of course been at his happiest in India and would always be glad he had come here, but yet he knew did not belong here.

His deep reverie was suddenly disrupted by a shout from Kempie down below:

'Oi, Akbar! C'mon, you mighty Mogul you, we're movin' on, boy!'

The sun was now high in the sky. Its searing whiteness beat down upon the palace, and drove the lurking shadows from every corner. As the friends walked back towards the gates, passing the now green and brackish waters which lay undisturbed in the abandoned Turkish baths, they realised they were now very hot and very thirsty. The youth guided them to a tea shack under a clump of trees over by the main road, where their *tonga wallah* and his starved horse were sleeping in the shade. The men ordered pots of the sweet, milky tea

107

and some fried snacks for themselves and for the youth. Then they settled themselves beneath the trees to doze away the afternoon.

A few days later, the three friends began their preparations for their trip out of Agra. Their plan was to head back up to the hills, by train, to a hill resort named Simla. They had chosen this spot as there was a reasonably priced 'soldier's home' there. They thought there would be no shortage of soldierly company there during this summer season, since it was the one of the main Hill Stations used by the military in this part of India. There would however be no exhausting route marches for the next ten days, and no uniforms either.

Each of them had had *shalwar kameez* made up by the *durzee*. These cotton suits, comprising long loose shirts and loose baggy trousers, were what the locals wore. The friends had also had Afridi-style leather sandals made to measure by the local shoemaker. Kempie had been delighted to find he could at last obtain comfortable shoes for his non-regulation size feet. The shoemaker had taken two large sheets of purple sugar paper and had motioned Kempie to place his feet firmly on them, so that their outline might be traced in pencil. The shapes were then cut out, marked with his name and regiment and saved, not only for this, but for any future footwear requirements he might have. These templates would be kept, quite possibly indefinitely, alongside those bearing the footprints of Mitch and Prof, and doubtless those of every soldier who had ever set foot in the Agra cantonment.

Setting off early one morning, the three friends took a *gharee* to the station where they caught a train to Delhi. They allowed themselves a couple of hours for sightseeing in the city, which they found intolerably hot and crowded, before catching the night train from Delhi station to Kalka. The seats in 2nd class were only moderately comfortable but they had a compartment to themselves. Once they had eaten the mutton curry and rice served up on board and had closed up the blackout blinds, they slept fairly well, despite the airless atmosphere of the carriage.

Mitch was awakened by the comparatively fresh morning air, which told him they were now a long way north of Delhi. It was just getting light when he lifted the window blind and looked out onto lush green fields. It was pleasing to be back once more in the Punjab – the land of the five rivers. Mitch could recite the names of all five of the mighty rivers which flowed down from the Himalayas into the valleys of the Punjab District. These rivers, together with the two annual rainy seasons, were what made the district so fertile and its people so strong and vigorous.

Looking out across the many acres of wheat and tobacco, he saw a gathering army of peasants heading from their villages and spreading out into nearby fields. As he watched, he saw each native find a lone spot and squat down on their haunches. Baffled at first, he suddenly realised they were attending to what the native troops referred to as their 'morning call' – using nature's latrines.

He shook Kempie and Prof awake and indicated the unusual sight which lay to each side of the train. As their carriage rattled along through the countryside, they could see the fields dotted with numerous figures, as far as the horizon in each direction. The heads of the natives were modestly covered with white gauze turbans, but, by contrast, their brown posteriors were plainly uncovered. The friends were astonished and bemused at the sight.

Soon, they reached Kalka, where they transferred to the waiting Kalka Mail – a much smaller train which ran on the new narrow gauge railway. The Kalka-Simla line had been constructed just eighteen months before. Prof had been reading about it in the *Hindustan Times* and so was very keen to ride on it. He explained that the new line was designated 'the British jewel of the orient'. It was indeed a miraculous feat of railway engineering, since it conquered gradients hitherto thought impossible for rail travel. The line also boasted more than one hundred tunnels and eight hundred bridges. Kempie thought this unlikely and started counting them but soon tired of this, as the passing scenery was far too distracting.

Although the carriages were smaller than usual, and the seats quite hard, the friends perked up enormously when, shortly after the little train had set off, a squad of boys came around offering breakfast trays to the passengers. Included in the price of their train tickets were pots of tea, bowls of porridge and buttered toast with jam. The teapots and mugs which accompanied their repast were made of enamelled tin, which seemed most practical, and no milk jugs or sugar basins were required, since, as per the local custom, the milk and sugar were already brewed up with the tea. Already, the air streaming in via the open carriage windows felt infinitely cooler and fresher than the hot soupy air of the plains.

The ascent into the hills took longer than they had anticipated, but they passed the time playing cards and consuming the inevitable snacks and tea which appeared at every station halt. The new narrow gauge trains might have been more modern, but the toilet facilities on board were no better than on other Indian trains, and still afforded the user an unimpeded and dizzying view of the sleepers rushing away beneath the train.

Eventually, they drew into Simla station, where an army of red-turbanned porters besieged the still-moving train, each setting his eye on a passenger or three. One wiry porter roughly conveyed the friends and their canvas rucksacks to one of the many waiting *tongas*. The friends had to rush to keep up with him and not lose sight of him in the crowd. The pony which drew their *tonga* appeared little more than skin and bone and it was soon clear why this was, as the poor creature struggled to take them up almost impossible slopes. Soon however, the road levelled out and they found themselves following the line of the long ridge of pine-clad hills which towered above them.

They arrived at The Mall – a long road which opened out into what was unmistakeably a military parade ground, flanked by a rather grand white stone church with elegant stained glass windows. The scene looked very English they thought as they noticed the many timbered, Tudor-style residences bearing names reminiscent of English seaside boarding houses. They arrived at their lodgings, which were not in the most elegant road in the town, but were nonetheless quite adequate.

They were immediately greeted by the proprietor, who introduced himself as Foggy Armstrong. He re-negotiated the price of their fare with their rogue of a *tonga wallah* and touchingly, he slipped an apple from his pocket into the mouth of the grateful pony. Next, he showed the friends to their large shared room which was fairly basic but wholly clean and comfortable. He pointed out the views from their veranda and left them to settle in and to decide who would occupy which of the room's one double and two single beds. Kempie immediately claimed the double which, when he lay diagonally across it, was a perfect fit for his huge frame.

As the three friends joined their host in the small garden for a welcome glass of beer, Foggy explained he had been with the Northumberland Regiment. As a time-served veteran of the Sikh Wars, with no family left back in *Blighty*, he had decided to stay on. He had used his savings to buy the guesthouse, he explained, and the income from this, combined with his army pension, afforded him a comfortable existence.

'How come you're called Foggy,' Mitch enquired.

'Well, the locals call me *Fauji*, which I'm sure you know means 'soldier', and somehow that got changed into 'Foggy' by all my visiting British soldier guests,' he explained good naturedly, 'and though I'm Alfred Armstrong really, everyone calls me Foggy nowadays, even the wife, who is a local girl by the way. Oh, and most of the kids you'll see runnin' about the place are mine. 'Must be seven or eight of 'em by now. Can't be too sure though, as every time I look at the wife she seems to be expectin'. That's what comes of having time on your hands – that and the Murree beer. No matter though, for out here, your children are your wealth. What else but children is a common soldier going to leave of himself on this earth, anyway?'

Foggy proved to be most affable and entertaining company and Prof was keen to ask him about his experience of 'staying on', since he still fancied he might do that himself one day. Foggy asked if they would be partaking of the dinner on offer at the guest house, as this would be his wife's local-style cooking, and they agreed they would. He sent one of his sons, whose name he seemed hard-pressed to recall, to tell his mother. The men continued to chat until the sun went down and they were called to the small dining room for their meal.

Mrs Armstrong's variation on the local mutton curry was highly satisfying, and the friends purchased a case of India Pale Ale from Foggy and carried it back to their room, where they sat on their veranda to consume it. It had been a long time since they had felt so relaxed, and the prospect of not having to rise early the following day was most appealing.

When they did awake the following morning, Mitch and Prof declared they had slept like the dead and felt greatly refreshed. Kempie however said that, despite his comfortably large bed, he had barely slept a wink, as he was convinced he had seen men climbing around in the trees all night. He had glimpsed red, devilish eyes staring in at him from the darkness, he claimed. Knowing that they were out there, and hearing their rustling amongst the branches all night, had prevented him from going to sleep, despite all the beer he had consumed. Mitch and Prof felt this was a shame, given that this was the first time Kempie had ever found a bed big enough to accommodate all of him.

At breakfast, the men were given a choice of an English style breakfast of porridge, followed by eggs with toast made from the local, English-style leavened bread they called *double roti,* or alternatively, an Indian style *chota hazri.* Unanimously, they chose the Indian style breakfast of charcoal-charred chuppatis soaked in hot, creamy milk. They had long been looking forward to sampling the Indian breakfast and it did not disappoint, and nor did the pot of *Ispahani* tea – served Punjab style.

Kempie mentioned his nocturnal ghosts. Foggy laughed and explained they would have been the local monkeys who lived in the trees all around them.

'It may look like the Surrey Hills up here,' he chuckled, but it's not England, and there's some rum creatures about. The holy men up at the *Hanuman Mandir* – that's the temple devoted to the Hindu monkey god, Hanuman – they feed the monkeys. You must make sure you keep your money and valuables with you, as the little blighters will steal anything they can get their thieving hands on if they get into your room – the monkeys, that is, not the holy men! Watch out for snakes as well, as there's a few poisonous varieties around here, though they normally slither away if they hear you coming.'

Armed with Foggy's advice as to what to see and what to avoid, the friends set off to spend the day walking around Simla. They climbed up through the trees and walked the mile and a half, along shady paths, from one end of The Ridge to the other, from Prospect Hill to Jakhoo Hill, where the monkey temple was located, and where Kempie now saw his 'ghosts' from the night before. Foggy had been right about the stealthy dishonesty of the monkeys, who were, Mitch observed, the slickest pickpockets he had seen east of *Bamsie.* The friends then strolled back again, this time along The Mall.

There appeared to be a level of British wealth and culture in Simla which the friends had not witnessed elsewhere. The town was also cleaner than any other they had visited in India. It boasted a *Gaiety Theatre* and numerous shops selling high class wares. The three-storey, English style residences, sat on plots delineated by purple rhododendrons which gave way to pines as the gardens blended into sloping hillsides. The houses were not set in neat rows, but rather each residence was carefully angled to make the most of the far-reaching views of the many pine-clad hills which extended as far as the eye could see.

When their stomachs told them it was time for lunch, their noses led them to a tea garden in *Lakkar bazaar* where corn cobs were being roasted over a charcoal burner. The aroma of hot corn was irresistible and they ate their fill and drank tea. While they sat in the little garden, watching the hustle and bustle of the market stalls around them, an old man approached them. At first, it wasn't clear what he wanted, and Prof was about to dismiss him as a beggar, when the teashop proprietor hastened over and explained the old man was a *Jyotishi* or soothsayer.

'He is verra good *Jyotishi*,' the *char wallah* explained, 'he is seeing all tings – the future and beyond.'

The friends laughed. What, they wondered, was beyond the future? Prof, whose Welsh mother used to read people's futures in their tea leaves, was intrigued and decided to give the soothsayer a go. He handed over the small requisite fee. The elderly man grasped Prof's hand and turned it over to scrutinise his palm. Squinting hard for a few moments, he began to utter his prophesy, and the *char wallah* translated:

'Jyotishi says the fruit of your tree will ripen under the Indian sun, Sahib, and your tree will have many offshoots. You and your beautiful wife will have many children together – all Indians. One of your children will have a different father and mother, however. You will enjoy long life and prosperity, God be praised.'

Prof seemed happy enough with his future, as indeed it was what he would have wished for himself. Kempie decided to have a go also and stretched out his palm with coins arranged upon it.

'Ask him what horse will win the Calcutta Cup next season, will you, boy,' he joked.

The soothsayer checked out Kempie's palm for a moment or two, then clicked his tongue, shook his head and closed up Kempie's hand, declining the coins.

'He cannot read your future. Not all hands may be read,' the *char wallah* explained

Kempie was mildly disappointed but pocketed his money. Mitch fished out his own coins and held them out. The soothsayer glanced at Mitch's palm also. This time, the soothsayer simply looked up and stared Mitch in the face for a few moments, before shaking his head and declining Mitch's money also.

'What's the problem?' Mitch asked, 'isn't my money good enough, or is it my palm he doesn't like?'

113

The two natives exchanged verbal rapid fire which neither Mitch nor Prof could follow. The *char wallah* became irritated and the soothsayer responded with equal irritation, until at last the *char wallah* rose to his feet and ushered the old man away.

'He is not seeing your future either, Sahib,' the *char wallah* told Mitch, 'it is not always working, or sometimes he is not feeling like saying what he sees.'

'What do you mean?' Mitch asked, feeling irritated himself now, 'does that mean he sees something he doesn't like – something bad, maybe? What did he say? I want to know, either way.'

The char wallah rocked his head from side to side in the classic Indian gesture, which could mean 'yes', or it could mean 'no', or it might simply indicate he had not a clue. It was a gesture familiar to Mitch and one he always found annoying.

'Come on,' said Prof, rising to his feet, 'that old faker couldn't see his dick if he was holding it with both hands! You'd best save your money anyway – for all the christening presents you'll have to buy for all my Indian children!'

The three friends set off to wander around the bazaar, examining all the local crafts; the carved and inlaid wooden boxes and footstools, and the lavishly embroidered linens, and soon the annoying incident with the soothsayer was forgotten. Kempie and Prof chose some pretty embroidered woollen shawls as gifts for Connie and Millie. They prompted Mitch to buy one for Irene too. For some reason, Mitch felt uncomfortable buying her a gift, but Prof suggested a pretty cream-coloured shawl with jade green embroidery, to match Irene's eyes.

After all, he pointed out, it wasn't as if it were an engagement ring, and the Grovers had been very kind to them, so it would be most unkind to leave Irene out. He said if Mitch didn't buy it for her, he would. This made Mitch feel unreasonably mean and so he gave in and bought the shawl.

After some haggling, they also bought some pretty embroidered tray cloths and napkins for Mrs Grover, knowing how much she liked to set out a pretty tea table. For themselves, they each bought one of the hand-woven, striped woollen blankets as souvenirs of their trip. They liked the way the locals wore these when they sat out in the evenings. Then it was time to head back to the guest house to consume Armstrong Begum's tasty home-cooked supper.

114

Their stay in the pseudo-Surrey hills passed all too quickly and soon it was their last evening at the guest house. Having consumed some rather small, but very tasty, charcoal roasted, spiced chickens and flatbreads with yoghourt *raita* and chutneys, the friends repaired, well sated, to their little veranda, with plenty of beers to while away their last night. They sat, comfortable in their loose cotton *shalwar* suits with their souvenir blankets around their shoulders, watching the big Indian moon rise and the huge fruit bats circling deftly above their heads.

Kempie had the air of a relaxed and pampered millionaire, as he sat with his large feet resting upon the low veranda wall.

'You know, this has been the first holiday I ever had,' he confided.

'It must have been like a holiday living on a farm in the country though' Mitch yawned, 'what with all that fresh air and scenery and starlit skies at night.'

'No, boy,' said Kempie sadly, 'it wasn't like that at all. It was all long hours and hard labour, especially after my folks died and I became a *Barnardo's* boy. *Barnardo's* rescued me from poverty and taught me some skills, but then I was back working on someone else's farm, for just my board and food, and no money for myself. I worked from dawn till dusk. Backbreaking it was, and exhausting. I slept in the farmer's barn and would get just a couple of hours sleep before it all started off again. And the food they gave us was not enough for a working boy. God knows how I got this tall on just bread and cheese!'

'Things were no better in mining,' Prof added, nestling down into the wooden reclining chair, 'same long hours and hard work, but it was all in the dark. We got paid, but it was a pittance. And some terrible accidents they had down there. Sometimes, when they had a cave-in like, it'd be most of the men in a village as would be killed. A village full of widows and orphans would be left. Not much help would be given by the parish and none at all from the mine-owners. Shocking exploitation, it was. I couldn't wait to get out and head off to London. Trouble was, I had no money to live on while I tried to get into something better, leastways not till the army took me on.'

Mitch, swathed in the warmth of his colourful blanket, agreed:

'We fell on our feet when we joined up, didn't we? I don't know about you two, but I bloody love the life, I do. I can't see myself ever wanting to do anything else. I never thought I'd get out of Bermondsey, and here I am, on the other side of the world, having a holiday in a guesthouse and in Simla no less, the resort where all the *toffs* stay. Who'd have thought it?'

The three sighed contentedly, as they sat, quietly star-gazing. Eventually, it was Kempie who broke the silence:

'Listen, I want to say, somethin'. You know, I never, in the whole of my life so far, had such good pals as you two boys. And that's not the beer talking, neither. Prof, you've helped me with the writin' and stuff whenever I had to do anything like that. And Mitch, well, I wouldn't have got through some of the manoeuvres and that without your help. I mean, I'm strong enough, that I am, but I'm not as nimble as the two of you. Mitch, you're the best man I've ever seen at the horsemanship and the firing, and you got me through the field trials, you did. I wouldn't have kept up with it but for you. I probably never said nothing like this till now, but I just want you both to know that you're the finest friends a man could have. And that's the honest truth.'

Kempie's emotional speech fell on deaf ears however, as his two best friends in all the world were now snoring heartily.

Back in Agra once more, their holiday in the hills seemed just a happy memory as the friends struggled to get back into the routine of life in the camp whilst the fierce summer heat persisted.

The following Sunday, Prof assisted Kempie to write a long letter for Connie, telling her all his holiday news. He also drafted his own tender missive for Millie. They would parcel up the letters along with the gifts they had brought and take them the following day to the despatch office to be posted to Sialkot. Mitch declined to write to Irene however, but asked them to send his good wishes to all, and to include his gift to Irene in their parcel.

He felt increasingly uncomfortable at the thought of continuing his friendship with the Grovers when he knew now that he had not the slightest intention of marrying their daughter. He did not know how he could impart this decision to them either, for he felt sure they would take it as an insult, especially as he had been walking out with Irene for quite some time now. If he were honest with himself however, he knew it was Irene's disappointment which he most could not face. She would be heartbroken and he was too cowardly to tell her how he felt. He banished thoughts of Irene to the back of his mind however and took himself off for a cooling swim instead.

The rainy season of 1908 was very late in coming. The dry heat increased to unbearable levels. Around the cantonment, the coppersmith birds burrowed desperately on the hard parched earth, in a vain search for insects. Also known locally as 'brain fever birds', they lived up to both names by their habit of banging their heads incessantly against the ground and uttering their repetitive metallic cry: '*doink, doink, doink!*' Vultures circled hungrily overhead each morning and, by midday, only the heat-loving lizards were venturing out to bask on the stone walls around the camp.

The bulk of humanity, soldier and civilian, remained in exhausted torpor in their respective quarters. The discomfort of the men in the cantonment had almost reached fever pitch before the unbearable heat suddenly broke and the blanket of stifling cloud above them began to release its random drops of water, grudgingly and tepid at first, then in an almighty, chilling deluge. The rains lasted for several interminable weeks. Now, mostly confined to barracks, the men were beset with a sort of cabin-fever. There was little to do in their off duty hours but drink and play cards. They felt listless and bored and arguments broke out often.

Some drilling was undertaken on the parade ground, albeit in heavy rain, but this was eventually curtailed, as the *dhobees* could not keep up with the demand for clean, dry clothes, as nothing could be properly aired in the damp monsoon atmosphere. Mitch discovered that putting away his still damp laundry resulted in its developing a fine white mould. He found his treasured scarlet cotton mess tunic was beginning to rot, and to his annoyance, he learned that the cost of a replacement would be stopped from his pay.

There was much cleaning of rifles and repair of equipment but not enough tasks could be found to keep the men busy and maintain morale. Moreover, the nature of the food changed noticeably, there being few vegetables harvested in the rainy season. Meals seemed to feature mainly rice or semolina. The men's health gradually began to deteriorate. Each day, more and more men were reporting to the Medical Officer, who in most cases diagnosed enteric fever.

Kempie had now developed an irritating cough which kept the rest of the men in his barracks awake at night. In view of Kempie's imposing bulk though no-one complained, of course. When Kempie started to experience alternating chills and sweats however Prof suggested he should report to the MO but the big man was most reluctant to do so. Like Mitch, he had a morbid fear of hospitals and medics. He explained, weakly and raspily, that his father had sought treatment in the workhouse hospital and had died there, to be followed to the grave very soon after by Kempie's mother. Mitch could understand his reluctance. However, when their friend began vomiting and had become so weak that Mitch and Prof could barely support him between them to get him out of bed, they insisted the time had come for him to seek medical assistance. He was duly admitted to the cantonment's sanatorium.

Even the mail, when it was delivered, had begun to turn mouldy and had a musty smell about it. 'Thank You' letters had arrived from the Grovers, and Mitch and Prof took them along to the sick bay to read them to Kempie. They found him looking no better for his twenty four hours under the care of the MO and, indeed, he was unable to sit upright to read his mail, so Prof read out to him his letter from Connie. It seemed to cheer him temporarily, but by the end of their visit to the sick ward, Kempie was sleeping uneasily, with beads of sweat on his brow, and his breathing was noisy and laboured.

No letter had come from Irene, but Prof advised Mitch that Millie, in her own letter, had written that Irene was anxious for Mitch to get in touch.

'I can't, Prof,' Mitch said, 'it wouldn't be fair to encourage her. I don't feel the same way about her as she clearly does about me. I don't know why. I just don't.'

Prof said he understood, but he felt Mitch ought to consider writing to Irene to tell her so and not keep her hanging on to a vain hope. Mitch said he would think about it.

Over the course of the next week or so, Mitch and Prof visited their friend as often as they could and became increasingly alarmed at his deterioration. He too had been diagnosed as suffering from enteric fever and the friends were shocked to see how quickly it was taking its toll on their big, strong comrade. Kempie was losing weight at a staggering rate and appeared also to be delusional. His huge arms and hands now seemed incongruously thin and spidery and he continually waved them around, as if fighting off invisible insects. He did not recognise his friends. He was delirious, and no-one could make sense of his ravings. His face was gaunt, with dark rings around his eyes, and his teeth appeared more prominent than before, which gave his head a skull-like appearance.

118

'Mitch,' Prof said fearfully, as they sat by Kempie's sick bed one day, trying to pour water between his friend's tight and cracked lips, 'I hate to say this, but I think he's dying!'

Indeed, it was the very next day, less than two weeks since the onset of his illness that Kempie joined the growing number of men who had succumbed to this untreatable disease. Mitch and Prof could not believe they had lost their big, strong friend, and so suddenly. He had never properly regained consciousness after they had read him the letter from Connie. They took comfort from the fact that the last words he had registered were those of his sweetheart.

Kempie's large but now skeletal frame was laid in the Indian earth at the local Christian cemetery, during a shared funeral service for the twenty two latest victims of the epidemic. Since Kempie had no family the company commander decided his few modest belongings should be disposed of by his two friends. The holiday clothes and the shoes he had had made to measure, were sent along to the church for the use of the parish poor, though Mitch could not imagine that any local impoverished person would be big enough to fill them.

They decided to send the balance of his pay and also his cherished souvenir blanket, which had so recently been wrapped around his big, cheerful person, to Connie, along with a letter of condolence carefully composed by Prof. The friends felt gloomy for a long while after the funeral. Somehow the big man's departure seemed to have left a large hole in their world. It had also somehow changed the dynamics of their relationship.

There was no response from Connie to their sad missive and Mitch supposed her to be wrapped up in shock, grief and disappointment. Prof received a long letter from Millie however, and the envelope contained a letter from Olive, expressing her and Basil's sincere condolences. They said they felt the loss of Kempie as keenly as they would have the loss of a son of their own. Prof drew Mitch aside as they sat in the mess canteen. He indicated the letter he had received from Millie.

'Mitch,' he said, his tone subdued and his expression one of determined seriousness, 'I've asked Millie to marry me, and she has accepted.'

Mitch was surprised. He uttered his awkward congratulations, but wondered if his friend had considered this thoroughly.

'It'll be a bloody long engagement though, won't it? After all you signed up for a ten year stretch, didn't you? They won't give you

119

permission to marry till your time's served. Still Millie's young. I'm sure she'll wait for you. Then you'll get your army reference and you'll find a good position out here, just like you planned.'

Prof shook his head:

'We won't be stationed here forever. They could move us on anytime, maybe even back to *Blighty*. I'd never be able to afford my passage back here. Millie might get tired of waiting, and there'll be others sniffing around her. She's a beautiful girl, Mitch, a stunner. I'd never find so beautiful a girl back home. I've got some savings and I think I could find myself work. 'Always fancied trying my hand at journalism. And, with a steady income, a Welshman could live like a king out here.'

Mitch had the sudden urge to say 'but what about me?' but then checked himself. He had just lost one good mate and now saw another slipping away from him but this wasn't about friendship. This was about Prof's future. Prof always had one eye looking to the future. That Mitch was the sort who lived for the present was something he supposed set them apart. Then again, Prof was usually the sensible one. He wouldn't do anything silly, would he? Mitch thought it must be the shock of Kempie's death which had suddenly got Prof thinking that life was too short. Mitch wanted to tell his friend not to make any hasty decisions out of grief but he didn't think he had the right to give Prof advice.

The two sat in silence for a while. Mitch wondered if Prof was hoping to be supported in his intent, or talked out of it. Eventually, Prof broke the silence:

'Millie had some more news, by the way. It's not good news though,' he looked around him to ensure they were not being overheard, 'it's Irene, Mitch, she's just found out she's in the family way.'

Mitch felt as though he had been pole-axed. He did not know what to say. He knew of course that the child was his.

'You'll have to do the right thing by her, you know, else she'll be ruined.' Prof urged, 'Her whole life will be ruined. Life's hard enough out here for mixed-race girls without the added stigma of having a child outside wedlock.'

Mitch was stunned. He had not expected this to happen. He promised Prof that he would think about it.

'Don't think about it *too* long, Mitch,' Prof warned.

120

The rains eased eventually, though the post-monsoon period brought its own dangers. The floodwaters were slow to recede and snakes lurked in every damp corner of the camp, often venturing into the barracks at night. Several men sustained snake bites, a couple of them fatal. The men were warned to check their clothing, shoes and bedding, in particular for the presence of the *krait*, one of the smaller yet most venomous of snakes. Also the many pools of surface water now became breeding grounds for vast swarms of mosquitoes which were almost impossible to eradicate or to exclude from the barrack rooms. It was one of the most unpleasant seasons Mitch and Prof had experienced.

Eventually however, the humid and pest ridden season gave way to the cooler and more refreshing days of the approaching Indian winter. Mitch felt that, for the first time in several months, he was less obsessed with the daily struggle to maintain personal comfort and could perhaps start to think clearly again. Two events now occurred which saved Mitch having to agonise any longer over his decision regarding Irene's predicament. Firstly, it was announced that B Company would be pulling out of Agra at the beginning of December and proceeding to Deolali for detached duty, in preparation for leaving India. Secondly, and most surprisingly, Prof suddenly disappeared.

When Mitch awoke to the sound of reveille one morning, he noticed that Prof's bed was empty. It did not appear to have been slept in at all. Then he noticed that Prof's wooden locker, at the foot of his *charpai,* was unlocked and propped open. It was empty, except for a sealed letter addressed to Mitch. Fearfully, Mitch opened the letter and read its contents:

'Mitch,

I have decided to stop travelling along life's great plain. India is the point at which I am going to stop. There is nothing for me back in Blighty but as you know I have found a veritable treasure out here. I will find a job of some description and settle down. It may not be as good a job as I could have expected with my service completed and a good conduct reference to my name, and I know I will lose my army pension, but I will find something, I'm sure. Anyway, it's time I got started on producing those children the soothsayer promised me. Please don't let on where I have gone, but do drink to my health and wish me well, as I do you.

121

All the best,

Ever your friend,

Thomas Lewis (Prof).'

Mitch's first reaction was anger. Prof had gone *AWOL*! How selfish of him. India had claimed the life of one of Mitch's two best friends and had now seduced away the other. Mitch was alone. He was deeply hurt that Prof had not told him of his plan to leave and that he had not even said goodbye in person. Surely the army would find him in Sialkot and would bring him back?

Then it occurred to Mitch that only he knew Prof was likely to have gone to Sialkot. The military police would not look further than the local bars and brothels. Mitch would not tell, of course. He owed Prof that much. It now occurred to him that at least this saved him from having to make a decision regarding Irene. In a couple of months, the company would be leaving India, probably for good. It would be a good thing if Mitch too moved on. Maybe he would make new friendships, new relationships.

B Company arrived in Deolali on the seventh of December. Mitch had forgotten about the strange, unsettled atmosphere which pervaded this transit station. Of course, he had been only vaguely aware of it when he had arrived there more than four years earlier. The station saw regular arrivals of eager, fresh-faced recruits, who usually spent just two or three weeks there, having their enthusiasm and innocence tempered by the old hands. Most of those old soldiers were time-served and were heading home. Others had been prematurely discharged, some due to illness, others to misconduct, but all were awaiting repatriation to an uncertain future. For whatever reason, most of the experienced soldiers waiting around at Deolali were jaded, exhausted, disillusioned and downright unhappy.

Once again, Mitch found himself rubbing shoulders with men who were veterans of frontier campaigns, men who had engaged the enemy and had survived. He was keenly aware that he had seen no action whatsoever himself. It was greatly disappointing. For all the training, the horsemanship and the musketry drilling he had undergone, none of his skills had actually been used in the service of

122

his country. He attributed this to his having been in the wrong place at the wrong time – or perhaps it had been a case of right place, right time. After all, some of the veterans had suffered severe wounds, some were blinded and some were limbless and, for them, the future wasn't in doubt. Unemployment was a certain prospect.

The air of impermanence at Deolali prevented Mitch striking up any new friendships. It seemed to him in any case that whenever he got close to anyone they either died or left him suddenly. He didn't know if he wanted to experience that sort of pain again, for pain was what it was. It was the pain of bereavement. He felt almost as bereft in losing Kempie as he had felt when he had lost his beloved Rose. The pain of losing Rose had been even more acute than his anguish over the death of his little brother Johnnie. No, he told himself he would not be so quick as to put himself through that kind of hurt again, not anytime soon at any rate. If he wanted companionship, there would always be a cluster of his fellow soldiers propping up the mess bar. He could associate with them, without getting close to anyone in particular.

The weeks passed slowly at Deolali, and it was during his time here that he started to notice some of the inequities of life in the service. His pay was a shilling a day and out of this he had a halfpenny stopped for his laundry and a further three pence stopped for 'messing'. This three pence from each man was given to the Lance Corporal, who would use the accumulated 'messing funds' to buy extras, such as butter and jam, which the men shared between them.

This seemed a more than adequate amount to Mitch, who now began to take note of mess prices and the amounts of such extras which were apparently being consumed. He wondered how it was then that, by the end of each week, the Lance Corporal had managed to get the mess book into debt. The men would be drinking tea without milk and eating dry toast by the end of the week unless they quickly stumped up extra contributions to the mess funds. However, the Lance Corporals and Corporals never seemed short of money themselves for drink.

There were also frequent stoppages from the men's pay, ostensibly for 'barrack damages'. This might imply that the men were getting drunk and destroying the barrack room furniture in the course of fights, but in fact this was not the case. These 'damages' charges seemed to be used to cover what was in fact natural wear and tear to glassware, crockery and other items in the mess, and indeed there was not that much wear and tear. The unfairness and lack of accountability of this system caused Mitch to conclude that some, if not all of the NCOs were misappropriating the stoppages to fund their own drinking. The NCOs did not fraternise with the privates and so it was difficult for the other ranks to observe what the NCOs were spending in the mess, but they could estimate this roughly, judging by how drunk they managed to get. Mitch started to sense a widespread conspiracy to defraud the other ranks.

He shared his misgivings with some of the men in the mess one evening. It seemed others had come to the same conclusions as he – that they were being cheated by the NCOs. Someone pointed out that everyone above the rank of Sergeant, all the Quartermasters included, were freemasons, and didn't everyone know how the masons stuck together. In fact many of the local tradesmen were masons too and, by that association, were able to attain and retain their contracts to supply the camp with victuals. It was suggested that the tradesmen might be rigging their prices too, with the connivance of the Quartermasters.

The discussion, kicked off by Mitch and well fuelled by drink, created strong feelings amongst the other ranks present. No-one was sure what, if anything might be done about the situation, but some strong opinions were expressed on what might be done to some of the NCOs. The men felt comfortable in expressing their views, since no NCO was present, and their discourse was not overheard by any outsiders, apart from the native mess staff.

That the loyalty and discretion of the bar staff might not be relied upon had not occurred to Mitch but it became apparent at the end of the evening when, as one of the last men to leave the mess after 'stop tap' was called, he started, a little unsteadily, down the steps to cross to his barracks. He felt a sudden, sharp push from behind, which caused him to fall flat on his face. Before he could stir, let alone rise to his feet, he was set upon by, he guessed, three or four individuals. He could not make out who they were in the dark, but they assaulted him not only with kicks and fists, but also with steel-tipped cane *lathis,* of the type carried by NCOs.

The fact that he now had no friends was something which also became apparent to Mitch when he eventually regained consciousness in the hospital ward. No-one visited him in hospital as his broken ribs and his many bruises mended. As Christmas came and went, he realised he had made no effort to cultivate new friends, but he had clearly attracted some dangerous enemies. He decided he would keep his own counsel in future, and not trust anyone around him.

On 6th January 1910, the order came at last for the Battalion to pack up and move out. They were going home, back to *Blighty* – 'dear old *Blighty*', as the song would have it. One Major, one Captain, three Subalterns, eight sergeants, ten corporals and one hundred and fifty-six privates, Mitch amongst them, embarked from Bombay on RIMS *Dufferin*.

As they set sail, Mitch recalled the optimism and excitement he had felt on his outbound journey to India. Somehow, he did not feel any such optimism on his return journey. Stopping at Aden, to collect some of their units who had gone there back in November of 1908, the ship now set a westward course. With a brief pause for the burial at sea of B Company's Private Ford, who had died of natural causes during the voyage, and despite their progress being checked somewhat by fierce storms in the Bay of Biscay, *Dufferin* docked at Southampton during late afternoon on 20th February.

As the troops steadily queued for the slow and orderly disembarkation, before entraining for their new billet at camp in Warley, Essex, Mitch turned up the collar of his woollen home uniform jacket and looked sadly at the dismal, leaden English skies. Somehow, it did not feel at all like a homecoming.

Chapter Eight – **Mutton Chops**

The summer of 1911 had taken every Londoner by surprise. The press said there hadn't been such a hot summer since eighteen eighty-seven, the year of Mitch's birth. Although it was early evening, the heat had scarcely abated. Mitch carried the jacket of his grey made-to-measure suit folded over his arm. The sleeves of his Indian cotton shirt were rolled up and he wore his grey hat tilted back on his head, in a vain attempt to take advantage of any passing breeze. He wondered if his parents would recognise him with his bulked out frame, his India-weathered face and his smart clothes. It was six years since he had left home, a thin, poorly-clad and frightened youth. Now a well-dressed and self-assured twenty-four year old, he was heading home again, wondering if indeed London would feel like home.

It had taken him most of the day to get from rural Essex into South London, hitching lifts to the city and walking along the side of the Thames. There was no public transport to be had, as the rail workers were still out on strike. As he strolled down Long Lane, a few curious heads turned to wonder what this relatively affluent looking young man might be doing, sauntering along with the confidence of a local, here in down-at-heel Bermondsey. He returned their glances with a look which said he could look after himself. He guessed they were probably strikers and maybe in need of some cash. It wasn't going to be *his* cash however.

He now turned into Crosby Row. The neighbourhood was unchanged and the stink for which Bermondsey was renowned hung even heavier in the stifling air than he had remembered it. The tenement buildings showed the same signs of landlord neglect. The same shoeless, snot-nosed kids still played the same games in the familiar dirty streets.

As dusk was now falling, those who were still in work were beginning to plod their weary paths home from tanneries and glue works and from the one or two food processing factories which remained operational. He could hear none of the usual sounds of cranes and other heavy machinery from the direction of the docks, so he guessed the dockers were amongst the million or so who had either walked out on strike or had been locked out by their employers.

The door to number 22 was ajar so he walked straight in and tapped on the door of his parents' rooms. To his surprise, it was a stranger who answered. Seeing the suited caller, the alarmed occupant took Mitch for a rent collector and tried to slam the door, but Mitch's reactive combat training ensured his boot insinuated itself between door and jamb first. He allayed the man's fears by calmly enquiring what had happened to the Mitchells, Joe and Georgina, who had been living here when last their soldier son had seen them. Reassured, the man nodded, released the door and went to find the slip of paper with the Mitchells' new address written upon it. Mitch was duly re-directed to Hardy Street, a short distance away.

Westminster House was nothing like as grand as its name suggested, though it might once have been so. It was a small boy who opened the door. At first, Mitch thought him another stranger and supposed his family might have moved on once again. He asked the child if the Mitchells lived here and the shy little chap ran inside to ask.

Georgina now appeared, wiping her hands on her apron. She had not aged in Mitch's memory, but in reality the lines on her face reflected the passage of time. Her harried face took on an immediate start of recognition however. Soon Mitch was being hugged by his tearful mother and gazed at in awe by his now eleven-year-old sister Jessie. That Mitch had yet another little brother came as something of a surprise to him. It took a little while for a shy little Freddie to emerge from behind the armchair however.

'Mitch! Why didn't you tell us you were coming? How long are you going to be home? Where have you been since last we saw you? Why didn't you write?' Georgina's questions tumbled out all at once.

'Whoa,' Mitch laughed. I'm home on leave for a bit, ma. 'Been overseas, in India most of the time, but I've been back about a year and a half now.'

Mitch soon had his small siblings enthralled with his accounts of thieving *Pukhtoons*, poisonous snakes and mosquito-infested monsoons and also of the remarkable journey Crosse & Blackwell's Piccalilli had made from Bermondsey to the tables of India.

Soon, Mitch's dad Joe arrived home, with fifteen year old George in tow. Mitch learned that Joe now worked at Smithfield meat market and George was an errand boy for one of the market's retail butcher's. Next to arrive home was twenty-two year old Joe junior, now a builder's labourer. Naturally, Mitch had to re-tell the stories for their benefit.

'Where's our Margaret?' Mitch enquired, realising there was someone missing.

'She's out cycling for the day with her young man, David,' Georgina told him.

'Our Margaret's courting, already?' Mitch asked, surprised.

'Of course she is,' Georgina laughed, 'she's twenty now, and working at Pinks' Jam factory in Long Lane, or at least she would be if she weren't on strike. The strike started here in Bermondsey, you know, and, what's more, it was the women of Bermondsey as started it. Now it's nationwide. Our Margaret's a union steward an' all. She got the girls out an' she's been standin' up to the bosses. She's a great little organiser, our Margaret.'

Mitch decided he would not mention the fact that he and his unit had been sent from Warley to man the railway signal boxes in Leicestershire where four thousand rail workers were out on strike. He feared Margaret would call him a strike breaker if she knew.

'What's my cousin Artie up to these days, d'ye know?' Mitch asked cheerily.

'Sure, and we haven't seen hide nor hair of him, not since his Ma died,' Georgina said, sadly.

'Aunt Jessie died?' Mitch asked, astonished.

'Oh yes,' Georgina nodded, 'Artie got work labouring at the docks after your Uncle Danny died, as he had to keep them all, and then just a couple of years later, my poor sister Jessie gets that *dimension.*'

'What *dimension?*' Mitch asked, puzzled.

'You know when the brain is gone soft. *Senile dimension* they call it. Of course she didn't eat no proper meals after Danny died and she had the TB quite bad too. Then she went into Dublin's *Rest for the Dying* hospital on Camden Row, but she didn't last long in there,' Georgina added.

Mitch shuddered at the thought of the hospital.

'So what happened to Artie and Annie and the little ones?'

'Well, when the dockers came out on strike, Artie had no money coming in at all, so he went off somewhere looking for work – probably came here to London. He hasn't been in touch with us though, and we didn't hear a peep from him since then. Annie left school and got a job as a servant in a big house in Dublin. Of course she doesn't earn enough to raise the younger ones and she isn't home to rear them anyway, so they got sent to orphanages all around Ireland. We'd have taken them in only we barely have enough room for ourselves and we couldn't have afforded their fares,' Georgina said, sadly.

Mitch recalled the fun and games he and Artie had had together as youngsters, at least until school had separated them. He was very sorry to hear about his Aunt Jessie. Georgina had lost her favourite sister. Mitch wondered if he would ever see Artie again.

'Those orphanages,' he asked, 'they weren't the ones run by the nuns, were they?'

'Oh no,' his mother reassured him, 'they was Protestant orphanages that took Jessie's children.'

Later on, after Georgina had fed them all, Joe and Mitch settled down in the kitchen's two easy chairs. Mitch recalled there had only been one such chair when he had left home.

'How long did you say your leave was, son?' Joe asked.

'Three weeks,' Mitch replied, his gaze dropping to the floor, as he remembered how, on the last occasion he had been untruthful to his parents, Joe had seen through the lie.

'We're based in Essex now,' he said quickly, 'but the best bit of being back in *Blighty* wuz last year, when I got to go to Windsor to provide a guard of honour for the King's funeral procession. It wasn't just *The Queen's* doing the guard of honour, there wuz a huge military presence in the town. I think they wuz expecting trouble, maybe from Irish anarchists or German fifth columnists or something. They never said for definite. Any road, I got to see all the crowned heads of Europe, so I did.'

'You never did!' Georgina gasped, 'tell us all about it.'

'Straight up, Ma, we wuz billeted in the Victoria Barracks and they marched us up the town to the castle, an' Missus Mitchell's best boy got to stand on High Street, with my back to the Castle, so I saw the whole cortège as it came from the station up to the castle for the funeral.'

The family was enthralled to hear Mitch recount how he and the rest of the Surreys had been up since half past five that morning, polishing boots, brass buttons and weaponry and, although they had been given a generous breakfast, they didn't get any lunch and were quite starving long before the royal train had arrived from London. They had stood, at ease in close ranks for hours upon end waiting, but had held their line, whilst the eager crowds of civilians began to swell behind them. Civilians and servicemen alike had been glad of the dense cloud cover that day, which had prevented their wait from becoming too hot and uncomfortable.

When, at last, the strains of a slow and solemn march drifted across on the breeze from the military band at the station, masking the churning and growling of the servicemen's empty stomachs, they knew the funeral party had arrived. Mitch explained what a great feat of logistics would have been involved in entraining and disembarking all the horses, troops and dignitaries, not to mention the big naval gun carriage which had served as the funeral bier. All had to be disembarked in exactly the right processional order, of course, as etiquette and practicality demanded.

As the cortège had passed out of the station approach and onto the High Street, the band at the station had ceased playing and the crowds had fallen silent. It was an eerie silence, Mitch said. Then, like a rolling tide, men's hats were doffed and the heads of all the onlookers, civilian and military, were respectfully lowered at the gun carriage's approach.

Mitch estimated there must have been some hundred and fifty straw-hatted sailors around the dead King, some drawing the ropes attached to the gun carriage as they made the uphill climb, others restraining it from behind as they passed up over the brow of Castle Hill and down the other side.

Joe reminded him of the incident at Queen Victoria's funeral only nine years earlier, when the horses drawing the Queen's gun carriage had been startled and had suddenly bolted. A disaster had been averted only by the naval ratings, who had rushed forward and secured control of the horses and gun carriage. This, he explained, had earned the senior service the honour of leading the deceased monarch's coffin for all time to come.

Mitch described how the scarlet coated men of the Grenadier Guards, their tall ceremonial Bearskin headwear lending some pomp to the sombre occasion, had flanked the sailors at the King's funeral, whilst the mounted household cavalry had followed behind. He said how lucky he had been to have had a front row view of the entire procession as it passed, just yards in front of him. Georgina said he would be able to recount the event to his own children one day.

Seeing how impressed his younger siblings were, Mitch further regaled them with colourful descriptions of the Emperor of Japan and the King of Persia. The youngsters chuckled at his regal gestures and comic facial expressions. Mitch listed some of the Princes and Grand Dukes who had passed before him, not that he could have identified one from another. The slow cavalcade had taken an age to parade majestically past the suitably solemn-faced statue of the late Queen Victoria, along past the Guildhall and the parish church, before circling around into the castle precincts, for the service and burial within St George's chapel.

'And they kep' you waitin' there all that time, wid no food in yer bellies?' Georgina asked.

'Yes, they did Ma, but when we eventually got back to barracks, the royal household had sent over a huge amount of food and drink for all the servicemen, so we dined well that night, I can tell you,' Mitch reassured her, 'on roast chicken, ham and tongue and all sorts of dainty food.'

'Mind you, I very nearly didn't get to the funeral at all, as *The Queen's* had a bit of a punch up the night before with the sailors and marines at *The Royal Oak*. One of them marines gave me a right shiner, he did. The next day the Sergeant says I can't go on duty in front of all them crowned heads with an eye as black as a fuzzy-wuzzy's arse!'

Freddie exploded into giggles at Mitch's colourful turn of expression, but Mitch carried on regardless;

'But the sarge fixed me up with some white oxide cream and then I looked presentable enough to turn out for the old King.'

Joe laughed too;

'We wuz up at Westminster that morning, to see the Old King orf on his way to the station. If we'd known you wuz in Windsor, we could have 'itched a ride with the coffin on the royal train and come out to see you.'

Georgina had a sudden thought and asked whether Mitch had seen or heard of the appearance, the day before the funeral, of Halley's Comet. The papers had been full of the fact that the comet would pass between the earth and the sun. Some scientists had predicted that a cloud of gas, trailing in the comet's wake, would pass over the earth, killing many of the planet's population in its choking poison.

'Huh, scientists!' Joe Mitchell exclaimed, 'wadda they know, and what's more, there wuz that eclipse of the sun a few days *after* the King's funeral an' all. 'Seems that also got a lot of people jumpin' up and down, wailin' that the world was gonna end.'

Mitch had not heard any of these portents of doom. However, that was hardly surprising, since he had been drunk for most of his time in Windsor. *The Royal Oak*, the riverside pub at the bottom of Castle Hill in Windsor, had become the hostelry of choice for the men of *The Queen's* during their brief stay in the town. It was the 'tap' for the Windsor Brewery, whose ales were of infinitely greater quality than the Murree brews Mitch had drunk in India. However, the pub had also been discovered by the sailors and marines who were billeted in the town for the royal funeral and, as Joe Mitchell would often say, oil and water just don't mix. There had been inevitable rivalry between the old sweats and the old salts.

Mitch told Joe he had been surprised to note that, unlike the army NCOs, the naval Petty Officers were allowed to fraternise with their ratings and would be seen drinking with them, and buying their rounds too. By contrast, from the day a soldier was made Lance Corporal, he could no longer walk out with his former comrades and nor could he drink or gamble with the other ranks. The newly appointed army NCO must not even allow the other ranks to call him by any former nickname he might have held. If he didn't immediately command respect in this way, he might be charged with 'conduct unbecoming' and might lose his stripe. When the fight had broken out at *The Royal Oak* between the senior service and the men in khaki, Mitch had been surprised to see the Naval Petty Officers joining their ratings in the fray.

Joe nodded in agreement,

'That's NCOs for you – bar stewards the lot of 'em!' he declared, with a sideways glance to ensure Freddie hadn't picked up on his veiled profanity.

It wasn't just in Windsor that Mitch had been drunk however. He had spent most of his off duty hours drinking himself into a stupor in the mess at Warley ever since his return from India. That had been the cause of his most recent trouble, though he wouldn't mention this to his parents, not yet at least.

'Wuz you at the coronation too?' Joe asked.

'No, Da. Some of my company was in town for it, but I wasn't. Some of us had to stay back at barracks.'

Mitch omitted to explain that the reason he, in particular, had remained back at Warley was that he had been doing a month in the glasshouse at the time.

Things had not been the same since Kempie had died and Prof had gone *AWOL*. Kempie's absence had made Mitch realise just how much he had relied on his big friend to keep him out of trouble. He had never seen Kempie lose his temper or threaten anyone, of course. Kempie had never needed to. It was enough for the big man to raise himself to his full height and to appear irritated and any potential aggressor would immediately back down.

Mitch did not know why he had become involved in the fight at the Windsor pub at all. It wasn't as though he had any mates to protect. He didn't feel the same sense of comradeship with his fellow soldiers at Warley as he had felt back in India. He supposed his participation in the punch-up had been solely due to the drink he had put away.

'Well now,' Georgina interrupted his thoughts, 'Freddie can bunk in with yer da and me tonight and you can sleep in the big bed with Joey and George. The girls have their own bed. And 'tis time our Margaret was back and getting into it. I'll wait up for her.'

Freddie, who had come out of his shell completely now, complained loudly that he wanted to sleep with his big brothers and hear more of Mitch's stories, but Georgina silenced him with a cuff around the ear and packed him off to bed. Mitch was suddenly tired of all the talking anyway and he fell easily into bed with his brothers.

Given that the family now occupied a different tenement from that which he had left, he didn't really feel as though he had come home. He had been away so long, he had forgotten what it was like sleeping four to a bed and with a pail in the corner to serve as a toilet. He had managed to down a couple of beers on his way over to Bermondsey, and Joe had sent George out for a few bottles for them to have with their dinner. Despite the strangeness of the tenement rooms and the fact that he had to get up once in the night to avail himself of the bucket, Mitch managed to sleep well enough.

The next morning, still functioning on army time, he awoke at first light and lay thinking as his brothers snored beside him in the bed.

133

He didn't recognise the bed. It was new – well, not new perhaps, but different. With three more wages coming into the house, the Mitchell family had clearly been able to afford a bit more furniture, hence the second easy chair in the kitchen.

'Joey,.. Joe!' he now elbowed his brother awake.

'Wha..?' Joe junior mumbled.

'Where's our other bed, you know the big brass one we used to share?' Mitch asked.

'S'gone,' Joe murmured, only half awake.

'Whaddaya mean 'gone'? Where has it gone? Have the girls got it in the other bedroom?'

'There isn't another bedroom,' Joe pulled himself up onto his elbows and squinted at Mitch through half-closed eyes, 'we've only two bedrooms and the kitchen, and the girls sleep on the put-you-up in the kitchen, 'cause they're better at getting up early than we are, and that way they get the first wash.'

'So where's the brass bed?' Mitch asked, alarmed now.

'Uh, we got rid of it,' Joe said, 'we changed it for this wooden one. Ma said she was sick of banging her shins on the brass one. Da and I sold it to the rag and bone man for a few bob. Jayzus, but it was heavy though, it took four of us to get it down the steps and up onto his cart.'

Mitch sat upright now in his brothers' wooden bed, remembering the small fortune in notes and coins he had stuffed into the hollow brass bed frame before he had left home. No-one else had known about it. He had kept it hidden as it represented his ill-gotten gains from the thefts he, Harry and Benny had carried out. His money must have been given away along with the old bed. He suddenly felt sick to his stomach at the thought of its loss.

That evening Mitch toured some of his old haunts. Eventually he spotted a familiar face in the smoky interior of *the Tanners*. There was no mistaking Harry Bailey's smart apparel and general air of affluence. He was the only man in the place drinking brandy. Mitch sidled up to the bar and stood quietly at Harry's elbow for a few moments, wondering if his *old china* would know him. After a few suspicious sideways glances to reassure himself the stranger standing uncomfortably close was not the law, Harry suddenly gave a start of recognition.

'Bloody 'ell!' Harry exclaimed, shaking his old friend by the hand and slapping him warmly on the shoulder, 'if it ain't Mitch isself, as I live and breathe! Where the 'ell did you spring from after all these years, eh? Wocher avin' ta drink, my son?'

'I've been out in darkest India, Harry, as it happens. I took the King's shillin', didn't I? Seein' as yer askin', I'll have a drop of what you're having, ta mate.'

Harry shouted his order for a couple more brandies to Albie, the landlord, and, with the drinks in hand, he steered Mitch to a vacant table.

'Well, I must say, yer lookin' well on it, Mitch lad,' Harry grinned, 'the army life must 'ave agreed with you. You must 'ave enjoyed all that spit and wossname.'

Mitch realised how much he had missed Harry's appealingly toothy grin and the way his eyes creased into crows' feet when he smiled. Harry still had the floppy blond locks too. He looked slightly heavier, but was otherwise unchanged. It took Harry a while to recover from his astonishment.

'I couldn't believe it when I heard you'd joined the *Kate Carney*, though I guessed why. I 'eard you'd signed up for a ten stretch though. 'Didn't think we'd see you back so soon. You on leave then are you?' Harry asked.

'Well, no,' Mitch confided, 'as a matter of fact, I've left the army.'

'Ev yer? I didn't think you *could* leave the army, leastways not till yer time's up,' Harry looked puzzled.

'No, you're right, you can't just walk away, but, as it happens, I wuz thrown out – a dishonourable discharge. Don't get me wrong, Harry, I don't regret having joined up. I loved the life, I did. I saw places I'd only ever dreamed about. I saw everything from the Taj Mahal to the Himalayas. I spent more than three years in India and I loved every minute of it. I loved the horsemanship, and the weapons training. I learned to speak Hindustani and even won a silver medal in the all-India field exercises. 'Had the time of my life, I did. I made some really good mates an' all. Then one of them, Kempie – a real big lad he was – he gets the enteric fever and dies, all of a sudden like. It wuz quite a shock how quickly he went, and him as strong as an ox. My other good mate – we called him Prof, on account of how he wuz so knowledgeable and read books and everythin' – he fell in love with a local girl and did a runner.'

Harry nodded. He could relate to that – a man giving up his freedom for a good woman, or even a bad one – but he would hear Mitch's news before he recounted his own.

'After that,' Mitch continued, 'well, it sort of all went downhill for me. The regiment came back to England and we wuz based over in Essex. There didn't seem to be much to do but drink, and I wuz drunk a lot of the time. Then I managed to wind up some of the NCOs and somehow ended up in the glass house a couple of times. 'Course, they wuz out to get me after that. I went out on a bit of a bender one time with some of the hard drinking crowd and found myself *AWOL* for a week. I'm not even sure why I did it. I suppose the army just wasn't working out for me after I lost my two best mates. We broke out of barracks, a couple of the men and me, and went tearing up the local pubs. That led to a court martial and a longer spell in the glass house – eighty-four days' worth that time. I even managed to break out of the glass house a couple of times and finally, after another court martial for the offence of 'desertion whilst under open arrest' and for what they call 'conduct unbecoming', I was given a dishonourable discharge – the order of the boot.'

Harry whistled in awe;

'Phew mate, what did yer dad say? I'll bet he didn't half give you some earache.'

''Aven't told the folks yet, mate. 'Told 'em I was on leave, didn't I? I wanted to buy meself some time, so's I can pick the right moment and break it to them gently like. My company's gone to Bermuda now. I could have been out there with them,' he reflected ruefully.

A sudden peal of female laughter from over in the pub's snug stirred Mitch's memories of his earlier Bermondsey days.

'Here, Harry, whatever happened to those two tarts you and I used to knock around with? Right pair of *gutties* they were,' he asked, realising he had used a Dublin word for 'prostitute', a term with which Harry might not be familiar.

'Who? H'Edie and Lily, you mean?' Harry asked, taking a sip of his drink, 'well, as a matter of fact, I married h'Edie.'

'Oh Christ, Harry, I'm sorry,' Mitch spluttered, 'I wuz just jokin' around.'

'Nah, 'salright, Mitch,' Harry gave a wry smile, 'I hadn't planned on settling down but, well, h'Edie was ... wossname ... pregnant, wasn't she? I 'ad to do right by the gel, didn't I?'

Mitch nodded. He found himself remembering Irene Grover and he felt a sudden twinge of shame. Harry might be a thief, but he had some principles – more principles than Mitch, perhaps.

'We got *three* nippers now, all boys, and all in good 'ealth, too' Harry said proudly, 'not bad for a h'orffnidge lad, eh Mitch?'

Mitch bought another round of brandies, to toast the continued health of Harry's brood.

'So, what will you do, now yer out of the *Kate* and back on Civvy Street?' Harry asked, 'only, if yer short of cash, I can put some work your way – not *kosher* naturally. It'd net you a few shekels an' it'd be you, me an' Benny, the same old team, just like the old days, Mitch. Wotcha say?'

The motor van drew up slowly, its lights out and its engine running, at the service entrance to the rear of Smithfield market buildings. The market was deserted at one o'clock this morning, as indeed it was at this hour most mornings. It would be a couple of hours yet before the traders arrived and the day's business kicked off. Benny Hyman hopped out and checked the address on the piece of paper. Confirming he was at the correct premises: *13 - 15 West Smithfield,* he glanced around to ensure there was no-one around to observe before he stepped up to the entrance of *W. Smith - Meat Wholesalers* and rapped on the big wooden service gate.

A moment later he heard Mitch on the inside drawing back the bolts. Putting his weight to it from the outside, Benny helped move the heavy gate. He signalled across to the van, at which Harry Bailey leapt out of the front passenger's seat and opened the van's rear doors. Moments later, Mitch and Benny emerged from the cold store within the darkened premises, each carrying a huge lamb carcass, which they manhandled into the back of the van.

'There's plenny more to come 'arry. 'Wanna give us an 'and?' a perspiring Benny gasped at Harry.

'Nah mate, summun's gotta keep their minces open, ain't they?' Harry replied, straightening his tie, 'besides, I got me best clobber on, ain't I?

After several more trips between cold store and van, Mitch closed the van doors and Benny hopped into the driver's seat alongside Harry.

'You comin' wiv us Mitch? Benny asked through the open window, as he removed his hat briefly and wiped the sweat from his forehead with the sleeve of his jacket.

'No mate,' Mitch replied, 'we start trading at four. That gives me just a couple hours' kip before I have to open up. I'll meet you down *the Tanners* later though.'

The van drove slowly away and Mitch headed back in through the gate, closing and bolting it behind him. He lit the lamp on the desk in the corner, took a fountain pen and the large ledger out of the desk drawer and settled down to complete his employer's accounts. He smiled to himself at how easy it was, balancing, or perhaps more accurately, 'cooking' the books.

Of course, Joe had yelled and stamped about for quite a while when he had finally learned of his son's dishonourable discharge, but eventually, he had calmed down and had agreed to help find Mitch work locally. Wally Smith had been pleased to interview the son of one of his hardest working meat porters, Joe Mitchell. It had been a porter's job for which Mitch had applied initially, but Wally Smith had been impressed with Mitch's neat handwriting and his skill with arithmetic. The fact that Mitch was an ex-soldier, with a silver medal and a third class army certificate, had persuaded Wally to offer this tall and well dressed young man the storekeeper's job. Joe had threatened Mitch however, on pain of death, to keep his nose clean and be on his best behaviour.

Naturally, Mitch had been sincere when he had promised his father that he wouldn't let him down again. However, Mitch had soon learned, over drinks with the other store men at the meat market, the way accounting was traditionally conducted in Smithfield.

In short, as it had been explained to him and as he in turn had explained it to Harry and Benny, all the store men down the market were 'at it'. There was much money to be made by ensuring that not all the carcasses coming up from the slaughterhouse via legitimate routes were recorded in the ledgers, and that those unrecorded carcasses left the premises covertly, via non-legitimate means.

Some of the store men had accomplices who would collect the unregistered meat. Others relied on the complicity of some of the market's delivery men. This was a networked scam of long standing and it was made plain to Mitch that, were he to buck the trend, it might be bad for his health, whereas participation would be good for his pocket.

138

Mitch had not found the early starts at the market too onerous, especially in summer. In any case, since leaving the army he had not been able to kick the habit of awaking early. There were all night coffee stands around the market and places where a market man might, in friendly company, eat a sustaining breakfast in the early hours. Mitch enjoyed both the bustling atmosphere in the market hall and the frenetic pace of the morning's trading. Smithfield was reputed to be the world's most successful meat market, and *W. Smiths of Smithfield* was a respected and reputable firm of long standing.

Smithfield was an amazingly well designed enterprise. Live animals were brought in from the country via a railway line which ran right beneath the market building itself. The animals were herded into the basement to be slaughtered and their carcasses were then hauled up in lifts to the various wholesalers' establishments, to be butchered and then traded, both wholesale by auction in the market's main halls, and also to the public via the numerous retail outlets around the market's outer circle.

The meat and meat products were sold at ground level, whilst down in the cellars the hides, hooves, horns and discarded bones were transported out again by the trains across to Bermondsey's tanneries and glue factories. Mitch liked to think that, in Civvy Street, he had progressed up the production chain, from the hide processing stage to the meat trading point. He wondered where life would take him next.

He had continued to impress Wally Smith with his capacity for work and his enthusiasm, to the point where Wally had given him his own set of keys to the premises. Mitch might now spend several nights a week sleeping on a palliasse in the back of the shop in order to be there to open up for the start of trading at 4am. He liked exploring the deserted markets after hours, especially the vast labyrinth of underground tunnels and charnel houses. He discovered dark and secret places where one might hide items that could not be accounted for and, of course, having his own keys enabled him to indulge in some late-night trading of his own – the sort of trading in which Harry and Benny were involved.

At the end of each day's legitimate market trading, which was generally all over by midday, Mitch would head home to Hardy Street, occasionally with a paper of chops, mince or sausages, which his grateful employer would slip him by way of a bonus. Sometimes, if Wally forgot to be generous, or if he wasn't around, Mitch would help himself to something a little better, a nice shoulder of lamb or half a dozen steaks. Mitch almost felt guilty cheating Wally. However, he liked being in a position to slip a few shillings to his brothers and sisters now and again.

Little Freddie thought his big stranger-brother a hero. Margaret was glad of her brother's generosity too, especially as the strike-pay had long since dried up, and naturally Georgina welcomed his contribution to both the family's housekeeping and the meat ration. Mitch would also give her enough for an occasional small indulgence for herself, such as some good-as-new shoes which did not let in the rain. Georgina bought herself a new coat down Bermondsey Market and even had Margaret cut her hair for her into a shorter, more fashionable style. Joe was pleased to see his family happy and his eldest son apparently treading a path on the straight and narrow at last.

All in all, everyone seemed very happy to have Mitch home again. The family rubbed along together quite harmoniously. As always in Mitch's life however, his contentment did not last long. Margaret announced she and David were to marry and they had found their own rooms in a tenement just off Southwark High Street. Then Joe Mitchell sustained a back injury when he skidded on some Smithfield offal and both he and the large portion of a cow which he was carrying had landed heavily on the flagstone floor. Joe now found himself slightly lighter work as a porter at Lambeth Hospital. Pushing around wheelchair-bound patients and wheeled laundry baskets proved less taxing than hauling animal carcasses.

Harry Bailey's usual cheery exhortation to his friends to 'be lucky' did not seem to work in Benny's case. Benny and his father, Israel Hyman, were observed by the police at their Paradise Road yard, in the act of unloading a consignment of mutton carcasses, for which, of course, they had neither purchase receipts nor explanation. Any worries Mitch might have harboured that the Hymans would implicate him were ill-founded however. Benny and his dad were tried, convicted and committed to *The Scrubs* without having revealed the identity of their source of supply.

Edie Bailey had presented Harry with a fourth son. She also presented him with an ultimatum. Although, on several occasions, Harry's collar had been felt by the local constabulary, he had managed thus far to avoid being charged with any offence. Edie now insisted he cease pushing his luck and take up a form of employment less likely to result in arrest. Harry agreed. Of course he would not eschew *entirely* the process of making easy money. He now established a small second-hand clothing and household goods shop in the Jamaica Road. Using his business negotiating skills to acquire items cheaply via house clearances and doorstep collections, he sold them on at a modest profit. Of course, his network of useful connections meant he might still fence the odd consignment of dubiously-sourced items via his legitimate business outlet. What Edie didn't know wouldn't hurt her.

Given Harry's conversion to *kosher*, or mostly *kosher* dealing, and without Benny's muscle, Mitch's nefarious meat trading activity was now curtailed. Heisting carcasses and getting away with it no longer thrilled him to the same degree in any case. Mitch could not risk visiting Benny in *the Scrubs,* lest he be identified as a likely criminal associate, and he now found he was seeing less of Harry, whose legitimate business dealings and family responsibilities took up more of his time. To his disappointment, Mitch felt he was somehow losing his friends yet again.

He had renewed his casual arrangement with Edie's obliging friend Lily, of course, but he knew he was not the only recipient of her favours. For this reason, and to ensure he did not fall into the same trap as Harry, he and Lily invariably took precautions. Lily wasn't exactly good company however, and he found no great satisfaction in their jaded and mechanical relationship. He now felt disenchanted also with the daily, bustling routine of the market. His memories of India and the camaraderie of his early days in the army still held a special place in his heart and mind, and he wondered if he might ever recapture the joy of those times. He recalled Prof's advice, about never going back but always moving forward. Maybe Prof had been right. Perhaps it had been a mistake coming back to Bermondsey.

Chapter 9 – **The Somme**

The tension along the line was palpable as the men stood ready. Some swayed in fearful anticipation; some pressed their foreheads against the damp, cold clay to steady themselves. Mitch could hear someone fairly close by muttering a prayer. Further down the trench someone was taking a piss. The tension affected each man differently. The months of training – training which Mitch had not needed in any case, and which had mostly involved horseback charges, plunging lances into sandbags – had not prepared them for this moment. The horses and the lances were now far behind the lines. Only the sandbags had come with them to the trenches. As a groom, Mitch had until recently been assigned to stay back behind the lines and care for the horses whilst others in the regiment went up to the front. The men of the 16th had taken a hammering though. The Lancers were effectively infantry now and it was a case of all troops to the front line.

Unlike others of his new comrades therefore, Mitch had little idea what would confront him when they scrambled over the parapet. However he guessed the chances of coming back alive and in one piece were not great. Someone in the company had described these last minute nerves, in the moments before an attack began, as being just like the stage-fright he had experienced in his acting career – wishing he had relieved himself before the curtain went up, wishing he had chosen any occupation but this. For some, however, quiet resignation and making peace with God was their natural response to the fear.

The waiting was the worst part, worse perhaps than the actual charge out into the total darkness. It would not be too long before that darkness would be illuminated by the angry glare of the enemy's artillery fire. Mitch was already familiar with the rattle of machine gun fire and the thunder of artillery as it was plainly audible even from well behind the lines. Soon though he would see what it looked like close to. This would be his first experience of engaging the enemy.

He had never seen a German. He wondered if they would look so very different from the British. Would they be little weasel-faced fellahs, like the 23rd Manchesters, those underfed but determined little bantam chaps who shared the trench with the men of the 16th? Or perhaps they would be tall and blond, like the Vikings Mitch recalled from the illustrations in his school history book. The stories he had heard about the Germans bayoneting Belgian babies made him think they must be less than human. That image should make killing them easier. He had never killed anyone and wondered if he would be up to it.

The silence before the assault was uncomfortable. He suspected that soon the noise would be deafening and the smell of cordite sickening. The men were not absolutely clear on what they were actually supposed to do once they were out there. 'Run to the enemy and engage him', Captain Evans had said. He made it sound like a tea dance. With a personal allocation of just six rounds for his Lee Enfield, Mitch hoped there would not be too many of the enemy. He guessed that, once he was out there, whatever happened next was all down to luck.

Perhaps it wouldn't be as awful as he imagined. Things rarely were. For now, however, the waiting was interminable. His bayonet was fixed. When his ammo ran out, which it would within seconds, assuming his rifle did not jam as it was prone to do, he would be pig-sticking again as in his India days, though not from horseback this time.

Mitch had been disappointed not to have seen any action during his service in India. He had been hopeful of rectifying this when his new regiment had arrived in France, but for months now, it had been nothing but training and waiting, digging trenches and standing to, and waiting. The area around the bay of the Somme was nice enough, modest villages with pleasant stretches of farmland in between. He had spent his off duty moments getting acquainted both with his fellow soldiers and with the local wines, which were cheap. He had strolled along the river at St Valery, watching seals out in the estuary and drinking coffee at a local estaminet. Now however, he had been sent up the line at last.

What characterised life in this particular army was the continual mantra of 'hurry up – and wait'. Galloping from one French village to the next, corralling the horses, digging trenches and dugouts, unloading shells and sandbags and then what? Wait. Hurry up and wait. Hurry up and wait. It was the waiting which the men could bear least. They were raring to go. At last however the moment had arrived

– the death or glory moment. 'In for a penny, in for a punnet' as Mitch's barrow boy mate Benny would say. Right now, selling fruit seemed a most desirable occupation.

From his position in the line, Mitch could not see Captain Evans, but he knew he was waiting there in the dark, his Webley in one hand and, in the other, the whistle which he would blow as soon as the signal to attack came down the line. Hurry up and wait. As they waited, and swayed, and prayed and pissed, each man had his own vision of what sort of hell awaited him over the top.

Somewhere down the line, in an attempt at humour, someone began to sing a cheery song in a feeble and tremulous voice:

'Tiddey-iddley-ighty, take me back to Blighty ...'

The singer was immediately silenced by the Lance Corporal's bark:

'Shut it!'

The minutes ticked by. No signal came. No sign of movement along the British line. No sign of an attack coming from the German side. What were they waiting for? Would the Tommies be starting the show or would Jerry? All they could do was wait and see. Hurry up and wait. Mitch decided to add his own words to the silenced singer's tune:

'Take me back to Monto; I want to be there pronto ...'

'Shut up Mitchell, you Irish fucker!'

Lance Corporal Skinner had recognised Mitch's voice. Of course he had. He ought to, since he had heard it often enough. Mitch and the Lance Corp had had several run-ins. The Lance Corp wouldn't forget Mitch's voice in a hurry. Mitch had told Skinner what he thought of him, the officers and their bloody silly waiting-around war. The silence resumed. Hurry up and wait. Hurry up and wait. The man standing next to Mitch leaned across and whispered in a Liverpool accent:

'Where's Monto, Mitch?'

'You don't wanna know, Scouse. Not a place you'd wanna visit, mate.'

The waiting was too much. The men became restless.

'Curtain up!' a disembodied voice demanded.

That would be the actor, Mitch guessed. Not only had he read many plays, he could recite them – not a skill he needed in this theatre though.

'Overture and beginners please!' another cultured wag shouted.

The Lance Corp's neck shot out like a telescope as he tried unsuccessfully to identify the jokers. Suddenly a lone rat came down along the trench, rattling swiftly past like a bullet beneath their feet. Several of the men took a swipe at it with their rifle butts as it scuttled past but it managed to evade death by dodging under and around the duckboards. A successful technique, Mitch thought.

'Jesus!' Billy Jackson breathed, 'the rats are leaving. They've got more sense than us!'

The waiting continued however. Hurry up and wait. Hurry up and wait. Why did it always take so long to start the show? Mitch had a vision of some fat General sitting in a dugout further up the line, finishing off his supper and dabbing his greasy chin with a linen napkin, while the men awaited his order to begin. 'Permission to die, sir?' 'Not yet, damn it, I haven't finished the port. Just wait, will you?' Hurry up and wait.

Mitch scratched at his ribs. The damned itching had started up again down his left side. He wasn't sure whether it was a nervous itch or whether the lice had come back again. The itch now spread to his left leg too, in the area of his trouser seam. It probably was lice then, since that's where the blighters laid their eggs. *Chats*, as the lice were called out here, were a frequent irritation in the trenches, but were just one of many. He would have to get the candle stub out and burn them off his clothes later on when he came back – if he came back. It was enough that the coarse khaki wool of the uniform irritated his skin, without him having to share the uniform with *chats*.

When he had joined his father's former regiment back in August of 'fourteen, he had looked forward to wearing the scarlet tunic and the *czapska* such as his father had worn during Queen Victoria's visit to Dublin. He had hoped to regain that sense of worth and pride from being in uniform again and to experience once more the camaraderie of barrack life. However, despite the 16th being known as the 'Scarlet Lancers', they and every other regiment in this miserable war, had been sent to the front with basic khaki combat uniform only. It was cheap and mass produced and it itched. It also seemed to double in weight when soaked with rain, which it often was, since the men mostly slept under canvas or in dugouts. So far, he had not recaptured the glory of being in uniform. Perhaps then it was death, not glory, which awaited him this time around?

145

Mitch had been amongst the first wave at the recruitment office back in Bermondsey. The prospect of getting out of the stink, of going overseas again, had seemed most appealing. He had volunteered details of his previous service and his knowledge of horses to the recruiting Sergeant, hoping he would be assigned to a cavalry regiment. Naturally, he had not mentioned his dishonourable discharge but had given his reason for leaving the army as having been time served. He suspected, rightly, that they would either be too busy to check this out or perhaps would overlook it, since war had been declared and they needed every volunteer they could get. They had indeed jumped at the chance to recruit a former soldier with recent experience.

He had expressed a wish to join his father's former outfit and his wish had been granted. He was now a groom in the 16th, the Queen's Own Lancers – the Scarlet Lancers. His mother had drawn his attention to an ironic quote in the Irish newspaper she bought regularly. Some politician was assuring potential Irish volunteers that the trenches were safer than the Dublin slums. He guessed the man who thought that up might have been to Monto but had certainly never seen the trenches. Now, and not for the first time since arriving in France, he cursed his own poor judgement. He regretted having exchanged the tedium of Bermondsey for the extreme tedium and intense discomfort of Northern France. Standing in a damp trench was not the kind of warfare for which he had been trained.

Suddenly the order came, disrupting his reflection. It was not an order to attack however, but an order to stand down. The assault was off – for tonight at least. There was a collective groan of disappointment from the ranks, though in truth none was too disappointed. No doubt the confrontation would be rescheduled anyway. For now however, a brief respite was welcome.

Mitch and his comrades had yet to see the enemy close to. They had spent months in training at *The Curragh* and had undergone yet more training in France, with screamed instruction and savagery from 'the canaries' – that particularly inhuman bunch of NCOs whose qualification for inducting new recruits was not battlefield experience but a yellow armband and a complete lack of humanity

'Wonder why they've stood us down this time?' Scouse complained, to no-one in particular, 'course, they never tell us nott'n. Was Jerry supposed to be attackin' *us*, or were we supposed to be having' a crack at *him*?'

146

'Dunno, but I'll bet it's 'cause they want to save on ammo,' Billy opined.

'Yeah, well they could save even more if they sent us home.'

The chronic shortage of ammunition on the Western Front was an issue which was causing great frustration for both officers and other ranks. Regular train loads of British armaments were passing through France almost daily. The men had seen huge consignments pass them by en route south, but they weren't for use in this northern theatre of war.

Mitch's enquiry of Lance Corporal Skinner had been met with the curt explanation that the shells were needed for the campaign in Turkey. Mitch's insolence in suggesting that it was insanity to be fighting the Turks when they hadn't enough ammunition to fight the threat so much closer to home had earned him seven days' of what was termed 'field punishment number one'.

This punishment was so prevalent now that it was referred to simply as 'FP1'. He had spent his week of FP1 behind the lines, strapped to the wheel of a gun carriage, and with bread and water rations only. When released from punishment and returned to the front, he had learned that the allocation of twenty rifle rounds per man per day had been further restricted to six rounds. Scouse had a point. For all the good they might do here, they might as well pack up and go home.

In early October, Captain Graham came around and asked for thirty volunteers for 'clearing up' duties. Mitch and his mates Scouse and Billy weren't too sure what this would involve – trench clearing perhaps? Whatever it might be, surely it would relieve the boredom. Mitch had forgotten his ex-soldier father's advice never to volunteer for anything.

The friends were ordered to take their entrenching spades, groundsheets and bedrolls and were each given five days' iron rations. As they reached the makeshift stables, saddled up their horses and headed up the line, the Captain stopped to gather the same number of men from each of the three squadrons until there were around a hundred or so volunteers. This must be a bloody big clear up job in a bloody big trench, they thought.

They rode south east for a couple of hours, across flat lands, criss-crossed by canals. It was evident this had been a coal mining area, but many of the industrial installations had been almost levelled

147

by shelling and the inhabitants had fled. As they came near to the spot where they were to bivouac, all seemed eerily desolate and there was an unearthly silence. Mitch thought it odd that there were no stray dogs and no birds singing, but then dogs followed people, and birds needed trees. This place had neither.

The village of Vermelles seemingly existed in name only nowadays. There was not a house left intact in the whole of the village. Around the village and for as far as the eye could see stretched acres of abominable wasteland. Captain Graham advised that these were the fields which had seen the worst of the fighting during the previous month's battle of Loos. He explained it was the volunteers' task to clear the battlefields of bodies for burial and to retrieve weaponry, ammunition and any other items which might be of value or use. They must not be left for the enemy to use, in the event that they later re-took this area.

The men of each squadron group were assigned specific sectors to clear and the task was to be completed as methodically as possible. Sections of corrugated tin which had once made up the roofs of farm buildings were now turned into make-shift sleds, or *skids* as the captain called them, for the horses to pull along. This was a practical measure as no wheeled vehicle would be able to negotiate the thick muddy terrain or the shell-cratered roads.

The men firstly set about removing the bodies, using the *skids*. This proved to be a sickening job, for many of the bodies were no longer intact. Mitch guessed many of the poor sods must have encountered nine inch shells at close quarters. These men had almost made it to the enemy lines. Quite a few of the corpses were missing heads and limbs and some had to be disentangled from barbed wire fences or extracted from beneath collapsed buildings or mounds of heavy earth. To their horror, the men also found the battlefield was overrun with legions of rats which were feeding on the corpses. Within a short time of commencing their gruesome work, each of the men had found cause to vomit. However, the men gradually resigned themselves to the horror and retching soon gave way to calm application to devising ways of making the task easier and less disturbing.

It quickly became apparent that the best way of doing the job was if the men worked in pairs. Mitch and Scouse had started out trying to match up severed heads and limbs with their respective torsos, but after a while it occurred to them that this was too difficult and time consuming, and that it probably did not matter anyway. None of the bodies would be sent home to England. Nobody would notice if a body was buried with the wrong head. Nobody would complain.

Mitch knew there were Mahommedan soldiers fighting on the Western Front. He had met men from the Sialkot Brigade returning exhausted from the front for a spot of rest and recuperation. He wondered how they felt at the prospect of dismemberment and consequent exclusion from paradise. Such sights as this would perhaps disturb them even more than it would the British Tommy, and yet, knowing the native troops as he did, he knew that they would go fearlessly into battle anyway.

The weather of early autumn had been consistently warm and swarms of flies had arrived to lay their eggs on the corpses. The shock of lifting a body, only to dislodge the millions of white maggots which fell from its abdomen like an apron of Brussels lace, gave the men fresh cause for retching. The volunteers tried to banish the thought that they might have known some of the unrecognisable corpses, or, God forbid, that they themselves might one day end up as part of a similarly obscene display. They laboured on, mainly in stunned silence, for the longer they undertook their grisly work and the more horror they observed, the more they became inured to the sights and the less they felt the need to utter expletives.

It seemed to Mitch that there was no grotesque attitude into which a body might not be contorted and no mutilation too awful to befall a human being. The volunteers tied handkerchiefs around their faces to keep the flies from their mouths. The foul stench of death and decay was overpowering however and did not abate but grew stronger as the sun rose higher in the sky. Mitch wondered why the battlefield had not been cleared weeks earlier, whilst the corpses had been fresh. Perhaps the *brass hats* had been waiting for a lull in the fighting.

On the easternmost side of the quagmire, they now started to encounter German corpses. In amongst them were the bodies of British troops who, they guessed, must have made it to the German trenches but had been slaughtered there. They wondered if the men had taken the enemy positions but then had been let down by a lack of back up or whether they had been killed by British shelling. That sort of thing wasn't uncommon in this type of confused and ill-executed warfare.

The volunteers had no instructions to bury the German dead, so they left them in the field. Some of the men took Jerry helmets, badges or belt buckles as souvenirs. Somehow, robbing the enemy's dead didn't carry the same taboo as robbing your own. It was interesting also to see what sort of weapons they might be up against. Mitch saw that the German bayonet was different from the British model. It was heavily serrated on one side, probably to inflict more damage coming out than it had going in.

He was trying to extricate a Gordon Highlander from the midst of some German dead when he noticed one of the German corpses was wearing an intact pistol holster. He checked it and was pleased to find a Luger P09 still firmly tucked within. He removed the hand gun, which he saw was still loaded, and pocketed it, taking also a few handfuls of bullets for the Luger from the dead German's belt.

Whilst moving the bodies, the volunteers simultaneously gathered any weapons and ammunition they found and piled these on separate *skids*. Mitch found surprisingly few personal items on the bodies of his fallen comrades however, and he wondered if others had been there ahead of them. There might be some truth in the rumours that the stretcher bearers and medics were partial to relieving the dead of their valuables. Some now alleged that RAMC no longer stood for Royal Army Medical Corps, but for 'Robbing All My Comrades'. He preferred to think, more charitably, that they retrieved such items in order to establish who had died and to return the personal items to the fallen men's families. Some referred to the stretcher bearers as 'the body snatchers' but Mitch now decided that theirs must be one of the worst jobs going, worse even than fighting in the front line.

As he pondered on this, his attention was suddenly diverted by a loud gasping sound from somewhere behind him. Startled, he turned around but could not at first see the cause of it. He and several others ran forward to where they thought the noise had come from, in case there might be a live casualty among so many dead. They came upon a vast, shallow depression in the earth, a very wide shell crater with many bodies lying scattered within it. Lying in amongst them however was one of their own party.

Private Johnnie Parsons lay writhing in agony and clutching at his throat. Mitch's first thought was that he must be having a heart attack and he made to jump down into the crater to rush to his aid. He checked his impulse however when another of the men, correctly interpreting the situation, called out 'gas!' Mitch now spotted several discharged blue cross canisters scattered about. He realised that the gas released in battle must have sunk to the lowest levels of the battlefield and was still lying there in pockets. Parsons must have inhaled some when he bent down to move a body.

They all stood around now, watching their stricken comrade, at a loss to know how to help him without putting their own lives at risk. Mitch and Scouse and a couple of others made several attempts to take deep breaths and clamber down into the pit, but soon they realised the distance to where Parsons lay was too great and strewn with too many obstacles for them to retrieve him and return before they needed to catch their breath again. Parsons was kicking and fighting for breath himself and so the return would not be easy in any case. All they could do was stand helplessly by and watch Parsons, contorting agonised and blue-faced in his death throes.

As the young private eventually gave up his struggle for life and lay still, Mitch wondered it if had crossed the mind of the dying youth that, because of the gas, his comrades would not be able to retrieve *his* body, but that he too would be left for the maggots and the rats to pick clean. Mitch prayed to God this had not occurred to Parsons. The manner of Parsons' death had shocked the already traumatised men. They had no option but to return to their work however, ensuring they now avoided any low-lying areas where gas might still linger. They also tried to avoid disturbing the dead men's clothing, lest the gas be trapped there also. Mitch realised that in fact the much maligned stretcher bearers risked meeting Parsons' fate every time they turned out.

As the light began to fade, Captain Graham conceded the men could achieve no more that evening, and so they headed back up the road until they found some derelict farm buildings where they pitched a very basic camp, in the shelter of what remained of a farmhouse wall. They lit fires and made tea to drink with their tinned bully beef, stale bread and jam. It might not be so bad were the bread fresh but it very rarely was. In the trenches, whenever the army bread ran out the troops ate 'biscuit' – a rock-hard, dried ration, which was most unappetising but which might at least be made a little more edible by being dunked in tea or water.

The jam supplied to the troops however was pretty poor. Pink's plum jam, it was, from the Bermondsey factory, and it came in seven pound tins. It was bland and starchy and plainly contained more thickener than fruit. It was always plum too, never strawberry or blackcurrant, and never marmalade, which would have been a real treat. The men wondered if someone at army HQ had taken a bung for giving Pinks the contract to supply this low quality, highly detested, plum jam. At least one meal taken each day in the field included plum jam.

Their supper having been consumed quickly and without enjoyment, the exhausted men arranged their bedrolls around their fires and turned in. No-one got much sleep however, partly because of the horrors they had seen but mainly because the rats were not content just to eat the dead but would occasionally creep up and have a nibble at the living also. Scouse said it was a shame rats weren't edible, as they could have roasted a few.

The volunteers spent much longer than had been expected sorting out corpses and burying them in clusters out in the fields, with rough wooden crosses to mark their graves. Two weeks later, they were still at it. They had retrieved a sizeable amount of weaponry and unused ammunition and this was drawn on the *skids* up to what remained of the road and stacked up for collection by the wagons which each day brought them fresh drinking water and extra tinned and dried rations.

Mitch had gradually become used to the sight of so much dead humanity. For some reason however, the presence of so many dead horses on the battlefield was the only thing which still moved him to tears. The scene and the smell reminded him of Smithfield. He felt angry that the faithful horses, who had neither the right nor the wit to accept or decline frontline service, had met the same fate as the men who had signed up to it. The volunteers were thankful when at last Captain Graham said they would rejoin the battalion. They were not sorry to be leaving. Billy Jackson had been convinced there were legions of ghosts around the place – the spirits of the fallen. The men had cause enough for sleeplessness without adding ghosts to the list.

Mitch had not expected to be pleased to return to his unit, with the prospect of being sent up to the front again, but he now thought perhaps there were worse things a man might be asked to do than fight. At least the problem with the supply of ammunition seemed now to have been resolved. Armaments were beginning to arrive from England again. It seemed safe to assume therefore that the men of the 16th would be actively engaging the enemy again very soon. For the moment however, Mitch, Scouse and Billy, and some of the others who had been involved in clearing the aftermath of Loos, felt they had earned the chance to dull the images they had seen and wash the taste of death from their throats with some of the local red wine down at the *estaminet*.

The word circulating amongst the troops they met at the bar was that the Gallipoli campaign was proving to be an overwhelming disaster. Opinion generally was that the allied armies were sustaining great losses but not gaining any ground on either Eastern or Western Fronts. The feeling was that the British and Colonial troops had fought hard and had suffered greatly, but that the weakness lay with the Generals and their indecisive strategy. The men's strongest condemnation was reserved for Commander-in-Chief of the British forces, Sir John French. In the popularity stakes, he was as detested as Lance-Corp Skinner and many others of the NCO breed.

Madame Calmar, proprietress of the *estaminet*, managed to rustle up a plate of stew for each of them. It wasn't the meatiest stew, but it was far more palatable than the tinned version they had been eating for the past fortnight. The *Machonochie* ration, as it was known, was a tinned stew of turnips, carrot and black-spotted potatoes. Provided in bulk as trench fare, it was even more unpopular than the plum jam, and it attracted the same speculation regarding its supply. The men felt better for having let off a bit of steam and, whilst none of them was particularly drunk, they were all now quite weary and so they set off back to the lines, hoping for a better night's sleep. It was unfortunate that on their return the first person they laid eyes on was Lance Corporal Skinner. Skinner greeted them with even less sensitivity than usual:

'So, 'ere's the bleedin' ladies of the cleaning up brigade! Done a good job 'ave yer, ladies? An' I s'pose you've been out spendin' what you found in the dead men's pockets, 'ave yer?'

The men were outraged. Mitch pictured Johnnie Parson's death struggle, and a red mist came over him.

'You hard-faced bastard!' he spat, as he made for the Lance Corporal, his fists ready to hammer home his feelings.

Billy Jackson and Scouse quickly restrained him. Skinner laughed.

'Well it's you, is it, you Irish fucker? Always got too much to say for yourself, 'aven't yer? Well, there's another detail going out to morrow to Vimy to do the clear up there. I'll make sure you're on it, Mitchell.'

'No way, Skinner, you son of a hooer,' Mitch's Dublin anger surfaced, 'no fuckin' way!'

153

Predictably, Mitch was duly awarded FP1 again, twenty-one days' worth this time, for using insubordinate language to an NCO and for refusing to follow an order. Of course, the order in question had been that he should volunteer. Mitch suspected this offence wasn't covered by the King's regulations, but he was quite sanguine about the injustice. At least he wouldn't have to look at Skinner's ugly face for the next twenty one days. As his comrades marched off to take their turn at the front once more, Mitch found himself again spending each day behind the lines, tethered to the wheel of a gun carriage, under the continual scrutiny of a sentry. The main thrust of this type of punishment was that he should be humiliated in front of the rest of the men. There were increasing numbers of soldiers undergoing field punishment however, so it was becoming a more common sight and therefore less shameful.

He was untied several times a day for ten minute periods in order to eat his bread and water ration or to be taken to the latrines to relieve himself. At the end of each day, he was handcuffed and escorted to the guardhouse to spend the night in a cell. Being brick-built and roofed, the guardhouse was actually warmer and more comfortable than either the tents in the camp or the dugouts in the trenches. In some ways, the intended humiliation, starvation and discomfort of the field punishment seemed preferable to the extreme conditions up at the front. One of the worst effects of the inactivity and inadequate diet on FP1 however was constipation. In theory, Mitch was not allowed to spend longer than ten minutes on a visit to the latrines, but the sentries understood the effects of FP1 and gave him some leeway and some privacy. This gave him an idea.

On his final day of punishment, whilst the sentry waited patiently outside the latrines, Mitch quickly scrambled over the back wall of the block and absconded. He returned just an hour and a half later from the village *estaminet*, where he had polished off a meal and a bottle of wine, and promptly surrendered himself to the guardroom. It was not exactly desertion, but the act of absenting himself whilst undergoing field punishment now earned him an additional twenty one days' FP1, to be served consecutively. As he slept relatively comfortably on a cot in the warm, dry guardhouse, he wondered how his comrades were faring at the front.

It was late December when Mitch finished his sentence. His release coincided with his comrades' return to base camp, as the 16th had now been relieved in the trenches by some other poor sods. Scouse and Billy Jackson recounted details of their experiences to Mitch. To some degree, he regretted not having been with them, but he was glad that, purely by luck it seemed, they were still alive. The 16th had come under attack on numerous occasions in recent weeks, though the attacks had been neither as heavy nor as prolonged as had been expected. Scouse said the word was that the attacks were an attempt by the enemy to distract attention away from a build-up of troops behind their lines in preparation for a much larger offensive to come. These minor attacks had inflicted relatively little damage on the regiment. One private had been killed and the wounded included just two officers, Lieutenants Hays and Davies, and five other ranks.

Christmas came and was met with very little joy or celebration in the camp. Most of the men received letters and parcels from home. They were very good at sharing whatever treats their relatives had sent. Billy's sister had sent him socks and chocolate. He kept the socks of course but shared out the chocolate. Scouse's Mum had managed to parcel up a huge lump of bread pudding. Scouse willingly sliced it with his trench knife and handed it around.

'I haven't had bread puddin' since I left Bermondsey,' Mitch laughed, 'd'you know back there you can buy it by the slice from the baker's. We call it 'dustman's wedding cake'! Wouldn't it be grand though with a spread of butter on it?'

Real butter too was a distant memory of course. Mitch had not received either a parcel or a letter from home in all the time he had been in India and so he did not expect to receive one now. However, to his great surprise, a sizeable and heavy Christmas parcel had arrived for him too. It was postmarked Bermondsey and the sender's name on it was that of his sister Margaret. He was touched.

'Look at the size of it Mitch,' Scouse enthused, 'I hope it's a big Christmas cake.'

'If it is, you'll all get a cut of it,' Mitch promised, tearing open the wrapping.

His face fell clean to his boots however when he held aloft the gift from home.

'Ah Jayzus, I don't believe it! A seven pound fuckin' tin of Pink's fuckin' plum jam!'

Chapter 10 – **Rouenation**

Trench warfare continued for the next six weeks, though it consisted mostly of an intermittent exchange of mortars and some opportunistic sniping rather than close combat. Captain Evans had a brilliant idea and sent the NCOs around to select men for a 'listening party'. They were to creep over towards the enemy lines to listen to what the Germans were up to. The brilliant plan had a major flaw in it though. The NCOs could find not a single man in the company who had adequate hearing. Mitch hoped his own hearing loss was just temporary and that it would return to normal if the shelling ever stopped. Scouse suggested to Skinner that the Germans might be asked to speak up a bit.

In the second week of February 1915, the regiment was ordered to mount up and head up towards St Omer. They were to rest up for a while at the camp at Wavrans, letting another outfit take a turn in the trenches. The men of the 16th set off under heavy skies. The weather in northern France had begun to take a severe turn and it felt too cold even to rain. Indeed, as they rode north it began to snow. Mitch was glad of the fact that mounted troops got to wear the British warm', the heavy woollen coats that were otherwise only issued to British officers.

The wind was blowing hard from the north and both men and horses had to contend with the constant sting of sleet in their faces and ears. Some were lucky enough to have been sent hand-knitted balaclavas from home and they wore these beneath their caps. Mitch enjoyed no such luxury however and the wind continually threatened to whip the cap from his head. His eyes streamed and his hands turned blue as he clutched the reins in one hand and his symbolic but fairly redundant lance in the other.

They passed several villages with sizeable old barns, and Mitch wondered why Captain Evans did not give the order for them to dismount and take shelter until the worst of the weather passed. It seemed the ever indecisive Evans was still thinking about it. The barns would have made quite acceptable temporary billets for both man and horse, yet still they rode on. Eventually, as the countryside became more open, farms became scarcer and the snowfall began to deepen, it became obvious even to their chinless Captain that the poor progress they were making was not worth the risk of frostbite.

The order was given eventually to dismount. They were to bivouac in the nearby open fields. This seemed sheer madness to the men, given that they had passed much better places, but Evans was loath to turn back. The site he had chosen was much exposed to the wind and snow and it was not possible to dig in as the earth was now iron hard. The men struggled in vain to erect canvas tents against what was fast becoming a blizzard. The best they could manage was to huddle down and cover themselves with the tenting. There were no materials to hand to turn into windbreaks for the horses but some of the men used their own blankets to cover the beasts. They hoped the storm would soon pass over and they could continue and try to reach shelter before nightfall.

The blizzard continued into the night however and, even were it possible to light fires, which of course it was not, the men had neither rations nor drinking water with them. It had not been anticipated that the journey to Wavrans would take this long. Several scouts were dispatched around the district to look for farmhouses or any sources of food, but they found only deserted ruins. The men passed a miserable and sleepless night huddled beneath the sheets of wind-whipped canvas, trying to keep warm.

In fact, the storm continued for two miserable days, during which time neither man nor beast had food or water. The continuing strong winds meant it was still impossible to light fires, so the men and horses had to slake their thirst by eating snow. It was the most uncomfortable experience they had endured thus far in the war and the men wished themselves back at the front. They cursed Captain Evans' poor judgement in making them continue in such bad weather. All agreed they should have turned back at the first sign of snow.

When, by dawn on the third day, the storm had finally abated, the men were able to emerge from their makeshift shelters. They immediately went to assess the condition of the horses. Tragically, nineteen of the horses had died of exposure, and a further twenty eight were suffering badly. Mitch's heart broke when he saw the extreme pain of his own mount. He rubbed her stiffened limbs and brushed the ice from her muzzle but there was little he could do to ease the animal's suffering. She whinnied piteously, her eyes rolling back in pain. He now heard several loud retorts and saw that Captain Evans and several of the NCOs, armed with pistols, were putting the ailing horses out of their misery.

Mitch could only stand back and avert his gaze as Skinner – it had to be the detestable Skinner, of course – shot Mitch's horse in turn. Mitch recalled the loaded luger in his pocket and had a sudden urge to place it against Skinner's head. It was his frozen hands, rather than any sense of self preservation, which prevented him from doing so. A number of the men were also suffering from frost bite but no medical attention would be forthcoming until they reached the rest camp at Wavrans. There at least there would be medical facilities.

The men were disappointed to find their accommodation in Wavrans was also under canvas. The leisure facilities went a small way towards making up for this though and there were a number of reasonable *estaminets* close by. Unlike in India, the army did not provide official brothels for the troops, and many of the men soon beat a path to the local *bordel*. Mitch however determined not to follow suit. He knew only too well what might befall the men, and indeed the women too, in such an unregulated establishment. He was happy enough to spend his off duty time drinking.

One of the little local restaurants served *poulet de Liques*, a wonderful dish which Mitch and his comrades believed was chicken with leeks. At least it *sounded* like chicken with leeks, except there weren't any leeks in it. They later heard from one of the NCOs, who'd got it from Captain Evans, that Liques was not a vegetable but was in fact a place a few miles west of Wavrans and was renowned for the quality of the chickens bred there. Mitch envied the captain his public school education, though the officer clearly knew more about chickens than he did about horses and men. All the officers seemed to speak French well. Many had spent their summers in France before the war and were at ease talking to the locals. The same could not be said of the NCOs of course. According to Scouse, they spoke only 'shite'.

Reports were now coming into camp of heavy fighting between the French Tenth Army and the Germans over in the east at Verdun. Apparently, it was an almighty bloodbath, but the British were leaving the French to get on with it. This made it all the more frustrating that, after a few short weeks of relatively tame action, the 16th were kicking their heels at the rest camp. Mitch was disappointed at what he had seen of the war so far. Although he never wrote home, he felt it would be good to have experienced the sort of action one might want to write home about. The French must be having a bad time of it though. Rumours were circulating that some of the French troops had deserted because of the incompetence of their leadership and that others, who had dared to refuse orders, had been shot by firing squad.

Scouse remarked, to the agreement of his fellow soldiers, that the French generals must be as hopeless as the British ones. The ineptitude of the British military leadership was a popular topic of conversation amongst the soldiers at the local watering holes. Limiting the discussion to such issues was a useful way for Mitch to avoid learning too much about his drinking pals. Although he liked Scouse and Billy in particular, he determined he would not again forge such close friendships as he had with Kempie and Prof in India. Mitch felt he might just be lucky and survive the war, but even if he did it was unlikely all his new comrades would. When the day came that he lost a comrade to a German bullet he might not feel their loss so keenly if he had not formed too close an attachment.

In March, a drink-fuelled disagreement with Lance Corporal Skinner, the details of which Mitch could scarcely recall, earned him what he referred to dismissively as 'another spot of crucifixion'. This time however he was tethered to a stout fencepost. At least it made a change from a gun carriage, he blustered. The seven days' FP1 kept him out of the local bars for a week and also kept his money in his pocket. At least he would have a bob or two more to celebrate with when Easter came around.

As April came to a close however, word filtered through from contacts back at *The Curragh* of an uprising which had occurred in Dublin during Easter. The incident was now a major subject for discussion amongst the men of the 16th, a significant number of whom were Irish-born or of Irish descent. To the Irishmen, it was a rebellion; to the British press an uprising. Whatever the view taken, it caused rumblings of alarm. Rumour now suggested the Connaught Rangers had mutinied, rather than be sent out to quell their fellow Irishmen. Out here on the Western Front, although the tide of battle had now turned in favour of the French at Verdun, Frenchmen continued to desert and to refuse orders, and the word 'mutiny' was now being whispered about this campaign also. The twin issues of Dublin and Verdun were the cause of some unease amongst the officers at the Wavrans camp.

When, following his latest bout of drunken indiscretion, Mitch was again paraded before Captain Evans, he detected a hardening of attitude on the captain's part. Skinner related the details of the offence, somewhat exaggerated and embellished, Mitch thought. The officer put down his pen and regarded Mitch with some disdain. Mitch was wondering whether the captain was weighing up his current offence in the light of his previous ones, when the seated officer suddenly fired a curt question at him:

'Ahrrish?' he said.

'What?' Mitch replied, uncomprehending.

'Beg pardon, SIR!' Skinner corrected him.

'You Ahrrish?' Evans repeated, louder this time.

'Oh, *Irish*, yes, I am ... sir.'

'Your sort are born troublemakers, aren't you? And I note from your record that this is not an arseolated incident. Well, I intend to put a stop to your shenanigans. Your sort of scum should be skimmed orf and kept away from decent soldiers.'

Mitch was still wondering, through the haze of his hangover, what 'arseolated' might mean and so he missed the conclusion of the captain's diatribe. Outside the tent, he asked Skinner how long he had got this time and the Lance Corp told him gleefully that he would be spending twenty-eight days on FP1.

Mitch was released from his latest punishment on 17th June. Two days later he and the regiment left Wavrans and rode due east. Despite the distant sounds of battle, it was a pleasant ride. The trees were all in leaf and the fields were carpeted with buttercups. They halted briefly in the town of Hazebrouck, so that the quartermasters could buy fresh food supplies. Mitch, Billy and Scouse bought themselves some fresh bread, real butter and a few dozen eggs which they stowed away in their packs to supplement the army food.

The lancers then rode on until they reached Sec Bois, a smart little hamlet with an attractive church. Mitch thought this red-brick and stone edifice resembled the church at Sialkot, but on a much smaller scale. The men were ordered to dismount as they were to be billeted in the tiny hamlet, which in fact was scarcely more than a crossroads. The officers were accommodated in some of the local houses whilst the other ranks were allocated a warm farmer's hay barn on the Route de Barre.

'Right,' Scouse directed, as he started laying a small fire, 'let's get them erfs cookin'. 'Shame we 'aven't got no bombardier fritz to go with 'em. This looks like a crackin' place to bivvy up though. 'Should get boko scran 'ere.'

Billy and Mitch agreed, there seemed to be plenty of good food, or 'scran' as Scouse called it, in the district. Soon, they were tucking into their fried eggs, albeit without Scouse's longed for chips, but with fresh buttered bread. The butter was yellow and delicious, unlike the dubious spread which appeared sporadically in the cooks' wagons and was christened 'axle grease' by the men.

Later, some of the locals joined them and brought wine and bunches of flowers. They seemed pleased to have the Tommies in their little *hameau*. The men were glad of the wine, but a bit baffled by the flowers. As friendly and genial as the villagers were however, they seemed to have hidden away their daughters. There was a limit to their hospitality, it seemed.

The 16th remained in readiness at Sec Bois for the rest of the month and although the front was a few miles distant, the sounds of battle could plainly be heard. Indeed the odd stray shell landed in the village from time to time. The men thought it the strangest thing to see the farmers and their horse-drawn carts still working in their fields, as they probably had since medieval times, but with the occasional stray 15 inch howitzer shell landing alongside them. There was something quite surreal about the villagers pursuing their ancient and traditional ways with the thunderous noises of modern warfare so close by. It seemed the cavalry were to wait backstage in case they were needed. The villagers' disregard for the war appeared to be infectious. The other ranks now played football or cricket on the village green. Some of the officers went off hunting game in the forest of Nieppe both to pass the time and to exercise the horses.

The relentless din of warfare continued all month, by day and night, but it did not stop the men of the 16th sleeping soundly in their comfortable billets, at least not until the night a shell landed right next to the hay barn, setting it alight. Some of the men grabbed pitchforks to drag the burning hay out of the barn, whilst others formed a human chain to pass buckets of water along from the nearby stream. The fire was soon extinguished and the exhausted men had to spend the rest of the night in the smoke-filled barn. The next day however, the farmer and his wife expressed their gratitude with more gifts of eggs and cheese. The *scran*, as Scouse would say, was certainly *boko*.

On the first of July, the men heard that a major battle had commenced on the Somme, though, disappointingly, the Cavalry Corps was to take no part in this action. The men of the 16th lamented their own exclusion from 'the bun fight' as they called it. They saw many ambulances pass, conveying huge numbers of casualties from the field dressing stations to the military hospitals further west. It seemed a shame the cavalry could not also do their bit. The 16th soon had a casualty of its own however, when Captain Evans was injured falling from his horse whilst pursuing a fox into the woods. Scouse could not imagine why anyone in his right mind would want to chase a fox, especially when Billy informed him that foxes were no more edible than rats.

It may have been the pain and indignity of this injury which was the cause of the captain's subsequent irritability, or perhaps it was his continuing fear of possible Irish insurrection which decided him to subject Mitch to a field court martial following his next bout of plain speaking with Lance Corporal Skinner.

On 17th July, Mitch pleaded guilty to the charges of 'using insubordinate language to an NCO and conduct to the prejudice ... etcetera.' He was expecting to receive the usual field punishment but, to his surprise, when the 'guilty' verdict was endorsed by the GOC of the 3rd Cavalry Brigade, the sentence he had been given this time was one year's imprisonment. Mitch was shocked. He thought this harsh for his offence, even given the cumulative nature of his misbehaviour.

He wondered where this sentence would be served. He could not imagine they would erect a guardhouse especially for him here in the French countryside, and even if they did, who would guard him when the regiment was sent to the battlefront? A further ten days would elapse before the location of Mitch's forthcoming imprisonment would be made known to him. He was to be taken under escort to Abancourt Number One Military Prison, at Blairgies in the city of Rouen.

At the edge of the woods bordering the north east corner of the town of Longueval in the département of the Somme, the South African 1st Infantry Brigade is coming under heavy fire from German artillery. From a depression, which is little more than a shell-scraping in the now exposed and scorched interior of the Bois d'Elville, a German machine gun crew scythes through the ranks of the fearless South Africans as they charge into the woods. As the bodies of the determined colonials begin to pile up, a lone figure crawls on his belly

162

through the mud a few hundred yards to the left of the machine gun post. There are no longer any trees left standing. The once dense forest canopy is gone. Only charred stumps now remain of the lofty oak and elm which formerly characterised the Picardy landscape, but the dead infantry men's corpses provide some cover for the lone soldier's stealthy progress.

He observes the sweeping pattern of the enemy MG08 on its bipod, as it spits out four hundred rounds a minute, taking out everything within a range of four thousand feet. Taking advantage of each hollow and depression in the muddy earth, the soldier continues to circle around until he is almost behind the machine gun crew. Suddenly, he springs to his feet, his fingers wrapped around a mills bomb, and sprints across the open ground towards the machine gun emplacement. The gunner spots him from the corner of his vision and wheels the gun around, just seconds too late, for the tall, square-jawed man in the mud-caked sergeant major's uniform launches the missile directly at the gun crew. The MG08 begins to stutter its venom at the soldier but is immediately silenced, as the mills bomb explodes.

As he hurls himself in amongst the German dead, the square-jawed man sees that one of the gunners, thrown onto his back by the blast, is still alive. Producing a trench knife, the sergeant major leaps astride the gunner, beating him about the head repeatedly with his brass knuckle-duster, before plunging the thin, triangular blade of his knife savagely into the German's abdomen. He thrusts the knife into the gunner's warm body again and again and again. He gasps and grunts with the effort of taking the young man's life. At last, he sits back on the corpse. His eyes are closed and a wry grin spreads across his square jaw. He is oblivious to the thunder of the heavy guns around him. His breathing is laboured but gradually subsides, as his lust is spent.

Abancourt Military Prison presented a forbidding edifice, as befitted its notorious reputation. Mitch had been surprised to see that the prisoners were accommodated, not in cells, but in tents. However, it was clear that the security of the perimeter was sufficient to prevent escape. He noted also that the ratio of guards to prisoners was high. No lone and disinterested sentries guarded these men. There would be no slipping over latrine walls in this establishment. The prisoners seemed a real rag-tag-and-bobtail rabble dressed in a variety of uniforms. The guards were soldiers of the Military Provost Staff Corps.

Mitch recognised the various insignia of some of the Scots regiments and also a few Welsh ones. Given the preponderance of colonial slouch hats however, he gained the initial impression that many of the prisoners must be *ANZACs*. It was a man in the uniform of the Australian infantry who first approached, sizing up the new arrival as Mitch walked hesitantly into the throng of weary and desperate looking men. There was a very tangible atmosphere; a pall of resentment and menace, which hung heavy in the air.

'Which outfit you with?' it sounded more of a challenge than a civil enquiry.

'The 16th the Queen's Own Lancers,' Mitch replied, matching the man's curtness.

'Aw look, a donkey-walloper, boys! One of the Queen's own donkey wallopers, mind!' he declared, for the benefit of the other prisoners, 'What you in fer?'

Mitch thought for a moment before replying. He didn't much care whether or not he befriended the man but equally he didn't want to antagonise him.

'Well, I didn't see eye to eye with my Lance-Corporal. But then, he was a bit of a short-arse, after all. I got twelve months.'

The man nodded, approvingly. Placing his hands on his hips, he glanced around him at his fellow prisoners, many of whom were taking an interest in the exchange.

'You English, then?' he made it sound more like an accusation than a question.

'Irish,' Mitch informed him.

'I'm Jack, Jack Braithwaite,' the infantryman said at once, his sun-creased features now breaking into a smile as he stepped forward, shook Mitch's hand and led him across to a group of other slouch-hatted men.

Rough introductions were made. It seemed many of the *diggers* had nicknames which they used in preference to given names. Jack, or 'Jack the Journo' as he was referred to by the others, was not quite as tall as Mitch and was slightly built, but there was something about his swagger and the intense scrutiny of his grey eyes which gave him a distinct presence. Mitch noticed his hands did not seem to be those of a sheepshearer. You never could tell where the *Aussies* fitted into the social scale, Mitch thought, since they all seemed to speak with the same accent and none had any edge to him.

Jack informed him he had been a journalist back in Sydney. He went on to say that he was one of four brothers who were fighting, his younger brother having been badly wounded at Gallipoli. The men who had served at Gallipoli were referred to reverentially by the Aussies as *dinkums*. Indeed there were a couple of *dinkums* incarcerated here in the prison. They had a lot to say about the way the generals had handled that particular campaign. There had been no trenches at Gallipoli. The *dinkums* had used their bare hands to scrape shallow hollows out of the stony ground. They had drunk dew and rainwater from those hollows. Many of them had died in those hollows, mostly from dysentery.

The Australians had plenty to say also about the prison management and the guards here at Abancourt. Mitch appreciated the instant openness and plain speaking of the Antipodeans. The atmosphere in the yard now felt a great deal less menacing.

'Mitch here biffed a lance-jack,' Jack advised the others, assuming Mitch's transgression to have been more severe than it was. This was a reasonable assumption, given the length of Mitch's sentence. Mitch did not correct him. The others nodded their approval.

Jack explained the prison routine to Mitch. The prisoners, all of whom had been sentenced to hard labour, worked from dawn till dusk each day except Sundays, and most of them did so out in the fields. No-one had escaped from a work detail, he warned, but several had been shot trying to do so. The provost guards, Jack explained, were trench dodgers, posted here to abuse their fellow soldiers who *had* been up the front, and thus they were the most detestable cunts who walked the face of the earth. They would shoot you quicker than Jerry would.

Jack said he too had been a lance-corporal once, but had 'gone walkabout' a couple of times and consequently had done spells in several 'spudholes' before being stripped of his stripes and ending up in prison. He warned Mitch not to give any thought to escaping, as all who had tried it had failed.

'Lie *doggo*, mate, and do yer time,' he advised.

Glancing around at the various uniforms sported by his fellow prisoners, Mitch spotted a small group of men sheltering in a corner of the yard who were not in any uniform at all. In fact they were stark naked.

'I see you have a problem with the *chats* in here, same as up in the trenches,' Mitch remarked.

165

'*Chats*?' Jack puzzled, 'aw you mean *cooties*? Aw yeah, there's plenty of lice in here, but that's not why those *Kitchies* are naked. They're English *conchies* – conscientious objectors, non-combatants, mostly Quakers, Congregationalists and the like. They refuse to wear uniform, and the cunts won't give them anything else to wear so they go naked.'

Mitch liked the way the Australians referred to the British troops at *Kitchener's boys*, or *Kitchies*. He hadn't heard of conscientious objectors however. He himself had attested voluntarily but he understood that conscription had been brought in back in January. He hadn't realised a man might object to fighting in the war. Jack explained that the conchies had been enticed over to France with a promise of being given 'non-combatant status' and an assurance they would not be involved in any task directly connected with killing. That promise had been broken. When they had refused to fight, they were imprisoned.

'How long did they get?' Mitch asked.

'Not long,' Jack replied sardonically, 'they've been sentenced to death.'

The food at Abancourt was even worse than that served up to the men at the front. The *hard-tack* biscuits here had live weevils in them and the grey concoction served up with these, which was nominally some sort of stew, was rancid. Jack was one of the mess orderlies which in other circumstances might have been a cushy number but no-one in his right mind would want access to extra rations of this quality. Jack seemed to be in his right mind. Mitch liked him.

Right after supper, the men were herded into their tents for the night. Jack made a space for Mitch in the tent he shared with some of the other *ANZACs*. Another sort of 'biscuit' was now rolled out. These were thin straw pads, roughly two feet six inches square, and each man was allocated three of these to form a mattress. It was the same type of bedding the troops had in the trenches. Each prisoner, except the *conchies*, was given a small blanket and they all settled down for the night. Mitch soon realised the 'biscuits' and blankets were alive with lice.

'When do we get de-loused?' he asked of his new companions.

'We don't, mate,' was the reply, 'you'd better start giving your little *cooties* names, 'cause they'll soon be your closest friends!'

166

The next morning the men were roused whilst it was still dark. They were served some sort of thin porridge and then were divided up into work details. Since he was sharing a tent with the *diggers*, Mitch was grouped with them. They were shackled together and herded into secure transport. After a half hour's drive, they arrived at a quarry where their restraints were removed and they were given lump hammers and were put to breaking up flints. Mitch understood the flints would be sent off to re-surface some of the roads destroyed in the shelling.

The men set to their task, under the watchful eyes of half a dozen armed guards, but they had been going for just a short while when some sort of disturbance broke out. As he glanced around him, Mitch saw the fuss involved one of the *conchies*, who, presumably to avoid upsetting any passing locals, had been given grey underpants to wear when outside the prison. The *conchie* was refusing to work.

The well-spoken Englishman could be heard politely but firmly expressing his reluctance to undertake any work which would contribute to the war effort. His polite refusal was met with a savage beating and kicking from two of the guards however. Mitch suspected this was a daily occurrence for the man, whose thin body was already marked by half healed scars and old bruises. He found the lack of dignity with which the half-naked man was being treated quite disturbing.

The rest of the prisoners had ceased work and gathered around to watch. They winced at every kick and blow inflicted upon the *conchie*, who had now fallen to the ground. He made no effort to protect himself or to retaliate. The guard standing nearest to Mitch also winced visibly and clutched his rifle tightly to his chest in case of further trouble. The *Conchie* soon lapsed into unconsciousness and was left, where he fell. One of his attackers cracked a tasteless joke about him being an '*unconscious* objector' now. There were murmurings of disapproval from the bulk of the prisoners.

'Quiet now! *Chipperow*!' the nearby guard barked at them.

Chipperow was a word Mitch hadn't heard since his India days. The bastardised Hindustani term was familiar to him, but so was the voice. He sneaked a few sideways glances at the guard, whose face he now recognised. A few more instructions from the guard gave away a County Cork accent, though it was a while before the man's name would come to his mind. As the guard's vigilant perambulations brought him a little nearer, Mitch ventured to whisper;

167

'Bussell? Is that you, Bussell?'

'Who is it wants to know?'

'It's Mitch, William Mitchell of *The Queens Royal West Surreys*. You are Staff Sar'nt Bussell, aren't you?'

'Mitchell! Jayzus, an' who did you kill that you wound up in prison?'

'I might ask you the same, Staff. Last time I saw you wuz in Sialkot. What're *you* doing here?'

Bussell came nearer and, looking around him, indicated Mitch should keep on swinging his lump hammer.

'Sure an' I got sick of Injah and wanted to come back home, so I did. I had the idea of transferrin' to the military police. I was in your neck of the woods for a few years, at Dublin's Arbour Hill military prison. Then when the war started, I came out here with the expeditionary force and I've been here ever since. It isn't how I'd hoped to be spending the war, and that's the truth. But who did you kill, then?'

'I didn't kill anybody yet, Staff, – neither an Alleyman nor a Tommy. I just sort of threatened to fix a Lance-Corp, or he says I did. I don't remember it though for I was off me head at the time.'

'God an' they're after sending men up here for very little these days. Usually they send indisciplined men to the bull-ring at Eatapples for the trainers to sort them out.'

'Is that easier than prison?'

'Well, I do hear tell it's just as bad. Them *canaries* is vicious types altogether, worse even than them two,' he gestured at the guards who had delivered the *conchie's* beating, 'and these are terrible times, so they are. They're shooting men for cowardice and the like. There's boys in their teens, never been away from home before and sent to the front. They're shell shocked and wanderin' off, callin' for their mammies, and the bastards are shootin' them for desertion. This is a terrible sort of war altogether. You just try to keep yer head down Mitchell, and do yer time aisy.'

It was just two days later that the next lot of trouble broke out. Of all things, the row involved Scotsmen and porridge. Mitch did not witness the start of the fight over breakfast, but he caught the gist of it. As bad as the gruel was, the Scotsmen were unimpressed to find that there was not enough of it to go around. They refused to go to work until they were fed. As mess orderly, Jack was involved in the fracas, though he seemed to be trying to pacify the Scotsmen. The Scots were taken out of the work detail, arrested and taken away for charges of mutiny to be entered against them. Mitch and the rest of his work party took the transport and went off for the day's labour at the quarry as normal.

As usual, they returned after dark, too tired even to have a wash before they ate the meagre supper. The toilet and washing facilities at the prison were woefully inadequate in any case. There was only cold water, no clean towels, only damp, shared ones, and there were very few razors available to the men for shaving. One razor had to be passed around two dozen or so men in turn. Shaving rashes were common, but Mitch awoke one morning to find he had developed large fluid-filled swellings on his face and neck.

He reported to the guard and was sent to the infirmary where there was already a queue of men with identical swellings. The MO diagnosed impetigo. Mitch reflected that, as poor as his family had been back in the Monto slums, they had always managed to keep clean. They certainly never had lice or any disease caused by dirt. The insanitary conditions in the prison however turned his stomach.

The men suffered on until mid October, when again there was a show of resistance from some of the men one lunchtime. This time, a contingent of guards came to arrest an Australian prisoner for some misdemeanour or other. His countrymen, and also the New Zealanders, immediately gathered to him and began to protest. Mitch saw Jack trying to defuse the situation by coaxing the Australian away to the yard and sitting him down in his tent to eat his meal before the guards would take him away for the inevitable beating.

The heavy-handed response of the guards was to arrest both the Australian in the tent and Jack. Jack Braithwaite was now a marked man since he had been involved, albeit in a conciliatory role, in the earlier row involving the Scots. Other *diggers* and *enzedders* who came to protest were pistol-whipped and were also taken away. Men who should have been leaving with their work details now sat down on the ground, refusing to go. The protest was spreading.

There was a great deal of confusion and shouting and suddenly more armed guards came flooding into the yard and began striking the seated protesters about the head with their rifle butts. As blood began to flow so the vocal protest rose to a fever pitch, with Mitch lending his own outraged voice to the dissent. Suddenly, he felt a hand upon his arm, pulling him back inside the canteen block. It was Bussell.

169

'Keep your head down Mitch. Don't be getting involved in this business. This is mutiny and it will end badly.'

Mitch hoped his father would not find out he was in prison. There was no reason why he should though. Joe Mitchell had spent some time in the glasshouse himself on a couple of occasions for 'high spirits', but being sent to military prison was a different matter. This was something which might affect Mitch's job prospects back in Civvy Street. His mother's words of long ago came back to him, as mother's words are apt to do: 'you'll be the ruination of me, so you will, the ruination!' Ruination. Rouenation. He had indeed reached a shameful low, he realised.

Bussell had been right, of course, and Mitch was glad he had heeded his advice. The more vocal Australians and New Zealanders in the yard had been taken to the cells and subjected to some savage beatings. Moreover, a few days later, Mitch learned that six of the principal protagonists had been sentenced to death for the crime of mutiny. Rumours circulated around the prison that the British military authorities would not be allowed to execute the Australian soldiers, since there was a written agreement between the two nations that no Australian would be hanged without the express authority of the Australian government. In any case, the *diggers* said, Jack's uncle was a brigadier, so he'd be all right.

On 29th October however, two men, one of them British, were taken into the prison yard at dawn and were executed by firing squad. All the prisoners heard the execution. The British man had been a gunner in the Royal Field Artillery. The other executed man was Jack Braithwaite. It turned out that, although he was an Australian resident, serving in the Australian infantry, Braithwaite was in fact a New Zealander. Unlike Australia, New Zealand had no non-execution agreement with the British.

Mitch reasoned that if the nephew of a serving brigadier could be executed without trial, then a recalcitrant Irish nonentity like himself could die in here without a ripple of protest. He determined he would indeed try to keep his head down. After the October incident, he did not see Bussell again, either around the prison or out on the work detail. He took Bussell's advice to heart though and now tried to avoid trouble.

The weather in northern France that November was particularly atrocious, yet still the prisoners at Abancourt Military Prison slept out in the prison yard under canvas. Mitch had never known cold like it. Thankfully, the naked *conchies* had been given *civvies* to wear and had then been sent back to England to serve out their sentences, now commuted from death to ten years' hard labour. Of those prisoners who remained at Abancourt, most, like Mitch, had been convicted for offences of disobedience or repeated minor misconduct.

In the now sub-zero temperatures, sleep was impossible. The prisoners' requests for more blankets were ignored. Their demands for more humane treatment were met with more beatings. When Mitch tried to rise one morning he found he was unable to stand. One of the guards accused him of malingering but then it became apparent he was shivering uncontrollably and that his joints were stiff and swollen. The MO confirmed he was suffering the effects of exposure and so Mitch and several other prisoners similarly afflicted were admitted to the infirmary. A few days later, Mitch was deemed fit to resume work at the quarry, though the rheumatic pains in his joints did not, and never would, leave him.

He paid several more visits to the infirmary over the coming months suffering from a variety of complaints. On one such visit, he heard from one of the medical orderlies that Bussell had been transferred to Military Prison number four, where he had shot himself dead – accidentally, an enquiry declared – although some suspected he might have committed suicide.

On 12th August 1917, a month short of Mitch's expected release date, he was informed that the remainder of his sentence had been remitted. He was not told why this should be, and of course he did not argue the decision. Within the confines of the prison he had heard nothing of the war's progress. He wondered whether things had reached so critical a stage that all men were needed at the front, even people of his ilk, experienced soldiers who, when in drink, had the temerity to talk back to a bullying NCO.

He rejoined his regiment at Epehy, where the 16th were standing in readiness to move up to the front in support of the 2nd army, and where he now learned that some of his squadron had bought it in the trenches at L'empire back in June. Their trench had been blown in and several of the men had been killed instantly. Happily, Scouse and Billy were still alive and kicking, though their experiences at the front had sharpened their sense of fatalism.

'C'mon lads, let's get bladdered tonight,' Scouse urged 'cause you never know, we might get slaughtered tomorrow. I fancy a bit of skirt an' all. How about it?'

The more Mitch thought about it, the more it occurred to him that Scouse was right. He might die tomorrow. Fuck it, he might die *today*. The prospect that lay ahead of him of miserable and squalid trench conditions, added to the squalor he had just experienced in the prison, was depressing to contemplate. A little comfort and a little fun was what they needed. Mitch had some drinking to catch up on in any case. He agreed to go with the lads to the *bordel* that evening, and maybe not just for the booze. This evening, he might just take a look at what the women upstairs had to offer the battle-weary, and indeed the prison-weary soldier.

The local bordello was a shabby place, devoid of any atmosphere but rendered slightly more enticing by the sheer number of men frequenting it.

'Beers,' Mitch demanded, holding up the relevant number of fingers.

'Il n'yen a plus,' the plump, elderly man behind the bar shook his head, 'du vin blanc?' he proffered the house white to the soldiers instead.

'There's *napoo* neck oil, mates,' Mitch informed his comrades, but there's wine.'

Turning to the Frenchman, he slapped coins upon the damp and sticky bar top, 'no plonk, mon sewer, van rooj, boko van rooj!'

A dusty bottle of rot-gut red wine was soon opened and placed on a tray with four mis-matched and greasy glasses. The four soldiers took a corner table by the empty hearth. Although it was August and no fire was needed, there was something unaccountably miserable about an empty hearth.

Mitch poured the wine. Filling his own glass last, and slowly to retain the tea-leaf like dregs in the bottom of the bottle, he quaffed the dark liquid. It was bitter with tannins and it coated his tongue, but after a few swallows it began to hit the spot. He thought it ironic that the word the French used to describe red wine was the same word used to describe that red muck the tarts in Piccadilly smeared on their faces. As the song suggested however, they had said their farewells to Piccadilly. They were a long, long way from Tipperary too, not to mention Monto and Bermondsey, which Mitch had never thought he would miss. The men drank slowly and in silence.

172

'So, whaddya think?' Scouse asked at last, 'shall we give the *prozzies* the once over or wha'?'

Mitch caught the eye of the patron and lifted his gaze ceiling-wards. The Frenchman nodded and gestured for them to go upstairs. The friends headed for the foot of the stairs, where Mitch paused and bent down to untie his mud-caked boots. Scouse tapped him on the arm and shook his head.

'Don't bother, mate,' he advised, 'these ain't ladies. You won't be takin' yer boots off. If you do, they won't be here when you come down again.'

The patron's wife, also plump but not quite as old as her husband, sat knitting in an armchair on the upstairs landing. Wearily, she put aside her knitting, took the men's money and ushered each into a different room. Mitch found himself in a small, cold and dingy bedroom. A blanket covered most of the window but what he could see of the glass was cracked and caked in dirt. He guessed it was only the dirt which was holding the broken shards of windowpanes together.

There was a rickety looking iron bed in the room and an old dresser with a jug and basin upon it, but very little else. The room reeked of sweat and stale cooking smells. The bed linen was grey and the pillows, indented from recent use, lacked any plumpness. He had no intention of using the bed however. This was his first visit to a French brothel. It was not at all like the kip house he recalled from Dublin. At Nellie Brannigan's, the girls had the place personalised with their dolls and fancy cushions. Brannigan's had been homely. This place was depressing.

The girl looked about twenty, he thought, not very tall and slightly built, but definitely not a child, thankfully. She wore a grubby, pearl-grey satin dressing gown, which she now removed and threw over the bed. She wore nothing beneath the gown and she stood before him, not in any way self conscious about her nakedness. She was thin and pale and her skin sagged, which he thought unusual in such a young woman. He guessed it was the effect of poor nutrition.

She looked up at him, her face expressionless. For a second, he thought of undressing, but, remembering what Scouse had said about keeping his boots on, he realised this would be inappropriate. The idea of introducing himself had also flitted briefly across his mind, then he realised how ludicrous that would be. If he did so, she would realise this was his first time as a paying customer. She probably didn't speak

English anyway, and this was to be a purely commercial arrangement. No small talk was necessary.

He made a rotating gesture, to indicate she should turn away from him, and he unbuttoned his trousers. Resignedly, the girl turned her back to him and bent over the bed. He realised he felt nothing and so was not ready to perform. He leaned forward, reached around her and cupped her small breasts in his hands. He rubbed them rhythmically and closed his eyes. The girl moved her hand behind her and took hold of him, to try to move matters along. Gradually, desire arose in him. He took hold of her hips and she bent further forward, resting her hands on the bed as he entered her.

As his action quickened, unwelcome thoughts now came into his head. He suddenly thought of his Rose, his love of a lifetime ago. Perhaps it was several lifetimes ago? He wondered if things had been like this with Rose and *her* clients. Had she assumed the same numb indifference, the same resigned co-operation? When he and Rose had made love however, it had been so passionate, so animated, so loving.

He glanced at his upper arm and the red rose he had had tattooed there in memory of his first love. He now felt his desire abate. This wouldn't do. He gazed out of the window, over the grey slate roof of the neighbouring cattle byre, to the bleak landscape beyond. He regarded the desolate acres of dark grey mud fading into a paler grey sky in what should have been a summer scene.

On the horizon, a lone tree trunk stripped of its foliage and branches arose erect out of the wasteland, crooked like a dead man's accusing finger. Closing his eyes did not help. In his head the tree became a real dead man's finger, like the ones he had seen poking out of the earth in the trenches.

Trying to ignore the unpleasant odours in the room, he focused on that erect tree trunk. It stood in witness of life which had once existed hereabouts. Life, and love, had once flowed through his veins too. Perhaps it would again. He concentrated on the task in hand. His desire returned. He quickened his pace and pumped for all he was worth. He just wanted this over with now. It would not bring him pleasure but it might bring him some relief.

He must not think of Rose. Think of anything but Rose. Rose ... I miss you, Rose. He glanced down at the bony girl beneath him. Her skin was grimy and white. He now noticed her hair. It was lank and greasy and damp. Suddenly a vision came to him of Rose in the killing hospital, her hair damp and her skin pale with red sores. The girl

174

beneath his grasp had the same red sores around her buttocks and thighs.

'Jesus Christ!' he recoiled, pushing her away from him.

His business was not yet finished but he could not continue. The girl looked up at him and shrugged. Mitch quickly adjusted his clothing and moved over to the washbasin. He poured some water into it from the jug and looked around for soap to use to wash himself. There was none. Suddenly, Rose was back in his mind again. He thought also of the drunken mariner he had beaten up in the alley in Dublin. He now thought himself no better than that rough, greasy seaman. He pictured that man coupling with his Rose. In his vision, the seaman was alive but Rose was dead. Poor Rose. Mitch's heart cracked. Death was in this room. Something within him gave way. He felt his gorge rise and the next moment he was vomiting into the china basin.

'Fuck!' the girl exclaimed angrily. Evidently she had at least one useful word of English in her vocabulary.

'Van rooj,' he muttered by way of explanation, as he left the room and clattered down the wooden stairs. He didn't care what she thought. He would not be back anyway.

Mitch feared he might have left it too long before presenting himself to the MO. His condition was recorded on his medical card however as 'Venereal Disease, Syphilis – mild' and he was sent to number 9 General Hospital. He experienced mild alarm at finding himself en route to Rouen again and he wondered briefly whether they intended to shoot him for his 'self-induced' condition. What was it his late Aunt Jessie had misnamed the process of mercy killing? *Euphemism.*

The treatment during his twenty day stay at the hospital was far less frightening than he had been led to believe. Neither 'clap traps' nor umbrellas featured in the process, only simple injections, in the buttock, of Salvarsan. The MO reminded him that he must continue his treatment when he left hospital, and possibly even when back in England, unless given full clearance at his final medical at the war's end. He was pleased to leave the hospital. Seeing other patients around him awaiting amputation of their gangrenous trench feet; nursing their shell wounds or enduring the constant tremors and stammering of neurasthenia, had made him feel extremely guilty, given the mild nature and sordid cause of his own ailment.

Mitch caught up with his regiment at Ribecourt, near Cambrai that autumn. The weather was again foul and the terrain was a muddy morass. Some of the regiment rode off to billets at a place called Fins. Mitch and his comrades however were assigned to a detachment of two hundred dismounted cavalrymen, under the leadership of Captain Tempest-Hicks.

On 24th November the dismounted men were moved up to support the defence of Bourlon Wood. The Welsh and Scots regiments had been engaged in heavy fighting and were fending off a fierce enemy counter attack when the cavalrymen arrived. The 17th Welsh in particular had suffered heavy losses, including all their officers. With help from the dismounted cavalry, they set about trying to recover the eastern portion of the wood. They were not successful in this endeavour but by dusk they were managing at least to maintain the stiff resistance against the enemy's continued bombardment.

Whilst Mitch had been in prison at Rouen, the British troops had been issued with regulation tin hats in place of their cloth caps and Mitch was now allocated one also. The pressed steel 'soup plates' were far from impenetrable, but at least fewer men seemed to be losing the tops of their heads to snipers now. If a sniper got you, it was more likely to be in the face or the neck.

It was rumoured that smokers stood a greater risk of being killed by sniper fire than non-smokers. It was common for three men to light up their cigarettes from the one Vesta. It seemed the sniper would be alerted by the flare of the smoker's match; would take aim as the second man lit his fag from it, and would fire when the third man moved in for a light. The third man would be killed, usually. Therefore it was considered most unlucky to be the third man lighting up. That in fact was exactly how Billy Jackson was killed two days later. Scouse remarked that he had always told Billy those foul woodbines would be the death of him

By midnight on the 24th, they had been joined by a battalion of Scots Guards and some Kings Own Royal Lancs and together they attempted to re-establish a line around the edge of the woods. Fighting continued non-stop through the 25th and, by afternoon, progress was being achieved by the Scots on the right and the 119th Infantry Brigade on the left, so much so that by midnight that night a strong defensive position had been achieved on the high ground in the wood. In the early hours of 26th, the 16th were relieved by the 62nd Division and now headed wearily back behind the lines, minus three dead and with six wounded in tow.

During the slow march back, whilst resting up in a trench behind the lines on 4th December, the exhausted men of the 16th found themselves being strafed by enemy aircraft. Mitch threw himself into the bottom of the trench. As soon as his face hit the ice-cold muddy water and filth, he realised this was not a smart move. A plane was flying low, following the line of the trench and firing directly at them. He was a sitting duck. He now realised he'd have been wiser to have pressed himself flat against the side of the trench, as he had seen Scouse do.

Someone now fell on top of him however, pressing him further down into the water. The plane was now taking a second run at them. The strafing began anew and machine gun bullets were now throwing up the mud along the length of the trench. The man on top of him was a dead weight however so Mitch had to stay put. When the strafing stopped, Mitch glanced up over his shoulder to see who it was who was pinning him down. Mitch now saw that it was Scouse, and he could see from the vacant expression that Scouse wasn't just a dead weight – he was dead. Mitch thought Scouse must have slipped in the mud and landed on top of him, inadvertently saving his pal's life.

In total, five other ranks, Scouse included, were killed outright in the air attack, as was Lieutenant Pargeter. Although inured to the sight of dead comrades, Mitch wept as he helped remove five dead horses from the carnage. Eleven more men were added to the growing list of the wounded. After burying their dead and patching up the wounded, the 16th Lancers continued their journey, uneventfully. By 6th December, they reached Buchy, where they went into billets for the rest of the month. Captain Cheyne was now in charge of the regiment, having been promoted temporarily to the acting rank of Lieutenant Colonel.

Another very cold and fairly cheerless Christmas came and went, this time without Billy and Scouse. This year however, the army food was slightly better and more plentiful. As Mitch ate possibly the most acceptable Christmas dinner he had eaten so far in France, he thought how much Scouse would have praised the repast. *Boko scran* it was – *napoo* turkey mind, but *boko scran*.

As he ate his meal Mitch thought of his comrade for the first time since Scouse had been killed. The memory of happier times, with

Scouse cooking them eggs outside the barn in the little French village, now caused him pain.

'Oh Scouse,' he thought, 'you poor sod.'

On New Year's Day 1918, the 16th headed back to the front again where they went into the trenches east of Vilaret. It was more of the same, the men enduring heavy shelling and trying to be constantly vigilant against snipers. The new British tanks were now brought into action. Neither the men of the 16th nor the enemy had ever seen their like before. Mitch didn't know what effect these lumbering metal monsters would have on the enemy, but they scared the shit out of him. As it turned out, the tanks quickly proved highly effective against the German positions. After only six days in the front line, the 3rd Cavalry Brigade was relieved by the 5th Brigade and the men of the 16th were sent into reserve at Vendelles. They understood the enemy was now on the run. All along the road to Vendelles, Mitch noticed the retreating Germans had cut down all the apple trees and telegraph poles. No-one was sure what the enemy had done with the all the wood, but much of it had been cut up and used as crosses to mark the graves of the many German dead who lay in the surrounding fields.

Mitch thought back to his early days in France, when he had been detailed to bury the British dead after Loos. He thought of Scouse and Billy who now lay in the French earth too. At least they had been buried and not left out in the open as easy meat for the flies and rats. He wondered how their families would learn of their deaths. He did not even know where they lived, for he had not allowed himself to become close to his comrades. Mitch was greatly fatigued now, but he was alive.

Each lancer now rode his own horse but also led a spare horse in tow. These were their dead comrades' horses and they were now heavily laden with shells. The huge, heavy brass shells were slung across the animals' backs and they hung down, four each side. Every now and again, the weight of the shells would cause a horse to slip in the mud and the poor beast would have a desperate struggle to get up again. Mitch felt for the beautiful, dumb creatures. This wasn't their war after all. More horses, pulling field guns, brought up the rear.

At Vendelles they were to occupy the intermediate trenches. Mitch assumed, wrongly, that this would be a safe position. They came under heavy shelling almost immediately and this continued, day and night until the end of January. He wondered what the cavalry were doing here at all, since this seemed to be mainly the artillery's show. The men returned the enemy's sporadic rifle fire, but this was just a supporting act to the big guns. In the Vendelles trenches, a further six men were wounded and two killed, without any ground apparently being won.

In contrast to the waiting around at the beginning of his war, Mitch now felt there was perhaps too much action, too much noise, too much mud and very little gain. To the best of his knowledge however, he had still not killed anyone, and nor had he engaged the enemy in hand-to-hand combat. When the men of the Lucknow Brigade arrived at Vendelles on 28th January to relieve them, Mitch was very pleased to see them. The Indians were surprised to be greeted in Hindustani by a mud-caked Tommy.

Things seemed to go a little better for the British and French troops during February. The allied advanced pushed slowly eastwards until, in March, it ground to a halt once more. Mitch found himself in reserve trenches by the village of Grandru, five miles north east of Noyon. Major Brooke had now taken command of the regiment from Captain Cheyne and there seemed to be regiment after regiment of soldiers pouring into the area. The 16th found themselves sharing trenches with the Northamptonshires; the 7th Queen's; the 7th Buffs and the East Surreys. There was a distinct feeling that something big was brewing.

The talk amongst the men, as evening fell and they sat down on the cold earth to eat, was the build up of German armaments behind the enemy lines. It was clear to all that the Germans were no longer on the run but were dug in. The belief was that there was to be a big push, another major German offensive. The men suspected the enemy would await the arrival of the spring weather, however.

Rumours also suggested the British had run out of manpower and now faced the serious prospect of defeat. A hundred thousand troops had been pulled back from the Eastern Front and also from Italy. This wasn't idle rumour either, since men fighting on the Western Front had seen thousands of their comrades being entrained back towards the channel ports. Word was that they were to be based on British soil, in case the enemy should succeed in breaking through to the channel. The outlook seemed very bleak indeed.

Each night now, the instruction was given to extinguish all fires in the allied trenches, since enemy aircraft were carrying out continuous surveillance now, and the possibility of an attack, from land or air, was never far away. Visibility was down to zero as Mitch felt his way back to his dugout from the latrines one evening. His walk seemed to take longer on the return than it had on the way out, and he now realised he had taken a wrong turning in the dark and had lost his way. He suddenly thought how unlucky it would be, were he to have stumbled into the enemy trenches by mistake.

He called out to ask where he was. Unfamiliar but helpful voices responded. He had stumbled into the East Surrey's zone, apparently. He had overshot and would have to turn back. Retracing his steps, he collided with another soldier who was invisible in the pitch darkness. The other man must have been a few inches shorter than Mitch, for the sharp edge of his tin hat struck Mitch hard on the bridge of his nose.

'Jayzus! You all but broke me snot!' Mitch exploded, lapsing into vulgar Dublin vernacular, as he often did in moments of stress.

'Ah, Feck off and watch where yer goin', ye gunner-eyed shite!' came the coarse reply.

'D'ye want a rap in the snot locker yerself, ye gobshite?' Mitch spat back, grabbing the other by the lapels.

'Is it a Dubliner who's mouthin' off at my, by any chance?' the shorter man asked, 'what's yer name?'

'William Mitchell of the 16th, the *Queen's Own Lancers*, an' what's it to you?'

'Mitch? It's never you?'

'Who's askin'?'

'Jayzus an' it's me, Artie Shields!'

Mitch could not believe he had stumbled across his own cousin, here, in the dark and so many miles from home. The two men laughed fit to burst as they embraced each other. So, Artie was in the army too.

When the cousins had found a quiet dark corner to get re-acquainted, Artie explained he had left Dublin to look for a labouring job in London and had ended up in Guildford working in construction. When the war started he had tagged along to the local recruitment office with some of his fellow builders and had joined the East Surreys. Mitch told him that, ironically, he himself had served with the West Surreys before the war, but was now with his da's old outfit, the 16th Lancers. Mitch said how sorry he had been to hear about Artie's parents.

'What about you though, Mitch, is yer bake broke, or wha'?' Artie asked him.

'No, 'tis the same shape it always was,' Mitch said, rubbing the bridge of his nose, 'no thanks to these feckin' helmets though. They're no use whatsoever. They're too shallow and dangerously sharp at the edges. They don't protect yer head and they don't fit tight. Feckin' soup plates is all they are.'

'The *Brodie*,' Artie informed him, 'that's what the helmet's called. It's named for the man who designed it, some arsehole named Brodie, and d'ye know it's based on the design of the British helmet worn by the pike men five hundred years ago at the Battle of Agincourt? It's the most useless bit of kit yet – not fit for purpose at all. I'd rather wear one of me late ma's auld woolly hats. At least that'd keep me ears warm. D'ye think someone took a bung for givin' out the contract for these feckin' things?'

Mitch laughed. The same topics were being discussed in the same way in every British regiment in every corner of France. It was great to have found his cousin again though, and out here in France of all places. Mitch now said he had to hurry back to his own trench soon, before they reported him as a deserter.

'After coming this far in one piece,' he laughed, 'I wouldn't want to get shot by me own side.'

The expected German offensive began at ten o'clock on the night of 20th March with a bombardment that continued steadily until around four thirty in the morning. A noticeable increase in the intensity of enemy artillery fire suggested an infantry attack was imminent. Captain Cheyne, now promoted permanently to the rank of Major, took Captain Allen, seven Lieutenants and two hundred other ranks, Mitch included, as a dismounted party. They set off to march to La Bretelle, from where motorised transport took them to Le Pateau. Mitch was frustrated about the lack of information. It seemed to him they were heading away from the fighting, not towards it. They were ordered to entrench in the southern quarter, below St Quentin to await the enemy's advance. They waited all day.

'Hurry up and wait, hurry up and wait. We're back to that bollicks, again,' Mitch complained as he and the rest of the party squatted in the old, vacated trenches by the Crozat canal. Word came through on the field telephone that the big push, the expected German offensive, had at last begun, but it was happening further north.

'I don't believe it!' Mitch exclaimed, to the amusement of the others, 'I'm in the wrong fuckin' place yet again! I *nearly* saw the action. *Nearly*! Story of my fuckin' life!'

They sat in the trenches all afternoon and, as night fell and with it a heavy fog, the infantry unit which had accompanied them into the old trenches was withdrawn and sent up to where the action was. The dismounted cavalrymen were to sit tight however. The fog became thicker and thicker and the men of the 16th hunkered down for a long, cold night.

At dawn, word came down for the dismounted men to remain vigilant as it was thought some stray Germans might take advantage of the fog to float across the canal on makeshift rafts. Several German deserters had already done so in the days leading up to the offensive apparently. The men sat alert, ready and waiting. They waited and waited and watched the stillness of the canal.

Squinting into his field glasses, Lieutenant Stephens cursed as he could see nothing beyond the water. All was eerily quiet as the rolling waves of dense, grey fog continued to billow across the canal towards them. Mitch heard a sudden soft noise – a sort of 'phut' followed by the tinkle of breaking glass. Puzzled, he looked to his left along the trench where the Lieutenant now lay back motionless against the parados. He looked as though he was just taking a peaceful nap, yet he was obviously quite dead. He had been shot in the eye, right through the lens of his field glasses.

Even more puzzled now, Mitch looked to the water. Where the hell had that one come from? He now saw the clear outline of helmets in front of him, looming larger and larger, like ghosts out of the fog. There were dozens of them, hundreds perhaps. The helmets were not soup-plate shaped. They were German shaped. The Germans were crossing the canal!

'Here they come! Look to the water!' Mitch yelled as loud as he could. His voice echoed back eerily at him in the dense fog.

Suddenly, all hell broke loose. The sound of rapid fire rang out. Mitch couldn't tell whether it was the echo of their own volley or the Germans returning fire, but it was certainly loud. He just kept firing wildly. He now heard a sudden savage burst of automatic fire. Jesus! The Germans might only have makeshift rafts but they had machine guns mounted on them.

Their infantry unit having left them, it was now all down to the one hundred and ninety-nine remaining dismounted men of the 16th to

182

hold off the attack. Mitch could see the Germans more clearly now. They were on this side of the water already, spilling out all along the canal bank, and firing as they ran. Mitch and his comrades fired back for all they were worth. Mitch could fire thirty or forty rounds a minute if he put his mind and muscle to it. He knew he could. He had a silver medal that said he could. This was it – death or glory. Now, at last, surely he would kill somebody.

'This is for you Scouse, and for you Billy!'

Now shells were being launched at them from the opposite canal bank. The German heavy artillery had arrived. The show had really started now. Firing wide of the mark at first for fear of hitting their own men, the German artillery men gradually got the range right and the shells were dropping nearer and nearer to the lancers, who had only their rifles with which to retaliate. This was the nearest Mitch had ever been to shelling and the noise was the worst thing he had ever heard. This was hell! This was Armageddon!

The noise and the smoke, the shouting and the smell went on interminably. He still did not think he had hit anyone, but surely he must do so sooner or later as Germans were all around him now. He fired at anything that moved in the space between him and the canal. He was now awaiting what the diggers had called *the last crump* – a shell which would mean the end of the war, for him at least. He was now convinced he was about to die.

He saw the final flash, the last he would ever see in this war, and heard his last explosion, just seconds before he felt the fires of hell in his head. His right eye suddenly felt as if it were burning its way out of his skull. The pain was unbearable. It wasn't just his eye which had been hit. His right arm was actually on fire. He screamed as he started to beat out the flames with his left hand. The smell of burning wool and flesh was the last thing he remembered before he lost consciousness.

Chapter 11 - **Alice**

Brune Place was not easy to find. Mitch had copied and saved the address from the note that came with the parcel of Jam he had received in the trenches a couple years back. He wasn't even sure whether his family would still be living there, since, like most tenement dwellers, the Mitchells moved house often. He showed the address to the tobacconist on Newington High Street however and was directed through a small opening between the shops which led into an alley just off the High Street itself.

He was surprised to find that the houses here were not lofty tenements. Brune Place was an entry comprising just a dozen or so small, flat-roofed, Georgian terraced houses. The red-brick houses on the right hand side opened directly out onto flag-stoned pavements whilst those on the left boasted small gardens with washing lines and low piquet fences. There was no-one home at number twelve, but Mitch did not have too long to wait.

When she returned from her shift at the pickle works Georgina was pleased yet tearful to see her eldest son again, after his latest absence of almost five years. Mitch was astonished to learn that his mother now had a job. She had always been a housewife. It was inconceivable to him that she should be working in a factory. How times had changed. Georgina was taken aback to see her son's scarred face. She had not recognised him at first at the door, for his hair had turned very white, whiter than her own, in fact.

He assured her, as they sat waiting for the kettle to boil on the little kitchen range, that he had not lost the vision in his right eye, though it no longer seemed to be in perfect alignment with the left one. The skin was a little burned and crêpy around the eye socket and down over his right cheek. He said he was grateful to have got off so lightly, compared to most other wounded survivors he had seen in the hospitals. Margaret would be able to dye his hair for him if he wished, Georgina said, for Margaret had made a grand job of touching up her mother's now greying hair.

She insisted on seeing the damage to his right arm too. The skin of his upper arm had bubbled like toasted cheese, he told her, owing to the red hot shell fragments. Indeed, it was still a livid red colour. There was virtually nothing left of his rose tattoo. Poor Rose had been obliterated entirely. He showed his mother the jar of thick ointment he had been given to use on his arm and cheek. Georgina put on her spectacles and spent a few moments studying the small print on the label. He wondered how long she had been wearing spectacles.

He told her how he had been taken firstly to the field hospital to be patched up and then to Military Hospital Number Nine at Rouen where he had been operated on. Most, but not all of the shrapnel had been removed. He described the moment of relief when he had learned he had, as they say, 'copped a *Blighty* one'. He had then been transferred back to England, to the Eastleigh clearing station in Hampshire. Once the medics were satisfied he was beginning to heal and had nothing infectious, they had sent him on to London, to the Mile End Military Hospital. After twenty six-days' recuperation, he had been discharged – honourably this time – both from hospital and from military service.

He said he had only vague recollections of the attack which had left him injured, and even less memory of the slow homeward journey through France. It was all somewhat hazy, but he was certain he and the other casualties had passed again through Sec Bois, the little hamlet where once his mate Scouse had cooked them the best eggs he had ever tasted and where a German shell had almost burned down the barn.

He said he thought he must have been delirious at that point on the journey however, for he had a vague idea he had seen the lovely church, the one that looked like a miniature Sialkot Cathedral, standing as a splintered ruin. He also thought that the local peasant farmers who had earlier given them wine and flowers had now shaken their fists and cursed the wounded soldiers as they had passed through. Then again, he told her, so many of those little French villages looked the same, as did the little French villagers.

'So you'll be able to speak French now, as well as the Hindustani, I suppose?' his mother asked.

'Like a native, Ma,' he laughed, 'a native of China!'

'Let me just wet the tea, and will I make you a bit of a sangwich to keep you going till we all have our supper later? What would you like in yours, a bit of cheese and pickle, mebbe?'

'Anything at all Ma – anything but plum jam, that is.'

The atmosphere down the Smithfield market was unchanged. Mitch got there for midday in hopes of catching Wally Smith before the day's trading came to a close. The familiar bustle, the shouts of the delivery men and the incessant tuneless whistling of the porters were all so familiar. Even the odour of the carcasses did not seem too bad, after the stench of the battlefield at Loos. Back in nineteen fourteen he couldn't wait to leave Smithfield. Now however he was happy to be back. Wally Smith was not there. It was a stern-faced Mrs Smith who demanded to know what Mitch wanted. He explained who he was and said he was hoping to have his old job back.

Wally's widow explained her husband had been killed at The Somme, as had many of the men who worked in the market. She was now running the business herself. She indicated a young woman, clad in a smart straw boater and a white coat, sitting marking up the ledger at Mitch's old desk at the back of the shop.

'That's my store man now, and a highly competent one she is too,' Mrs Smith said.

'But, she's a woman!' Mitch protested.

'Yes, she's a war widow same as me and she has four little 'uns to support. I'm sorry Mr Mitchell, but I don't have need of your services. I recall Wally mentioning your name a few times when you worked for him. No doubt you executed your duties to the best of your ability, but I won't be getting rid of my girl – especially as the profits have become markedly healthier since she started doing the books. I'm very sorry, but that's how it is.'

Mitch felt a momentary anger. His facial disfigurement was obvious to all but it was evident also that this badge of honour would win him no sympathy here. He was not after all going to slip back into his lucrative little number in the meat trade.

The army MO had decided Mitch's injuries represented only a twenty per cent incapacity and that in turn merited only a modest conditional pension which would run for just twenty six weeks. He had assumed his old job would be kept open for him. It had not occurred to him that women might have taken on many of the men's jobs during the war, nor indeed that they might not be made to give them up for the homecoming heroes. Presumably, the women and boys, who now seemed to be working everywhere in the market, had not inherited the

186

traditional dishonest ways of their male predecessors. The power of the crooked cabal had been broken. The world had changed.

The large lorry negotiated its way clumsily and hesitantly along the narrow, winding country lanes. Mitch slowed down at several crossroads so Benny could check the inadequate wooden signposts against the sketchy directions Harry had scribbled down for them. Mitch was loathe to come to a complete halt since starting up again involved much grinding of the gears. He was still getting the hang of driving motorised vehicles and had certainly never handled anything quite this big before. Benny had never been to rural Essex before and Mitch had only a sketchy recollection of the area from his time spent in camp at Warley.

Just outside Romford, they finally found the little hamlet of Squirrel's Heath. It was all so tranquil, Mitch thought, a beautiful landscape, not unlike France, but with not a trench or howitzer in sight. Benny hated it.

'I ain't *never* been in the country in all me life, Mitch,' he complained, 'there ain't no 'ouses around 'ere, just trees an' sheep. It's not *natural*!'

'It's *entirely* natural, Benny. Don't worry; we won't be here too long, just long enough to load up the lumber. Have you got the paper work? Are you happy to do the talking whilst I stay with the lorry? If the gaffer gives you too much earache, we'll just say we think we got the wrong place and we'll take off.'

Mitch brought the lorry up the gravel track and came to a squeaky halt just by the field gate. Benny got out and opened the gate. Over by the edge of the nearby woods, the laughter of a small group of Land Army girls rang out unexpectedly. As if taking Mitch and Benny's arrival as a signal to stop work, they now downed their axes and gathered around one of the felled tree trunks to take out their packed lunches. The two friends got down from the lorry. Mitch left Benny to speak to their supervisor whilst he strolled across to where the girls sat.

'Good day, ladies,' he called out chirpily, 'it's a fine day for it.'

The young women giggled. They were a fine looking bunch, he thought, all slim and healthy looking from their outdoor labours.

Clearly, it was these young women who had felled the nearby pile of tree trunks which Mitch and Benny hoped to collect.

'Where's the usual fellah, then?' Mitch heard their male supervisor call out to Benny, 'we were expecting him tomorrow, in any case.'

Benny launched into his rehearsed explanation about the rush order for government timber needed for the repair of bridges over in France.

'Our injineers are still patchin' up the place for the frogs, you know,' Benny said plausibly.

One of the girls in particular caught Mitch's eye immediately. She wore the brown Land Army uniform jodhpurs, brown woollen jumper and cream shirt beneath her fawn, belted mackintosh. Her slim legs were encased in the regulation, knee length leather boots and around her neck she wore a cotton neckerchief to keep the perspiration from her collar. Mitch knew about the Land Army girls from the posters at the recruitment offices, but this was the first time he had seen any of them. He hadn't believed women capable of undertaking heavy farm work, and yet the pile of felled trees stood as irrefutable proof of their ability. He wondered how it was that a girl might work as hard as any man, felling trees and ploughing fields, and yet still look so feminine and attractive.

The attractive girl threw off her uniform hat. It was a slouch hat with one side pinned up – almost identical to the ones the Australian troops had worn in France. In Mitch's mind the slouch hat stood for independence, daring and an uncompromising attitude. The girl's dark auburn, collar-length curls bounced free in an independent sort of way. Mitch had observed that these days many young women wore their hair bobbed. It was more practical, he supposed, if the girls were going to do the same work as the men, and it suited her fine.

This girl was a stunner. He moved closer to her and guessed she was around five feet four or maybe five five. She took little notice of him but sat down, produced her own wax paper lunch pack and started to eat her sandwich. The other girls passed around a bottle of water. Mitch sat beside her on the tree trunk and cheekily sidled right up to her.

'Do I know you?' she asked sharply, 'have we met before?'

'No,' Mitch retorted instantly, 'I'd have remembered.'

The other girls giggled at his impudence, but the object of his attention remained unmoved. She was a cool one.

'I'm Mitch,' he continued, ignoring her coolness, 'until recently, of the 16th, the *Queen's Own Lancers*, back from the front, wounded in action and broken of spirit, with a heart that needs mending – any takers, ladies?'

The girls giggled again. They clearly appreciated Mitch's patter and his looks, which hadn't been totally spoiled by German shrapnel. The auburn beauty was still paying more attention to her sandwich than to him however.

'You see before you a wounded serviceman, ladies, a man in need of love and comfort,' he persevered.

The beauty looked at him for a second before she spoke:

'You'll be a man in need of medical attention if you don't get your arse off my hat!'

The other girls laughed as Mitch leaped to his feet and she snatched her hat from beneath him, pummelling its crown back into shape.

'These don't grow on trees, you know, or perhaps you London boys don't know what grows on trees?'

'I admit, I am fairly ignorant about country ways, but I'd be delighted to have you teach me. I have to run now though, but I'll see you again soon,' he said, looking over his shoulder and noticing Benny was ready for them to start loading the timber.

The girl had placed her hat back on the log, so, on impulse, he snatched it and took several steps back.

'You can have your precious hat back, but only if you tell me your name!' he called.

To his alarm, he saw she had picked up her axe and was moving towards him. He continued to back away, still clutching the hat.

'Don't kill him, Alice,' one of the girls called out in jest, 'you'll only blunt your axe!'

His curiosity satisfied, Mitch flicked the hat in her direction and ran over to the lorry to assist Benny in loading the felled timber. When they had loaded up the lorry and secured the timber as well as they could, they hopped into the truck and Mitch started up the noisy engine. With a loud grinding of the reluctant gears, they started off down the gravel lane again. All the girls, with the exception of Alice, returned Mitch's friendly wave.

The following Friday afternoon saw Mitch driving up the same gravel lane, but this time in an open-top Vauxhall A-Type. He arrived just as the Land Army girls were packing up for the day. Having driven all the way from Bermondsey, he was relieved he had not missed them. The girls set off on foot down the lane and so he coasted along behind them and sounded his horn.

'Any of you ladies want a lift home?' he shouted cheerily. Five of the girls immediately leaped into the vehicle. Only Alice continued to walk ahead, ignoring him.

'Oh, come on Alice!' he called out.

'Yes, come on, Alice!' the five girls chorused.

Mitch rolled along beside Alice, who continued to ignore him.

'Come *on*, Alice!' her five friends implored.

Alice gave in and climbed into the car.

'Where to?' Mitch asked, gaily, and the girls directed him down the lane for about a mile until they came to a row of agricultural workers' cottages. He pulled up outside and the girls, Alice included, all hopped out, laughing.

'Alice! Alice, don't go, come for a drive with me. I've driven all the way from Bermondsey to see you. Please say you'll come out with me,' he pleaded.

Alice slowed down and let the other girls overtake her, before she turned and came back towards the car. She looked stern and he steeled himself for a refusal.

'I can't stay out late, and you'll have to wait while I have a good wash and change,' she said.

When she emerged, Alice was wearing a dress. She looked beautiful. The girl who followed behind her was pretty too, but her appearance was not perhaps so welcome.

'This is Emma,' Alice explained, 'she's my chaperone.'

'Chaperone?' Mitch was taken aback.

'My escort. I don't go out alone with strange men. If you want to take me out, you have to take Emma too.'

'I'll be as quiet as a mouse,' Emma enthused in her privately-schooled Home Counties accent, 'Look, I've brought a book to read. You won't know I'm here. What a super car you've got. How thrilling! Where are we going?'

Mitch set off for a tour of the Essex countryside, with the girl of his dreams beside him – and her friend in the back seat.

It was dark when they got back to the house. Deciding her chaperoning duties were fully executed, Emma hopped out of the car and ran into the cottage. Mitch turned to Alice and thanked her for the pleasure of her company. He asked if he would be seeing her again.

'Well maybe you will,' she said, 'that is if they don't arrest you for stealing the timber.'

Mitch assumed a look of shocked innocence.

'I suppose you're going to tell me you didn't know you were stealing it?'

Mitch vehemently denied the offence. He had simply been paid to drive the lorry, he insisted, and he had never met that chap Benny before that day. He added that work was hard to come by since his return from the war, as his job at Smithfield had been taken by a war widow.

'So you don't have a proper job, then?' she looked unimpressed.

He told her that, since his return from France, he had had some success finding casual work, doing a bit of driving here, a bit of book keeping there, and so on, but that he hoped to find a permanent job sooner or later. He assured her he was a hard worker and was trusted by his temporary employers, so much so that they had allowed him to borrow their motor for the day. He hoped she would not query his definition of the word 'borrowed'. Some might have said 'stolen'. If pressed of course, he would concede 'taken without permission', since he would be returning it later. He could hardly be seen driving such an expensive car around Bermondsey. It would attract too much attention. He quickly drew the conversation around to the timber again.

Alice told him he was lucky, as her 'Super' had not got a good look at Mitch, though he was sure he would know Benny again if he ever saw him. The supervisor hadn't even had the wit to note the number of the lorry it seemed, so luck was on their side. Alice, on the other hand, might be just twenty-one, she said, but she was nobody's fool.

She had left her East Anglian village five years earlier, to go into service in London, and she had regularly experienced men lying to her and trying to take advantage. She had hated London and had missed the country life. When the WLA had been recruiting, she had naturally seen it as a chance to get back into the country again. Despite the hard work, and the false assumption by some farmers and farm hands that the WLA were easy prey for men's baser attentions, she did enjoy the life.

Mitch told her he had been born in Dublin but had moved to Bermondsey and had joined the army at seventeen, serving in India. He told her all about the thieving Pukhtoons; about the hot Indian nights made fragrant with jasmine; about the hot spicy food he loved so much and about the Taj Mahal, and how the splendour and timelessness of India had made him feel so insignificant. He watched her eyes widen at the breadth of his experience and the magic of his description.

She told him she was a carpenter's daughter, and that she too came from a large family, so she had to make her own way in the world. Her mother had died a few years ago, and she had lost two of her brothers in the war. Mitch told her how his little brother had died in infancy; how he had lost his two best friends, one to fever and the other to the love of a pretty Anglo-Indian girl, and he told her of the others in his life whom he had lost; Scouse and Billy, and of course Rose, his first sixteen-year old love, though he didn't go into detail about Rose.

He was just wondering if the moment was right to move in a little and try to kiss her, when, to his surprise, Alice took the initiative and kissed him. He stroked her face and her hair. Both were so soft and so very fragrant. He slipped a protective arm around her and she eased herself into his embrace, her head against his shoulder. He kissed her again and felt her tremble gently. She did not resist when he gently slipped his hand around her waist and drew her closer to him. His hand found its way slowly up towards her breast when suddenly she shot bolt upright and slid away from him.

'Right! We'll have none of that, Mr Mitchell!' she admonished him, as she made to get out of the car.

'Alice, I'm so sorry, please don't go. I don't know what I was thinking of. I couldn't help myself,' he pleaded.

'What sort of girl do you think I am?' she flared, 'I expect the kind of girls you're used to are a bob a time in London, well, I'm not like that. Where I come from a girl expects to be treated with respect!'

'I'm so sorry, Alice,' he tried his best to look and sound contrite, 'I do respect you, and won't try anything like that again, I promise. Please forgive me.'

Alice did forgive him and she did agree to see him again. In fact, they saw a lot of each other over the next few months. Mitch turned up regularly to court her, sometimes in a 'borrowed' car, but on other occasions he would catch the train to Romford and walk or hitch a lift the rest of the way. Some days, they were able to borrow a couple of horses and saddles from the man who owned the estate where Alice worked and Mitch and Alice would ride together.

Horses were now in very short supply throughout England since none of the animals taken to France in wartime had been brought back. He supposed those unfit for farm service had been eaten by the French. The landowner had sent six horses and two sons to France but none had come back. He had kept only two young foals which were now fully grown and he was only too glad to have someone exercise them.

Mitch would try to perform some of his lancer tricks, retrieving his hat from the ground using a pitchfork for a lance. He was now out of practice though and sometimes he would fall off. He would play dead so that Alice would dismount and run to his aid, and as she bent over him, he would steal a kiss – just a kiss, mind.

He was pleased to see that Alice loved horses as much as he did. There were a lot of things he liked about Alice. She was petite and feminine, yet she was also strong and feisty. He liked her independent spirit. She had all the spontaneity and sparkle that he had found so exciting in Rose, his first love, and so much of Rose's generosity of spirit, and yet she had more of an instinct of self preservation. She was not the sort of girl to sacrifice her reputation, as Irene his girlfriend in India had done. Alice had firm and unswerving principles. He knew his parents would approve of Alice. In fact, one of his mother's favourite phrases kept coming to his mind. He felt Georgina would have said of Alice 'she'll be the making of you'.

It was when Mitch and Alice were strolling in the fields late one afternoon, watching the sun set and discussing how wonderful it would be to live in Ireland and keep horses, when it suddenly became clear to Mitch that he wanted to spend the rest of his life with this beautiful, principled, spontaneous girl. In fact, he couldn't think of anything he wanted more. He felt a deep happiness he had not felt since he had left India. He thought he should show Alice how spontaneous he could be too. He asked her to marry him.

Alice glanced up and down the street before closing the bedroom curtains. She loved the fact that the front bedroom of their terraced house had not one but two big sash windows. It was a lovely house and Waldeck Grove was a quiet and respectable road. She liked West Norwood. Her doubts about coming back to live in London had been dispelled quite quickly by West Norwood. It wasn't really London at all, more suburban Surrey. She would have preferred to live right out in the country of course, but then they had to live where the work was. There were fields and farms aplenty not too far away from West Norwood, in any case. She wished her new husband didn't have to go to work in the middle of the night though, but then that was how Smithfield Market operated.

She was not afraid to spend nights alone, as their neighbours were quiet and respectable too. Her neighbours had nice, respectable jobs – clerical work and civil service, that type of thing. Most of them worked up in the city. None of them worked unsociable hours as Mitch did. Of course he was just a storekeeper at the meat market, so he had to work when others slept in order to earn the sort of money they did, so that he could afford to rent the sort of house they had. The neighbours were good people though, so they didn't look down their noses at a storekeeper and his wife.

She climbed into bed with a sigh. It was lonely having to go to bed on her own, but she liked it when Mitch came home in the afternoons and went to sleep. Sometimes she would join him in bed for a little while and he would make it up to her for not always being there to cuddle her at night. The neighbours understood the reasons why their curtains were drawn in the afternoons, well, one of the reasons, at least.

Alice was proud that Mitch had a good, steady job which paid well. Well, mostly it did, but it seemed his pay depended upon the profits the market traders made and these sometimes fluctuated. Sometimes, Mitch explained, he had to wait for his money but at other times they would pay him a good bonus. Sometimes he brought home chops or sausages for their tea, sometimes steaks.

She made a mental note to ask him if he could get some liver and kidneys. She had heard offal was good when you had a baby growing inside you. She would soon tell him about the baby, now that she was sure. She thought of the nice things she would buy for their first child, and how she would get Mitch to decorate their little back bedroom. These happy thoughts soon had her deep in sleep.

She awoke with a start. She had no idea what had caused her to wake and nor did she know what time it was, but it was very dark, so it must be the middle of the night and she had heard something. There it was again, a faint creaking sound. There was someone in the house! She sat bolt upright, alarmed now. There was another creak, louder now. It was on the landing outside the bedroom door. Someone was outside the bedroom door! She had feared this might happen, that they might have burglars when Mitch was out at work.

She slipped quietly out of bed, pulled on her dressing gown and flattened herself as best she could against the wall by the bedroom door. If the thief came in he might not notice her behind the door. She glanced around in case there was something to hand which she might use to defend herself if he did see her.

She now heard someone say 'shhh' outside on the landing. That was odd. Why would a burglar say 'shhh'? There must be two burglars! She was fearful now, not just for herself but also for her unborn baby. A footfall on the landing caused that loose floorboard to flex, which in turn caused the bedroom door to click open. How many times had she asked Mitch to nail down that floorboard? She held her breath. She sensed the burglars were holding theirs too. Soon the creaking resumed however.

She risked taking a peep through the open door out onto the landing. The moonlight pouring in from the small skylight above the landing revealed the indistinct figures of two men. Her heart pounded wildly. She hoped they would not hear it. One of the men had a ladder and was positioning it beneath the trapdoor which led to the roof space. She wondered what on earth they could want up there. There was nothing up there but the water tank and some dusty old items of furniture left by previous tenants. Of course the burglars would not know that. Perhaps, having found nothing of value downstairs, they had thought there might be treasure hidden up in the loft.

It occurred to her that, when they found nothing of value, they might come into the bedroom. She decided that, if both men went up the ladder, she would make a run for it downstairs and out of the house. As one of the men reached the top of the ladder, he turned around, bracing his back against the ladder, to push open the trapdoor. She now saw his face in the moonlight. It was Mitch! What on earth was doing? He had frightened the life out of her. Why wasn't he at work? Why was he creeping around in his own house? She would ask him, but not yet. She had no idea who the other man was, and she was in her dressing gown, after all. She would watch them for a bit and find out from Mitch later, when the stranger had gone, what it was they had been up to.

Mitch and the stranger were up in the loft for a good ten or fifteen minutes. Though they were clearly trying their best to be quiet, the floor boards up there creaked worse than did those on the landing. Soon she heard them coming down again. She slipped back into bed. A little while later, she heard the stairs creaking and the front door closing. She rose again, went over to the window and looked out. Both Mitch and the stranger were walking off up the road. They were each carrying something, several overcoats perhaps. How very odd. Despite the disturbance she managed to go back to sleep.

When Alice awoke later that morning, she arose and checked the rest of the house. Mitch had not yet returned. Still in her nightwear, she determined to solve the mystery of Mitch's nocturnal visitor. She slipped barefoot out through the back door and retrieved the ladder from where it hung on hooks on the outside wall and she manoeuvred it up the stairs. Only once before had she seen inside the loft space, and that had been just briefly on the day they had moved in, some six months earlier. She climbed the ladder carefully, as she knew a fall would be bad for the baby. She raised the trapdoor. Poking her head gingerly into the loft, as she would have died of fright had she met a spider, she saw the loft too had a tiny skylight.

Hauling herself up into the loft, she glanced around. She could see nothing amiss. She pulled open one of the drawers of an old chest. The drawer front was loose and it came away in her hand. The drawers were empty. She then turned her attention to an old single wardrobe tucked away over against the party wall. She opened the door slowly, in case this was where the spiders lurked. There were clothes hanging in the wardrobe. In the limited light, they seemed to be coats. She reached out and touched one. It was a fur coat. Astonished, she pulled it out. It wasn't dusty like the wardrobe, but felt new and very, very luxurious.

She had to try on the fur, naturally. She had never in her life tried on a fur coat. Clearly designed for a taller woman, it came down to her ankles but it looked and felt really good quality. But what was it doing here? Had Mitch bought it as a gift for her? Surely not. He did not earn *this* much money. If he had, she would certainly have him return it, as they had better things to spend their money on than fur

196

coats. But, oh my, it did feel luxurious. She looked into the wardrobe again and now saw there were about a dozen such coats hanging there. What in God's name was this all about?

Searching further, she found a large, wooden cigar box pushed right to the back on the wardrobe's upper shelf. Had Mitch bought himself cigars? But he did not smoke – something to do with snipers and the trenches, she recalled. A friend of his had been killed lighting a cigarette. It was something to do with superstition about a third man lighting his cigarette from the same match, and it taking just the right amount of time for a German sniper to take aim and fire at him. So, why the cigars, she wondered? She opened the box. To her horror, she saw that it held not cigars but an evil looking black pistol and some bullets. She quickly replaced the box and the coat back in the wardrobe, before hurrying down the ladder and securing the trapdoor behind her.

Mitch had never hit Alice before. He had not hit her hard, just a bit of a slap really, but he regretted it the moment he had done it. If he had ever regretted anything he had done in his life, and if there ever was anything he wished he could take back, this was it. Alice had been unusually quiet when he had come home and she had let him get some sleep before confronting him with the issue of the furs and the gun. They had had the most almighty row, naturally.

She had accused him of being a petty thief and he had accused her of being naïve if she really thought a storekeeper's wage would pay the rent on *this* sort of house in *this* sort of neighbourhood. No, he had not set out to deceive her; he simply had not wanted her to be a party to his criminal activities. He had wanted to *protect* her.

Protect her? She had laughed in his face. He had also wanted to give her everything he could, everything she deserved out of life, but there was no way, as an ex-soldier, with no trade to his name, he could do so without resorting to dishonesty. Ex-soldiers were ten a penny. *She* might be content to scrape by, but he wasn't. He had wanted better – for her and for himself.

She had wept, she had shouted. He had told her not to shout in case the neighbours heard. She had said it didn't matter, as they wouldn't be her neighbours for much longer, for she would be leaving him. She would not live with a petty criminal, a common thief, a thieving, deceitful, lying bastard. That was when he had slapped her.

197

He had wept too. He had fallen to his knees immediately and begged her forgiveness. He had pleaded with her not to leave him. He would kill himself if she left him. He loved her more than life itself. She was the only thing that had meant anything to him in his miserable life. He would never, ever raise a hand to her again. He would cut off his own hand first. To prove he meant it, he had taken up the bread knife from the table and had slashed his arm.

That was when she had told him about the baby and they had both wept together. He had not left the house that night. The pretence was over. His lies were exposed. There was no job at Smithfield and never had been, at least not since before the war. He had been frightened she would not marry him if she knew he had no job. The furs were stolen of course, and they had not been the only stolen goods to have been stored in the attic.

The Luger had been a souvenir he had brought back from the war. No, he had never even fired it. He had never killed anyone. The gun was just a 'persuader' which he took with him when he broke into warehouses in the early hours of the morning, a precaution in case he got caught. Everything he had done, he had done for love, he said. He adored her. He needed her to forgive him. He would stop thieving, he promised. He would do *anything* she asked of him, if only she did not leave him. She bandaged his arm. Then she forgave him.

Mitch had been sincere in promising to find an honest job, but he could not find work where there was none. As things turned out, it was Alice who found a job. She had made friends with a lovely couple who lived in their neighbourhood, a Danish couple, the Pedersons. Alfred Pederson had found her a job at the dairy farm where he worked. Alice had skills even if Mitch had not. She could milk a cow. It did not bring in much money, but it would do for now. Obviously, she would only be able to work at the dairy for seven or eight months or so, and in the meantime, Mitch walked the streets of London looking for a job. Although Londoners were trying to put the war behind them, the new decade which had just begun did not give cause for optimism.

The nation's economy, and indeed the wider global economy, had not recovered as everyone had hoped. The London to which the men who had fought the Great War had returned was not the London they had left. There were few jobs for the able-bodied, a great many of whom tramped the streets with diminishing optimism. The city's streets were also filled with the mutilated men of war, many of whom were now reduced to begging. It seemed to Mitch that the only people who seemed to enjoy any affluence at all were those engaged in crime and profiteering. Mitch became daily more and more despondent. The winter was here now, and their baby would be born in the spring.

Alice came home one day, tired out from her work, but with a possible solution.

'How do you fancy becoming a policeman?' she asked.

Dismissing a distant, disturbing memory of a long ago Dublin police sergeant and his own distressed mother, Mitch took the leaflet Alice had brought home. He read aloud the salient points:

'*Do you want a Job?* – yes, I bloody well do! *Pay: ten bob a day, twelve bob for married men; allowances: one and a tanner a week; quarters: paid for; free uniform; a month's leave for every twelve month's service,* blah, blah, ... *pension better than in any other police force...* blah, blah...*promotion, compensation* ... where is it?'

'It's in Ireland, Mitch. *Ireland.* It's with the Royal Irish Constabulary. It says if you don't like the job, you can leave after giving a month's notice. If you did like it though, maybe I could come out too and we could live there. I've never been to Ireland, Mitch. Housing is cheaper over there, and maybe we could have horses one day. Mitch, what do you think?'

'I think you're going to love it in Ireland, Alice.'

Chapter 12 - **The Wicklow Warriors**

The drive from the camp at Gormanstown down to Dublin gave the dozen temporary constables in the back of the personnel carrier a chance to get acquainted. Although they had all been undergoing the same two weeks of induction at the Royal Irish Constabulary's training camp, the instruction had been so intensive that most of the RIC's new recruits had not had a chance to socialise.

Mitch knew only one of them slightly. George White, Blanco to his mates, had arrived at the Gormanstown camp on the same day as Mitch. Blanco had been a professional soldier before the war and had been made up to corporal whilst in France. Despite Mitch's extreme distrust of NCOs, he thought Blanco seemed decent enough. The twelve men had been advised that six of them would be posted to the Dame Street barracks in Dublin but the other half dozen, Mitch and Blanco included, would be posted to a place called Dunlavin in County Wicklow.

As the wintery countryside of County Meath gave way to the smoky outskirts of Dublin, Mitch speculated on what might be expected of them once there, for no-one had really spelled out the precise nature of their duties as yet. As part of their training, the new temporary constables had been read the text of a newspaper cutting from Freeman's journal. The trainers explained it was a report of a speech made by RIC Divisional Commissioner for Munster, Lieutenant Colonel Smyth. It was the nearest thing to clarification of their rôle which the recruits had so far received. Mitch could recall a particular line of that speech:

'The more you shoot, the better I will like you, and I assure you no policeman will get into trouble for shooting any man ...'

All the recruits had been surprised at the liberty these words appeared to give them. Their trainers told them Lieutenant Colonel Smythe had been assassinated for his words just a week after they had been reported in the press. His murder by Republican gunmen had caused ripples of anger not only around Gormanstown camp but around every RIC barracks, the trainers said.

The job of the new recruits, they gathered, was to bolster the ranks of the RIC and to support the regular constables in the execution of their normal police duties. That said, it wasn't even clear to the recruits what constituted normal police duties, for these were not normal times and a great number of policemen had already been killed carrying out those duties.

Lieutenant Colonel Smythe's own brother had also served in the constabulary. It seemed he had been some sort of intelligence officer, working at Dublin castle, when he too had been assassinated by the IRA. This had happened whilst Mitch and his fellow recruits were at the camp, and they had read all about it in the press. It occurred to Mitch that, if the IRA could get to the men at the top, then the constables on the ground would be highly vulnerable. He understood now why the temporary constables' pay was so generous.

The training had been largely in self-defence tactics, how to avoid being surprised in an ambush, how to subdue and disarm a suspect, and so on. Mitch had already learned such techniques in the army in India, of course, since the Pukhtoons were inclined to jump a man from behind too. Mitch had learned a very good technique to use if someone should attempt to grab him from behind. This involved delivering a sudden sharp elbow backwards into their stomach whilst simultaneously scraping the heel of his boot down their shin and stamping down hard on the top of their foot. The pain this would cause would make the assailant leap back and relinquish his grip immediately. Mitch had only tried this out in training, but he knew it would work, for the soldier who had executed these moves on Mitch had left him winded, helpless and in agony.

Not much time had been devoted to learning about legislation however. They had not been instructed in how to make an arrest nor had they even been advised what constituted an offence under the law. In fact, they had been told they need not concern themselves with the letter of the law, since most of Ireland was now under martial law anyway. Should they identify someone they believed ought to be arrested, they were to summon the military and the military would carry out the arrest. Conversely however, the constables were allowed to shoot and kill any suspicious looking locals on sight. This seemed illogical to the new recruits.

It had been emphasised to the new boys that the situation in Ireland was war. The new temporary constables, all of them ex-combatants, could relate to war. The trainers had warned though that the current state of Ireland was not the kind of war situation to which they were accustomed. The enemy did not wear uniforms and nor did they fight from behind lines of barbed wire or from battleships, but were in fact civilians walking the streets. They walked amongst, and were indistinguishable from, the regular law-abiding citizens.

The enemy in this particular war was known as the Irish Republican Army. The IRA was not a regular army but comprised a series of loose bands of irregular combatants. According to the trainers, they would be ready to attack the moment a constable's back was turned and indeed were prepared to kill in the most cowardly and brutal way. The recruits had been warned that the most innocuous looking group of civilians might suddenly produce weapons and turn on soldiers or police, killing them in cold blood. It was necessary to remain vigilant at all times. Any broken-down vehicle or upturned cart by the roadside might be an ambush. Weapons and messages were carried around by the most innocent-looking of women and children. Therefore the constables must not turn their backs on someone they had just searched, lest he suddenly procure a weapon from a passing child.

Not for the first time in his life had Mitch bitten his tongue when an officer had offered to 'put him in the picture about the Irish'. The training officer had given Mitch and his fellow recruits the benefit of his views on the ingratitude and treachery of the Irish, whom he considered to be a sub-human species. Mitch thought that perhaps the officer had not detected the lingering remnants of his Dublin accent, or then again perhaps he had, and maybe that was the reason for the lecture seemingly being delivered in Mitch's direction. The trainer may have found the direct gaze and unswerving attention of this particular pupil gratifying, not realising that Mitch had been wondering just how much resistance a bayonet would encounter from such a thick skull.

'Ah well,' Mitch had consoled himself, 'it's not the whole Irish race that's the enemy, and if he can't see that, then he won't see the enemy coming.'

The trainee constables had already been on several raids out of Gormanstown. The raids had been led by newly recruited police officers, known as temporary cadets or auxiliaries. The raids had involved roaring into villages and, taking advantage of the element of surprise which the motorised tenders afforded them, raiding houses to look for suspects, arms or any other evidence of the inhabitants' involvement in subversive activity. The outcome of the raids had not lived up to the raiders' anticipation however, as little had been found apart from frightened villagers and the odd illicit *poitín* still, the product of which the auxiliaries had naturally confiscated and consumed. Mitch had been surprised to see that there was as much poverty in the villages as there had been in Dublin. Somehow he had expected country people to be eating better fare for their supper than gruel.

He wasn't sure he liked the tactics employed by the auxiliaries, such as hammering on doors and yelling out: 'it's the military', when they were in fact just policemen – and policemen without powers of arrest, seemingly. When, as was usually the case, the searches yielded nothing, some of the auxiliaries found it difficult to suppress the steam they had worked up and would resort to beating up any hapless man or boy who didn't give his name or get out of their way quickly enough.

One of the auxiliaries with them had lost control and had given an old man an unnecessarily savage beating, whilst the recruits had looked on uneasily. It was the old man's failure to answer the questions put to him which had been the cause of the officer's ire. The man's equally elderly wife had made feeble attempts to beat off her husband's uniformed attacker with her walking stick.

'Let him alone!' the old lady had protested, 'Sure he's deaf and cannot hear you. Let him *alone* will you, you bloody black crows!'

The old lady too was knocked to the ground. Her protests still rang in Mitch's ears – bloody black crows indeed. The constables' dark-coloured uniforms and the swooping nature of their raids were highly intimidating. Equally intimidating were the auxiliaries' military-style berets and other non-regulation embellishments which made them look like a rabble of gun fighters of the Wild West. The auxiliaries in question had even taken to calling themselves 'the Gormanstown Raiders'. The incident with the old couple had brought it home to Mitch just how bad were relations between police and people. He hoped this would not be the sort of work he would be expected to do at Dunlavin. He felt he would rather be facing German artillery than terrorising elderly villagers.

Mitch's thoughts were interrupted as their driver now announced he would be driving them around the streets of Dublin to give those men who were to be stationed there an idea of the layout of the city centre and the location of the Republican areas. They entered the city and drove east along the quays, crossing the Liffey via Carlisle Bridge before heading up Sackville Street. The driver pointed out the sights, including the famous Guinness Brewery. Blanco commented that the blackness of the Liffey water must be the cause of the Guinness being so black.

Another of the recruits, a clean-shaven young Scot with a sailors' kitbag wedged between his knees, commented that the Liffey also had a top crust of tan coloured foam, just like the beer did. Was that the reason, he asked, why a pint of Guiness was referred to as a pint of *Black and Tan*? Mitch informed him that in fact a *Black and Tan* was a mixture of stout and pale ale. He asked the Scot if he was aware that the Irish also referred to temporary RIC constables like themselves as the *Black and Tans.* He explained that the odd mix of dark-coloured police jackets and khaki army trousers, which had been issued to their hastily assembled ranks, was the reason for this. The Scot hadn't heard this, and nor had he heard of the black and tan coloured hunting hounds of Limerick which Mitch advised him bore the same descriptive name. He had never been to Ireland before, he said.

As they reached the Liffey's north bank, the driver indicated a large bullet hole just above the breast of one of the bronze angels at the foot of the O'Connell monument. To the amusement of the recruits, he explained that a bored British soldier, anxious for some action during the standoff outside the General Post Office five years earlier, had 'tried to shoot the tits off' the bare-breasted female. They all laughed, though Mitch thought it a shame to have despoiled such a beautiful monument. He suspected any Fenian who dared show similar disrespect for a London monument would probably be hanged.

The grander buildings and smart shop fronts of Sackville Street presented an elegant vista. Mitch recalled walking down Sackville Street with Rose, gazing at the ornate hats in the windows. The vehicle now turned sharply westwards again. Now, Mitch found himself gazing out at streets which were far less attractive but even more familiar. What the driver now described to them as a 'hotbed of Republican activity' was of course Mitchell's former home turf. Lower Gloucester Street was little changed, apart from the barbed wire barricades at each end. The driver slowed down to have a look at some police activity which was going on – a search of one of the houses apparently. Mitch thought the auxiliaries involved seemed to be using their rifle butts rather liberally on both doors and occupants.

He now glanced down the length of Lower Gardiner Street towards his boyhood home, and saw, if not familiar faces, certainly familiar types. He suddenly felt uncomfortable, for it occurred to him that he would be ashamed were a former neighbour to spot him riding in the back of a police vehicle and indeed wearing the uniform of the *Tans*. He pulled the peaked cap lower down on his forehead but then he realised it was unlikely anyone would know him, so long had he been away. He supposed his appearance was now much altered anyway.

He wondered if he ought to feel some affection for the place. Somehow he did not. He felt only the loosest connection; nothing remotely resembling nostalgia. It was as if his childhood had happened to someone else. He had come from here, yet he had never belonged here, no more than he had belonged in Bermondsey. He noticed there were still barefoot children running around and prostitutes still paraded the streets of Monto.

The Scot called out some obscenity to some of the girls. Mitch didn't understand what he had shouted, and he guessed the girls would not either. For a second or two Mitch found himself scanning the girls' faces, looking for a familiar pale beauty with long auburn curls and a laugh like a trickling stream. He could not recall Rose's face to mind however. It was Alice's face which had supplanted Rose's in his memory. He dismissed the painful remembrance of Rose.

'Another time, another life – a boy, not me,' he thought.

The wheels of the Crossley tender now bumped him back to the present, as they bounced over a temporary security ramp and headed back across the Liffey, passing through Temple Bar until they reached Dame Street. Here, prominent atop the hill, stood Dublin Castle, the unmistakable symbol of seven centuries of British rule in Ireland. The tender drove slowly past the guards and into the castle precincts, coming to a halt in the lower yard where the twelve recruits now alighted.

The six constables who had been allocated to the Dame Street barracks were taken into the government buildings by a sentry. The driver was told to await the sentry's return as there would be some mail to take for the Head Constable at Wicklow. The driver and the remaining six men, Mitch included, were left to kick their heels outside for a while. They smoked as they got acquainted and stamped their feet in an effort to stave off the January chill.

Suddenly, two police vehicles roared into the yard and braked violently to a halt alongside them. Mitch admired the smart lines of the new Lancia vehicles with their anti-grenade netting on top. He wondered if the barracks at Dunlavin would have Lancias. Perhaps he might get to drive one. A number of armed men now leapt from the vehicles. They all wore the distinctive military-style berets of the auxiliaries rather than the standard police cap issued to the temporary constables.

Mitch's knowledge of the auxiliaries was not just confined to having accompanied them on raids. Their exploits were featured in the press almost daily now. Recruited from war veterans, just as the temporary constables were, the auxiliaries were however drawn from the officer class. As Mitch understood it, the original intention had been for the auxiliaries to provide leadership and supervision to Temporary Constables like himself. At least that had been the theory behind it. In practice however, they had become a separate strike force, capable of exercising particular brutality, but perhaps without the constraints of conscience and empathy which held many of the regular and temporary constables in check. Mitch thought it was probably an issue of class; a feeling of superiority, which enabled these former officers to operate with such indifference towards the Irish working class and peasantry.

The press reporting on the auxiliaries' almost daily outrages had reinforced Mitch's view of a certain type of officer and the contempt which that type held for the Irish. Despite these differences in both social class and uniform, all these imported police, whether auxiliary or constable, were all deemed by the Irish to be *Black and Tans*.

The Scot now remarked that the bandoliers of ammunition with which the temporary cadet-auxiliaries were festooned, and the side arms which they wore strapped ludicrously and impractically low on the thigh, gave them the look of Mexican bandits. He asked if anyone knew what was denoted by the 'TC' badges which the auxiliaries wore. Before Mitch could volunteer the information, the driver beat him to it with his own interpretation:

'Them Cunts!'

The constables sniggered. Mitch wondered whether the auxiliaries had heard them.

The recruits watched with idle curiosity as the auxiliaries now dragged two harassed looking, suited civilians from the back of the vehicles and manhandled them towards the ramped incline in front of the castle entrance. As they passed close to Mitch, one of the prisoners stumbled and almost fell. His captor manhandled him roughly to his feet, causing the man's hat and spectacles to fall to the ground.

Another of the auxiliaries, a tall, well-built man with a square jaw, stepped forward, crushing the spectacles beneath his foot, and drew his pistol from the holster strapped to his thigh. At the sight of the weapon, Mitch and his fellow constables stepped smartly aside. With sudden and unexpected ferocity, the square-jawed auxiliary smashed his pistol into the prisoner's face. There was the unmistakable, dull crunch of splintering bone and an arc of blood turned to steam in the cold air. The prisoner slumped into unconsciousness and was dragged off, the toes of his polished boots leaving tracks in the dust.

The sudden viciousness of the assault shocked even the battle-hardened onlookers. To Mitch, the civilian had the look of a harmless clerk. Mitch was reminded of the *conchie* he had seen being beaten and robbed of his dignity at Abancourt Military prison. He decided the driver's name for the auxiliaries was wholly appropriate. Stepping forward to retrieve the man's hat and shattered spectacles, Mitch held them out in a vague gesture in the direction in which the auxiliaries and their prisoners had gone. The group had now disappeared into the building however.

He examined the hat and saw it was a fairly smart one, a brown felt slouch-type hat. It was a good quality, stylish hat. He recognised the label inside from his Bermondsey days. *Christy's* exported hats around the empire. Harry Bailey used to wear *Christy's* hats, though of course Harry never paid for his. A *titfer* Harry would have called it, as in 'tit fer tat' – hat. Smacking the dust off the hat, Mitch placed it and the broken spectacles on the low ramp wall in front of him, thinking their owner might retrieve them when he left.

'No point leaving those there,' said the driver, 'that poor bastard won't be coming back for them.'

Before Mitch could enquire why that might be, the sentry appeared with the mail bag and some canteen rations for the constables to eat on their journey to Dunlavin. The driver signalled to the six recruits to board the Crossley once more. On sudden impulse, Mitch retrieved the slouch hat and folded it away into his pocket.

Inside the dungeon-like 'intelligence room' beneath the castle's administration building, the tall, square-jawed auxiliary removes his great coat and hangs it behind the door. Two of his men force the prisoners onto wooden chairs and bind their hands and feet. Another auxiliary now enters the cell. Wearing police badges on his Connaught Rangers officer's uniform, he is small of stature and has a very pronounced limp. The interrogation commences. Square-Jaw begins firing questions at the civilians. He wants to know details of their operations and who else was involved. The prisoners protest their innocence. Small-Man begins to scream at them, his voice reaching a shrill crescendo. Spittle flies from his curled lips. He slaps the prisoners about the face. He whips them with his riding crop and he kicks their shins with his small, shiny-booted foot. He then draws his revolver, spins the barrel and places it against the head of one of the prisoners. The prisoner begins to shake as he feels the cold steel against his temple and hears the chamber revolve. The dull click of the firing pin against an empty chamber brings the prisoner a brief second of relief. 'Cunt!' he curses Small-Man. Small-Man discharges the revolver once more, this time against the prisoner's leg. A sharp puff of smoke arises from the prisoner's singed trousers as the bullet enters his thigh. He screams, shudders for a moment or two then lapses into unconsciousness.

Small-Man turns to the second prisoner now and positions the revolver against his temple. Demanding answers but receiving none, Small-Man again pulls the trigger. The prisoner screams out in anticipation of death. No bullet comes however. Tired of watching the game, Square-Jaw now steps forward and produces a brass knuckle duster which he eases onto his hand. He begins to beat the prisoner about the face until he feels the man's jaw dislocate. Breathing heavily now, Square-Jaw buries his fist in the man's stomach and steps quickly aside to avoid the explosion of blood and vomit which experience has taught him will follow.

The first prisoner has revived slightly and is now groaning in agony. He invokes the intercession of the Blessed Virgin Mary: 'Jesus, Mary, Mother, help'.

Square-Jaw now turns his attention to him and repeats his well choreographed sequence of jaw breaking and abdomen crunching. He deals the prisoner one final, backhanded blow and the man's head flops backwards as his neck breaks with a sickeningly loud crack. The second prisoner now soils himself as the two interrogators turn their combined attentions towards him.

The tranquil scenery on the drive out of Dublin had been most pleasing, with the blue beauty of the Wicklow Hills trailing them along the way. Mitch was relieved to be free of the ghosts of his past which he felt still stalked the city. Now the daylight was fading as the Crossley pulled up outside the police barracks at Dunlavin. The recruits could see Dunlavin was a rather smart market town, nestling comfortably in the foothills of West Wicklow. The main streets were very wide and led to a main square, with an imposing church. There was a railway station, several grocers' shops and a post office. More importantly, there were several bars; enough Mitch thought to provide distraction for him and his fellow constables.

Some of the men expressed their displeasure at finding themselves posted out in the sticks. They would have preferred the city. They could not imagine there would be much action in a place like Dunlavin. Mitch didn't care particularly. It was all the same to him. There was nothing to bind him to Dublin these days and France had provided him with enough action anyway, albeit somewhat late on in the war. So what if this was a quiet place? His pay was generous, regardless of whether he had to shoot anyone or not. Why would he mind where he was posted? He noticed that the building immediately to the left of the barracks was a pub, *The Railway Hotel*. Convenient, he thought.

Mitch and Blanco were first out of the tender. They and the four other recruits filed into the police barracks. It was a two storey building in the middle of a terrace. With its grey slate roof and regular sash windows, it looked as though it had once been a private house. Mitch now remembered another snippet of the late Lieutenant Colonel Smyth's speech; something about, if there were no police barracks, or if the barracks were destroyed, they should commandeer any suitable house, throwing the occupants out onto the street to die, if necessary. He had assumed that was just posturing on Smythe's part. Now however, he wondered if the Dunlavin barracks had once been someone's home.

Inside, they were met by one of the regular constables, a man who clearly fell below regulation height. Seemingly startled at their appearance, the little constable hopped around behind the thick oak counter and into the back office. He returned almost immediately, accompanied by a senior officer, a taller man in his early fifties.

'Good morning men,' the older man greeted the recruits as they all trooped in.

He smiled affably: 'Gather round now, and welcome to Dunlavin Barracks. I am District Inspector Laurence Delaney and this is the orderly of the day, Constable Thomas Cuddy, who will shortly register you all and assign you to your accommodation. We do not have a sergeant attached to the station at present, but Cuddy here has recently passed his sergeant's exam.'

Cuddy reddened slightly at the attention focused on him, but the DI continued:

'Firstly however, a few things you need to know: Dunlavin Barracks is the headquarters for the district. Head Constable Daniel Haughey, who is based here, is the senior officer in this district. He is not here today but you will meet him in due course. The district encompasses six additional stations: Baltinglass, Blessington, Donard, Hollywood, Kiltegan and Stratford. Our County Headquarters is in Wicklow town itself and that is where our county inspector is located. However, you will all be stationed here in Dunlavin. The barracks is where you will work and where you will live. Now, I understand you have all seen active war service, despite which you have volunteered to return to uniform to fight again on another front. Well that is commendable enough, for don't they say that one volunteer is worth twenty laying hens?'

The mixed metaphor made the newcomers smile though they did not know whether or not it was deliberate. The inspector went on;

'Now, whilst we are grateful to have you here, I should point out that your presence here will double our complement. Operationally speaking, that is a good thing of course, but it means accommodation will be tight. All constables will now have to double up, two to a room, whereas formerly each man had his own room. As they say, familiarity breeds distemper, so I would ask you all to bear this in mind and try to get along.'

The men tried to look interested in the DI's words, though most of them were focused on the prospect of washing the road dust from their throats at the public house which was situated so obligingly next door. Delaney continued his speech:

'A further factor is that you men are, I understand, being paid ten shillings or more per day. Our regular constables also receive ten shillings, not for a *day's* work however, but for a *week's* work. So, whilst I hope this will not lead to any resentment on *their* part, I would urge you to be discreet and not flaunt your comparative wealth in their faces. We also enjoy good relations with the local people of the district and although we had a bit of trouble here last year, things have quietened down over the past few months, so please do not upset the apple pie.'

Delaney rubbed his hands together and continued;

'Now then, my personal philosophy is, if a thing is worth doing it is worth delegating, so I will now hand you over to Cuddy, who will take down your perpendiculars, and then, once we have you settled in, we'll all get a cup of tea.'

Delaney nodded to Cuddy, who blushed again and started to write the date in his large register. He beckoned Mitch forward:

'Name, date and place of burt, please.'

'William Mitchell, thirty-first of December, 1887, er ... in Donneybrook, Dublin,' Mitch volunteered.

He had decided against giving his true district of birth, since he was not exactly proud of it. The city was only thirty miles or so distant and people here would have heard of Dublin's poorest and most shameful district. Donneybrook was one of its slightly more rural suburbs, with a better reputation than that of Monto.

'Tuesdah,' declared Constable Cuddy. He had a west of Ireland accent which was slightly unfamiliar to Mitch's ear.

'What?' asked Mitch, puzzled.

'The turty-furst of December 1887, 'twas a Tuesdah,' the orderly said confidently, 'you were borrun on a Tuesdah – Tuesdah's chile is full of grace.'

'Was I?' asked Mitch, 'I wouldn't know what day of the week it was – I wuz very young at the time.'

Inspector Delaney cut in: 'Oh, it would be. Cuddy is very good at working out that type of thing in his head. It's a rare sort of a gift he has. You can tell him any date and he'll tell you what day of the week it was. He has an extraordinary memory for dates and details.'

'I suppose you could tell me what won the Grand National that year too?' Mitch jested.

Cuddy scratched his head briefly, before replying: '*Gamecock*, 'twas.'

They did not know if this was accurate, but the recruits were suitably impressed at Cuddy's apparent power of recall.

'Very good, Cuddy, but not now, there's a good man,' the Inspector cut in, 'you have to process them all and allocate the rooms. Then there are the new items of uniforms to dispense, so you'll need to hurry up, Cuddy.'

'Hurry up, Cuddy!' Cuddy repeated, blushing again, and he set about recording Blanco's details in the register. He next advised them which room they would be allocated. Mitch was to share a ground floor room with Blanco. The two men passed along the counter to another of the regular constables, who checked their sizes and handed them the long overdue dark-coloured trousers to match their jackets and caps. They went to inspect their new quarters whilst Cuddy processed the rest of the new men.

Mitch and Blanco's room was very basic, with cream-painted walls, a small fireplace and two iron cots with thin mattresses, upon which fresh bedding and towels were neatly piled. They donned their new uniform items. They were now fully uniformed as RIC constables, in fully matching jackets and trousers, of the same type as those worn by the regular constables. Mitch hoped this would help them integrate better with the regular men.

'The Irish'll have to stop calling us the *Black and Tans* now,' Blanco mused.

'I'm sure we'll be called a lot worse when they get to know us,' Mitch laughed.

Mitch and Blanco headed back along the corridor to the day room, where a cluster of impatient constables waited for Cuddy to serve up the tea.

'Hurry up, Cuddy!' the regulars demanded of the flustered Cuddy.

'Ah, hurry up, Cuddy!' Cuddy repeated as he quickly dispensed the welcome mugs of hot, strong tea.

The six recruits and the three regulars who were on duty began to get acquainted. The new men were given a tour of the barracks and an introduction to the procedures, rules and routines.

There were rotas for food shopping, meal preparation and cleaning of the barracks, and the newcomer's names were added to these and to the shift rosters. Whoever was the orderly of the day had to man the counter, maintain the daily occurrence book, and make regular pots of tea for the rest of the constables. Cuddy informed them that Larry Delaney liked a biscuit with his tea and that his office was up on the first floor, next to that of the head constable.

Although Constable Cuddy was helpful enough, Mitch detected a degree of stiffness on the part of the other regulars. He sensed they did not entirely welcome the newcomers.

The first week passed uneventfully for the new recruits. The only callers at the barracks seemed to be illiterate locals who wanted a letter or some official document read out to them. Although this was not part of their official duties, it seemed the regular constables were always happy to oblige. Such callers provided the only diversion in the constables' otherwise dull day and also brought in village gossip. Some brought in the odd gift of firewood or a few sods of turf for the barracks and Mitch glimpsed one local producing a small, unlabelled bottle from his pocket which one of the regular constables quickly consigned to his own pocket. Mitch guessed it was probably *Poitín*. The regulars seemed generally content to spend most of their time with their feet up on the desks, reading the sports papers and drinking endless mugs of tea

The regulars managed to upset the young Scotsman at an early stage in their acquaintance by referring to the temporary constables as 'The English'.

'Listen, you fuckers can call me Arthur or you can call me Constable Hardie,' he said, with ill-concealed irritation, 'but fer Chrissake stop calling me English!'

One of the regulars whistled softly at the rebuke, whilst another commented mischievously from behind his paper:

'And you can call me when you have the tea made.'

Hardie was unsure if the comment was intended to imply the temporary constables were not pulling their weight with the housekeeping duties or that they were only fit for domestic work.

'Fuck off!' was the Scot's considered reply.

Mitch had detected some small quirks about Hardie's accent. It was not purely Scottish, but had overtones of something else. When quizzed, Hardie explained he had spent most of his youth in his birthplace of Stirling but had moved to Stockton-on-Tees, on the Yorkshire-Durham border, when his father had found work as a moulder in the iron foundry there. Having started work himself as a boy apprentice in the Stockton shipyards, Arthur Hardie had soaked up mixed elements of the local Yorkshire and Durham accents. To further confuse the issue, he said, he had married a Lancashire lass the previous January and they had been living with her folks in Blackburn, so he thought it surprising that he had anything left of his Scottish accent at all.

Mitch wondered whether, like himself, Hardie had tried to suppress his native accent in order to fit in. He commented that Hardie looked a bit young to be married. Hardie said he was all of twenty-three, and indeed his twenty-fourth birthday was only days away. Mitch said he too had recently married, just a month after Hardie, in fact. In that case, Hardie replied cheekily, Mitch must have been on the shelf to have been getting married at so late an age.

'Perhaps no woman wanted to marry an over-the-hills Englishman with a squint,' he suggested, 'couldn't you have worn an eye-patch or summat?'

'You cheeky bastard!' Mitch laughed, 'I'm only thirty-three, and some of us wuz away fighting a war whilst you wuz at home in short pants – or was it a kilt? And I'm not English, any road. I'm Irish as it happens, despite the London accent. And, what's more, this isn't a squint. I copped a bullet in my eye at The Somme.'

Hardie protested that he too had been to war. He had joined the navy at seventeen, he said, and had seen plenty of action at Jutland.

Mitch began to feel a degree of rapport with Hardie. Perhaps it was because, despite the ten year age gap, the two men had more in common with each other than they did with the other constables. The other four temporary constables, Blanco White, John Linward, Tom Alston and Bill Lindsey, *were* all Englishmen. Mitch felt they didn't share his and Hardie's experience of being from everywhere and yet from nowhere in particular. The young Scot's forthright manner also reminded Mitch of the uncompromising *diggers* and *enzedders* he had met and admired at Abancourt.

'So what should *I* call you,' Mitch asked him, 'do you get called 'Artie' at home?'

'No pal, it's Arthur to you, but you can call me anything, just so long as you're buying the beer!'

Their second week in Dunlavin brought the temporary constables a brief respite from the boredom of hanging around the barracks and trying to avoid upsetting the regulars. Four of them,

Mitch and Hardie included, were assigned to provide an escort for one of the local magistrates who also served as auctioneer at the local cattle market. Mitch guessed that the DI had sensed the antipathy between the temporary men and the regulars, as he had decided it best if the two groups were assigned shifts and tasks as separate entities, rather than working together. Cuddy told them the same arrangement had been introduced at the other barracks in Delaney's district.

Since Cuddy seemed to take no objection to *The Tans,* as the regulars now called their temporary colleagues, he was put on shift with them in order to provide them with local knowledge and to ensure they followed normal police procedures. Procedures were something Cuddy was good at. He could quote the police manual at the drop of a hat. The temporary constables were a little wary of him, until they satisfied themselves he was slightly odd but fairly harmless and was not acting as a spy in the camp for the regulars.

Mitch and his squad were issued with rifles and handguns for the escort duty and had to sign individually for each weapon and for their ammunition, which was carefully counted out. Cuddy was most assiduous in completing the log in this regard. He seemed to take all his duties seriously. Following Cuddy's very precise directions, the four constables took the Crossley and drove over to the magistrate's house at Milltown, about a mile away on the edge of Dunlavin. Cuddy, as barracks orderly, remained behind to hold the fort.

Mr Robert Dixon was awaiting them and was glancing at his gold pocket watch when they turned into his carriage driveway and so they only had time for a fleeting impression of the Dixon residence. From what they saw however it appeared to be a very large and imposing two-storey whitewashed farm house. Beyond it were farm buildings, barns and quite a lot of land. There were only three houses out at Milltown and they all enjoyed lovely views clear across to the hills. Mitch found himself wondering what a house out here would cost, as he could picture himself and Alice riding Irish stallions around these beautiful fields.

The constables accompanied the magistrate to the auctions and had to stand guard all morning, observing from the sidelines and also checking all comers lest they be armed. Delaney had already briefed the men that, all over Ireland, a number of local magistrates had been killed by the Republicans who, understandably, considered them agents of British oppression.

Martial law, which included a system of trial without jury, had recently been introduced in most counties of Ireland in order to protect the administrators of justice and to obviate the intimidation and murder of jurors and trial witnesses. Despite this, the threat to the magistrates had not abated, since there were many friends and families of imprisoned and executed rebels who wanted revenge. Mitch now began to realise how difficult the position of the regular constabulary must be. As Irishmen, they must surely have some sympathy with the Republican cause, and yet it was their sworn duty to uphold the law. Having the world 'Royal' on their police insignia must surely mark them out also as instruments of the British state. They must be as much at risk as the magistrates yet they seemed fairly sanguine about their own safety.

Mitch gained the impression that Delaney was fairly shrewd and knew how to keep his men in check and the locals onside. He regularly visited all the barracks in his district but spent the greater part of his time at Dunlavin, since that was district HQ and was where his boss was based.

Conversely, Delaney's superior, Head Constable Haughey, seemed to concern himself mostly with supervision of the barracks' administration. He rarely left his office and seemed to spend his time checking Cuddy's calculations of the mess bills and provisions bills, signing off the accounts and reading the constables' reports. Although he was the senior officer at Dunlavin, he seemed to be more of a figurehead, and he stood in Delaney's shadow to a great degree.

Cuddy was the man at the lower end of the administration chain, who knew where everything was located in the barracks and who recorded conscientiously every scrap of useful information, both in log books and in his head. With his eye for detail and his curious straightforwardness, Cuddy applied himself unswervingly to his duties. Mitch wouldn't have thought Cuddy's accounting needed such thorough checking as Haughey gave it. Then again, Haughey was typical of the sort of leader whose lack of confidence in his own ability was accompanied by a lack of confidence also in those who served beneath him.

Mitch had met his type in the army. He would bet money on Haughey not appreciating Delaney's worth either. Delaney would have made a better army officer than many he had met, Mitch thought, for Delaney could identify a man's abilities and utilise these effectively, even in the case of a quirky character such as Cuddy.

216

The provisions, for which the temporary constables paid out of their daily allowance, did not include alcoholic beverages. Moreover, consuming alcohol within the barracks was against the rules. Neither Haughey nor Cuddy drank, and nor did they approve of drink, but Delaney was rather more understanding in that regard. When Haughey and Delaney went home at the end of the day, that was when the drinking would begin in earnest in the barracks, for indeed there was only so much tea a man could absorb. Tea would keep one awake, yet the power of beer to induce sleep was universally acknowledged. It seemed the regular constables had spelled out graphically to the teetotal Cuddy what would happen to him if he ever told Haughey about their drinking.

If Haughey were not around when Delaney was ready to leave for the day, the district Inspector would sometimes ask: 'Is that Guinness I smell?' and of course a bottle would be found for him. In Delaney's amusing brand of personal philosophy, it was not laughter which was the best medicine, but porter.

By midday, the Dunlavin auctions were concluded. As the farmers from around the region made noisy arrangements to move out their cattle, Dixon and his police escort made a more discreet withdrawal back to Milltown. En route, Dixon had the men stop at a local baker's shop where Hardie and Blanco stood guard in the shop doorway as the magistrate made his purchases. Hardie grumbled at what appeared to be improper use of a police escort, until Dixon emerged with several boxes of pies and cakes which he gave to the men for their lunch. Blanco raised a finger to his forelock and thanked the magistrate for his thoughtfulness. Hardie however remained unimpressed.

'Did you see the commission fee that *toff* Dixon got?' Hardie asked Mitch, as the six temporary constables sat in the Railway Arms later that evening, 'he had a wad as'd choke a Blackpool donkey?'

'I expect he makes a packet from his farming too,' Mitch said, 'since he's one of those who call themselves *Anglo-Irish*, though there's no Irish blood in them at all. They're English really. They call themselves farmers too, but they don't get their hands stuck in the soil. They hire others to do that for them. It's not muck but money that sticks to their sort.'

'Well, I wish some of it would stick to me.'

'The English gentry own the land and the Irish are allowed to farm it for them,' Mitch continued, 'that's what all this unrest is about. It's not a new thing. It's a war which has been going on one way or another, for seven hundred years now.'

'They did the same thing in Scotland, Mitch. The Scots fought them, and lost. I can't stand Dixon's sort, all privileged and looking down their noses at the rest of us.'

'It was decent enough of him to buy us the pies though, wasn't it?' Blanco said, 'He didn't have to do that.'

'I imagine he could afford it well enough,' Hardie smirked, 'and it was the very least he could do.'

The men at Dunlavin Barracks were not sure when it had happened, but it was Cuddy, with his sharp eye for detail, who noticed one morning that, where formerly a necklace of telephone lines had stretched between the telegraph poles outside the barracks window, there now stretched only an expanse of cloudy sky. He decided the missing wire was sufficient reason to immediately disturb the senior officers. Delaney, Haughey and all the men on duty poured outside to have a look. Someone had indeed cut all the village telephone lines, including those to the police barracks.

As Delaney stood assessing the situation, it occurred to him that whoever had done so must have brought a ladder to climb to the top of the poles, and, if they had a ladder long enough to reach the top of the poles, they could easily have climbed over the back wall of the barracks. He voiced his concerns to Haughey. The Head Constable contemplated this for a few moments then tasked Delaney with an immediate review of barracks security before he headed back inside to bury himself in his paperwork.

Delaney despatched Cuddy down to the hardware store for some bags of mortar, whilst Mitch and Hardie went next door to the Railway Hotel to requisition all their empty bottles. Patrick Lawler, the landlord, guffawed. He said it was the first time in all his born days he'd had a policeman in there demanding *empty* bottles. He wasn't best pleased about this though, as the bottles were worth money to him, but Hardie squared up to him and made it plain it was not a request but an order. Mitch pacified the publican however by reminding him that the safety of his own premises depended to some

218

degree on their reinforcing the security of the adjacent barracks wall, and for that they would need some glass.

Returning to the barracks yard, Mitch and Hardie put the bottles in old flour sacks and, using half bricks, smashed them into jagged pieces. The constables then spent the afternoon concreting the shards of glass all along the top of the back wall. Having worked in construction in Blackburn after leaving the navy, Hardie was able to show his fellow constables how to mix and apply the concrete.

'Good fences make good labour,' Delaney chirped, as he and Haughey watched them work.

'Sir, is this the first bit of trouble you've had around here?' Mitch asked him.

'No, good Lord, no. Last year we had someone try to break into the barracks. We think he was after weapons. He came across the roof from the pub next door and had started taking slates off our roof to get in. Lord knows, he'd have managed it too, but for a passing army patrol that saw him from the road. They fired a few shots off at him and Cuddy thought the barracks was under attack by gunmen, didn't you, Cuddy?'

'Yes, I did so,' Cuddy flushed, as he always did when addressed directly by his superior, 'and when they got him down, sure wasn't it Paddy Lawler's cousin?'

'Well the army took him straight away,' Delaney said, 'it saved you a lot of paperwork, didn't it Cuddy? Also last year the Republicans set fire to Saundersgrove, the Tynte family residence. Luckily the family weren't here but were over in London. No-one was hurt, though a lot of valuable paintings and books were destroyed. That was the same night there were simultaneous attacks on five police barracks around the county.'

'The eighth of May, 'twas,' Cuddy chimed in, with his usual obsession for accuracy, 'and in September someone broke into the Molyneaux house and stole their guns, and then ....'

'All right, well now let's see if you can't talk and work at the same time Cuddy, or you'll still be going at it when the night shift starts. Least said, fences mended, so hurry up now, Cuddy.'

Delaney went off, chuckling at his own little joke.

The discussion about the troubles continued later that night, as the temporary constables sat in *The Railway Hotel*, celebrating

219

Hardie's birthday. They had got the lad playing the upright piano in the corner to play 'Happy Birthday' and Blanco was soon regaling his comrades with some gory gossip he had heard about the kidnapping of a magistrate by the IRA the previous year.

'The kidnappers shot him in the head and took him to the beach where they buried him in the sand up to his neck. They left him there so's he'd drown when the tide came in,' he informed them.

'Jesus, that's a nasty way to go,' Tom Alston shuddered, 'he'd have been watching the tide come in and he would have drowned slowly. What sort of bastards are they?'

'Yeah, but the thing was, when the IRA returned the next morning, he was still alive. They hadn't buried him far enough down the beach, so the tide hadn't reached him. They dug him up and reburied him further down, so he had to wait *another* twelve hours till the tide came in again.'

'Where did you hear that?' Mitch interrupted him, 'That's a load of bollicks! Firstly, if the bullet wound to the head hadn't killed him, he'd have died in the night from exposure. And have you any idea how difficult it would be to dig a hole five feet deep in wet sand, without the sides caving in, *and* to then get a struggling man down into it? How long would that have taken them? Why would they bother? There's more than one way to skin a magistrate, as Delaney might say. Why didn't they just shoot him dead?'

'Well,' Blanco shrugged, 'I'm just sayin'. It's what I heard, that's all.'

'It wouldn't bother me if the IRA skinned *our* local magistrate,' Hardie added, 'toffee-nosed arsehole that he is.'

'Delaney says Dixon's the son of a gentleman, a Dublin aristocrat or some such,' Blanco added, 'and his own son James, who lives at home still, he was an officer in the war, a lieutenant in the Royal Irish Fusiliers. 'Got the military medal *and* the Serbian Cross, he did. The daughter's a good looking piece though.'

'Daughter?' Hardie perked up.

'Yeah, you must have seen her riding her horse into the town, not that she'd give you the time of day. She's in her twenties and she's still living at home as well. 'Waiting for the right man to come along, I suppose, someone as wealthy as the Dixons, and the same class, naturally.'

The men had consumed a fair amount of drink by last orders and there were still a few locals sitting in the pub, nursing their last drinks.

When the publican announced closing time Hardie went over to the bar, slapped his coins down and demanded more drink, but Lawler declined to serve him. Hardie suddenly began to shout and swear at the publican. Mitch and the others were surprised at the quickness of his temper and tried to calm him down. To their alarm, Hardie now produced a handgun and started waving it around. The barmaid screamed. She and Lawler ducked down behind the bar. Mitch tried to take the gun from Hardie but it went off accidentally, raising more screams from the terrified barmaid. Not content with having sneaked a gun out of the strong room, Hardie also had it loaded. Luckily, the discharged bullet buried itself harmlessly in the wooden beam overhead.

'Just who the feck do you think you are?' the landlord fumed.

'Who are *we*?' Hardie asked, still waving the weapon, 'Who are *we*? We're the fuckin' Wicklow Warriors, that's who we are!'

'Well yiz are all barred, so feck off, the lot of yiz!' the landlord shouted – from his refuge beneath the bar.

Mitch and the other constables managed now to wrest the gun from Hardie and ushered him out of the pub. Once the situation was defused, the drunken constables found the image of the angry publican, uttering threats from his hiding place, quite funny. Mitch wondered how Hardie had managed to get hold of the weapon without it being booked out to him, but he wouldn't ask him about this until Hardie was sober.

As they walked away from the bar, they heard the chatter of the locals resume and the young man who'd been playing the piano struck up the tune he usually played when *The Tans* left the bar – *Oro, sé do bheatha a bhaile*. The political sentiment hidden in the Irish lyrics, in essence wishing the English would go home, was lost on the temporary constables, though not on Dubliner Mitch.

The incident served to get, not only Hardie and his comrades, but the whole Dunlavin contingent of the Royal Irish Constabulary barred from *The Railway Hotel*. Naturally, this blanket ban did nothing to enhance relations between the regulars and *The Tans*, as the regulars now called their temporary colleagues even to their faces. The temporary constables tried to ease the tension by arranging for crates of beer and bottles of whisky to be delivered to the barracks by the local spirit grocer, at *The Tan*'s expense, of course.

221

The Tans passed their day shifts in perusing the newspapers, drinking tea, chatting and dozing, and of course trying to put the wind up their Irish counterparts.

Despite Delaney's exhortations to them to maintain good relations with their Irish colleagues, Hardie used a monkey wrench to tighten all the taps in the barracks, so that when the regulars arrived for their shift, they would not easily be able to turn them on. He also bolted, from the inside, the door of the toilet in the yard, and then climbed out of the toilet window. He hoped the regulars might not discover this until after they had drunk a skinful and might therefore be incapable of climbing in through the window to unlock the doors.

The English constables thought it all rather childish, but Mitch quite enjoyed Hardie's sense of mischief and his ingenuity. For his part, Hardie was encouraged to bolder stunts by Mitch's obvious enjoyment of his antics. He was baffled though as to why Mitch sometimes called him 'Artie' instead of Arthur. Naturally, the Irish constables found small ways of getting their own back. No-one seemed to take great offence however, and it certainly served to lessen the crushing boredom of life in the barracks.

The night shifts passed with only slightly less tedium than the days, owing to the consumption of copious amounts of alcohol in the barracks. That the constables both lived and worked within the same building was the cause of a sort of cabin fever which made them by turns indolent or restless. It reminded Mitch of being confined to army barracks by the Indian monsoons. For some reason however, the inactivity did not seem to affect the regulars to the same degree. The Irish constables seemed more inclined to accept the deadly dull routine of barrack life, whilst the senior officers, Delaney and Haughey, were not at all affected by the barracks claustrophobia, for they worked only day shifts and were permitted to live with their families in rented houses nearby.

The recruits' third week at Dunlavin progressed with the same monotony as had the previous two. The men had little to do but drink and play cards to relieve their boredom. They read the press reports of the latest Republican outrages around the country and of the equally outrageous reprisals taken by the auxiliaries, yet no such atrocities seemed to be happening in Wicklow, thankfully.

The highlight of the week was the arrival of workmen to further reinforce the barracks against any potential attack – the sort of attack which the bored former soldiers thought might not be *wholly* unwelcome. Reinforced steel shutters, with special defensive firing slits, were fitted to all the windows, and a section of the roof was removed for a machine gun emplacement to be fitted.

'Look, a Belgian rattlesnake!' Mitch exclaimed, as he saw the Lewis gun being fitted to its mountings, 'I haven't seen one of those since the Somme. Maybe things are looking up?'

Later that evening, after much beer had been consumed by the constables, Hardie suggested they should test out the barrack's new defences. Delaney would be grateful if they showed some initiative, he suggested. It seemed a good idea at the time, and Linward, as evening orderly, was persuaded to sign out a rifle and rounds of ammunition to each of them. Cuddy and the regulars had retired to bed hours since, so there were no objections to the plan. The temporary constables lined up outside and kicked off a prolonged volley of fire at the steel shutters on the front windows of the barracks.

All around the town, terrified citizens bolted their doors and closed their own shutters against what sounded like a full scale IRA attack. The local dogs began to bark and crows deserted their roosts and took to the night air cawing in alarm. When at last the ammunition ran out, Hardie went over to examine the shutters and declared that there was not a single bullet hole in them. They must indeed be impenetrable. Laughing, they all went back inside the building.

Inside however it was a different story. Firstly, they found the regulars, who had retired to bed following their day shift, now emerging from beneath their cots where they had been cowering in terror. They too had thought themselves under attack and were understandably furious to find *The Tans* were responsible for the firing which had deafened them. The temporary constables had completely forgotten that their Irish colleagues were in the building. Nor had they foreseen the possibility that some of the many rounds they fired at the shutters might enter the building through the firing slits. They now found that both the day room and the DI's office had actually sustained a significant amount of damage.

The men spent the rest of the night shift trying to clear up. The list of casualties included DI Delaney's mantel clock and the framed portrait of the King which had hung above it but which now lay, its glass in shards, in the grate. They would be in *terrible* trouble when Larry Delaney saw that, Cuddy informed them.

Partly as punishment for their high-spirited shooting up of the barracks, but also because of a directive from Dublin about increased vigilance regarding personal safety, all of the constables were now confined to barracks at all times other than when on patrol or escort duties. A counter-insurgency campaign, mounted in recent weeks by the auxiliaries out of Gormanstown and including raids on local civilian-owned businesses and homes, had increased the likelihood of IRA reprisals against the RIC.

As a further precaution against sudden attack on the barracks, each man was now issued with a handgun, for which he had to sign. Surprisingly however, they were not issued with ammunition. In the event of such an attack, it was the day orderly's responsibility to grab sufficient ammunition and quickly issue it to the men. If going out on patrol however, the men would be issued with six rounds apiece, which if unused must be surrendered on their return.

The men tried to busy themselves with small tasks around the barracks. The barracks windows were washed, men's boots were polished and personal laundry was washed and ironed. Mitch borrowed Hardie's sewing kit – he was surprised to learn all sailors had one of these – and he set about re-stitching the hat band which had come loose on the slouch hat he had picked up at Dublin Castle. As duty orderly, of course he also made lots of tea. Cuddy gave him a hand in the small kitchen off the day room.

'A woman's work is never done, is it Cuddy?'

Cuddy did not seem to understand irony.

'No, I imagine not.'

'Still, they're paying me a lot of money to make tea, so I shouldn't complain. I hope we get to do some real policemen's work soon though.'

'Larry Delaney says it could all be over soon enough, for there's likely to be a truce coming, and then he says we'll see the back of you *Latchicos,* thanks be to God.'

Mitch laughed, 'is that what Larry calls us?'

'Yes, it is – *Latchicos* and *Tans.*'

Mitch smiled at Cuddy's innocent frankness, 'You're a very open and honest sort of a bloke, aren't you?'

'Yes, I am.'

'And you remember everything, every little detail, and never make a mistake?'

224

'Yes, that's right.'

'No wonder you passed the sergeant's exam. How did you get into the police, though? There's a height requirement isn't there? No offence, Cuddy, but you're not exactly tall?'

'My father was a policeman. If your father was a policeman you can get into the constabbalery without having to meet the reggalations. 'Tis in the rules, in the section on eligibility ...'

'That's okay,' Mitch stopped him, 'I don't need chapter and verse.'

'Mitch? Can I ask you something?'

'Ask away.'

'What's a *Jackeen*?'

Mitch laughed again, 'A *Jackeen*? Why, is that what the regulars call me?'

'It is so.'

'Well, a *Jackeen* is what some Irish country people call a Dubliner. Out here in the country they don't trust Dubliners. They call us *Dublin Jacks* or *Jackeens*. It's maybe not a very polite thing to say.'

'I see. And what would the *Jackeens* be after calling us country people, then?

'Well, I suppose I'd call you *Culchies*.'

'And what does that mean?'

'Well, you'll know this better than me, as you're a Mayo man, so correct me if I'm wrong, but isn't there a similar sounding phrase in Irish which means 'back of the house'?'

'Yes, *cúl an tí*.'

'That's it. Well, it's maybe to do with the fact that people who came from the country to Dublin to work as servants for the gentry weren't allowed to use the front door, but had to come in at the back. Or some people say it's because in the country everyone comes in at the back door, instead of the front, as it's more neighbourly. Whatever the reason, in Dublin we call the country folks the cúl an tí, or *Culchies*.'

Mitch could almost hear Cuddy's logical brain assimilating the information and storing it for future recall. Hopefully, it would get back to the disdainful regulars. *Jackeen* indeed!

'And, they do call Constable Hardie *The Jock*,' Cuddy volunteered.

'Do they? And what else do they say about us?'

225

'They say *The Jock* has a terrible quick temper. They say he's a loose cannon waiting to go off. They wouldn't want to be out on patrol with him.'

'Who's the loose cannon?' Delaney asked, as he came into the kitchen behind them, 'Ah good, the tea is mashed, I see. Is there a biscuit going?'

'*The Jock* is the loose cannon, Sur,' Cuddy honestly informed him as he opened the biscuit barrel.

Mitch hoped the DI hadn't heard them referring to him with inappropriate familiarity as 'Larry'.

'Ah, that would be Constable Hardie, I presume' Delaney took a biscuit, 'the loose cannon responsible for the incident at Lawler's bar.'

'It was his birthday, Sir, and we wuz all in high spirits,' Mitch excused his colleague.

'Yes, well it seems to me *his* spirits manage to rise higher than anyone else's. You would be well advised to avoid that one, Mitchell,' Delaney said, in a kindly tone, 'for they say that if you lie down with dogs, you get up with fleas. Cuddy, would you ever put a splash more milk in my tea. And don't hold back with the sugar, now. Sure, faint heart never won fair coconut.'

Delaney glanced out of the window at the newly repaired telephone lines.

'Ah good, the engineers've put the lines back up, and would you just look at that indignant looking flock of crows back up there again too. The way they're looking at us, you'd think we'd taken away their perch for spite.'

'It's a *murder*,' Cuddy said.

'Where?' Delaney's eyebrows shot up over his mug of tea, 'who got murdered?'

'No, sur,' Cuddy explained, 'a lot of crows together, 'tis called a *murder,* not a flock. Like, you're supposed to say an *exaltation* of larks and a *deceit* of lapwings, and so on. They're collective nouns, so they are.'

'Really? And I suppose it would be a *hangover* of constables then, would it?' Delaney smiled, helping himself to another biscuit and leaving Cuddy to scratch his head over that one.

'So what's the story with this truce, then?' Mitch asked, when they all sat down for a hand of cards that evening after supper, 'D'you think they'll reach an agreement?'

'Never,' Alston said, 'this fight's been goin' on too long. The Irish don't want to give away the north; the Protestants in the north don't want to be a part of an independent Ireland, and Westminster doesn't want to agree to independence for Ireland anyway. If we lose Ireland, the rest of the dominions will want out. Imagine if we lost India. It would be the end of the empire. There'd be a lot *more* soldiers out of a job. Why, someone would have to start another war.'

'I dunno. I reckon it could all be over by the end of the year,' Hardie said, 'and we'll be out of a job. I knew this money was too good to last.'

'I think you're right. We haven't even fired a shot since we've been here,' Mitch complained, 'well, only at our own barracks! Apart from the telephone wires going down though, we haven't seen any trouble around here. When the missus asks me what I've been doin' whilst I've been here, I can tell her I've fixed the garden wall, washed dishes and made tea, – oh yes, and acted as nanny for the magistrate. She'll have me washin' dishes at home next, and nannyin' for our baby, come April.'

Hardie opened some bottles of beer from the crate and handed them around.

'Well, with a bairn on the way, you're gonnae need a job. I can't see this one lasting the year out. We'll all be back in England, looking for work. My Jessie'll give me earache when I turn up back home jobless again.'

'You know,' Mitch looked regretful, 'I had hoped this police job might even lead to something permanent. Alice and I had dreamed of living over here in Ireland – nice little whitewashed cottage, a little garden for the chiseler to run around in, maybe a couple of horses to ride.'

'You'll have to get yourself a job as an auctioneer then,' Hardie declared, 'that way, you'll have a nice big house, with wads of cash hidden all over it, and all the horses you want.'

'What was that about wads of cash?' Lindsay's ears pricked up.

'Dixon, the magistrate over at Milltown, he keeps big wads of cash at home. He must be worth millions,' Hardie informed him.

'How do you know that?' Lindsay asked.

'Well he must do, 'cause Mitch, Blanco an' me escorted him back from the auctions last month, and he had an enormous amount on him. He asked us to stop at the bakery, but he didnae ask us to stop at the bank, did he? It stands to reason he keeps it at home. He's probably got it stuffed under his mattress or behind his mantel clock. There's been a few banks robbed by the IRA, and I think our auxiliaries did one over in Cork an' all, when they burned the city that time. Dixon probably disnae trust the banks to look after his money. Otherwise they would pay his fee straight into the bank, wouldn't they? When you think about it, that's probably the real reason he wants an escort. It's no' his skin we're protecting, it's his money.'

The constables fell silent for a moment, variously contemplating Mitch's rural dream or the magistrate's millions, and then Linward tottered to his feet:

'Well, if I'm going to be unemployed and broke soon – and that's a sobering thought – I'm going to get drunk whilst we've got the beer in. Any more for any more?'

The men continued drinking into the small hours. Alston had fallen asleep in one of the hard wooden chairs in the day room, Lindsay had disappeared off to bed and Linward was throwing up in the kitchen sink. Mitch and Hardie were still going strong however.

'Well, that's the beer finished, Arthur,' Mitch yawned, 'time to hit the hay.'

Hardie grinned however, as he produced a bottle of Bushmills' whiskey.

Chapter 13 – **A Dead Man's Hat**

On the Tuesday evening, the six temporary constables presented themselves for their night shift, relieving the regulars as usual, and conducted their formal roll call. This was a process Mitch thought fairly pointless with a shift of only six constables, but Cuddy was the evening orderly and he was a stickler for routine. In fact, Cuddy would get rattled if there were any divergence from established procedure. It was just another of the little man's many quirks. The head constable had left for the day and DI Delaney was standing in the lobby, buttoning up his civilian coat over his uniform in readiness for his own discreet departure.

Mitch had wanted to speak to Cuddy at the counter, but thought he would wait a moment or two until Delaney had left the building. He caught the tail end of a conversation Delaney was having with Cuddy and one of the regulars. It was obvious that the regular was complaining about *The Tans,* so Mitch hung around to hear what was said.

'Well, yes, I suppose you and *The Tans* are as different as chalk and chips,' Delaney was saying, 'but when the county inspector comes over next week for his routine inspection, I want you all to try to present a united front. It won't do any of us credit to let him know there's any disharmony. And make sure there's no crates of beer knocking about, or empty bottles. You know how he feels about drinking in the barracks. He's another pledge man himself, just like Daniel Haughey.'

'Yes Sur,' the regular said, 'but, Sur, you might want to have a separate word with *The Tans,* for they're the ones likely to cause trouble. They're not like us. They don't care a jot for a county inspector 'cause they're not going to be here for the long term. They're a quare bunch, so they are, not like us at all. Like a herd of ignorant wild goats, they are.'

The DI now spotted Mitch at the counter and cleared his throat:

'Ahem, yes well, I suppose our differences may simply be regional. As Rudyard Kipling once said; east is east and west is Meath. Well, goodnight to you now, Constables.'

Delaney nodded at them both, put on his gloves and stepped out into the cold air to set off for home. The regular constable headed up the stairs to his own room.

Mitch now turned to the orderly:

'Cuddy, I'll be going out of barracks for a few drinks later this evening and ...'

'Oh no,' Cuddy shook his head, 'the headquarters directive said no constable is to leave the barracks except on official duties. You can't leave the building.'

'It'll only be for a short while.'

'Well, I'm telling you mustn't go out, but if you do go out, it'll be logged in the daily occurrence book and Larry Delaney will see it tomorrow, so he will.'

'All right, all right. Well, in that case I'll stay in. I'll just go into the storeroom and get some more wood for the fire in my room though. It's freezing in there.'

Blanco was stretched out on his bed reading and didn't look up as Mitch entered, with the bundle of firewood. Mitch put some of the sticks on the fire and gave it a poke to liven it up a bit.

'I see you've got your *civvies* out,' Blanco said, nodding at Mitch's grey suit which hung from the hook on the back of the door, 'going to a dance, are you?'

'I was thinking of going to the pub, but Cuddy's put the *kaibosh* on that. Anyway, I'll give the suit a bit of a clean tomorrow, if I can get hold of some petrol or white spirit. Arthur borrowed it and the trousers are too long for him. He's managed to get them in a bit of a mess.'

'I wouldn't lend my clobber to that nutter. You won't be cleanin' it in here will you, mate? You'll stink the room out.'

'No, I'll do it out in the yard.'

'Isn't that the hat you got at Dublin Castle?' Blanco pointed at the brown slouch hat which also hung on the hook.

'Yes, well, I don't think the previous owner, has a use for it now. From what I hear goes on up there, I'd imagine he's probably dead.'

'Blimey, you wouldn't catch me wearing a dead man's hat! You won't 'ave no luck wearin' that.'

230

'It's quality velour though. It's a *Christy's titfer*. It's too good to throw away, mate, 'specially now I've put the band back on it. Any road, I'm starving. Are you coming down the kitchen and see if Cuddy's got supper on the go?'

Cuddy was in the kitchen peeling potatoes when the constables, both temporary and regular, began to gather together for supper.

'Where's the supper, Cuddy?' one of the regulars demanded.

'There's stew tonight. I just have to boil the praties,' Cuddy said.

'Well hurry up, Cuddy' the regular shouted.

'Ah, hurry up, Cuddy! Hurry up, Cuddy!' the red-faced orderly parroted as he dropped the potatoes into a pan of water.

One of the regulars mentioned Delaney's instruction that all the beer would have to be cleared out of the barracks before the county inspector's impending visit.

'Maybe we could ask Paddy Lawler if we could store the crates in his yard during the visit,' Alston suggested.

'Sure, he's not likely to agree to that, not since that feckin' eejit shot up his pub,' one of the regulars glowered at Hardie.

Hardie removed the Webley from his holster, spun it around on his thumb, wild-west style, and spat 'Pow! Pow!' in the regular's direction.

'Jayzus! I hope that's not loaded,' the regular said, as he ducked .

'It won't be,' Mitch assured him, 'and Paddy Lawler's all right with Arthur and me now since we went and cemented glass on top of his walls as well as ours. We used the leftover cement and did it for him for free, as a favour.'

'Right then,' Hardie beamed, producing his half full bottle of Bushmills, 'we'd better make sure we drink all the stuff we have on the premises before the visit. Pass us some of those glasses Mitch. Now, who'd like a wee chaser to go with the beer?'

It was a little after midnight as the two men approached the Dixon house at Milltown. The house was in darkness as the household had retired for the night. The shorter of the two men rapped on the front door. He tried the door handle but the door was locked. After a few moments, a man's voice called out from within:

'Who is it? What do you want?'

231

'It's the military. Open up now,' the shorter man demanded.

'It's the middle of the night!' the public school voice from within protested.

'This is an emergency, open up now!'

'Wait a moment,' the occupant replied.

The shorter man squared up to the front door and the second, slightly taller man stepped to one side into the shadows. After a few moments, the door was opened. In the moonlight, thirty-year old James Dixon, the magistrate's son, could see the man in front of him was not in uniform but in civilian dress. The second man now stepped forward out of the shadows and shone the flashlight in Dixon's face, disorientating him and preventing him from seeing them clearly.

'What's wrong?' Dixon asked, shading his eyes from the glare of the torch. He now noticed the two Webleys pointed in his direction.

'We want money,' the second man said, 'we won't hurt you, we just want money.'

'There's no money here, we don't keep money in the house ...' Dixon started to close the door.

The first man who had spoken now sprang forward suddenly, pushing the door open.

'Don't give me that,' he yelled, waving the gun in the young man's face, 'don't fuckin' give me that! Get the money now, or I'll put one in yer 'ead!'

He pushed Dixon back into the house. The second man followed, closing the doors behind them.

The second man now flashed the torch beam around the darkened hall. He saw James Dixon was wearing trousers under his dressing gown. Over by the foot of the stairs, the magistrate stood, also in trousers and a dressing gown. The first man, who was clearly taking the lead, demanded money once again. Again, James Dixon denied there was any in the house.

Suddenly, there was a flash and a shockingly loud retort, as a gun went off. The noise reverberated around in the dark confines of the hallway. The second man flashed the beam of the torch around the hallway again and saw nobody had been shot. It seemed his accomplice had just let off a warning shot.

'Right, if you don't cough up the money, we'll get the women and kiddies down here!' the leading man yelled.

He manhandled the magistrate back up the stairs, leaving the second man keeping James Dixon covered in the darkened hallway. The second man kept both the flashlight and his gun trained on the younger Dixon. He now noticed the young man kept his right hand behind his back.

'Wait a minute, what's that you've got behind you?' Give it over!'

Dixon produced an iron poker from behind his back. The second man went to grab it from him. Dixon took advantage of the distraction however and smartly snatched away the man's revolver. Ex-officer Dixon's self-defence training now came back to him as he wrestled the intruder around, slipping his left arm around the man's throat to secure him in a chokehold. The man yelled out, but Dixon held firm. Now, the leading man came cursing his way back down the stairs, pulling the magistrate along behind him.

Still maintaining his grip on the second man, James Dixon pointed the Webley at the leading man and pulled the trigger. The firing pin clicked but the gun did not go off. The leading man raised his own gun however and moved towards Dixon. Dixon let drop the useless gun and manoeuvred the second man around, positioning him like a shield between himself and the leading man.

The second man now called out to his accomplice, warning him not to shoot. The leading man strode forward however and thrust the Webley over the second man's shoulder, aiming it at point blank range into James Dixon's face.

'No, don't shoot him!' the second man cried out again.

Maintaining his grip on the second man, Dixon now threw his right hand over the leading man's gun hand, forcing the weapon down and angling it around towards the second man's back. This was not an easy manoeuvre, as the leading man was shorter than both of them. The leading man pulled his arm away however, wrenching both his hand and his weapon free from Dixon's grasp. With Dixon thrown off balance, the second man now managed to break the chokehold and tried to make for the front door, but James Dixon held onto his jacket with both hands and was pulled along with him.

Two women now appeared at the top of the stairs. They were in their nightgowns. They stood for a moment, trying to make out what was happening down in the moonlit hall. When they realised it was a robbery, they both came running down. The elder of the two females rushed to the umbrella stand by the front door, grabbed a metal knob-handled walking stick and began raining blows down upon the now bare head of the second man, whom James Dixon was still restraining by the jacket. In doing so however, she also caught James Dixon a hefty blow on his head, causing him to lose his grip. Finding himself free, the second man tried to open the front door, but the elder woman was right behind him. She continued to beat him about the head with the heavy end of the cane.

'Mother, please, have pity, let me out!' the intruder cried out, but the old lady kept up her blows with the walking stick.

James Dixon now ducked to the floor and retrieved the second man's dropped revolver again. Hoping it was merely jammed rather than unloaded; he raised it once again and tried to fire it at the leading man. Again however nothing happened. Suddenly, there was another loud retort and a sudden sharp burst of flame briefly illuminated the gloom of the hall. James Dixon reeled back, clutching at his left shoulder. Another shot rang out, hitting Dixon lower down in the body, and he fell to the floor. There was a stunned silence for a few seconds.

'Quick, fetch a lamp,' the second man called from the front door. Shocked, the magistrate ran back upstairs, to reappear a moment later with a lighted oil lamp from one of the bedrooms.

The flickering oil lamp sent ghostly shadows darting around the hall. This seemed to unnerve the leading man and he swung his gun wildly from side to side, as if fending off invisible foes. James Dixon could now be seen, lying wounded on the floor. The magistrate made to go to his son's aid, but the leading man raised his gun.

'Just get us some money and nobody else will get hurt,' he ordered. His neckerchief had now slipped down around his throat and he had lost his hat in the struggle. He quickly pulled the neckerchief back up over his nose and mouth again.

Robert Dixon put his hand into his trouser pocket, withdrew a handful of coins and threw them on the hall floor.

'There, that's all I have. I have no other money in the house. Take it, damn you!'

Suddenly, several more shots rang out. The magistrate now slumped and fell to the ground. The leading man had shot him as well. The younger woman now screamed very loudly. She too made for the umbrella stand, grabbed a walking stick and began attacking the leading man with it, trying to knock the gun from his hand. The magistrate groaned loudly from where he lay on the floor, alongside his now semi-conscious son. The leading man cursed loudly. It was all going horribly wrong.

The second man now succeeded in making his escape through the front door. The younger woman continued to beat the leading man with the walking stick, but the metal handle now came loose and fell to the floor. Taking up another cane from the umbrella stand, she resumed her assault on the leading man. He snatched the cane from her however, broke it in two and threw the pieces at her, and then he too ran to the front door, opened it and ran outside.

'Shit!' the second man cursed as he reached the front gates at the top of the drive, 'my hat!'

He set off again, running into the lane and disappearing into the darkness. The leading man, also hatless, emerged from the house. He struck a match and began searching around on the path but he could see neither hat nor torch. Several matches later, he realised it was no good. Abandoning the search, he too ran off into the darkness.

It was around five in the morning when Mitch arose, disturbed by the comings and goings in the barracks. Blanco appeared to be asleep still. Putting on his uniform trousers and shirt, Mitch went down to the day room. Cuddy was manning the counter and was looking more flushed and flustered than usual.

'What's going on, Cuddy? What's all the noise about?'

'There's been a shooting out at Milltown, so there has.'

'Who's been shot?'

'It's the magistrate, Mr Dixon. He's dead, and his son is badly wounded.'

'Dixon? That's the man who's also the auctioneer, isn't it, the one who sends us in food and things sometimes? Who would want to kill him? Do they know who did it?'

'Not yet, but I went up the road for Danny Haughey and he called out Larry Delaney and they've taken the night officers over to investigate. He left me in charge and said you *Tans* are to remain here and look after the station. What happened to your head, Mitch?'

'My head?'

Mitch put a hand to the top of his head. It was tender.

'Oh yes, I tripped up last night going out in the yard. I'd had a skinful of Hardie's whiskey. 'Musta banged my head in the dark. I'll go and see to it. Give us a shout when the tea's brewed, will you.'

Blanco was now awake and lying back in his bed when Mitch returned to their room.

'Blimey, Mitch, you missed all the fun and games in the early hours. You musta slept through it all. 'Seems someone's done for the magistrate.'

'Yes, Cuddy just told me.'

'I woke up around two as that Dixon girl and the doctor was hammerin' at the front door. So, I sends Cuddy to Haughey's house to fetch him and I gets the tender started up, but then Haughey arrives with Delaney and Delaney says he wants the Irish constables to handle it. Us *Tans* are to stay here, he says. Then they all heads off to Milltown. So I thought, fine, let the buggers get on wiv' it. I'm goin' back to bed. You wuz snorin' away and you missed all the excitement.'

'Terrible business. So they think it was the IRA?'

'Bound to be, innit? Mind you, Delaney wanted to know if anyone here had left the barracks during the night.'

'What did you tell him?' Mitch asked.

'I told him *I* didn't hear anything. Mind you, now I think on it, I'm not sure I didn't hear that bloody squeaky back door going in the night.'

'It was probably someone going to the toilet. Maybe it would be best not to mention that though, in case they start thinking one of us did it, instead of going after them IRA killers. Hopefully they might have caught them by now anyway. They know who the local *boyos* are.'

'Yeah, maybe you're right, Mitch. Did that fuckin' *leprechaun* make a brew yet?'

'Not yet, mate. He's flappin' round the counter like a blue-arsed fly. I'm going back to my pit and catch another forty winks. He'll give us a shout when the tea's up.'

Cuddy and the temporary constables held the fort at the barracks for the rest of that day, whilst Delaney, Haughey and the Irish constables ran back and forth incessantly between the barracks and the crime scene out at Milltown. More constables were now brought in from other barracks in the district and there was a constant to-ing and fro-ing. All the hard work Cuddy had put in over the past few days scrubbing and waxing the barracks floors in preparation for the county inspector's visit, was now undone by the onslaught of additional

236

muddy boots, and the little man had worked himself up into a froth of frustration.

Delaney told Cuddy not to worry about the visit now but to busy himself instead conducting an examination of all the weapons in the barracks and also carrying out a routine search of all the men's rooms, checking their clothing in particular. He next directed Cuddy to inspect the exterior of the barracks and the outbuildings and, of course, to hurry up about it. Thus re-focused, Cuddy applied his usual thoroughness to the task and was soon able to put aside his distress over the state of the floor.

The following morning, Delaney had Cuddy summon all the constables to muster in the day room for the usual roll call in order to address them about the Dixon murder. Cuddy carried out the head count of the assembled constables and it was quickly realised that Hardie was missing. Delaney despatched Alston upstairs to look for him.

Almost immediately, Alston came clattering excitedly down the stairs again. He blurted out the shocking news that Hardie was lying dead on his bed with a Webley in his hand. It looked like he had shot himself through the heart, Alston said. The constables gasped in unison. Mitch was stunned. No-one had heard anything, or if they had they must have mistaken it for the banging of the iron back door. One of the Irish constables made the sign of the cross. Cuddy stood, red-faced and uncomfortable, his hands tucked defensively into his arm pits, looking like the schoolboy who didn't break the greenhouse window but feared he might be blamed anyway.

The District Inspector's gaze immediately panned around the assembled men and settled upon Mitch. Delaney's usually friendly features were now set in a disappointed frown.

'Ah, well now,' he said, 'that's thrown a sparrow in the works. Indeed it has.'

The Dixon house at Milltown, near Dunlavin, County Wicklow

Chapter 14 – **The Second Man**

In London, at the Eaton Square home of Field Marshall Sir Henry Wilson, Commander of the Imperial General Staff, the hall telephone rings. The butler answers it and summons Sir Henry to take a call from Dublin, from a Lieutenant Colonel Anderson at Military Headquarters. Sir Henry says he will take the call in private in his study:

'Anderson? Yes, I have the papers you sent on the Mitchell case. I am in complete agreement with you on the charges.

Now, I met with the Prime Minister and the Chief Secretary for Ireland yesterday and I have to emphasise to you that both Lloyd George and Greenwood consider this a case of great importance. The PM knows well my own views on his policy of reprisals. However, he has consistently disregarded military advice and has given his ... gendarmerie, as he calls them, free reign to do as they please. As for Tudor's so-called intelligence officers, what they're doing has nothing to do with intelligence gathering and it certainly isn't warfare. It's just government sanctioned murder, nothing less. How little they understand the Irish. Well, now the PM's chickens have come home to roost, I'm afraid.

You probably heard Greenwood had yet another roasting in the house the other day. The Labour Commission report hasn't gone away. That Labour MP, Clynes, demanded to know why, if the press reports are as inaccurate as he claims, Lloyd George hasn't publicly refuted them or censured the press. Anyway, doubtless you've seen all this in the Dublin papers too, but what you won't know, and what the press won't know either, is that the King has now become involved. This is strictly 'need to know', of course, but His Majesty has expressed his displeasure that we seem able to execute the Sinn Feiners with little regard for public opinion, yet so far no action has been taken against any Black and Tan who has murdered.

Well now Anderson, this is where we come into the picture. The PM is now looking to the military to sort out his mess. If order cannot be restored in Ireland, there must at least be some show of fair play. The press, the Americans above all, must be persuaded that, despite how it looks, we are trying to be even-handed. Since we, and not the politically appointed judges, are now in charge of justice in Ireland, then justice must be seen to be done. Of course, it won't help matters that Greenwood has put up five hundred pounds from his own pocket towards the defence of one of Tudor's auxiliaries.

And, speaking of that case, has the date of 'The Major's' court martial been set down yet? April? Fine. I presume the venue will be Dublin City Hall again, as per his previous court martial? Good. Well, given his acquittal in December for the last lot of killings, I imagine we can be confident about how his April trial will go? Good. Now, in view of the likely outcome of that trial, the Home Secretary feels it is imperative that Mitchell's court martial be scheduled for as soon as possible after 'The Major's'. Do you think you can arrange that? Good. 'The Major's' acquittal is fairly certain, whereas this chap Mitchell hasn't much of a hope. The PM's banking on that. Mitchell's conviction should keep the press at bay for a while and hopefully will satisfy His Majesty also. That is why I cannot emphasise too strongly the importance of the Mitchell case.

Of course, it wouldn't be helpful were the court to go for the lesser charge of manslaughter, but I doubt they will. With that possibility in mind though, I feel the Counsel and Judge Advocate should be supplied from England. This would be preferable to having the Attorney General for Ireland appear for the Crown. 'Don't want to take any chances, do we? Can that be arranged too? Excellent. Will you then write to the Judge Advocate General about this as a matter of urgency? Good. Excellent. Clarify matters for the JAG and make sure we're all dancing to the same tune, what? Good man. That should help clean up the Government's dirty laundry. Now then, the sooner the damned politicians, those useless fucking frocks, can get their peace process under way, the sooner we can all fucking well go back to being soldiers again.'

On Friday 15th April 1921, at Dublin City Hall, a tall, well-built, square-jawed man appears before his second General Court Martial to answer charges of murder. Once again 'The Major' is acquitted.

On Saturday 16th April 1921, Temporary Constable William Mitchell became a father. On Monday 18th April 1921, he became the sole defendant at a General Court Martial held at Dublin's City Hall.

Situated within sight of Dublin Castle, City Hall was a magnificent edifice. The beauty of its façade was marred only by its essential encirclement of untidy barbed wire barricades and equally untidy khaki-clad troops. As Mitch and his escort drove past the balustraded forecourt, dominated by vast classically reeded stone columns, and as they marched at the double through the cool and elegant marble interior, Mitch experienced a feeling he had last felt some years ago out in India. He felt small and insignificant, as powerless as a speck of dust in the vastness of a mighty universe.

Seated in the courtroom, he glanced at the name plates of the Judge Advocate general's representatives lined up before him. These were definitely *Top Brass*. The President of the court was Major and Brevet Lieutenant Colonel Montague Bates, CB, CMG, DSO of the Second Battalion, East Surrey Regiment. The other members were: Lieutenant Colonel Chapman, OBE; Major Heath, RGA of the First Battalion King's Own Royal Regiment; Major Langley, DSO, MC, RGA of the Wiltshire Regiment; Captain Sabben, also of the Wiltshire Regiment and Captain, Brevet Major Gurdon, MC of the Second Battalion East Surrey Regiment. Clearly, these proceedings would be a much grander affair than Mitch's earlier field court martial in France.

It felt as though the big guns were all lined up and he, as their target, was helplessly caught in their sights. Seated at a table over to his right, and appearing for the Crown, were Mr D.M. Wilson, KC and Member of Parliament, whose name plate indicated he was also His Majesty's Solicitor General for Ireland, and Mr Richard Best KC. Sitting alongside Mitch was his own representative, Mr James Ambrose Reardon. He had no nameplate. Mitch guessed Reardon to be in his late thirties, a Cork man from his accent, and there was nothing about his appearance to suggest any sort of military background. Mitch could not decide if that were a good thing or bad.

He had not met Reardon before setting foot in the court, but he knew the barrister would have been instructed by his solicitor. Reardon explained that the KC on the opposition's name plates meant 'King's Counsel'. They were 'Silks' he explained – in simple terms, the highest level of barrister. Mitch didn't like to upset Reardon by asking whether he had any letters after *his* name. He wondered whether Reardon felt as intimidated as he did by all the brass and the silks and the letters ranged against them.

He now noticed the posse of pressmen seated behind him. He wondered if they included the London hacks. If so, he supposed that not only his parents and Alice, but all their friends and neighbours, would soon be presented with every detail of the murder with which he was charged. His attention was now drawn back to the proceedings, as the members of the Judge Advocate's court were sworn in, one by one. Next the charges were read out by the Judge Advocate, P. Sutherland Graeme esquire, CBE:

'The Accused, William Mitchell, a constable in the Royal Irish Constabulary, is charged with committing a crime within the meaning of Regulation 67 of the Restoration of Order in Ireland Regulations, that is to say, murder, in that he, at Dunlavin in the County of Wicklow, Ireland, on the second of February 1921, feloniously, wilfully and of his malice aforethought did kill and murder Robert Gilbert Dixon. How say you, are you guilty or not guilty?'

'Not guilty,' Mitch declared.

The Judge Advocate next read out a second charge, which sounded identical to the first, except that instead of 'kill and murder' the charge read 'kill and slay'. His solicitor had warned him to expect two charges, one of murder and one of manslaughter. Mitch also pleaded 'not guilty' to the second charge. The Solicitor General now commenced his opening address, outlining the details of the robbery and shooting of the magistrate. The *top brass* seemed to be taking notes the whole time.

The first witness, the deceased's son, James Dixon, was called to the stand. Dixon's gaze immediately found Mitch. Mitch felt the entire court was watching his reaction to the appearance of the witness, so he avoided looking Dixon in the eye. At the Prosecution counsel's bidding, James Dixon recounted the events of the early hours of the second of February. It all sounded very familiar to Mitch, for he had had little to do for the past six weeks since his arrest but go over the evidence with his solicitor.

One part of Dixon's oral evidence now seemed unfamiliar however. Dixon described how, having disarmed and restrained the second man – allegedly Mitch – whilst at the same time angling, towards the second man, the gun hand of the leading man – allegedly Hardie – he had heard second man call out, urging leading man not to shoot. This much was familiar to Mitch from the written statements, but now Dixon added that the second man had next spoken the words:

'...in case you shoot *me*.'

Mitch glanced suddenly at Reardon, wondering if he would challenge these final words, since they had not appeared in Dixon's written statement. Reardon did not react, but from the witness stand Dixon had noticed Mitch's reaction, and he quickly added;

'Well, I cannot recall the *exact* words used, but they were certainly to that effect.'

Since this was a crucial point, and a very damning one, Crown Counsel invited Dixon to say why, *in his opinion*, the second man had asked the leading man not to shoot. Dixon said:

'Well, I understood it was to avoid him hitting his accomplice. It would have been: 'do not shoot, or you will shoot me,'... or something to that effect'.

Mitch expected Reardon to register an objection at the witness expressing an opinion, rather than stating fact. Reardon did not however.

Mitch glared at Dixon. This seemed to unsettle Dixon, who said again that he could not recall the *exact* words.

Dixon now recounted how he had grabbed the leading man's gun hand but the leading man had managed to snatch his gun hand away. In doing so, the leading man's gun had gone off, wounding Dixon in the hand. Mitch could not recall this being mentioned in Dixon's written statement either. In Mitch's recollection, Dixon had claimed the first shot fired had been the leading man's warning shot. Dixon now indicated a small scar on his hand however. Mitch was confused.

Dixon went on to describe how he had then been shot in the shoulder by the leading man. After this, he had fired the gun he had taken from the second man, but it did not go off. The leading man, had then fired again and had again wounded Dixon, through the hip this time, and the bullet had lodged in his stomach.

'I fell to the ground after that,' Dixon continued, 'but then I managed to pull myself upright and followed the second man, who was by now over by the door. I grabbed the second man's clothing and held onto him. Then, my sister and my aunt had come downstairs. My aunt had a walking stick with her and I urged her to beat the second man on the head with it, so that he might be rendered insensible.'

Counsel asked whether the aunt had in fact managed to beat the second man on the head, and the witness said she had indeed beaten him very hard about the head, several times.

'Unfortunately,' he added, 'in her enthusiasm she also hit me on the head at the same time.'

Dixon indicated a point on the top of his head where, he claimed, a scar had been visible for weeks after.

'Was there any light in the hall at any time during the incident?' Counsel asked.

'Yes,' Dixon replied.

'And can you therefore describe the men's appearance?'

'The second man was of a similar age, height and build to me. He had a grey suit and he had a moustache. The other man however was a man of slighter build.'

Next, Dixon said, one of the men had shouted that he was out of ammunition and that they should go. They had then left the house.

Mr Reardon now rose to his feet to commence his cross examination of the witness. Mitch noticed that Reardon's hand, and the papers it held, were shaking.

'How long did the incident last?' Reardon asked.

'Around ten minutes,' Dixon replied.

'Was there a light burning in the hall during *all* of that time?'

'No, there was no light at all in the hall for the greater portion of the time. I cannot recall exactly when the light was brought in, but it was after I was shot.'

'Was the light burning in the hall all the time you were struggling with the second man?'

'No, the light was not on during the struggle.'

Reardon now moved on to another relevant point.

'Can you confirm that, a day or two after the incident, you were asked to attend an identity parade and, at that parade, you identified as the second man, a man who was not the Accused but was in fact a local man from Baltinglass?'

Mitch began to feel a little more confidence in Reardon now.

'I cannot recall having identified anyone. The police did arrange a line-up of seven or eight suspects a couple of days after the incident, but I was feeling weak then and I do not recall having been able to identify any of them.'

Reardon now challenged the witness on another point:

'Is it not so,' he asked, 'that you described the second man to the police as having a sallow complexion?'

Everyone in the court now looked across at Mitch, clearly concluding there was nothing sallow about his face.

'Yes, but I am saying he had a sallow complexion *that* night.'

'When did you actually see the man's face and for how long did you see it?'

'I only saw his face at one point, when holding him near the door. My aunt was beating him with a stick at that point. Perhaps he was sallow with fear.'

Reardon next established of the witness that the gun Dixon had fired had been that taken from the second man.

'And is it not so that, in your original statement to the police, you said the revolver you had tried to fire was 'evidently unloaded'?'

'No, not unloaded, it was the case that it would not go off, and this might have happened if it was loaded in several chambers. I would not like to say one way or the other, why it did not go off.'

Mitch was pleased to hear Reardon press the point further. Reardon now read from Dixon's original statement, which had been presented to the initial military enquiry:

'I aimed at the man who held the revolver and pulled the trigger but nothing happened. The revolver was evidently unloaded.'

'Well,' Dixon retreated, 'whilst that may have been what I said, I had *meant* to say simply that the gun would not go off. I only pulled the trigger once, and then I collapsed.'

'Do you have previous experience with revolvers?'

'Yes, I was in the war.'

'And can you confirm that you saw only one of the assailants fire a weapon during the entire encounter, and that was fired by the man who shot you?'

'Yes that is correct.'

'And is it the case that, as soon as you were shot by the leading man, you saw the second man making off through the door?'

'Not exactly. Not making off *through* the door, but rather he was standing *near* the door.'

'And did you hear the second man say to your aunt 'Mother, let me go'?'

'Yes, I did, but this was *after* I had grabbed the second man again and was encouraging my aunt to beat him.'

'So the second man was anxious to get out of the house but you were hanging on to him and your aunt was beating him, and therefore he was being prevented from escaping?'

'Yes, I suppose so,' Dixon conceded.

Reardon now returned to the question of the words the second man had used when they had been grappling and asked Dixon if those words had been 'do not shoot'.

'Those are the only words I recall him saying, but the reason he would have said it must be because I had his comrade's gun turned towards him.'

'But the only words you actually heard him say were: 'do not shoot', spoken to his companion and 'Mother, let me go', said to your aunt?'

Mitch could see the way his counsel was going with the questioning and he suddenly felt a faint glimmer of hope.

However, the Judge Advocate now cut in:

'I think you have not put it fully, Mr Reardon. The note I have here is: 'do not shoot or you will shoot me'.'

Reardon corrected him:

'I believe the witness said that was the *impression* he got, but that the actual words which he remembered were 'do not shoot'.'

'Yes, yes,' the Judge Advocate said, impatiently, 'he said that at first and then Mr Best asked him further what words were used and the witness said those were the actual words.'

Mitch could tell Reardon was all set to argue the point further with the witness, when the President, glowering, now intervened:

'He also said that the second man called out to his comrade to come to his assistance did he not?'

'Yes Sir, but that was before ...' Reardon began to respond feebly.

'Mr Best, do you wish to re-examine?' the President cut Reardon off. Clearly, this was the end of Reardon's cross examination of this witness. Reardon sat down. He was still shaking, Mitch noticed. Mitch's glimmer of hope began to fade.

Best rose and asked the witness if the point at which both men had been anxious to get away had been after all the shooting was over. The witness confirmed that was so, and that he recalled one of the men saying he had no more ammunition. Of that fact, he was certain.

The next witness called was the late magistrate's daughter, Miss Kathleen May Dixon. In response to Best's questions, she gave her account of the incident, which was similar in most respects to that of her brother. As she described her assault upon the leading man with first one walking stick and then, when that had broken, with another, Mitch noted that her depiction of her own bravery was attracting glances of admiration from the all male court.

Miss Dixon added that after the incident, when she had run upstairs to dress before going to fetch the doctor, she had looked out of the window and had seen the two assailants still outside the house:

'The second man was standing down by the gate. The one who had attacked my father was still standing on the gravel drive, outside the house. He was lighting matches and groping around for something on the gravel drive. I heard them talking and several times he called the other man 'Bill',' she added.

Mitch sat bolt upright on hearing this. Never in his life had *he* been called 'Bill'. Did she really hear the name 'Bill' used? He hadn't seen this in hear earlier written statement. She would know from press reports that the Accused's name was William. Was she seeking to embellish her initial account by including what she assumed to be his nickname? He hoped Reardon would address this point.

'I then cycled to fetch Doctor Lyons. He lives on the other side of the barracks. As I passed the barracks on the way there, I saw a man wearing light coloured clothes standing in the street right outside the barracks.'

Mitch felt this was another embellishment. Why would anyone, either robber or passer-by, be standing in the street outside the barracks in the early hours of the morning.

'What happened when you returned to your house?' Best asked.

'I then spotted a flash lamp on the hall table and two hats lying on the floor.'

'Were those hats the same you now see here on the evidence table?'

'I could not say they are the same, but they were certainly similar soft hats. I also saw some bullets lying near them on the floor.'

In his cross examination, Reardon asked if Miss Dixon had heard the second man cry out to her aunt to open the door and let him out. She confirmed she had and that the second man had been let out. The door was closed behind him but the leading man had left soon after, opening the door for himself, she thought.

'When you looked out of the upstairs window, you saw the leading man lighting matches and searching the gravel but the second man was by then up by the gate. Is that correct?' Reardon asked.

Mitch could feel Reardon leading up to asking when, then, it could have been that she heard the leading man outside using the name 'Bill'. However, at this point, the Judge Advocate cut in yet again:

'Did you get a look at the second man?' he asked.

The witness said she had not. In answer to the Judge Advocate's further questioning, she said she could not describe the second man.

'Was this because they had something covering their faces,' The Judge Advocate asked, 'and did you see what that was?'

'No. I thought it felt like a handkerchief or muffler, and I understood from...'

'Ah,' interrupted the Judge Advocate, 'you must not tell the court what you understood or what you have heard, but merely what you observed.'

Mitch had the strongest feeling that someone had been discussing with this witness details of the physical evidence found.

The Judge Advocate now asked Miss Dixon to clarify when she had heard shots, whether it was after she had struggled with the leading man and he had taken her stick or later still. She could not confirm when she had heard shots fired however, but she had seen guns flash at both sides of the hall and so had concluded that *both* assailants had fired shots. In this respect, her account was at odds with that of her brother.

The Judge Advocate did not pursue this discrepancy but abandoned his questioning at this point and told the witness she might withdraw. Mitch glanced at his counsel. He wondered whether Reardon had the right to insist on continuing his own cross examination. Reardon too was still wondering this as he watched the witness leave the courtroom.

The Judge Advocate now announced the court would recess for luncheon. Everyone rose and the big guns withdrew. Mitch and Reardon had just a few seconds before the military police would take Mitch away.

'Mr Reardon, why didn't the Judge allow you to finish your questioning of the witness?' he asked.

'I don't know,' Reardon replied, 'I was never involved in a court martial before and they didn't give me a copy of the Judge Advocate's rules for this type of hearing.'

After lunch, Another Miss Dixon, Martha Jane Dixon, the late magistrate's spinster sister, was called as a witness. She gave her own account of the incident. Like her nephew and niece before her, she was accurate on the timing of the incident, which had started at precisely half past midnight and had lasted some ten minutes. Mitch thought the Dixon household must have a clock in every room, all of them accurate and all able to be viewed in the dark. Considering her age, Mitch thought the witness had remarkable recall, since she repeated not only the sequence of events and the exact words which had been uttered but also added her observation that the second man, the man whom she had hit over the head with the stick, had a moustache.

Asked what had occurred on the third of February, the day following the incident, Miss Dixon senior said she had been taken to the police barracks at Dunlavin and had been shown the body of a dead constable, whom she had identified as the leading man, the man who had shot her brother and nephew.

Asked if she recognised the hats and the flashlight now on the evidence table, she identified them unhesitatingly as being those items she had seen on in the hallway immediately following the incident, and she confirmed also that none of these items belonged in the Dixon household. In fact, she added, she knew the hat of every local resident in Dunlavin. Those hats found at the scene, which were now on the evidence table, did not belong to any local. Those, she assured the court, were the hats of strangers.

The family physician, Dr Lyons, now made a brief appearance on the witness stand. He testified that his house was situated some seventy yards beyond Dunlavin barracks, in the opposite direction from Milltown. He confirmed also his involvement in the events of the early hours of the second of April. He gave details too of the injuries for which he had treated James Dixon and of the post mortem examination he had conducted the following day on Robert Dixon.

Lyons had also been present on the third of April when James Dixon had been operated upon by Dublin surgeon Mr Pringle, who had removed from James Dixon's intestines the bullet which now lay on the evidence table.

The next witness called was District Inspector Laurence Delaney. Mitch wondered why he was wearing civilian clothes. He did not wonder for long though, as the Judge Advocate warned Delaney that, for obvious security reasons, he should not disclose to the court either the nature of his own rôle in the affair or his designation. Delaney wondered if his rôle wouldn't be obvious to a blind monkey on horseback, given the nature of the evidence he would be giving. The press were also directed not to report Delaney's name.

Delaney duly recounted what he had found when he had gone to the Dixon house at around five thirty on the morning of the second of April. He identified exhibit H as the flash light found at the scene and confirmed also that it was identical to those issued to the constabulary, though he could not say if it was one actually issued to Dunlavin barracks. The police had remained at the house until around nine o'clock that morning, he said.

On his return to the barracks, all constables had been instructed to muster and all had been examined, as had their revolvers. It was noticed that Constable Hardie had a fresh cut mark, around an inch and a quarter in length, on the top of his head. The bicycles in the barracks shed had then been examined. Two appeared to have been recently used and there were the damp tracks of bicycle tyres on the flagstones in the yard. Each constable had then been directed to produce his civilian clothing. Hardie's clothing appeared to be bloodstained, as was his revolver.

Asked about the examination of the Accused and his clothing and revolver, Delaney confirmed the barrel of Constable Mitchell's revolver was found to be fouled, his civilian clothing bloodstained and, when he had been asked to produce a civilian hat, he had produced the grey one which was now marked exhibit N. That hat had not been bloodstained. Delaney added that he had given the Accused's bloodstained coat, waistcoat and trousers – now exhibits 01, 02 and 03 – to Sergeant Brophy, an officer brought in from Baltinglass barracks.

Mitch wondered why some exhibits were numbered and some identified by letters. The Judge Advocate was puzzled by this also and had Delaney explain. It seemed the three items given to the Analyst had been marked by him, and the Analyst used a numerical identification system, not an alphabetic one.

'I gave directions to Sergeant Brophy ...' Delaney continued, but the Judge Advocate coughed suddenly, and, taking the hint, Delaney corrected himself;

'... that is, the sergeant then took the clothing to the Home Office Analyst for forensic examination.'

Crown Counsel asked Delaney whether he knew the Accused to possess more than one hat.

'I do not know. I would have no knowledge of his civilian clothing.'

Delaney continued, 'shortly after this however, both Hardie and Mitchell were relieved of their arms and placed under supervision in the barracks. The following day, it was discovered that Hardie had shot himself dead in his room with a service revolver. Later that same day, his body was identified by Miss Dixon senior as being that of one of the men present in the Dixon house when her brother was killed. I then arrested the Accused.'

Delaney looked across at the Judge Advocate, expecting to be warned again about disclosing his rôle. When this did not happen however, he continued:

'The Accused made no statement at that time, but he was examined and found also to have a fresh cut mark, around an inch long, on the top of his head.'

In cross examination, Reardon asked Delaney about the identity parade he had held.

'Can you confirm whether James Dixon ever identified a man from Baltinglass as being one of the men involved in the incident?'

'Well indeed, there was a brief military court of enquiry held, in lieu of a civilian inquest, and at that enquiry Mr James Dixon was shown a line-up of men, the Accused included, but he did not identify the Accused. In fact, he identified another man, another police officer from a different station. For security reasons, I imagine I should not say which station the man was from.'

'At any time, was a man from Baltinglass identified by anybody?' Reardon asked.

'The man from Baltinglass was not really identified as such, but he had said that man was *like* the man in the house.'

'Who said this?' Reardon asked.

'Mr James Dixon did,' Delaney replied.

'So James Dixon said that a man from Baltinglass was *like* one of the men in the house?' Reardon pushed the point.

'Yes,' Delaney faltered, 'though I should not say from what station the man was.'

The Judge Advocate now cut in:

'When was this?'

'At the court of enquiry held by the military in lieu of a civil inquest, the Accused was paraded amongst others before Mr James Dixon – on the morning of the fourth of February it was – for identification purposes, and Mr Dixon pointed out a man other than the Accused as being like one of the men who were there,' Delaney expanded.

'And was the man from Baltinglass?' Reardon asked.

Suddenly, Crown Counsel was on his feet:

'He does not SAY he was a man from Baltinglass!' he snapped.

'Do not get angry with me,' Reardon said calmly, determined not to let the police security requirements override the rights of his client.

'I am not,' Best muttered, sitting down again.

Reardon continued:

'I will call him a man from anywhere you like, but was the man, whom Mr Dixon said was *like* one of the men in the house on the night in question, a member of the RIC?'

'Yes, he was a member of the RIC ... stationed at Wicklow,' Delaney added quickly, with a mischievous glance across at Mitch.

Mitch smiled back at Delaney. Reardon concluded his cross examination by having Delaney confirm that James Dixon did not identify the Accused at all, either then or at any time subsequently.

Next, Head Constable Daniel Haughey was called. Clearly, the Judge Advocate had reconsidered his security strategy, for, though Haughey's name was not disclosed to the court, his position was.

Unlike Delaney, Haughey was able to positively identify the torch found at the crime scene as that belonging to the Dunlavin barracks and he added that the barracks torch was not at the barracks when he had returned from the crime scene, but it had last been seen in the barracks day room at eleven the previous evening. He was satisfied the torch he had recovered from the crime scene was the torch missing from the barracks. Mitch felt Haughey's level of recall of these minutiae surprising for a man who rarely left his office.

Haughey now identified some of the bullets found at the scene as belonging to a service Webley of the type used by the RIC. Other spent bullets, which had been found underneath the Dixons' hall sofa, had however been of a type only suitable for use in an automatic pistol. He was then asked to describe the layout of the barracks, the position of the strong room within the day room and the system for booking out weapons and ammunition.

Haughey confirmed he personally had checked the number of bullets in the strong room back in December when conducting an audit, and there had been five hundred and seventy one rounds in the strong room. When next he had checked however, after Hardie's suicide, there had been only five hundred and fifty one rounds left. Therefore twenty rounds could not be accounted for. Haughey confirmed that all the station constables had access to the room since firewood was also kept in that area, although it was the duty orderly's responsibility to ensure no-one took ammunition without it being booked out.

In his cross examination Reardon asked the Head Constable if it had been the habit of the constables at Dunlavin to drink heavily when on duty. Haughey said he had only once seen one constable under the influence of drink and that had been the previous Christmas Eve, but otherwise he had never seen any of the officers drunk, either in the barracks or in the nearby public houses.

Mitch thought Haughey was probably being truthful in this. From Haughey's office he would not have noticed that most of his constables had hangovers each morning. When pressed by Reardon, Haughey admitted he had suspected some were taking drink but said he had always cautioned them not to do so, as he did not approve of drinking himself.

Haughey confirmed that Mitchell and the other temporary constables had only been at the barracks for a month prior to the incident. He confirmed, in answer to Reardon's questioning over the ammunition, that this had not been kept in a locked box and so it would be possible for any constable to help himself. Asked if there were automatic pistols kept in the strong room, he said there had been once, but there were none kept in there these days, just some left over automatic ammunition. He said he had not thought the ammunition for automatics could be used in a Webley service revolver and yet, after the incident, he had tried to put some of the automatic rounds into a Webley – the Webley which had been issued to the Accused, in fact – and it had fitted the magazine but he had not managed to fire the weapon as it was fouled and would not fire.

Reardon asked Haughey when exactly he had found the Accused's Webley to be fouled, whether this was before he had tried using the inappropriate automatic rounds in it, or afterwards. Haughey admitted he could not recall. The Judge Advocate now chimed in and asked if any other weapons, an automatic perhaps, had been found at the Dixon household. Haughey replied that none had, however the Dixons had not been required to produce any guns of their own for comparison.

The next witness was Constable Thomas Cuddy. Embarrassed to be in the spotlight, he nevertheless stood to attention and gave his evidence honestly and thoroughly. He testified that another of the exhibits, exhibit R, a small torn piece of leather, had been found at the crime scene, and that he had advised the head constable that he recognised it as having been attached to the barracks torch, which was also found at the crime scene. He said he was familiar with that particular torch, that the piece of leather covering around the handle had been coming loose for some time and that, on one occasion, he himself had glued it back on. Mitch might have expected Cuddy's superior observation and memory skills to feature in the prosecution somewhere.

Cuddy confirmed he had been night orderly on the evening of the incident. He said both Hardie and Mitchell had separately expressed a desire to go out of barracks, but he had told them this was not allowed. He had then seen each of them in turn enter the store room, where the strong room was located, and emerge carrying bundles of firewood. Yes, other officers had also collected firewood from the store room, as it had been a cold night. No, he might not have noticed if any of the constables had concealed anything within the bundles of firewood, since he had not searched these. Cuddy had then brought his own bedding into the day room and had turned in at precisely two minutes to midnight.

'What were the other constables doing at that time?' Best asked

'Some were sitting chatting and drinking in the day room;' Cuddy answered, 'others were sleeping; one had gone to bed and one was being sick in the kitchen sink, for they had all taken a *skinful* of beer and whiskey and were fair *fluthered*. I had none taken myself, for I do not drink.'

Best asked Cuddy to examine the hats from the exhibits table and say if he recognised them. Cuddy had no hesitation in confirming which hat was Hardie's and that the other two belonged to the Accused. Best asked him to clarify then if the Accused had owned two hats.

'Yes, he had two hats. The grey was his usual hat. It matched his grey suit. The brown one was a *Christy's of London* hat. 'Twas one he took off a dead man.'

Mitch shrank at this, as felt the eyes of the court upon him. He would not have an opportunity to expand on his acquisition of the hat since Reardon had said he should not give evidence in his own defence, lest details of his adverse army record came out. The way Cuddy had put it, the court might think Mitch a robber of corpses. An unsavoury image suddenly came to his mind of the German corpses he had looted in France.

'How well do you know the Accused?' Best now asked.

'Well, I was the only one of the reggalars who would work with the English constables, so I know him well enough, I suppose,' Cuddy replied.

'And did you see the Accused associate with Hardie?'

'Oh yes, he did so. The District Inspector had told him he shouldn't lie down with Hardie though, because of the fleas and because Hardie was a *loose cannon*. He shot up the barracks, so he did, and the pub next door.'

'And what sort of a man is Constable Mitchell?' Best asked.

Before Reardon could leap to his feet to object, Cuddy helpfully informed the court:

'He's a *Jackeen*.'

Reardon did not cross examine.

A Doctor Brontë was now sworn in and he identified himself as a Licentiate of the Royal College of Physicians and Surgeons in Ireland and also as Home Office pathologist for Ireland. In a very wordy fashion, he went about identifying the clothing belonging to the Accused and Hardie, confirming that he had examined them and had cut out sections for testing. He also confirmed his conclusions that the blood stains found on the clothing belonging to both men were indeed human blood, though of course he could not identify whose blood it was.

The final witness of the day was Constable George White. Blanco confirmed he had joined the constabulary the previous November and had been posted to the same training course at Gormanstown with the Accused, but they had become acquainted mainly during the past month when sharing a room at Dunlavin barracks.

Asked to describe what he had seen and heard during the night of first to second of April, he said he and the Accused had retired to their room for the evening.

'Did you sleep soundly during the night or were you awake at any time?' Best asked.

'I slept like the dead, I did,'

'And in your statement made to the earlier hearing, did you say you had not seen or heard anyone leaving the barracks?'

'Yes I did, although ..'

'Although...?'

'Well, when my head cleared later on, I fancied I might have heard the iron door at the back of the building squeak in the early hours. I might have imagined it, but something awoke me and I then got up to go and answer the call of nature.'

'What time was that?'

'I'm afraid I have no idea. It was dark.'

'Did you pass anyone going out to the toilet in the yard?'

'Er, well, no. I didn't go to the yard. I'd rather not say where exactly I went to relieve myself, if it's all the same to you, but I didn't leave the bedroom.'

'So, was the Accused in the room when you got up in the night?'

'Well now, I'm not too sure. I had the impression his bed might have been empty, but I can't now be certain about it. I'd had quite a lot to drink and my head was not too clear.'

'So if the Accused was not there, how long after this do you think he might have returned to the barracks?'

Reardon leaped to his feet and objected to Counsel's leading the witness. The Judge Advocate did not react however.

'I really object to this,' Reardon reiterated, 'the witness did not say the Accused had left the barracks.'

The Judge Advocate continued to ignore him however and Reardon, unsure of whether military legal protocols afforded him the same rights of natural justice as did civil courts, and wary of angering the Judge Advocate, had little choice but to sit and be silent. Best now took his seat however, so Reardon rose again to cross examine. He would play the game by Best's rules;

'How much had you had to drink on the night when you *think* you may have got up in the dark to relieve yourself and you *think* the Accused's bed *might* have been empty?' he asked.

'Eight or nine bottles of beer and several glasses of whiskey,' Blanco replied.

'And you could not, when questioned just a few hours later, recall having heard anyone leave in the night?'

'No,' Blanco replied.

'Do you know how much Hardie and Mitchell had drunk that evening?'

'More or less. They'd certainly had more beer than me, and they were finishing off the whiskey between them when I turned in.'

'In your opinion, were they drunk?

'Oh yes, well gone.'

'By what name did you usually call the Accused?' Reardon took a new tack.

'We all called him Mitch.'

'Why Mitch?'

'Well, short for Mitchell. Like I'm usually called Blanco, as my name's White.'

'Did you ever, at any time, hear anyone in the barracks, including Hardie, call the Accused 'Bill'?'

'No, never.'

Satisfied, Reardon sat down.

The Judge Advocate asked Crown Counsel if he wished to re-examine and Best again rose. He asked Blanco if he could identify the hats on the exhibit table. Reardon shifted in his seat. He knew that, in a civil court, the prosecution counsel would only be permitted to re-examine on any *new* points of evidence which had emerged during cross examination, and not on any issue which he had overlooked in his examination-in-chief. It was a cause of extreme frustration for Reardon that he was unfamiliar with the procedures in courts martial. He felt sure they were obliged to follow the general precepts and procedures of civil law, but he was not sure enough to challenge the court on this. Mitch didn't fully understand how the proceedings were going, but he could sense Reardon's annoyance.

Blanco could indeed identify the owners of the hats. He said he recognised the brown slouch hat in particular because he recalled the Accused having acquired it when it was dropped by a prisoner they had seen being arrested and beaten by auxiliaries at Dublin Castle, and he also recalled the Accused sitting in the day room, sewing the hatband back onto the hat. He recognised the large, amateurish stitches the Accused had used. He remembered this, he said, because Hardie, who had learned how to use a needle and thread when in the navy, had teased the Accused about his poor needlework skills.

Mitch felt that Blanco's evidence had perhaps made him out to be more of an opportunistic thief than a rifler of corpses.

The court concluded for the day at five o'clock. Reardon was permitted only a few moments with his client whilst the military police escort stood impatiently by.

'Is there anything else you think might be helpful for me to raise when court resumes tomorrow,' Reardon asked, 'anything at all?'

'Well, you could ask the other constables about when Hardie took a gun to the Railway Hotel and fired off a shot. It scared the bar staff good and proper. There wuz another incident as well in another pub.'

'Did you ever tell anyone about this?'

'I gave a statement about it at the military enquiry, you know, the inquest thing. Didn't they give you a copy of it?'

The hearing resumed the following day at ten thirty. Constable Alston was examined, mostly regarding his discovery of Hardie's body on the third of April, for Alston could remember little of the night of the shooting. In cross examination, Reardon managed to get Alston to confirm that another of his colleagues, William Lindsay, was known as

'Bill' to the rest of the constables in the Dunlavin barracks, whereas he had never heard the Accused addressed as 'Bill'.

Temporary Constable William Lindsey, a tall man with a distinctly sallow complexion, gave evidence next and he agreed he was known as 'Bill' and moreover he was the only officer at the barracks ever addressed as such. Constable Mitchell was invariably referred to as 'Mitch', he confirmed. Lindsey was asked about the front and back doors of the barracks and he said the front door was always kept locked and only opened for callers who could identify themselves. He said the back door was supposed to be kept locked at night, but in practice it was often left open to make it easier for constables to use the toilet in the yard. He added that it was not the heaviest of iron doors and indeed would squeak loudly when moved by the wind. Reardon asked Lindsey whether, in his opinion, Hardie and the Accused were drunk when they were all in the kitchen together on the night of the shooting. He confirmed they were.

Reardon now asked that the Accused's statement, which had been given to the fourth of February enquiry but which he himself had not been shown, now be produced to the court. Courts Martial Officer, Captain Arnold Victor Dickinson, who had taken Mitch's statement, was duly sworn in, much to the Judge Advocate's annoyance. His irritation seemed to be directed at Reardon, as if Reardon's ignorance of the Accused's earlier evidence were Reardon's own fault.

Dickenson read out Mitch's statement:

'The Accused said: On the morning of first of February, I went around to a number of shops to collect the bills. I called into a public house where Constable Hardie was well known. Having heard in barracks that he had had a row with some people name Brennan who are employed in that public house, I called in and enquired from the young lady behind the counter and asked her what the row had been about. She refused to tell me exactly and said she did not want to get anybody into trouble, as Constable Hardie was just here to earn his living. Take no notice of him, she said, he is mad. He had on two or three occasions, threatened me with a revolver. I asked her if she would make a case of it and come with me to the district inspector or head constable, but she refused, saying she would not give evidence against anybody, so I could not make a case of it. I then returned to barracks about twelve fifteen.

I had been drinking in the morning and continued in the afternoon. I did not report the matter, but went back in the afternoon to persuade her to come to see the Head Constable. She still refused. I then had tea in the barracks. I continued drinking in the evening. I finished up in the hotel next the barracks. I returned to the barracks at 2200 hours. I remember being in the kitchen. I was talking to some of the regular Constables. The next thing I remember was being wakened up at 0500 hours on the second of February; someone was shouting 'Get up, they are here' or words to that effect. I immediately got up and found all the Irish police of the barracks had gone out, leaving the English ones behind.

I asked what had happened and everybody seemed to be confused. I recall Cuddy saying someone was shot. I then went back to bed and remained there until 0845 hours, until asked to come into the day room. We were then all asked to bring our revolvers, rifles and ammunition and then our civilian suits. Mine was kept by the DI. I did not know I was under supervision. The following day I was arrested.

I had always tried to avoid Constable Hardie, as he appeared to be of a wild nature. I have heard him being warned on several occasions in the day room about taking his revolver out with him, and I have made his rifle ammunition up for him often. To my knowledge, I have only been in his company a few times, and mostly on patrol. He has often asked me to lend him my civilian clothes. I told him I would not, and to leave my things alone. On the Saturday preceding this affair however, he told me he planned to go up to Dublin on Sunday February the sixth and so I agreed to lend him my clothes.

I have been in France for three years and was blown up on the Somme in 1916 and again in 1918. I was wounded and sent home, for which I got a pension. Since the war, when in drink, my nerves and head affect me, and I am easily influenced. I am thirty three years of age and have a wife ten years my junior. She and I have been married twelve months and have a child due shortly. During my time in the RIC, I have always been amongst the first to volunteer for any task required. I joined the constabulary to try to prevent this sort of thing and not to provoke it.'

Dickenson confirmed to Mr Best that the statement had been made back in March. Mr Reardon next cross examined Dickenson and asked if the statement had been taken under caution. Dickenson said it had. Reardon asked if the Accused had had access to legal representation before or at the time of making the statement, and Dickenson said he had not.

James Dixon was now recalled and asked to confirm that he had been in close contact with the Accused on the night of the incident and if so whether he had noticed if the Accused had been drunk or sober. Dixon said he had been grappling for quite a few minutes with the Accused but that he did not smell drink on the Accused and so could not swear to it that he had been drunk.

Reardon confirmed to the court that the Accused would not be giving evidence on his own behalf and nor would he be calling any witnesses to speak in his defence. The Judge Advocate therefore asked Counsel if they were ready to proceed to submissions and whether they felt they might complete these before the luncheon recess. Messrs Best and Reardon agreed they were ready.

Reardon now embarked upon a comprehensive submission. He began by expressing his deep sympathy with the relatives of the late Mr Dixon and complimented the witnesses on the great personal bravery which they had shown under the terrible circumstances of this most shocking crime. Next, he sought to remind the court that the Accused was facing the death penalty and said that he was sure the court, in its deliberations, would not fail to consider the dreadful consequences of returning a verdict of murder.

Turning to the evidence, he highlighted the fact that the defendant had not been identified by any of the family as having been present at the scene of the crime, and that all the evidence against him was circumstantial. This fact warranted particular caution on the part of the court, lest an innocent man be wrongly subjected to the ultimate penalty. Assuming that the Accused were to have been the second man in the case – and this had not been proved – could the court be completely satisfied, he asked, on the evidence given, that the Accused was engaged with the leading man in a common design to commit this crime of murder? In Reardon's submission, they could not be so satisfied, particularly in view of the fact that the second man's weapon was unloaded.

They had heard the fact that James Dixon, a man well used to revolvers, had stated the second man's gun to have been unloaded. He

261

had heard the hammer click and yet no shot had gone off. The natural conclusion to be drawn was that the revolver had been in good working order when Dixon had tried to use it. It had later been suggested the weapon was merely fouled, but the court should bear in mind that the revolver had been tampered with by the head constable *subsequent* to the incident, when he had forced inappropriate ammunition into it.

It had been suggested during the evidence of Miss Dixon junior that she saw smoke in two places in the hall, suggesting that both interlopers had fired their weapons, and yet James Dixon's evidence was that the leading man had fired once then had crossed the hall to fire again. This would clearly account for Miss Dixon's false assumption that she had seen both guns fired.

Reardon reminded the court that, as soon as the leading man had finished shooting, he had declared himself out of ammunition and had urged the second man to leave. Surely, this too was a clear indication that the second man had no ammunition in his gun. None of the witnesses had suggested the second man had fired a shot at any point. The police evidence confirmed that only six shots had been fired during the incident, which is the contents of one revolver and which was further indication that only one gun had been loaded. Clearly therefore, it had been the leading man's gun which had been fired.

That, Reardon declared, was the first fact which suggested that the Accused – even were he one of the men there than night – was not engaged in any common design to commit a felony. Moreover, once the first shot had been fired, the second man had shown every desire to run away from the house. He had never advanced further into the hall but had remained standing near the mat, where he was subsequently engaged in the struggle with young Mr Dixon, who admitted he had held on to the man's clothing, *preventing* him from leaving. The second man was also heard pleading with Mr Dixon's aunt to let him leave.

Reardon also highlighted the evidence that the second man, whether he be the Accused or not, had been heard shouting to his companion, exhorting him not to shoot. Indeed, the moment the door was opened, he had fled, leaving his companion behind. Killing was not a crime he had intended to commit, and he had tried to flee the scene from the time of the first shot. It was demonstrably not his intention to hurt or kill anyone in the commission of this robbery. He was seen already at the end of the drive, by the gates of the house, at the moment when his companion was only just exiting through the front door. He was clearly trying to dissociate himself altogether from a murder in which he had taken no part. He clearly repudiated it.

Reardon now took up a large legal tome and approached the *big guns*. If the court should accept these facts, he continued, and should accept that the second man entered the house with no worse intent than to demand money with menaces, and then the only verdict which might be reached was one of manslaughter. The law, he reminded them, was laid out very clearly in the ninth volume of Lord Halsbury's great encyclopaedia of the law, paragraph 1174, from which he read:

'Where several persons are engaged in a common design and another person is killed, whether intentionally or unintentionally, by the act of one of them, done in prosecution of a common design, the other parties are guilty of murder if the common design was to commit murder, or to inflict felonious violence, or to commit any breach of the peace and violently to resist opposition by force, but if the common design was merely to do an unlawful act involving violence, then the others are guilty of manslaughter only.'

Passing from the law, Reardon now turned to the question of whether the Accused had even *been* the second man. Not one of the witnesses was prepared to state that the Accused was one of the men present at the crime scene. The Accused had not been identified by anyone in the case, despite having been paraded before James Dixon soon afterwards. Indeed, he reminded them, *another* constable from Wicklow had been identified by James Dixon as resembling the man with whom he had grappled.

Moreover, Mr Dixon had described the complexion of his assailant as 'sallow'. Indeed, it might be said that the complexions of Constable Blanco White and William – or 'Bill' – Lindsay, as seen in court, might better be described as sallow, than might that of the Accused.

Reardon went on to mention young Miss Dixon's insistence that the leading man had called the second man 'Bill' several times, yet it had been positively stated that the Accused was never known or addressed as 'Bill', though there is indeed another man in the barracks who was known as 'Bill'.

Reardon urged the court to take account of the statement made back in March by the Accused – a statement made spontaneously, honestly and without benefit of legal guidance. They should note the sincerity of the Accused's words. The Accused had been wary of

Hardie's wild nature and had made every effort to avoid him. Hardie had asked to borrow the Accused clothes. The Accused had reluctantly agreed to lend these.

Reardon now drew the court's attention to the evidence, given by no fewer than three members of the Dixon family, that Miss Dixon senior had inflicted four or five heavy blows of a knob-handled cane upon the head of the second man. Indeed James Dixon himself had been caught in just the side swipe and yet had sustained a long-lasting scar from her onslaught, whereas the Accused had only a small scratch on his head when examined only hours later. It could not therefore have been the Accused whom Miss Dixon senior had hit with the stick.

Mitchell had unquestionably been drinking a great amount on the night of the robbery and was under the influence of it, and yet Mr Dixon said he could detect no smell of drink upon the second man when he grappled closely with him. Could a man have consumed the amount of beer and whiskey as it was stated the Accused had without it being obvious?

With regard to the forensic evidence, Reardon did not seek to dispute the findings of the good Dr Brontë. The fact that there was human blood found on a suit and hat belonging to the Accused was not in doubt. However, as long ago as March, and without benefit of legal advice, the Accused had said Hardie had sought to borrow the Accused's civilian clothes. Hardie, if indeed he were the leading man, though that had not been established, might well have taken the Accused's clothes to wear on the night of the crime.

And with regard to the brown slouch hat, also bloodstained, which several witnesses had confirmed belonged to the Accused, had not this hat, according to Constable White, originally been acquired by the Accused when dropped from the head of a man being beaten at Dublin castle? Was it not more likely the blood on this hat had belonged, not to the Dixons, but to the hat's previous owner?

Defence Counsel's submission continued, though Mitch's concentration was now beginning to wane. He was thoroughly impressed with his advocate's words and he hoped the court would be equally moved by them. Reardon was no longer shaking, he noticed. Mitch now had a very good feeling about how the hearing was going. The *big guns* were listening intently to Reardon. Reardon was confident, coherent and persuasive.

Reardon was now quoting *the Queen versus Pridmore*, *the King versus Jackson*, and the wise comment of one *Baron Bramwell* on the rule of law, though Mitch could not easily follow this. Further precedent was to follow: *King versus Price*, where six men had been charged when one of their number had stabbed a German sailor. Mitch tried to understand all this and how it related to the charges against him, but he was soon lost in the weighty and wordy turn of the arguments.

He recalled his father's descriptions of what Monto must once have been like, with the bewigged lawyers and their massive legal brains, being conveyed from their elegant Gardiner Street homes to the Dublin law courts. And now, here was Mitch, a boy from the Monto, himself being defended by an admirable Irish legal brain.

Eventually, it was the turn of the Judge Advocate to sum up the case, reiterating the points of law as well as responding to the points raised both by the Crown Counsel in his opening address and by Reardon in his closing submission. Mitch heard Lord Halsbury's book being quoted again, and also the recurring phrases 'common purpose' and 'common design', but the effects of so many hours of concentration had tired him. He gave up trying to follow the argument. He wondered how the lawyers could go for so long and not lose their wits entirely.

It was one o'clock when the Judge Advocate finally announced the court would rise to consider their verdict. The *big guns* rose. Everyone else in the court followed suit. Reardon excused himself and said he had to speak to someone outside the court. He returned some quarter of an hour later. Mitch noted Reardon was nervously biting his fingernails. If Reardon was nervous however, Mitch felt oddly calm. Though he had not understood all the proceedings, he now had every confidence that Reardon had done his best for him. There was little point in worrying about the outcome therefore. It was now beyond the influence of Mitch and his able counsel. His fate was in the hands of a much greater force. He only hoped that force would be merciful.

It was only thirty five minutes later that the court resumed. Mitch did not know whether to feel hope or fear, as he really had little idea how it had gone. The President of the court now announced that they found the Accused 'not guilty' of the second alternative charge.

That sounded positive. Mitch glanced at Reardon. Reardon was not smiling however. Mitch was confused. He could not recall which charge was which. Now Reardon was on his feet again, asking the President if, prior to reaching a determination on the first charge, the court would hear from the witness Delaney regarding the service of the Accused. The President agreed. Delaney was brought back into court.

Reardon asked Delaney if he were in a position to give the court any information regarding the Accused man's behaviour whilst he had been in the service of the RIC and, perhaps, of his army service record also. Delaney cast a sad and apologetic glance across at Mitch. Delaney said the only document he could produce was Mitch's army discharge paper. This was now handed to Reardon. Delaney stated however that Constable William Mitchell had joined the RIC on 19th November 1920 and had been posted to Dunlavin district on 1st of January 1921. Mitchell was just one month and two days in Delaney's charge but, said Delaney, he had always found Mitchell to be a clean and apparently a sober man. No complaint was made against him during that time and he had discharged his duties as a policeman efficiently and well. Delaney cast a faint smile in Mitch's direction as he left the witness stand.

Reardon now produced to the court Mitch's certificate of war service which confirmed that he had served as a Private for almost the entire duration of the war, from August 1914 until June 1918 when he was demobilised. Reardon advised the court that, under 'special remarks', the officer commanding the Third Cavalry Regiment had written: 'He is smart, intelligent and hard working.' Since they were all military men however, the men of the court were aware that this was a phrase used on all war service discharge documents.

The President now turned to Mitch and asked if he wished to address the court. Mitch just wanted to leave.

'No sir,' he said.

Chapter 15 – **As The Crow Flies**

The boat train from Rosslare pulled into Dublin's Westland Row station and the passengers, weary from the overnight sailing, poured out onto the station platform. One of the last passengers to alight was a petite young woman, clutching a young baby and carrying a small suitcase. She hung back to avoid the crush. One of a group of arriving soldiers broke away from his comrades and offered to carry her suitcase. Exhausted, Alice gratefully accepted the soldier's kind offer.

At the end of the platform, on the other side of the barrier, six men waited – six men who, despite the fact that it was not raining that pleasant June morning, were wearing heavy raincoats. They scanned the faces of the arriving passengers. They looked in vain for a small beady-eyed man with receding hair and a bushy moustache.

As the last wave of passengers approached the ticket collectors, the men realised, to their intense disappointment, their target was not on the train. They were armed and all fired up to take out their quarry, but he was not on the train. Deeply frustrated, one of them pulled out his weapon and began firing anyway in the direction of the British soldiers. Another of the men did likewise.

Instinctively, the soldiers unshouldered their rifles and dropped to the ground ready to return fire. Passengers scattered, screaming and diving for cover. Further back on the platform, the lone soldier dropped the suitcase and pulled Alice to the ground, shielding her and the baby with his body. The soldiers did not return fire, for fear innocent passengers would be hurt in the crossfire. The six men made their escape out of the main station entrance and sped off in the waiting car. The soldiers gave chase.

The kind soldier helped Alice her to her feet. Making sure she and the baby were unhurt, he ran off down the platform after his colleagues. Soon, it was apparent that the show was over. Nobody had been hurt. The gunmen had got clean away and passengers began tramping out of the station and disappearing into the surrounding streets, as if this were just another typical Dublin day. Maybe it was.

Alice had known Dublin was a dangerous place, but she hadn't expected to be caught up in a shoot-out just minutes after her arrival. Not knowing her way around the city, she hailed a cab outside the station and asked the driver to take her to any modestly-priced boarding house, as near as possible to Phibsborough.

The Rosary Guesthouse looked and sounded like a respectable establishment. The driver helped his passengers up to the door and deposited the suitcase in the hallway for them. He agreed to wait whilst she booked in and paid for her room. The landlady seemed kindly and welcoming as she ushered Alice in.

'How long will you and the child be staying, dear?' she asked.

Alice explained it would be just the one night then she would be returning to England on the boat train the following night.

'That's an awful short holiday for ye, and us havin' the best weather of the year so far,' the woman said, as she showed Alice into the room, which was small but seemed clean enough.

'Well, I'm not here on holiday. I'm just visiting someone at the prison, my husband in fact,' Alice told her.

The woman softened.

'Are you, indeed, and sure there's some fine boys locked up across there, and just for the crime of being Irish. Is your husband Irish then?'

Alice confirmed he was a Dubliner.

'Tis terrible times we're livin' in altogether,' the woman said, as Alice wrote her name in the register, 'but, I tell you what dear, whenever you come back this evening, I'll have a bite of supper kept warm for you. Don't worry if it's late. You can come and eat in the kitchen and I'll warm up some milk for the baby.'

Alice thanked her and put her case in the room then she and her baby took the taxi to Mountjoy.

Boyd apologised that he was not allowed to leave Mitch and his little family alone together, but he sent Dwyer off to make them all a cup of tea and he did his best to remain unobtrusive. Mitch took Alice in his arms, holding her and his infant gently to him. He buried his face in Alice's hair. He had forgotten the scent of her. He hoped she would speak first, for he had no idea what to say. He was both relieved and overjoyed that she had come. He had thought he would never see her again. Alice now showed him his daughter.

268

'What did you call her?' he asked, marvelling at the tiny, sleeping infant.

'Kathleen,' She said, 'Kitty, for short.'

'You chose a good Irish name,' Mitch smiled, 'and oh but she's so pretty. I'm glad she takes after you and not me.'

He examined his baby daughter's perfect little fingers and her tiny toes and he kissed her little downy head. Kitty did not stir but slept soundly on.

'She must be, what, seven weeks now?' he asked.

'Yes, and she's a good baby too. She sleeps right through the night – most nights,' Alice said.

'Have a look at her, Boyd,' Mitch enthused, 'isn't she the prettiest baby you ever saw?'

'Indeed she is, Mitch,' Boyd beamed, 'ah and will you look at the little turned up nose on her, like a cherub. A little angel, that's what she is.'

Dwyer arrived with the tea and he had to have a look also.

'Ah, she's a little doll, she is, and would you ever look at her little mouth. She has the latest fashion in lips, so she has,' he declared.

'And what are you on about now, eejit boy? Sure, what's the latest fashion in lips?' Boyd shook his head disparagingly.

'Tis the little pouty look, like that Mary Pickford or one of them fillum stars,' Dwyer informed him.

Alice laid her sleeping daughter on Mitch's bunk and they all sat at the table to drink their tea. The atmosphere seemed stiff. Nobody seemed to know what to say. Nobody wanted to mention Mitch's situation.

'Where is it you're staying, Mrs Mitchell,' Boyd enquired.

'*The Rosary*, a bed and breakfast just a stone's throw from here,' Alice answered.

'And will you spend the whole of today here with Mitch, for you know you're entitled?' he asked

'Yes I expect I will. Well, I've nowhere else to go,' Alice replied.

'Is this your first time in Ireland, Mrs Mitchell?' Dwyer asked.

Mitch smiled to himself as he noticed young Dwyer's little finger extended as he lifted his tea mug. Dwyer was affecting a degree of good manners because Alice was here. Mitch liked it that his wife was being accorded the respect a lady deserved, albeit that she was the

269

wife of a convicted and condemned criminal. It was but a small gesture, but one which assumed undue importance to Mitch in his final hours.

'Yes,' Alice answered, 'not that I'll be seeing much of Ireland though. I'll be heading back tomorrow.'

'Where will you go, Alice?' Mitch asked.

'Back to London. I had to give up the house when your pay allocation stopped coming. I've been staying with my sister since then, but I can't live on charity forever. I've decided to go back to London and try to find work.'

'But how will you manage on your own?' Mitch asked, suddenly feeling deeply ashamed that, so far, he had been preoccupied with his own desperate situation and had given scarcely a thought to how his wife and baby might fare.

'We'll manage somehow,' Alice gave him a steely look, 'we'll have to, won't we.'

Feeling uncomfortable, Boyd rose to clear the tea things.

'What would you like for lunch, Mrs Mitchell? If they have it in the kitchens, we'll order it. Pop along to the kitchens Dwyer, there's a good lad. Now Mitch, he can put in your request for supper for the both of you too. You know you can have anything you like. What about a bit of steak, or lamb, or maybe a nice steak and kidney pie, with a bottle of porter to wash it down?'

Boyd avoided pointing out that his was to be Mitch's last supper.

'Do you think they could do us a pan of stew?' Mitch asked, 'a nice Dublin coddle and a cut of bread, that would be great.'

Boyd gave the order to Dwyer and despatched him to the kitchens. He then stood in the cell doorway for a while, tactfully averting his gaze as Alice sat on Mitch's bunk to discreetly breastfeed her baby.

The day passed awkwardly. Neither Alice nor Mitch wanted to refer to the events which had brought him to this. It didn't seem right to spend the precious time which remained to him in recrimination, but nor did it seem right to be making small talk. Mitch eventually bit the bullet.

'I'm so sorry Alice, about everything. I don't know what to say to you. I failed you. You deserve better than me. You should forget me.'

Alice didn't reply.

270

'What will you tell Kitty – about me, I mean?' he asked.

Alice sighed.

'Well, I don't think I should tell her that her father was hanged for murder. I don't want her growing up with that on her shoulders. That's another reason for going back to London. Nobody cares to know another body's business there. We can make a fresh start, Kitty and me.'

'I didn't do it, Alice,' Mitch blurted suddenly, 'I didn't kill that man. I never killed anyone this side of the war, and I'm not even sure I ever killed anyone in the war either. I'm not a murderer, Alice.'

'No,' Alice said softly, 'I don't suppose you are.'

'I'm sorry about us, about the dream we had, the house in Ireland and the horses and the children and all that. I wanted all of that for us. I'm sorry I won't see Kitty growing up. I don't even have money to give you to buy something nice for my little girl. I have so many regrets, Alice. I can't turn the clock back, though. Maybe you'll find someone better than me one day.'

'Maybe I will. Maybe I won't. There's not many men would bring up another man's child though, especially a convicted murderer's child,' she responded with unexpected callousness.

'Ah, don't be nasty to me now, Alice,' Mitch pleaded, tears now running down his cheeks, 'for, after all, I'm going to be dead tomorrow.'

'And me and the baby are going to be destitute tomorrow, Mitch,' Alice began to sob also. She let loose the tears she had been holding back for a very long time.

'I gave birth to her all alone, Mitch. I was so frightened. And I'm going to be bringing her up all on my own too. That frightens me even more. I don't know how we're going to manage Mitch, I really don't. So don't expect me not to be angry with you. I have a lot to be angry about.'

Mitch arose, took her gently in his arms and they stood, just holding onto each other for quite some time. Neither had the words to express the heartache they shared, or their fear of what was to come.

When the supper came around, Alice said she couldn't eat anything after all. She was too tired. She wouldn't stay too late, she said, but would have something with the landlady back at *The Rosary*. Mitch didn't want her to go. He experienced a sudden surge of desperation, for he knew he would never see her or his little daughter again. However, he could see how exhausted she was. He hated himself for what he had put her through. He also hated the thought of her walking to the boarding house alone, but she assured him it was not far. She had got all the way to Dublin safely, she assured him, and so she would make it back to the boarding house a few streets away.

She now recalled the incident at the station earlier that day. She mentioned the shooting on the station platform.

'Oh yes, 'tis in all the evening papers,' Dwyer informed them, 'I just saw a copy in the kitchens. The *Boyos* were there to assassinate the hangman, Ellis, but he wasn't on the train. He usually arrives at the prison the night before the ..., well the night before, but Governor Munro was expecting trouble, so he had him come over two days earlier.'

'Well,' Mitch smiled ironically, 'I nearly got a temporary reprieve then, didn't I? Nearly – isn't that the story of my life?'

He held Alice very tightly, as if to imprint the essence of her in his memory, then he kissed little Kitty and wished them luck. Dwyer let him stand in the cell doorway to watch his wife and baby go. As Alice walked away down the wing, escorted by Boyd, she didn't look back. He couldn't blame her. Another chapter of his life was at an end, he thought – the final chapter, without a doubt.

It was already dark as Alice left the prison. She was surprised to see quite a crowd of people gathering outside the gates. For a moment, she wondered if they were here because of Mitch, then she realised that of course they would be here to keep a vigil for the other two Irishmen who were also to hang in the morning.

Physically and emotionally drained now, she walked the few blocks to the boarding house. Kitty had been so good all day. Alice hoped she would sleep well through the night also, since they had an early start the following day. As Alice climbed the steps the landlady opened the front door. Alice recognised her suitcase as the woman placed it upon the top step.

'Here's your money back,' she said, her earlier kindly demeanour no longer in evidence.

'I realise now who you are, Mrs Mitchell – you're the wife of the *Tan* they're hanging in the morning. Well I won't have a *Tan*'s wife staying in my house. I'm sorry.'

Alice remained, stunned, on the steps, as the door slammed. The noise awoke Kitty who began to wail. Alice turned around and sat down on the steps for a moment to rock her distressed infant and to think.

'Well, come on Kitty dearest,' she said at length, 'there's only one place we can go.'

The crowd keeping vigil for Maher and Foley had grown considerably when Alice arrived back at the prison. The anxious auxiliaries had moved the people away from the gates and back behind temporary barriers. The crowd was now softly intoning 'The Soldier's Song'. There were candles burning before images of the Virgin Mary and the Sacred Heart, and many people were on their knees praying. Alice found the atmosphere eerie yet moving.

Two lorry loads of armed soldiers had now turned up in case of trouble. The Lancashire Fusiliers had their bayonets fixed to their rifles but remained watching the scene from within their turreted, armour-plated vehicles parked at a discreet distance up the street. Alice hoped there would not be more shooting. She wondered if she had made a mistake coming back here, but where else could she go? After that morning's carry on, she didn't think the railway station would be any safer.

There were several braziers blazing and women were huddled around them so she eased her way through the crowd in the direction of the warmth. Seeing the baby in her arms, the crowd parted to let her through.

'Come on, this way darlin'. Let her through now,' one of the women by the brazier urged.

A space was made for her by the fire. Alice put down the suitcase and sat on it. She looked around at the faces of the women. Their cheeks were tear-stained like her own. She guessed they were the families of Maher and Foley.

'Are you Constable Mitchell's wife?' the kindly woman asked.

Alice nodded apprehensively.

'Then stay here with us the night, darlin' and sure we'll say the *De Profundis* for your man too.'

The sun rose on another Tuesday, despite Mitch's prayers that it should not – not yet at least. Naturally, he had not slept at all during the night. He had the impression Boyd and Dwyer had been unable to sleep too, but he had lain quietly as if in sleep, to avoid disturbing

273

them. His head had been full of thoughts and recollections. Voices had come to him from the past, Dublin voices mostly.

He had tried to picture his father's face, and his mother's, for neither had been to see him since his arrest. Perhaps they had been too ashamed. Perhaps they could not afford the fare from London. They had never met Alice. They wouldn't even know they now had a granddaughter.

He had pictured the tenement in Gardiner Street, which ironically was not too far from where he now lay. He had recalled his childhood in the Monto, with the japes and the mischief. He had even heard again his mother's long ago voice warning that, if he ran with the crows, he'd be shot with the crows. He hadn't listened of course. If he had, perhaps things would have worked out differently. He could have been exalted, like the starlings in Cuddy's collective nouns. He could have been many things. However, he had indeed chosen to run with the crows, the bloody black crows.

Oh, he had had his glory days in India all right. Those had been good times – mostly. He could have chosen to remain in the army and perhaps he'd have made something of himself. He couldn't say he hadn't had chances in life. Nor could he really blame anyone else for his misfortune, no matter how often he cursed the officer class. How often had his mother said he would be the ruination of her? Well, she'd been right about that too. He had been the ruination of others as well. He had ruined his own life and those of his soon-to-be-destitute wife and daughter.

He thought of his poor Alice. He wished she had turned to smile at him, just once, as she had left him. He now tried to call her face to mind, the face which he had held and kissed just hours earlier, but strangely it was not her face he saw in his mind's eye, but that of his long ago love, his Rose. Lying in the dimly lit cell, he had run his fingers over his scarred arm, where the almost obliterated tattoo was all that remained of Rose. Rose had now re-claimed him. Dublin had re-claimed him. Prof had been right. Mitch should never have come back to Ireland. His sadness was immeasurable, yet his self-loathing served to reconcile him to his fate.

He wondered if death would re-unite him with others he had cared for. Would he see again his little brother, Johnnie, and have a chance to say how sorry he was that he hadn't been nicer to him? Might he see Kempie, his big, gentle friend? Would Rose be there when he got to the other side? Was there anything at all beyond death, or was this all there was? He had no idea. He was suddenly gripped by a fear of the unknown and he began to feel sick. His limbs ached and there was pain in his head to match the pain in his heart.

He thought back to his Bermondsey days. He recalled the sting of the lime which used to coat his body and clothing and make him look like a ghost. He remembered once having heard that executed prisoners were buried in quick lime to hasten their decay. He wondered if that would happen to him. Would his body and the very memory of him be eradicated? Would his own daughter be told nothing of William Mitchell? He felt himself drifting uneasily towards sleep but the memory of the collective stench of rotting flesh from the Summerhill abattoirs, from the *Alaska* work's tan pits and from Smithfield meat market, and the idea of his own imminent decomposition kept drawing him back to wakefulness.

The solicitous Boyd was soon leaning over him with his usual good cup of tea however.

'Did you manage to sleep, Mitch?' Boyd asked.

'Not really, no,' he told him, 'for I have a headache and the old rheumatism is giving me jip too.'

'Ah, sure we all got a touch of that out in the trenches, didn't we?' Boyd empathised.

Mitch hadn't got his rheumatism in the trenches however, but in the military prison at Rouen. No, he couldn't manage any breakfast, he assured Boyd. There was a knot in his stomach the size of a boulder as he rose to wash, shave and dress himself for the last time. He accepted Boyd's offer of a final glass of whiskey though. He was aware that he hadn't long to wait now and it felt like being in the trenches again. The waiting was the worst part. Get up and wait. Hurry up and wait. He was aware that the other two, Maher and Foley, would be going over the top first. He was to follow them. No doubt they would be feeling just as apprehensive he did.

The tea soon soothed his headache, just as it always had when he was a child. The pains in his legs and shoulders remained however but served to remind him he was still alive. As the tea warmed him, his anxiety began to give way to an unexpected sense of calm resignation. Perhaps it was the whiskey on an empty stomach or simply the tiredness which now came over him in waves.

The two chaplains entered the cell and greeted him solemnly. They began intoning the prayers for the dying, the same prayers he had heard so often at the Somme. Not long now.

Governor Munro appeared next. Mitch quickly rose to shake his hand and suddenly felt slightly dizzy. Perhaps he had risen too quickly, or perhaps he was still asleep and dreaming all of this, for it felt most unreal. Not long now.

Another man appeared behind the Governor, a short beady-eyed man with a receding hairline and an unkempt bushy moustache. This would be Ellis, he guessed, the man who had unwittingly cheated death himself just twenty four hours earlier. Lucky bastard.

Boyd now stepped forward and embraced Mitch.

'Goodbye, Mitch,' he choked.

Mitch felt suddenly and unaccountably sad for Boyd. A white-faced Dwyer also came forward to grab Mitch's hand and pumped it up and down. Poor Dwyer. The lad could not speak. He looked thoroughly miserable and was unable even to summon up a word of farewell. Mitch thanked them both for their kindness.

Now Ellis was securing a leather belt around Mitch's waist and was pinioning his arms firmly to his sides. Mitch stood to attention. He was Lancer Mitchell again – the *Scarlet Lancer*; the crack shot with a silver medal to prove it. Not long now. Things were moving very quickly. This was it.

The Governor and a posse of warders led the way at the double down the length of the wing. They were followed by the prison doctor and some civil servant or other. Mitch walked in the midst of them, the executioner guiding him firmly by the arm. Hurry up. The two chaplains formed the rear guard. Not long now. Not far to the parapet, then over the top, with Billy and Scouse.

A red door at the far end of the wing was now opened and the party walked swiftly through it. Mitch had just several seconds to take in the sight of the interior of the hang house and the long steel chain with the leather lined noose hanging from it. It all seemed so unreal. Hands guided him quickly forward onto the stout oak trapdoors of the scaffold and his ankles were deftly bound together. A white cotton bag was now pulled down over his head, shutting out the view, and he felt a weight resting upon his shoulders. Hurry up and wait.

Panic began to grip him again and he began to breathe heavily, realising these would be the last breaths he would ever take. As much as he wanted to struggle, to try to make a break for it, yet he determined to go bravely and not to cry out or resist. He stood powerless and swaying. He swayed as he waited to go over the top. His fate was no longer in his own hands. The world is waiting for the sunrise, he thought. He would not see the sunrise.

There was a sudden and almighty bang, like a rifle shot, as the trapdoors were sprung. It caused him to jump. Now, to his surprise, he was flying.

Outside, a startled crow took off above the heads of the people and headed squawking into the rising sun. Below, the door of the prison opened and a warder emerged to pin three white notices on the railings at the front. The crowd, as one, made the sign of the cross. Women wept.

'Out of depths, I have cried to thee, oh Lord,' whispered the assembled in unison, 'Lord, hear my voice ...'

Soon, the crowds began to disperse and Dublin began to go about its business as best it could on an otherwise pleasant June morning. A petite, solitary figure carrying a small suitcase walked along the quickening streets towards the station at Westland Row. The baby slept innocently in Alice's arms as she made her lonely way to the boat train.

EPILOGUE

When I come to the end of a good story, I am usually curious to know what happened next. What becomes of the characters, whether real or fictional, once the author has done with them? In anticipation that you have found *Running with Crows* to be a good story, I have therefore continued my research a little beyond the end of my narrative. Here, then, is a little more background to some of the characters and an account of what happened to them next:

William Mitchell, formerly of the Royal West Surrey Regiment; the 16th Lancers and the Royal Irish Constabulary, was forgotten both by history and by his family. Like many soldiers, Mitchell did not kowtow to his NCOs. Ironically, in death also, he continues to challenge authority. His is one of the few unclaimed bodies whose presence in the unconsecrated grounds of Dublin's Mountjoy Gaol stands as an embarrassing obstacle to a proposed €100 million commercial development. I like to think Mitchell would have enjoyed his continuing rôle as a thorn in the flesh of the authorities.

Alice Mitchell remained true to her plucky nature. She did indeed go back with her baby daughter Kitty to South London, where, with the practical and moral support of her Danish friends, the Pedersons, she secured work as a post woman. A few years later, she met and married a good man a little younger than herself and went on to have more children and a peaceful life. She passed away equally peacefully at the age of ninety.

Kitty Mitchell grew up in the belief that her father was an Irish policeman who died a hero whilst keeping the peace. She also lived into her nineties.

'The Major', who came up through the ranks from private to acting captain during The Great War and was decorated for his daring feats of courage, enjoyed a brief but notorious period of service with the Royal Irish Constabulary's Auxiliary Division [ADRIC] between November 1920 and July 1922. Having been twice tried for murder by courts martial and twice acquitted, he was transferred to a different ADRIC station where he was subsequently involved in a further fatal incident. He returned to the army again after this and by 1940 he had attained the rank of 2nd Lieutenant. However, he never held the specific rank of Major, by which title he had long insisted on being addressed. He later followed a number of his former ADRIC colleagues into the new 'Palestine Gendarmerie' which was run by his former ADRIC commander, Sir Henry Tudor. Thrice married, 'The Major' passed away in Gaza in 1942, whilst again serving in an 'intelligence gathering' capacity with the Provost Marshall's office of the Palestine police.

The Small Man in the Connaught Ranger's uniform was a close associate of 'The Major' in 'F Company' of the ADRIC and, like 'The Major', had spent his early youth in Kensington. The son of a woollen merchant from County Down, his was a middle-class upbringing and he had enlisted as a professional soldier ten months before the outbreak of The Great War. Having been taken prisoner at an early stage of the war, he had attempted a series of escapes from several German Prisoner of War camps before succeeding in 1918. On his return to the front, he was badly wounded, losing a leg. Having been promoted to the rank of Captain and awarded the DSO, he later entered the banking profession and became a novelist. He gave false evidence at one of 'The Major's' courts martial and also intimidated prosecution witnesses. In one of his subsequent books, he freely admitted his and 'The Major's' involvement in various killings, including those murders for which 'The Major' had been tried and acquitted.

Jack 'The Journo' Braithwaite, born in Dunedin, New Zealand and son of Dunedin's mayor, Joseph Braithwaite, had volunteered to join the New Zealand Expeditionary Force in 1915. Having served in Egypt and been promoted to Lance-Corporal, he was transferred to France, where he lost his stripe for going AWOL from the front. Like Mitchell, he absconded from Field Punishment, for which he was sentenced to two years' imprisonment at Blairgie, Rouen's Military Prison. An escape attempt there earned him a two year extension of his prison sentence. On 29 October 1916 Braithwaite was executed by firing squad for the offence of mutiny. He was one of five *enzedders* shot for mutiny during the war. All the Australians sentenced to death had their sentences later commuted to two years' hard labour. In September 2000, Jack Braithwaite and the four other executed NZEF troops were granted a pardon by the British parliament.

Laurence Joseph 'Larry' Delaney had been employed as a railway signalman in the Queen's County (County Laois) before joining the Royal Irish Constabulary. He took early retirement from the RIC at the age of 53 on 12 May 1922, upon the disbandment of the constabulary. He passed away peacefully in Rathdown Co Dublin thirty years later, aged 83.

William 'Bill' Lindsay, the sallow-faced, 29 year-old, Middlesex-born former gravedigger, former soldier and temporary constable in the RIC, absconded from the Dunlavin barracks shortly after the execution of William Mitchell. In his absence, Bill Lindsay was officially dismissed from the RIC for desertion.

Blanco White, John Linward and Thomas Alston, former soldiers and temporary constables in the RIC, remained with the constabulary until February 1922 and were sent home to England with a gratuity of £50 each.

Robert Gilbert Dixon, farmer, magistrate and landowner, was the son of James Dixon, gentleman, of Wicklow Street, Dublin, and his wife Elizabeth Gilbert [herself the daughter of Robert John Gilbert, gentleman, author of a history of Dublin and benefactor of the Gilbert Library in Pearse St., formerly Great Brunswick St., Dublin]. Following his murder in 1921, Robert Dixon was buried in the family grave at the Church of St Nicholas, Dunlavin, alongside a daughter, Evelyn, who had died aged 19 in 1913, and a son, John Dixon, who had died aged 17 in 1915.

Martha Jane Dixon, spinster sister of Robert Dixon and witness at the court martial of William Mitchell, died aged 80 in 1930.

Linda Dixon, widow of Robert Gilbert Dixon, claimed £27,000 malicious injuries following the unlawful killing of her husband by a member of the Crown Forces. She remained in the family home at Milltown, where she passed away aged 75 in 1948.

James Dixon, son of the late Robert Dixon, holder of the Military Medal and the Serbian (gold) cross, who was wounded in the Milltown incident and testified at the subsequent court martial, never married but remained at Milltown running the family farm until his own death aged 59 in 1958.

Kathleen May Dixon, daughter of the late Robert Dixon and witness at the court martial, did not marry either. She served as a Petty Officer in the WRNS in World War Two, and returned to live at Milltown, where she too passed away in 1962, aged 68. She was the last member of this now extinct branch of the Dixon family.

Jessie Hardie, cotton weaver, daughter of Lancashire water colour artist Archibald John Walter Jones, and widow of Constable Arthur Hardie, remarried and went on to have children.

Field Marshall Sir Henry Hughes Wilson, First Baronet, Chief of the Imperial General Staff, Unionist MP and an outspoken critic of politicians, to whom he frequently referred as 'the frocks', resigned his post in February 1922 in protest at Lloyd George and Winston Churchill's negotiations with Sinn Fein over a settlement in Ireland and over their plan to send the ADRIC veterans of the Irish troubles to quell similar troubles in Palestine. Wilson was assassinated on his own doorstep on 22 June 1922, having returned from unveiling the Great Eastern Railway War Memorial at Liverpool Street Railway Station. He had drawn his sword to defend himself, but this proved ineffective against the guns of his hit-and-run assailants. The exact motives for his assassination are unclear. Unlike his two killers, England-born IRA men Reginald Dunne and Joseph O'Sullivan, Sir Henry was born in Ireland, in County Longford. Dunne and O'Sullivan were apprehended by passers-by and were executed that August by hangman John Ellis,

Lloyd George, a Manchester-born Welshman and Liberal politician, served variously as Minister for Munitions, Secretary of State for War and Prime Minister of the Coalition Government during World War One. He survived several scandals involving his extra marital liaisons and his selling of honours and knighthoods for cash, and in 1921 secured the settlement which established the Irish Free State. He resigned as Prime Minister in 1922 following disagreement with the Conservatives in the Coalition Government over Britain's foreign policy in Turkey.

Sir Hamar Greenwood, Canadian-born British lawyer and politician, was the last to hold the office of Chief Secretary for Ireland [1920-22]. As a supporter of the policy of reprisals carried out by the 'Black & Tans' and auxiliaries in Ireland during the Anglo-Irish War, he attributed blame for the auxiliaries' burning of the city of Cork in December 1920 to the Sinn Feiners and to the city's residents themselves. He lived at Onslow Gardens, Kensington.

John Robert Clynes, Member of Parliament and opponent of the British Government's policies on Ireland, was born in Oldham, Lancashire in 1869. One of seven children born to Patrick Clynes, an illiterate Irish farm worker and victim of the 1850s evictions in Ireland, John began work at the age of 10 at Oldham's Dowry Mill. Largely self-educated, he became a writer and later Labour MP for Manchester North East. A champion of rights for children employed in the textile industry and a supporter of the suffrage movement, he also exposed the activities of profiteers who, during World War One, engaged in food price fixing and provided dangerously sub standard shells and other faulty supplies to the troops at the front. He also led the opposition to Lloyd George's policy of reprisals during the Irish War of Independence. A lifelong member of the Labour party, he served as Lord Privy Seal and deputy leader of the House of Commons before rising to the office of Home Secretary from 1929 to 1931. He was widely regarded as one of the few honest and worthy men of politics in his time. He was also considered, not least by my aunt who worked for him, to be a thoroughly kind and decent man.

Edward Byrne, Mitchell's solicitor, continued to practise law in his father's legal chambers and served as President of the Dublin Bar Association 1967-68.

James Ambrose Reardon, Mitchell's barrister, continued to practise in the Dublin courts, undertaking many pro bono cases in order to uphold the rights of Dublin's poor and disadvantaged.

Dr Robert Matthew Brontë, 41 year-old Armagh-born Home Office pathologist, Crown Analyst in Ireland and former RAMC captain in World War One, was also a critic and opponent of Sir Bernard Spilsbury, the more famous, self-employed and self-promoting celebrity pathologist. Brontë, described by his own critics as 'a garrulous Irishman', may not have been the most succinct of court witnesses, but history supports the validity of his challenging of Spilsbury's evidence in the 1925 Thorne case (a controversy described as 'The Celt versus the Saxon'). He was related to novelist Charlotte Brontë, though historically their family name was Prunty.

John Ellis, the Rochdale barber turned hangman, carried out his final execution in 1923. Nine months later, he shot himself in the head in an unsuccessful attempt at suicide. He received no pension from the Home Officer for his duties as official executioner. He briefly trod the boards, acting in the rôle of executioner William Marwood, his nineteenth century predecessor, but the play was taken off, having been deemed in bad taste. As the economic depression took a hold on Lancashire, Ellis found it hard to make ends meet and it was perhaps the ghosts of his past which caused him to drink heavily. In 1932, he succeeded in killing himself when he slashed his throat in the front doorway of his home. His funeral and subsequent burial were attended by many curious locals, but no representative from the Police Commissioner's office or the Home Office attended. Ellis too died a forgotten man.

*Garda station at Dunlavin, County Wicklow, formerly the RIC
Barracks*

About The Author:

Born of Irish parents, in Manchester, England, DJ Kelly has lived and worked in 20 countries across 4 continents during a long career in government service and speaks seven languages. Briefly a member of *Creative Writers' Network of Northern Ireland* and *Metroland Poets,* before she co-founded *Chalfont Writers' Circle*, she now lives in Buckinghamshire, England, researching and writing historical fiction and publishing a successful series of local history books.

Also by the same author:

A Wistful Eye – The Tragedy of a Titanic Shipwright

Published in 2012, this novel is based on the true story of the murder of the author's great grandmother and of her great grandfather's rôle in building Titanic.

'A professionally produced book, *A Wistful Eye* is a fascinating and enjoyable story ... engaging ... a thoroughly enjoyable read with some facts about Irish history that I was not aware of.' – **The Historical Novel Society**

'A fact-based story of love, loss and injustice in which the author brings her ancestors, and the poor district of Belfast, to life, complete with speech in wonderful local dialect. Kelly's well researched and fictionalized account of her family history is a mighty fine achievement.' – **Family Tree Magazine**

'A lovely read. Well done. You've captured the time and place.' – **Sam McAughtry, author, journalist & broadcaster, BBC Northern Ireland.**

Follow DJ Kelly at:- website: www.djkelly.co.uk Twitter: @djkellyauthor

Lightning Source UK Ltd.
Milton Keynes UK
UKHW012009220721
387616UK00001B/5